Where is Home?

Where is Home?

MARVIN T COOK

ISBN: 978-1-4269-5596-9 (sc)
ISBN: 978-1-4269-5597-6 (e)

Trafford rev. 01/17/2011

 www.trafford.com

North America & International
toll-free: 1 888 232 4444 (USA & Canada)
phone: 250 383 6864 ♦ fax: 812 355 4082

CHAPTER I

The Trip

A young lady is driving south on I-95 in her 2009 red Dodge Viper alone. It is a cool late October Saturday night. The sky is clear with no moon. She decides she needs to use the restroom and sees an exit coming up. There is a sign that indicates a service station is at the exit for Mount Holly Church Road. She takes the exit but turns the wrong way—right—away from where the service station was one mile away to the left. After driving for about a mile, she sees a dirt road and felt the need to relieve her urge and turns right into the road. She drives a short distance and a deer runs in front of her car. To avoid hitting the deer, she makes a hard right turn and slams into a tree real hard. It demolishes the left front end of the car

In the accident, she hits her head on the windshield and bounces back hitting the back of her head on the door frame. The gal tries to restart the car. In addition to front end damage, the battery is damaged and the car will not restart. Still having the urge to relieve herself, she gets out of the car, takes a few steps and relieves herself which was real easy. She does not have underwear on. Seeing a cabin a short way back with a light on, she proceeds to go in that direction to seek help.

After a few steps, the lass stumbles on a rock and falls hitting her head again. In the incident, she loses her purse containing all her credit cards and $1000.00. The girl also loses her left shoe. She forgets about the cabin proceeding back towards the road she had turned off of. Once there, she collapses and goes unconscious. She lays there until morning.

Meanwhile, in the cabin is Henry Willington, a salvage yard owner. He is there to shoot deer out of season. It is a thing illegal in Virginia. He heard the crash and made up his mind to investigate what it was that caused the noise. He thought right away there was an accident. He would investigate as soon as he finished working on his deer shot illegally. After finishing the deer, he goes to the accident scene with his tow truck. Wellington hooks up the vehicle knowing the salvage of parts would be profitable in a large way. He tows it to his cabin for the night. In the morning he would haul it to his salvage yard.

A young man, the next morning, before Wellington leaves, sees the lady of the crash lying on the side of the road. He stops his 2008 Silver Dodge Viper, gets out and goes to see if he could be of some help. The young man is Conrad Thomas. He is 23 years old and already a Manager for Wachovia Bank. He sees that she was unconscious and had bled from her head. Conrad lifts her into his car and proceeds to Henrico County Doctors Hospital in Richmond.

Arriving there, he goes in for help. A nurse from the Emergency Room comes out. She is RN Victoria Gray on her way home for the day after working to replace a nurse that was off. They put her into a wheel chair and Conrad is told to go check her in. Going to the reception area, he realizes he did not know her name or whether she had insurance or not. Conrad tells the receptionist this little bit of information. He is eager to see if the young girl is going to be alright. She is admitted to the hospital. Afterwards, the doctor instructs the nurse on her duties to the lass and sends her to have an x-ray with an orderly pushing her bed. She remains unconscious.

At the x-ray, the woman is placed on the table and pictures are taken. She is taken back down to Emergency to await the reading of the film. After seeing the pictures, a doctor tells the nurse to give her oxygen and start an IV.

The lass is wheeled to room 213 on the second floor. A nurse, RN Valery Bass, comes into the room and starts the IV and places her on oxygen. Conrad finds out what room she is in and proceeds to it. Once there, he is told to wait until Valery is finished. Shortly, Conrad is admitted.

For the first time, he notices that she is a red haired, young beauty very similar to Maureen O'Hara of Hollywood fame. He becomes interested in the girl's state hoping she would awaken. The young red head does not. A brief time later, Conrad proceeds home to tell his parents of his adventure.

Once home, Conrad says "Mom, I'm home." His mother, Grace Thomas, arrives in the living room. His father, Hank Thomas, has not arrived from work yet. He is a lieutenant with the Henrico County Police Department. Conrad asks his mother where his dad is at. Grace says "He is still at work and I do not know why." Conrad begins telling his mother of his find on the side of a road in Henrico County. Conrad tells about finding the young woman, on the aid of the gal he had rendered and that she was unconscious the last he knew. His mother says "That is the son I raised."

Conrad's father, Hank Thomas, arrives in just a few minutes and Conrad proceeds to tell him of his adventure this October day. He tells his dad all the facts pertaining to the incident. His father asks, "Are you going to tell her that you were the one to find her?" "Yes dad, as soon as she comes around," speaks Conrad. The family, after a brief time, has dinner fixed by Grace. It is salad, steak, and baked potato. After finishing, Conrad goes upstairs to take a shower. His parents go into the Family room to watch TV. Afterwards, they all retired for the evening.

CHAPTER 2

The Stay

The next day after work, Conrad returns home to get a camera to use if she was awake. He, then, goes to the hospital to check on his find. The young red head was still unconscious. Conrad takes a picture of her for future reference not knowing why. He, afterwards, goes to the Nurse Station to ask of the girl's condition. Nurse Valery Bass asks "Who are you?"

Conrad replies "I'm the man who found her and brought her to this hospital." "Oh," she says in response. Bass goes on to say "She is still in a state of unconsciousness. We have no idea how long this will last. She is doing okay after being bandaged up. The girl does have three concussions."

Conrad returns to room 213 just to wait to see if the young one would return to a normal state of mind. He stays until closing time at 8 o'clock pm—two and a half hours after arriving at 6:30 pm. He leaves the room, returns to his Viper and drives back home. He reports to his mom and dad that the girl has not gotten over being unconscious. His dad asks "How long do you plan to see this girl?" "As long as it takes for her to awaken and I can tell her I was the one that found her and took her to the hospital. What's for dinner, mom?" completes Conrad. "Since we had steak last night, I think we will have pork chops for supper with mashed potatoes and green beans," returns Grace.

After the meal is fixed, all sit down to eat. The main topic of the evening is Conrad's attention and intentions with the young lady. The family enjoys the meal with Conrad and Hank taking second helpings of everything. Hank questions Conrad "Do you think it is wise to check on the girl every day? What if she is upset with you finding her? Maybe she had a problem with a drug overdose."

"How will I get to know when she is out of the unconscious state if I don't go every day? I'm sure that she will be glad that I took her to the hospital. I'm also sure she has no drug problem. She doesn't look the type. Besides, I did not see a purse and one shoe--the left--was missing. She may need some help," replied Conrad.

"Conrad, I do not want you to get involved with this lady. You do not know her or where she came from. She may have lived down the dirt road you told us about. You do not know her age or why she had no purse and missing a shoe. What condition were her clothes in? How did she look today?" showing concern for her son replies Grace. Conrad, eager to reply, states "When I found her, she was wearing an expensive looking green dress that goes down to her knees. She had nothing else to speak of. I noticed she had no jewelry on her hands or around her neck. She was in a hospital gown the time I saw her after delivering her to Henrico Hospital. The girl looked beautiful with her red hair."

Grace questions "Why are you so interested in her regaining consciousness? Do you have feelings for her?" Conrad tells his mom "I would like to know why she was lying beside the road on Mount Holly Church Road. I would also like to know why she was even traveling on the road. Most of all, I would like to know who she is."

"What if he is interested in her, Grace? It would be interesting for us to see where his fascination leads," responds Hank. "We do not need to know anything about this girl. When will I get my point clear? Conrad has not been interested in any girl for any length of time. Why now?" comes back Grace. Conrad interrupts the exchange between his mother and father "It IS my life and I will decide where this involvement will lead if I can get the lass to agree to some sort of dating. If she won't then I won't have much of an opportunity to get involved with her. I still want to talk to her." "Well then Conrad, do as you want. You are of age at 23 to make your own decision about her" reports Hank. Grace only replies "We will see about that."

Grace goes into the kitchen to prepare dinner. Hank and Conrad continue discussing the young lady. Both have found an interest in the direction the encounter will lead. Meanwhile, Grace is getting the pork chops out and begins to fry them. She also gets the potatoes out and puts these in the microwave to bake before mashing them. Getting the dinnerware out, she sets the table and then returns to the pork chops. These are one of Conrad's favorites to eat, but not the most favorite. That was Mexican food at his special restaurant. Getting the chops done is an easy task.

However, she had stated earlier that they would have green beans and mashed potatoes. She proceeds to mash the potatoes after opening a can of green beans and placing these in the microwave. Grace places the pork chops on a plate with the potatoes and green beans each in bowls. She announces "Come and get it. Dinner is served."

The men come in and immediately Hank asks "Where's the coffee?" Grace gave him "Still in the peculator. I will get it in a moment." Conrad says he would have a soft drink instead of coffee. After getting the coffee for Hank, Grace sits down with the other two to eat dinner. Conrad gets his Pepsi to drink. When dinner is over, Conrad thanks his mother for the pork chops. He tells her they were pretty good.

Once Hank is finished, he goes to the family room to watch television. Conrad joins him and Grace clears the table placing the dishes in the dishwasher and putting the leftovers in the refrigerator. She then joins the men in the family room. She, however, gets a book down to read from the built-in library. They all spend the rest of the evening, short as it is, doing their choices. After a while, all retire for the evening.

.   The next day, Conrad goes to work at Wachovia—a job he has had for 5 years. He had managed to be promoted to a Manager of accounts and finances. He had taken courses in Business Administration at Virginia Commonwealth University (VCU) to prepare for the job. He had not wanted to be a police officer as is his father—a lieutenant on the Henrico County Police Force. Hank had been at the job for almost 30 years. Grace goes to work at her job at VCU being an English teacher. She had been at her job 28 years. The three work out their day. Grace and Hank return home while Conrad goes to the hospital in his 2008 Dodge.

Conrad arrives at Henrico Hospital and parks his car in the lot. He walks straight to room 213 to see his find. She remains unconscious. Conrad asks Valery Bass "Has there been any indication she is going to wake up?" Valery replies "No. We have seen no change in her condition. Her heart rate is fine as well as her breathing capacity. Everything looks good for the time being."

"Does that mean there is a chance she will get worse?" inquires Conrad. Bass tells him "Well, there is always a chance of that happening, but we do not expect anything to get worse. We still are not sure how long she will remain in this state. It could be days, months or years. Each case is different. Normally, we expect an unconscious person to come out of it in about a month. Anything less would be considered something amazing."

Conrad is disappointed to hear the news that the young lady could be out of consciousness for a month. He keeps those feelings to himself hoping it would only be days. Conrad stays for the remainder of the visiting hours sitting in a recliner waiting—for what reason he asks himself. He knew he is getting more than interested in where she came from and why she was beside the road. After completing day two of watching the unconscious girl, he goes to his car and drives home. He is expecting dinner when he arrives there.

Grace has indeed prepared dinner for Hank and Conrad. Hank had been home about an hour before Conrad arrives. Hank was anxiously awaiting Conrad's arrival because dinner is barbecue. That was Hank's favorite food. Grace's favorite food is seafood at Red Lobster, mainly lobster. It has been a while since she last went and she is looking forward to going there again. Conrad arrives and his mother states "Dinner is ready boys. Let us take our seats and get our food." All three end their meal about the same time. Conrad tells his mother "I will clean up the kitchen for you tonight. That way, you can spend more time with dad." Hank and Grace decide to go upstairs to their master bath and get into the whirlpool.

Conrad does as he says he would. He, then, goes to his room to ponder the evening's events. He is still disturbed about what RN Valery Bass had told him about the time of unconsciousness. He is so down over the thing that he has trouble going to sleep. Conrad eventually does go to sleep. After their time in the whirlpool, Grace and Hank retire for the evening.

It is now day three for Conrad's efforts in learning about the girl. He has arisen with the intent of finding out more about being unconscious. Conrad tells his parents that he is going to VCU's Library to look the subject up for details about how long one could remain in said state.

After breakfast of fried eggs and bacon, the family leaves for their individual jobs. The day was really slow for Conrad. He was anxious about finding out more about unconsciousness than RN Valery Bass had told him and he desires to see his, now, future endeavor. Just as soon as his day is over, Conrad goes to the VCU Library. He knows the head librarian, Maryann Witten, from when he attended the university. She had been a student in Library Science and since landed the job of head librarian after being a part of the library staff for five years. Part of that time, she had been a student.

Arriving at the library, Conrad goes in and finds Maryann. She is at the computer for use by the staff where she is looking up a book for a student of Architecture. As soon as Maryann is finished, he asks "Maryann, can you help me find information on being unconscious?" "What in the world do you want that for? You were a Business Administration major," comes back Witten.

Conrad tells her the story of finding the girl and that she is unconscious. He adds that he is interested in when she might awaken. Maryann goes back to the computer and types in the *Find* box the words 'State of Mind.' Conrad says that is not what he wants to know, but Maryann tells him she was the librarian and to let her do her job. She finds listings for several books. Witten takes down notes for a few of the books to see which will best satisfy Conrad's quest.

The first turns out to be not of any use to Conrad. Maryann continues with her list until finally coming to a book titled '*The Mind and Its Problems.*' She found in the index a complete dissertation on unconsciousness. Conrad says "That seems to be exactly what I am looking for. Thank you, Maryann." Her reply "You are welcome." Instead of sitting down and immediately going through the book's section on unconsciousness, Conrad heads for his Dodge and leaves the lot for the hospital. His search for information having been completed, he knew he could read it while waiting to see if his 'friend' would regain her consciousness.

Arriving 20 minutes later, he notices that the time is now 7:00 o'clock pm. Conrad goes to the room and sits down. There was no change in the girl. He opens the book and begins to read about being in an unconscious state of mind. It was a very informative undertaking. Conrad is ready for what he will find out: be it good or bad. He sits there the full hour he has remaining for visiting time, but does not realize that the time is over.

Nurse Valery comes in to check on the girl and informs Conrad it is time to leave. He returns "I didn't know it is that late." He goes to the parking lot, gets in his Viper and calls his mother "Mom, don't hold any supper for me. I'll stop and get me something on the way home."

Conrad has made up his mind to go get some Mexican food at the Mi Hacienda Mexican Restaurant—his favorite food at his favorite restaurant. Arriving there, he goes inside and asks for Juanita to be his waitress. He is greeted by the manager, Jose' Emanez. Juanita has wanted to date Conrad for some time, but Conrad just thought of her as a good friend even though she had long, shiny black hair with just a few curls.

Juanita arrives at his table "Conrad, it's oh so nice to see you again. What can I get you?" "I'll have the usual: two tacos, a burrito and an enchilada with a Pepsi for my drink," states Conrad. There was no form of involvement on his part. He wants to keep it that way. He also thinks about his other 'friend' in the hospital.

Juanita eventually returns with his food and drink, asking "Can I join you for a brief, but enjoyable, moment?" Conrad says "Yes, but don't expect much. I have a lot on my mind." "About your job?" seeks Juanita. "No. I have a friend in the hospital and I am worried about the condition that she is in" gives back Conrad. "You have a friend in the hospital who is a girl? That is a shame. Do I know her?" inquires Juanita. "No." says Conrad. With that, he begins eating his food in a remorseful manner. Juanita notices and decides to leave Conrad alone. She gets up and goes to wait on other customers.

For some reason, he thought, the food was not as good as usual. He realizes that it is probably because of his thoughts for the girl and her condition. The thoughts were separate, yet combined. He finishes his meal, leaves a five dollar tip and heads for his car. He drives home still in a dismal mood. Once there, he tells his parents that he going to bed early.

Instead, he goes to his room and reads some more from the book he got at VCU Library. He finishes reading and learns that the normal time is indeed a month of unconsciousness, but he also learns there were reported cases of only ten days. One thing that scared him was that 99% of the people who have severe head injuries die. The other 1% tend to live because the medical staff does what they can to prolong life.

Conrad felt better somewhat having read the section of the book that is of interest to him. He decides to go to bed to get up early tomorrow morning. He has the intention of visiting the hospital before he goes to work. Visiting hours start at 8:00 o'clock am. He wants to be there.

It is now day four. Conrad arises at 5:30 am and takes a shower. He dresses and goes downstairs. He leaves a note telling his parents that he is leaving early to go by the hospital on this the fourth day of his visits. Conrad leaves in a hurry at 7:00 am proceeding to the hospital. He wants to be there before the visitor's time begins so he could have the full hour before he had to be at work. It would make him late for work, but he really did not care about that. He reaches his destination at 7:15 am. He decides to get a bite to eat from the cafeteria, but he would make it quick. He gets two donuts and a bottle of Pepsi Cola. With this in hand and it now being 7:19 am, He goes to room 213.

The first thing he notices is that she is still in her state of seemingly unending sleep. The next thing he notices is her hair had been done and looks even more beautiful than when he saw her last night. He asks a new nurse "Who made the request to have her hair done? I thought she would have to do that." The nurse says "I am Georgia St. John. I have been assigned to this girl for today and possibly tomorrow. Who are you that you need to know?" asks St. John. Conrad tells her all about the incident that he knew. She, then, states "I guess it will be okay to tell you. Nurse Valery Bass had the beautician come early this morning before going home."

Being satisfied, Conrad sat down in amazement at the beauty of this lass. He became adamant that he would continue to come until she was conscious. It is now an important event in his mind. He needs to know if she is married or single. Although, without any jewelry he thought most likely she is single. He guesses her age as 21 years old. He is beginning to have feelings for the young lady. He has made up his mind to get to know the girl as soon as she regains consciousness.

RN St. John left Conrad with the young lady. Conrad goes over thoughts in his mind thinking about what would be his first statement or question that he would put forth to her when she regains consciousness. He also thinks who would be first to speak and what might the girl say. His morning time being used, he leaves for work and arrives a few minutes late. He works the day at Wachovia and returns home before going to the hospital. Once there, he changes shirts and shoes to be more comfortable.

Leaving the house in his Viper, Conrad makes a quick drive of the distance to Henrico Hospital. After parking his car, he goes straight to, and into, room 213. The girl is still out cold. He just sits down and waits.

Nurse Georgia comes in and says "Good evening young man. Are you here again to visit Jane Doe?" "Yes. When did she get that name?" asks Conrad. St. John replies "It's been on her record since she was admitted. Didn't anybody tell you this?" "No" he answers. "Well, now you know" states the nurse. After checking the monitor, bandages, IV, and oxygen, she leaves.

Conrad just sits in the recliner and waits watching the television. The other patient had been discharged earlier that day leaving Jane Doe alone in the room. Conrad thought it a better situation. His time to leave arrives and he leaves her room heading for his car when RN Valery Bass asks him to wait a minute. He stops at the Nurses Station. Valery asks Conrad "Are you any relation to the young lady in room 213?"

Conrad wonderingly asks "No, why do you ask?" "We do not have anyone to contact if there is a change in her condition either way. Could we contact you as an option?" states Valery. Conrad returns "By all means. I am interested in when she will recover. Let me give you my name and telephone numbers." He writes out his name, office, home and cell phone numbers stating "The first is a daytime number. If I can't be reached there, then, call the cell phone. The middle number is my nighttime number. Call me at the first change in her condition, please." Bass, being glad for the information, says "Thank you very much Mr. Thomas. We will put this on her chart and word will be passed on to the other shifts."

Conrad leaves the building, enters his car and drives home somewhat disappointed that he had not seen any change in his 'Jane Doe'. He says to himself 'tomorrow is another day.' Arriving home and going inside, Conrad asks his dad "How was your day?" "Pretty normal. We had a stakeout that yielded us nothing and we'll continue to do it again and again 'til we get the two we're after they are robbery perks. Other than that, there wasn't much else. How was your day? You started awful early" Hank inquires.

"Yes, it was early. I went by the hospital hoping to see a change in Jane Doe as the hospital has her listed. After about an hour, I went to work and the day was a real drudgery. I kept thinking of her and when she will talk. After work, I went to the hospital again. She is still the same" Conrad relays to his dad. Hank, then, asks "Why did you call her Jane Doe? Is that her real name or just something the hospital came up with?"

"Dad, it's like the Coroners' Office. They don't know who the patient is so they just name them John or Jane Doe for the time being. I was a bit surprised. One of the nurses had a beautician fix Jane's hair and, dad, she looked downright gorgeous. I can hardly wait to see her again" excited is Conrad.

Grace enters with "What are you two fellows up to now? Is it that girl again?" "Oh, hi mom" Conrad continues "Yes, it was. I told dad about a beautician from the hospital fixing Jane's hair and how it drastically changed her appearance. The hospital did it without anyone from outside giving permission because she was still out of it. She has been resting quietly with no change in her condition."

"Drastically, huh. Does that mean you are increasing your interest in her? You do not know if she is married. You better leave well enough alone" rules his mother. "You're right about me not knowing if she is married, but she had no jewelry on. Further, she looks to be only 20 or 21 years old. And my interest in her has been heightened, mom, just because I don't know these things" her son comes back with.

"Your dinner is waiting for you in the kitchen. You did not call, so I assumed you would eat when you got home. It is corn beef, cabbage and cornbread. I have kept it warm for you. Do not get overly interested in the girl. Do you hear me?" orders Grace. Conrad's only reply is "Yes, mother." He goes to eat, although corn bread was not one of his favorites. He got himself a cold Pepsi from the refrigerator to go with his meal.

While he ate, his parents go into the family room. Hank sits down and turns the TV on while Grace got a book to read from one of the many shelves. She sits next to her husband and they enjoy their time before retiring for the night. Meanwhile, Conrad is eating and thinking of Jane—as he now thinks of her. She seems to be on his mind all the time. After eating, he puts the leftovers away and places the dirty dishes in the dishwasher. Conrad starts it to save the trouble for his mother. Then, he goes upstairs and retires for the evening as well.

The next day is day five of his indulgence into the mystery of Jane Doe. Conrad takes his shower, dries himself, gets dressed and goes downstairs to the kitchen. His mother is already there fixing breakfast. He had gotten up a bit late due mainly to yesterday's length. Grace welcomes her son with "Good morning. Are you still thinking about THAT girl?"

"Mother, please. I have told you and dad that I would continue to worry about her. It's as if she were my responsibility. I even gave my name and phone numbers to the hospital for them to call if there is any change in her status. They didn't have anyone else to call" informs Conrad and continues with "What's for breakfast?" His mother replies simply "Oatmeal with maple syrup. It will be done in a minute. I have poured you a glass of orange juice to go with it."

"Thanks mom. Where's dad?" queries Conrad. "You father has gone to the office. He has something important to get done early as possible. He did not tell me what. Get your bowl. This is done," tells Grace. Conrad does as he is told. After filling his bowl and taking it to the table, he gets a spoon and some milk. He sits down pouring milk on the oatmeal—just enough to thin it a bit. He begins eating and his mother starts again "You know you can get yourself in trouble with that girl in the hospital. Why has she become so important? Do you not have something else more important to do than go to the hospital every day? What if she never comes out of the coma? What then? What if she is married? What if she has a child and is not married? What effect would that have on you?"

"Mom, enough is enough. Okay? I will take it one day at a time. When I feel it is a hopeless case, then I will give it up. Until then, she is my responsibility. I did find her and I did get her admitted to the hospital. I really don't want to discuss it now. I am your son who you taught to be concise and considerate. That's all I'm doing," demands Conrad. He commences eating his oatmeal—his favorite type. Before he finishes eating, his mother gets her coat and leaves for work at VCU. She is in for a hard day. Conrad cleans the kitchen before leaving for work. He, then, gets his coat and leaves the house to find his car had been moved. He had forgotten that he was the last one home and had blocked his father's truck from leaving the driveway.

Conrad arrives at work to find people waiting to talk to him concerning some financial matters. They were interested in CDs, investments and a trust fund. This took his mind off of Jane Doe for the entire morning. It is almost normal as if he had never seen the girl. When he leaves for his lunch time, it all comes back to him. He is in turmoil over what his mother had said to him at breakfast. He tells himself 'that's not going to change my mind about anything'. He goes to McDonald's for lunch having the 'Big and Tasty Combo' that came with a medium Pepsi. He eats and returns to work. He has a lot of paper work to complete after the morning's encounter.

Back to work again takes his mind off of the young lady. He completes out his day's work and returns home. He is the first to arrive. So, as a treat to his mother, Conrad starts dinner. He takes hamburger and shredded Cheddar cheese out of the refrigerator first. Second, he gets a can of chili with beans. Third, he gets an onion. Last, he gets out a loaf of bread. Conrad begins to cook the hamburger in the form of patties bigger than what would be used for sandwiches. While these were cooking, he opens the can of chili and beans, placing these into a bowl and, then, into the microwave. He starts the microwave and goes back to flip the burgers. He, then, chops the onion and places it in a bowl. After cooking the burgers, he places a slice of bread on each of three plates. On the bread, he places the burgers. Then, he covers the burgers with the chili mix and finally spreads cheese over each burger. This is their dinner—Texas Burgers. The bowl of onions is set on the table for anyone wanting to add these to the 'Texas Burgers'. There is enough for each of them to have another helping. He finishes just in time for his mother to arrive and affectionately say "What have you done?"

"Well mom, I've cooked dinner for us. We can eat now or wait for dad to come home. It's your choice" replies Conrad. "We can wait for your father. He called me at school and told me he would be home on time" comes back Grace.

Just then, the door opens and it is Hank. He says "Uummm. It smells good. How did you cook dinner so fast, Grace?" "I did not cook. It was all Conrad's doing" states his wife. Hank orders "Let's eat then." Conrad had forgotten to make coffee for his mother and father. His father is first to say something about it. Grace gets up and goes to the kitchen counter to make the coffee and tells Hank to wait a minute. They eat a few minutes later and Grace says "The coffee is ready" and she pours a cup for Hank delivering it to him.

After dinner, Conrad tells his parents he is going to the hospital. His mom asks "What? Again? When are you going to stop?" "I don't know that I will stop. Will you stop complaining about it?" comes back Conrad. "Wait a minute, Grace. Our son is right. He is over 21 and you need to cut the apron strings because it is his life he is leading. We made our mistakes and managed to live through them. My mother says it was a mistake for me to marry you, but I did, didn't I? Besides, we have no idea how things will go until she does wake up. So what if he wants to have a single sided date every night with the girl? As I said before, it is his life" orders Hank in a grumpy tone.

"But . . . ." is all Grace could get out before Hank cuts her off with "No ifs, ands, or buts about it. Conrad can and will do as he pleases as long as it doesn't destroy the family's reputation." Conrad remarks "Thanks, dad. Don't fret mother. Dad and you have had faith in me all along. So, why change it? Goodnight people." Conrad grabs his coat and goes out the door. Fortunately for him, his dad had blocked in his mother's car. He figured that his dad knew he would go to the hospital.

Arriving and parking, Conrad gets out of his Dodge Viper and goes into the hospital. He stops by the cafeteria to get him a Pepsi to drink (he is not a coffee drinker). He heads straight from there to Jane's room. Upon entering the room, he finds Georgia St. John looking over the monitor. "Is anything wrong?" inquires Conrad. "No, Mr. Thomas. We did see Jane, here, move her fingers earlier today. That is a good sign. We are just checking to see if things are still the same in her status. It appears to be so. Tell us if you notice anything different—hand movement, eyes open, speaking, anything like that. We'll appreciate it" requests RN St. John just before she leaves the room.

Conrad takes his seat in the recliner and begins his, what seems like, dutiful watch. It is 6:45 pm. He sits and drinks his Pepsi all the while watching the lass as she lay perfectly still. That is until about 7:25 pm. She wakes up, takes off the oxygen mask and says immediately "Where am I?" Startled, Conrad tells her

"You're in Richmond in Henrico County Doctors Hospital in room 213. My name is Conrad C. Thomas. I checked you in to the hospital. Who are you?" Stuttering, she utters "I … I … I do not know. I cannot remember my own name. What am I doing here? What are these bandages for? Why and what is with this IV in my arm?" Conrad interrupts and tells her "Hold on. You're going too fast. Let me ring for a nurse." He grabs the button beside her bed on the rail and presses the button.

RN Valery Bass is the first to arrive followed shortly by RN Georgia St. John. Before entering Valery yells "WHAT IS IT?" Conrad anxiously states "She's awake and talking. She can't remember anything including her name. St John arrives. The two nurses commence checking the Jane Doe out after asking Conrad to step out. Valery checks the monitor. Georgia shuts off the oxygen and checks the IV. Valery checks the bandages.

Meanwhile, Jane Doe is full of questions. They each ask her repeatedly to wait a few minutes. Finally satisfied that all was okay with her status, Valery asks "What do you want to know first?" "The gentleman told me where I am at, but not why" says Jane Doe. Georgia tells her "I'm Georgia St. John and this is Valery Bass. You have three concussions on you head. You have been here five days. Your conditional status is stable. We don't know your name, address or why you were brought here."

"Who can tell me?" asks the lass. "You will have to ask the young man. He brought you here and checked you in" returns Valery. "Where is he? Can I talk to him? Where are my clothes?" inquires Jane Doe. "Your clothes and one shoe are in the closet. You only had the one on when you were admitted. We are through now and we will send Mr. Thomas back in to see you," offers Valery.

CHAPTER 3

The Name Game

Conrad reenters her room. The young woman immediately asks "Why did you bring me here?" "I found you lying face down on the side of Mount Holly Church Road. You were unresponsive and had bled from your head. You had lost a lot of blood. I didn't know what all was wrong with you. So, I brought you here to be checked out. That was on Sunday morning five days ago. Today is Friday" gives Conrad. Where is my other shoe and where is my purse?" she asked. Conrad confesses "I have no idea where either is at. I found you with only one black loafer. I didn't see the other."

The statement strikes an accord with her. She believes Conrad is sincere and states "You do not know my name? I guess not. I do not know you. As far as I know, we just met. I do not remember how I got hurt, where I am from or where I was going or why. I feel lost." "Let me fill you in a bit. I never met you before picking you up to carry to my car. I have never seen you in Richmond before, but that really doesn't mean you haven't been here before. Let me try to help you with remembering your name. Let's try your first name. Do you remember anything about it at all? Maybe you can remember what letter or sound it began with. Try to think."

"Well ... I think it began with the sound 'se'. Like in the word set," comes back the girl. Conrad says "Ooooh. That makes it harder. You definitely are not a Jane and I doubt you're a Doe. That sound is a soft consonant and could be a letter 'c' or 's'. Let me try a few and see if one sounds right. Let me say a list, then, you tell me to stop when you hear one that sounds like it. Cindy. Cynthia. Sally. Samantha. Sandra. Sandy. Sarah. Saundra. Sydney. Sylvia. Sissy. Summer. That's all I can think of at the moment. Did any sound familiar?"

"There were two. Cynthia and Sylvia. But, I really do not know," answers 'Jane'. "You need a name besides Jane Doe. Which do you like?" offered Conrad. The girl replies "I know a Cynthia and a Sylvia. I think. But, I do not know which one to pick." That statement about knowing the two girls strikes an accord with Conrad. "Well, thinking you know is close to remembering. Just pick one. You could pick Cynthia. That's close to Conrad alphabetically. Then again, maybe you should take Sylvia," Conrad puts forth. "That almost sounds like an order 'take Sylvia'. But since it came from you, I will pick Sylvia. It sounds sexier anyway. Did I just say 'sexier? I should not have said that. I don't know you YET! I do hope I will learn more about you," seeks Sylvia.

Conrad retorts "I hope you do too. Now that the first name is over, let's try for a last name. Any guesses as to what it might sound like?" "R" "But that's a big range of names. Can't you do better?" asks Conrad. Sylvia says "If I had a phone book, I could read the names." "There! You just said it. Reed. R…E…E…D. Your name will be Sylvia Reed. Push the button for a nurse," Conrad says as he takes her hand to shake it. Before pressing the button, Sylvia looks up at him and smiles, but he does not let go of her right hand. Instead, after a moment, she takes the button holder in her left hand and pushes the button with her left thumb.

The signal brings in Valery Bass in a rush saying "What is wrong?" "Nothing," says Conrad "Nurse Valery Bass meet patient Sylvia Reed," as he dropped her hand. "How did you get her to remember her name?" asks Bass. Sylvia responds first with

"We played a name game. I actually did remember something of my first name. I knew just the start of it. Conrad gave me a list of names that started with 'se' like in set. Two sounded like they might be right." "Sylvia was one. What was the other?" requests Valery. "Cynthia. Conrad at first suggested that I pick it. Then, he changes his mind and says I 'should TAKE Sylvia'. So, I picked Sylvia. The last name came as somewhat of an accident. Conrad asked if I knew anything about my last name and I told him 'R'. He said there were a lot of 'R' names. And I said if I had a telephone book I could READ it. Do you get it? R e a d versus R e e d."

The RN tells Sylvia "That was quite interesting. Do you remember the names of anybody else or how those might start? Maybe you might remember a member of the family or a relative. Think about it tonight. Mr. Thomas, it is almost 9:00 o'clock. That is well past the time you should have left. I must tell you to leave. Sylvia will be here for you tomorrow. We will change her name on her chart and the hospital's record. Goodnight, Mr. Thomas." Conrad takes Sylvia's right hand and holds it with his left in a caressing manner and says "Until tomorrow MORNING." He lets her hand go after a moment and then leaves.

Sylvia asks "Why did he visit me today?" "He has visited you every day since you were admitted five days ago. He even left his phone numbers to call if there was a change in your status. We noticed you moved your fingers earlier today. We did not think it serious enough to call him because we knew he would be in tonight. He has been very concerned about you even though he does not know you. Further, he was told that the average time a person remains comatose is about a month. He was prepared to come every day. He even had a medical book to read on your condition. By the way, you have set a new medical history for Henrico County Doctors Hospital. You have only been out four days. The previous record was 11 days. I will close your door as I leave so that you can watch TV. The control is on the right side rail near the nurse button. If you need something, just press the red button. Is there anything else?"

"Could I get something to eat and does this IV have to stay in my arm?" asks Sylvia. RN Valery's reply is "Yes, to both of your questions. You will have a tray in a few minutes." Valery Bass leaves for the time being.

Sylvia thinks over everything that has transpired since awakening almost two hours ago. The thing that struck her the most was Conrad's touching her hand twice. She was eager for him to touch her again. Sylvia did turn on the TV set after Conrad had turned it off just before she awoke. She wants to watch a movie and found one that would start in a minute. So, she waited for the program and her food. After ten minutes, a kitchen employee brought her a club sandwich, lime Jello and a can of ginger ale. She ate everything and wanted more, but did not ask for it. She watched the movie to its end and changed channels to a music station to listen to. Sylvia remained awake until 3:00 o'clock am when she dozed off with the TV still on the music channel.

CHAPTER 4

Washington DC

It is Sunday morning, the day after Sylvia's trip began. Mary Redman goes into her husband's office and says "Honey, Sylvia is gone. Her bed was not slept in nor is her car here. What are we going to do?" Her husband, Sylvester Redman, picks up the phone handset and calls his Under-secretary Eric Cook. Eric arrives "Good morning, Mr. President. What can I do for you?" "You can get me Charles Edwards, Director of the FBI. Have him come here immediately. Our daughter, Sylvia, is missing," says Sylvester.

"Yes sir, Mr. President," responds Eric. He leaves to call the Director. Mary says again "Honey, what are we going to do? She has never done anything like this before." "When Edwards gets here, we will start on finding her whereabouts. I am sure he can handle it" says Sylvester. "Well, she had a full tank of gas that would take her into North Carolina, West Virginia, New York or anywhere in between. Where would she go? And why would she want to leave last night. Yesterday was her birthday and we wanted to have that surprise party for her. We will have to postpone that now," says Mary. Sylvester comes back with "That is a minor thing right now. Do not worry about it. Eric can handle the notification of the invitees. I wish Edwards was here."

Charles Edwards arrives inquiring "What is this about Sylvia missing, Mr. President?" "Edwards, she was gone this morning and so was her red Dodge Viper. Her bed was not slept in. We really do not know when she left the House. I want you to get a team together to investigate. There is to be no media release of the information. Also contact Henry Travis, the D.C. Police Chief and have his men keep a lookout for Sylvia's red 2009 Dodge Viper.

In addition, I want you to contact the Maryland and Virginia State Police agencies. Do what I have told you today even if you have to contact Travis at his home," responds President Redman. "Yes sir. Understood sir. I will do the contacting of the police agencies first and get a senior agent to form a team after I do a briefing. Is that acceptable, Mr. President?" "Yes. Now go and get started," orders Sylvester. Edwards leaves.

Cook comes back to the President with "One of the staff says he saw Sylvia headed towards the garage at 10:30 last night. I have questioned the entire staff, sir, and he was the only one that saw anything." "What is his name? Bring him here to the office after you leave. Later today, contact the invitees to Sylvia's birthday party telling them it has been postponed for a while. Give no indication as to why. If you are asked, just reply there is a time problem with my schedule. And until further notice, there will be a time problem with my scheduling. Look over the next week and see what can be postponed for a while. If you feel that some event cannot be put off, then leave it scheduled, but advise me what you have done once you have completed this task. Are there any questions?"

"No sir. However, Howard James, the staff member I mentioned, is busy with duties at the moment. I will need to have someone replace him for the duration of the time he is with you, Mr. President," says Under-secretary Eric. Sylvester tells him "That is fine. You may leave now."

Eric leaves and heads to the other end of the White House to get Howard James after first getting another staff person to fill in for Howard. Arriving where James is working, he informs him that his work will be covered while he is with the President. "What have I done that I must go before him," asks Howard. Cook tells him "I will take you there. It is nothing bad. I think he wants to talk to you about Sylvia. Let's go." They leave for the other end of the House.

Meanwhile, Sylvester is comforting Mary "Dear, I know you are worried sick about Sylvia. We will get through this event as if it never happened. Just wait and see. I am sure Edwards will get things started soon, if not already. There is really no need to fret over the situation." He hugs Mary.

Under-secretary Eric Cook arrives with Howard James at the President's personal office (not the Oval Room office). "Here is Howard James as you requested Mr. President," advises Eric. Redman reaches out his hand to shake James' hand. James is a little hesitant. He had never been this close to the President before. Eventually, he does take the President's hand. They shake hands. Sylvester says "I want to thank you for your diligence in observing Sylvia last night and reporting it to Eric. You did nothing wrong in not stopping her. She was 21 yesterday and old enough to make her own choices. Have a good day and take the rest of it off with pay. See to it Eric. "Yes sir" Eric takes Howard from the office and escorts him back to his work station. He, then, tells James "Give Liz a list of the rest of your duties for the rest of the day. Then, you may do as the President told you." "Yes sir, Mr. Cook" responds Howard James. Howard, then, tells Liz his duties for the rest of the day and asks her "Are my duties harder than yours?"

"No. Actually, the duties difficulties are about the same. I do like the change though. What did Redman want with you?" asks Liz. "It seems I am the only one of all the staff to see his daughter, Sylvia, last night. I told Cook and he told Redman. After I got to the office, he shook my hand and thanked me. It was something neat. I also have the rest of the day off for being so diligent" informs James. Howard leaves.

About the same time, FBI Director Edwards sees Henry Travis, Chief of D.C. Police at his home and informs him "President Redman wants you informed about the missing of his daughter, Sylvia. There is to be no media leak. He wants you to have your officers to be on the alert for his daughter's 2009 red Dodge Viper. If it is found with her, escort her home. If it is found without her, report its location to me personally at FBI Headquarters and, then, have it towed to the White House's back gate. You are to begin immediately. Are there any questions?" Travis responds "Do I need to put out additional officers on patrol?" "That's up to you. You do what you think is best to serve the interests of President Redman," answers Edwards. Edwards, then, leaves.

Arriving at Headquarters, Director Edwards looks over his list of senior agents and picks Ginger Ales. He calls her at her office and tells her to come to his office as quick as possible. He waits impatiently for her arrival. About fifteen minutes later, she arrives. "Ginger, the President's daughter is missing. She has not been seen since around 10:30 last night. At least, that's what Cook told me. I'm appointing you in charge of a task force of ten agents. It will be your team as you pick them. Try and get partners as pairs. You may need a couple of single agents working alone.

I want reports every day until we find her. It may be necessary to force her home. We don't know why she left. There is to be no media leaks and the agents should not disclose why they are looking for Sylvia. I want you to start today with agents in the field by noon. Also, find out what personal info you can about Sylvia's friends and her interests at Georgetown University. She is taking Psychology. Get a young agent to do that so he can blend in with the students. Report back to me at noon."

Senior Agent Ales says "I will get on it right away, sir." Ginger arises to leave his office, but Charles stops her with "By the way, send me a list of who you pick and what their assignments are as soon as you get done with that." Afterwards, Ginger leaves heading for her office. There is no one around to interrupt her as she puts her list of ten agents together. She spends 15 minutes making the list and an hour calling all the agents telling them to report to the debriefing room, which was next to her office.

Senior Agent Ales' list included: Bill Bradford, John Asbury, Jim Duffy, Allen Jeffers, Sandra Lane, Ruth Magnus, Richard Peterson, Victoria Roberts, Glen Underwood and Ho Wong. She made their assignments and sent the list to Director Edwards as instructed. The agents arrived at different times. Some made it quickly to the debriefing room, while others took some time. But, by 10:00 o'clock am, all were present and wondering why they were called on their off day. They even talked about it amongst themselves until Ales arrives. She had been busy detailing the assignments so she can tell each agent what their responsibilities will be. She, also, had given the list of duties to Director Edwards.

Entering the room, Agent Ales introduces herself "I am Senior Agent Ginger Ales. I will be in charge of this special task force. Our task is not as simple as it sounds. We are to locate Sylvia Redman, the President's daughter. She has been missing since 10:30 last night as near as anyone can place it. She drove her 2009 red Dodge Viper and no one knows why she left or where she is going. When we find her, and we will, we will first ask Sylvia to call home. The agent with her will stay with her until she is off the phone. That agent will call me while Sylvia is on the phone. The agent will also stay with Sylvia until told otherwise. If she wants to drive somewhere, follow her. Do not lose sight of her. It may be necessary to take her into custody and I do not mean under arrest.

"Bill, Jim and Ruth, you will be responsible for canvassing the bars, dance halls, motels and restaurants. John and Sandra, you will be responsible for checking out her bank account and credit cards. Find out how much money was last drawn out and when. Also check her credit card usage, when and where used last.

"Richard and Victoria, you will be responsible for checking her cell phone records and White House staff to see if there are any connections where she may have told someone something. Especially, check out Bonnie Spenser for she has had dealings with Sylvia and some were not all that good. Glen and Ho, you will check on her computer, e-mails and papers. See who she contacted last.

Allen, I will speak to you in my office. Each team will be responsible for giving me a daily report of your activities and findings. When you have completed as much as possible, tell me and I will find other work for you. We will be at this until she is found. You can begin immediately," commands Agent Ginger.

Ales and Jeffers go to her office. "Please be seated. Allen I have saved you for last. You are our youngest agent that has attended Georgetown University. Your job will be to get her schedule and question her professors. Also, question some of the students discretely. Try not to disclose your cover. If it becomes necessary, then do it. Especially, hang out at the campus night club. I am sure she spent some time there. Any questions?" Ales asks. Bill says back to her "I wasn't all that active on campus. I may know some of her professors. I will do the best I can." "That is all I ask" states Senior Agent Ginger Ales.

The agents all leave to start their assignments after gathering any equipment they may need. Agent Allen gets a binder to appear as a student. Ginger goes to Director Edwards, who is having coffee at the cafeteria. She gets a cup of coffee and sits down with him. They are alone except for some vending machines. Ginger starts with "All the agents are on the job. If anyone of them finds her car or her, they are to call me immediately. I told them to check out things and give me a report daily. Is there anything else, sir?"

"Only, what will you be doing?" asks Edwards. Ginger says "I will be checking other agencies to see if she has contacted any of these. It just may be possible she got some information that can tell us where she is going." "Good point, Ginger. I had not thought of that. Start with the Department of Transportation. She may have asked for a specific map or set of maps. Get on that right away" "Yes sir." After finishing her coffee, she returns to her office and begins the calling the best she can. After all, it is Sunday.

Agent Allen Jeffers goes to Georgetown University only to find that there are not many students there. He does, however, go to the student night club which is open all day, every day. He notices some students scattered at different tables. He goes over to one and says "I am new here. Would any of you know Sylvia Redman? I know her personally and would like to talk to her." One of the students answers back "You mean the President's daughter. She is never here on Sunday. You should be able to catch her in her Psych class tomorrow. It starts at 8:00 o'clock. "

Allen, then, asks "Does she have any friends that might be around today?" Another student answers "You could try Marvin Cookson. He's spent a lot of time with her at the library. You might catch her there tomorrow. She is a volunteer. Cookson is probably in his dorm, but I don't know which one. Go to the library. It's open today and get on the computer. Look up the campus listing. It will tell you which dorm and what room."

"You both have been very helpful. Thank you so much," gives Allen as he leaves for the Georgetown University Library. Getting there was easy. He had used the library several times when he attended the university.

Once there, he goes to one of the available computers and goes to the web site for the university. Allen clicks the link for the student address list. He enters Marvin Cookson's name and sees where to find him. He goes to his dorm room, but Cookson is not there. Jeffers does see a picture of Cookson and Sylvia. Marvin's absence makes him wonder if the two of them have taken off together. He takes his cell phone and takes a picture of the picture on Cookson's bulletin board. Allen, then, heads back to the library to question the employees. He takes the walk to the library again. He wants his presence to be known. At the library, he sees a volunteer at the checkout counter and asks "What can you tell me about Sylvia Redman? I am new here and a friend of hers. I would like to catch up on things. "

The volunteer says "She was supposed to work today, but hasn't shown up yet. We brought in a cake to celebrate her birthday. It was yesterday don't you know. You might catch her tomorrow afternoon. She is to work again." "Thank you," is all Jeffers had to say. He goes to the cafeteria just to look around and maybe see Sylvia. There is no sign of her and it is lunch time. After his library visit, he returns to FBI HQ to file his report with the fact that Marvin Cookson is a friend and he got a picture of them together. Jeffers gets 100 copies made to pass out to the D.C. police to be on the lookout for both of them together or apart. Jeffers takes the pictures to Senior Agent Ales, who takes them to Director Edwards.

He tells Ales "Add Marvin Cookson to your list of calls to the Transportation Department. Maybe he got the map or maps instead of Sylvia. It may be possible they left together."

Agent Ales, after leaving the Director with Jeffers report, gives the job to Jeffers informing him what to do. Jeffers is pleased to have the task. He sets about it right away going to the Transportation Department. Arriving there, Allen asks "Do you have any record of Sylvia Redman or a Marvin Cookson requesting a map of anywhere?" The clerk responded "Let me check our records." After checking, the clerk continues "No, sir. We have no record of either one of them requesting anything. Sorry." He, then, returns to Cookson's dorm room to await his arrival, if he does come back today. There is the chance he took off with Sylvia. Agent Jeffers makes a call to Marvin Cookson's cell phone, but cannot get anyone to answer. So, he makes up his mind to try again in a little bit of time.

Agent Allen Jeffers waits in Cookson's dorm room for him. Around 3:30 pm, Cookson enters his room. Seeing a man there, he asks "Who are you, what do you want and what is it you are doing in my room?" Agent Jeffers goes to the same routine he used with the students in the student night club. He states and asks "I am a friend of Sylvia Redman. I'm new here and am looking for her. Some of your friends said that I should check with you. Can you help me?"

"I know her, but I don't know where she is. We were supposed to have breakfast together, but Sylvia didn't show. I wish I knew where she was so I could talk to her myself. We have a movie date for Wednesday at 7:30 pm" responds Marvin. Allen almost orders Cookson "Here is my cell phone number. Call me if you hear from her or just see her. I would appreciate it." Marvin tacks the note to his bulletin board. Allen leaves heading back to headquarters disappointed in what he just found so far. He wants to be the one that returns daughter to mom and pop.

Meanwhile, John Asbury and Sandra Lane are on a computer checking Sylvia's bank accounts and learned she had a $1,000 withdrawal from her checking account on Saturday, They learned of Sylvia's spending addiction and were sure they would find what they wanted--where her credit cards were last used. They had no luck on either account. They go to HQ to inform Senior Agent Ales.

Richard Peterson and Victoria Roberts are at the White House in Sylvia's room on her computer checking her cell phone records. They found no usage since last Friday where she called the university. It did not show to whom she talked to. They got a list of staff personnel from Eric Cook and began their interrogation of every employee. Agents Richard and Victoria want to know what anyone on the staff knew about Sylvia. They started at one end and would work their way to the other checking off names as they go. Under-secretary Cook had told them about Howard James. They crossed his name off their list first.

The first working person Richard and Victoria interviewed was Liz who had replaced Howard. She told them "I don't know anything about the President's daughter. Ask Bonnie Spenser. She's even had arguments with Sylvia." Victoria put a star next to Bonnie's name. The two continue the list, but learn nothing else, except most of the employees did not know the actions or interact with the President or his family.

Victoria and Richard finally get to Bonnie Spenser who is a secretary to the President's family. They find her typing an e-mail. They introduce themselves and ask "What do you know about Sylvia Redman?" "Why do you ask?" queries Spenser. Richard tells her "We have been assigned to ask everyone their knowledge of Sylvia's actions and activities. We were told by one of the staff that Sylvia and you have had arguments."

"Well, the times we talked were not all 'arguments' as you put it. We did have disagreements while talking about boys. There was one boy in particular. She e-mailed and telephoned a Marvin Cookson at Georgetown University. He is one of the boys that should be talked to." Victoria made a note to give to Allen. Victoria and Richard left going to Senior Agent Ales at HQ.

Glen Underwood and Ho Wong had gone to the White House as well. They go straight to the Lincoln Bedroom which was where Sylvia slept and her personal computer was at. The computer is off. They turn it on and it asks for a password. Wong is an expert at deciphering passwords. It took him only ten minutes and they were in. Checking her e-mails they could not see who she sent to because she had an MS Outlook block on saving any part of an e-mail sent. They were able to read those that she received. Sylvia had failed to erase some and failed to erase the deleted files. They found mail sent by Marvin Cookson and a boy named Harold Yodel. Glen and Ho had come across Marvin Cookson before, but Harold Yodel is a new name. There is no indication as to whether he is a student at Georgetown University or not. Glen makes a note of that. They search her room for any papers that may lead to finding her, but found nothing.

Bill Bradford, Jim Duffy and Ruth Magnus each took a picture of Sylvia with them. They stay in contact with one another to keep from duplicating coverage. They took all day to canvas just the bars and dance halls. At one of the bars, the bartender stated that the girl in the picture had been in with a boy, but being under 21 she just had a Diet Pepsi. None of the other bars or the dance halls had ever seen Sylvia. Bill, Jim and Ruth quit at about the same time. The motels and restaurants would have to wait until Monday. Getting back to FBI HQ, they each gave a report about what they had discovered to Ginger.

All the agents, except Allen Jeffers, were told to come to the debriefing room at 8:00 o'clock in the morning. Jeffers would stay with Georgetown University for the time being. He would talk to Sylvia's professors starting in the morning. Allen, particularly, wanted to talk to her Psychology professor He quit canvassing at 7:45 pm having not talked to Harold Yodel, who lives off campus. Allen did discover that Yodel was not in the student directory. It will be a task to find this Yodel.

The other nine agents arrive in the debriefing room by 8:00 am. Senior Agent Ginger Ales is waiting for them. She tells them to sit down and all did so. They noticed that Jeffers was not there. Ginger starts the day by debriefing the agents on what each set had done the previous day. She also mentions about Allen Jeffers having a lead on a Harold Yodel, but he had told her the Yodel was not a student. Yodel's address would have to be discovered. She gave that task to agents Glen Underwood and Ho Wong. She told them to use whatever means they could envision to find out his address and get him to the debriefing room. Six of the seven, Ginger Ales told to canvas the motels and restaurants and to work in pairs except for Jim Duffy.

Jim was given a special assignment of contacting the Smithsonian Institution for usage of their satellite monitor that could run film images of cars and people on earth. The satellite was currently being used to monitor terrorist training camps in the Sahara Desert, Afghanistan and Iraq. Ginger did not know if it could be gotten and/or used. The receiver of the satellite's signals is portable to some extent. It would require realignment with the satellite every time it was moved. Also, the pointing of the satellite was needed to where the GPS of the location to be viewed was stored in its memory. Jim Duffy was to get on it after dismissal from the debriefing room.

After being dismissed, all the agents set about their assigned tasks. The six assigned to the motels and restaurants were sent to hit the streets and canvas. Each couple was provided a picture of Sylvia Redman with which to aid in the canvassing. It will take all day for the teams to complete their assignments. Jim Duffy, on the other hand, will be done in two hours, maybe with a yes answer. That is what Ginger wants. She is going to see to its installation at the D.C. Police Headquarters so the police could monitor the vehicles in the area to see if there was a red Dodge Viper available to be investigated.

Jim goes to the Smithsonian Institution main facility at 1100 Jefferson Dr SW in Washington. After introducing himself and asking to see the director, he is met by the facilities director, Fred Ivory. They go to his office. Fred asks Jim "What is the nature of your visit to our main building?" Duffy told Ivory the nature of the dilemma the White House is in and the need to use the satellite monitoring system.

Ivory states "Agent Duffy, the satellite system monitor requires a skilled technician to use it. I will have to provide one with the monitor to set it up wherever your agency requires the monitor to be installed. If it is ever is ever a need to move it, the technician will need to come and do the process all over." Agent Jim reports "Our unit needs the monitor established in the main office of the D.C. Metropolitan Police." "We will have it there later today" responds Fred Ivory.

Jim's next task is to contact D.C. Police Chief Henry Travis. He will explain the use of the monitor and satellite system for viewing details of vehicles and human beings. Duffy shows his ID and requests to talk to Henry Travis. Jim is shown to the Chief's office. Jim identifies himself for the Chief and says "Your force is currently surveying traffic for a red 2009 Dodge Viper belonging to Sylvia Redman. There is a monitor that will be delivered here to your office for installation. It is used with a satellite for viewing people and vehicles. It will be your responsibility as long as it is in use here. A technician will set it up for you and teach you how to change the GPS location of the satellite's focus. Are there any questions?"

Travis responds "What will be my response upon seeing the red Dodge?" Agent Duffy says "You will report the location to one of your squad cars to tail the vehicle until one of our agents can join in the chase. Once the agent is on scene, he or she will take charge and stop the vehicle. You must also report the vehicle being found as soon as it is seen. This will give our agent the time needed to get to the site. FBI Director Edwards is aware of this endeavor and expects full cooperation. We may have an agent come here and be a screen watcher and watch as your assigned personnel as well"

Henry Travis says "I will be here awaiting the installation. You are sure the person doing the installation will be able to teach us how to use the monitor?" "The technician coming with the monitoring system is Smithsonian Institution certified meaning the person is fully capable of instruction. However, learning to use the system will be entirely up to you and your personnel. We want it monitored 24 hours a day. So, you will need at least four people to be available for training including yourself. Can you arrange that within the next hour? The technician is supposed to be on his way with the monitoring system now. Also, he needs help unloading the monitoring system. It is portable, but one person cannot handle the loading and unloading. Can you get the installer help?" queries Duffy.

Chief Henry replies "Can do. Give me a second to call the desk sergeant for some people to assist the technician when arrival takes place. I will have three persons to assist. The sergeant will place the officers on notice to not leave our facility. Is that enough people?" "Yes, that will do for the technician. A white five-ton truck will be the delivery vehicle. It will have the Smithsonian seal on it. Tell your people to be on the lookout for this vehicle.

One of them will need to show the technician where to park for unloading" says Agent Jim.

Meanwhile, agent Allen Jeffers has been at the university campus. He has also been waiting for notification that Harold Yodel has been found. Jeffers beats the students to the Psych classroom by getting Sylvia's schedule complete with starting times and places from the Administration Office. He is familiar with all the buildings having attended the university just three years ago. Nothing has changed. He finds Professor Jack Wilson in his office. Allen says "Professor Wilson, I am an undercover agent of the FBI. Here is my badge. I am here to determine what I can about the activities and encounters of Sylvia Redman. Can you help me? Do not give my ID away. I will be sitting in on your class to see who all attends. I may need to question one or more of the students. Could you specifically point out Marvin Cookson if he is in your class?"

Professor Wilson tells Allen Jeffers "I will endeavor to do what you ask about your ID and the sitting in on my class as a new student. As for Sylvia, she has been a good student. I have not seen her associate with any boys except Marvin Cookson. They share my class. I do not think they share any other classes. Marvin is not that good of a student. His behavior leaves a lot to be desired. If I could, I would have him expelled for his disrespectful actions. I will call Cookson by name to let you know who he is. I am afraid that is all I can tell you about Sylvia and Cookson. You might try some of her other professors. She carries a full load of 12 credit hours. That means she has four classes or three other professors besides me. You can get her schedule from the Admin. Office, if you like. There will be no charge for the service. Everyone on campus can get a schedule, if authorized."

Agent Jeffers tells Wilson "Thank you. I will do just that," not letting the professor know that he has already done the job. Allen takes his binder and gets a seat near the rear of the room so he can watch the door and anybody who comes through it to be a part of the class or for some other reason. He has his binder open with paper inside to take notes on. The students start to enter the room, but no one takes notice of Jeffers at the back of the room. Most of the students sit near the front to hear the professor's lecture. Jeffers noticed a man sitting next to Marvin Cookson, who had been called by name by Professor Wilson. He looked older than himself. It did not mean the man was not a student, but it did seem odd to agent Jeffers.

After class was over, Jeffers did the same with the rest of the faculty that were professors of Sylvia. They all gave him about the same information. Allen heads to the night club after class is over. He figures to get a sandwich there instead of going to the cafeteria. He sees Cookson and the man together again. He goes over and says to the man "I talked to Marvin here about Sylvia Redman yesterday. My name is Allen Jeffers and I am a friend of Sylvia's. Have you seen or spoken to her?".

The man tells Jeffers "I'm Harold Yodel. I'm a friend of Marvin's. We take classes together all day long. We only have four a day schedule. No, I haven't seen or talked to Sylvia at all. Sorry." Allen knows the man is lying, but 'why' is a question that Allen wants answered. He leaves the night club and calls FBI HQ and tells Ginger "Harold Yodel is here at the university night club. I asked him if he had seen or talked to Sylvia. He says he had not spoken to or seen Sylvia at all. He's lying. Being a friend of Marvin Cookson, he has most likely seen Sylvia in Cookson's company Send two agents to pick him up and take him in for questioning. Have them pick me up too. I want Marvin Cookson to see that so he will get the impression I am a student who might be involved in something that Harold is involved with. Cookson and Yodel are at a table near the end of the bar."

Senior Agent Ginger Ales states "I will do that as soon as I am off the phone. I will send Glen and Ho. They will pretend they only know you as a wanted person. Do not convey acknowledgement of them showing you know them. Say something like 'What am

I being taken for?' That should show Cookson exactly what you want. You can go back to the campus tomorrow."

After the call was over, agent Allen goes back inside and orders a drink. Not 15 minutes later Glen and Ho show up. They go to Jeffers first. He questions "What's going on here? Why am I being taken?" Underwood states "We have a warrant for your arrest. One of your fellow students turned you in." After cuffing Allen, the two take him and go to Yodel's table. Wong, this time, says "Harold Yodel, you are taken into custody for questioning." "For what cause?" asks Yodel. "Drugs" says back Glen. The two are taken out and placed in Glen and Ho's car in the back seat. Both were handcuffed.

With Jeffers and Yodel in the car, Ho drives to FBI HQ and both are taken inside. Yodel is put into one questioning room, while Jeffers is freed. But, Yodel does not know that. Glen begins questioning Harold about Sylvia. Yodel decrees "I don't know the girl." "We seem to think she may have gotten some drugs from you. So, you do know her."

"Yeah, but I haven't seen her since Friday in Psych class." "Why are you enrolled in the university? What is with the friendship you have with Marvin Cookson? Is he getting drugs from you or selling them to you?" "I'm not into drugs in any way. Sylvia wouldn't have gotten 'em from me. I only know her through Marvin. We have been buddies since he was in high school. We met at a gym when I was playing basketball. He wanted to join in. We let him because we were one short." "What relationship did you have with Sylvia Redman? She is the President's daughter," gives Underwood. "I didn't know that. And we have no relationship. As I said, I only know her through Marvin," explains Yodel.

Glen goes out and asks Jeffers if that was enough. "No. We need more out of him. Ho, you go in and play the bad guy. See what you can get out of him," demands Allen. Wong enters and immediately demands of Yodel in a loud voice "Tell ME about your relationship with Sylvia Redman, the President's daughter."

Being intimidated, Yodel says "Being an adult of a few years, she asked me last Wednesday how to 'get away' from her family. I asked if she had a car and she says 'Yes'. I told her to withdraw some money and just drive off. Is that what this is all about?" "I will ask the questions" shouts HO! He continues "That is not what this is about. It must have been more than you providing her with information. WHERE DID THE DRUGS COME IN?" Yodel, feeling threatened, says "Let's make a deal. I'll tell ya about the drugs and you talk to the police."

Ho was not aware that Yodel really was into drugs. It had been a ploy to keep him in the questioning room. Outside, Allen and Glen were dumbfounded. They had not suspected Harold to be involved with drugs at all. It was something that had to be dealt with. And they were wondering if Sylvia was somehow involved. Glen goes to the door and tells Ho to come out. Once outside the room, Glen says "We need to know if Sylvia was involved. Give him the deal so we can find out. Ho goes back inside.

Once again Ho starts talking to Harold "Okay the deal is set. Here is a pad and pen. Write what you know and sign it. Yodel writes down everything including the mentioning of Antonio Denario as the Italian Drug boss. Antonio operates from his restaurant Denario's Pizza and Italian Restaurant on the NW side of D.C. near Bethesda MD. There is no mention of Sylvia, but Yodel does mention Cookson and him sell marijuana and some Cocaine on campus. Glen calls the D.C. police to come and get Howard Yodel and the confession telling them about the deal being made where Yodel will get less time. The whole scenario is handed over to the police.

Allen Jeffers leaves for the night after giving a report to Agent Ginger Ales. Glen and Ho do likewise. About the same time, the other seven return giving their reports. The technician from the Smithsonian has installed the monitoring system and trained the D.C. Police personnel. They begin using the system. The Chief has gotten four officers as instructed.

CHAPTER 5

The Last Two Days

Conrad gets up early on day five and heads to the hospital. He is more than anxious to get to the hospital to see Sylvia Reed. Once there, he enters room 213 with a smile on his face. Sylvia is eating a breakfast of fried eggs, bacon, toast and coffee. She has not touched the coffee. Conrad asks "Good morning, Sylvia. Why haven't you had your coffee?" She says back "I do not drink coffee. I am a Diet Pepsi freak. Good morning, Conrad. It is nice to see you back again."

"I feel I have a yearning to get to know you better" asks Conrad in a pleasing voice. Continuing "How old are you?" "I do not know. My birthday was last Saturday, I think." states Sylvia. "Well, let's go with that. Are you married? Where do you live?" asks Conrad continuing to seek answers to the girl's history. Sylvia comes back with "I know I am not married. I would be wearing a ring if I am married. I do not know where I live or what I was doing at the edge of that road." "We will have to get you some clothes before you are discharged. Any word on that?" speaks Conrad.

Sylvia, laid back, gives "I wish I could tell you what I need other than a pair of shoes." Conrad responds "You will need a dress, coat, gloves and a hat in comparison with the shoes. It is quite cool outside for an October month. It will be my treat."

"That is very nice of you. I do not have any money to repay you with," says Sylvia.

Conrad states "I want to do for you as long as you need it. After all, it was me that found you on Mount Holly Church Road. I have already been responsible for you here in the hospital. Has the doctor told you when you may be released?" "No. I am supposed to see him later this morning. And I am supposed to have my hair done again today. I was told about it being fixed up while I was out," says Sylvia.

Conrad offers "I will pay for the beautician." Interrupting, Sylvia states "You do not need to do that." "Oh, but I do. I get to see your beauty when it is done. Besides, how else can I get to know you better if I don't treat you once in awhile," responds Conrad. He is beginning to get real feelings for the girl. He has it in his mind that she and he could court for a while.

Conrad looks at his watch and he decides it is time to leave to go to work. He takes Sylvia's hands and tells her "I've got to go to work now. Be sure the beautician does your hair up nice. I like its redness. I'll be back after work." He leaves and goes to the Nurses Station and asks "How much is the beautician for a patient? "$35.00" comes the reply from a nurses' aide. He gives her $70.00 and says "This is to cover Sylvia Reed's beautician for today and last time. Get me a receipt, please." He goes out to his 2008 Dodge and drives to work. Again, he is just a little late. But, no one says anything. He had told them of his find and visitation three days ago.

Conrad's day is a usual day. His father, however, has a different than usual for his day. Hank had been on a stakeout for two wanted men. This had been going on for a couple of days. But today, the two are seen walking towards the house that has been under surveillance. Hank gets out of his truck and tells the two men to halt and raise their hands for they were under arrest.

Both men pull out guns and start firing at Hank. Hank ducks behind his truck. Three slugs go into the side panel of his truck. Sergeant George Harris, having been on the stakeout also, gets out of his car and starts to shoot back. He had called for assistance. It arrives from the other end of the street. Two officers get out and draw their weapons. Hank has fired a total of nine rounds from his Gluck 9. George has fired four. The new officers have not fired a shot because the two shooters toss their guns into the street and give up. They know they are outnumbered.

Hank and George cautiously approach the two men with guns aiming right at them in case they try something. The other two officers approach as well. One of the officers takes his handcuffs and places them on one suspect. The man says "Hey man, ya got these things too tight. They's cuttin' my wrists."

"They're supposed to do that when put on properly. That's so you won't get loose" says the officer. Sgt. George gets the cuffs on the other guy. George tells the two officers to put them in their squad car and take them in. Hank looks at his truck and says "George that is the first time any vehicle of mine has received damage from another person. I wonder what this will do to my insurance payments. Let's get into the office and do the paperwork on these two characters."

George responds knowingly "You betcha." Hank and he have been friends for many years. A year after Hank joined the Henrico County Police, George signed up. They met shortly after that and became friends. Going back to the station, Hank must not only fill out the paperwork on the two desperados, but also on his truck. He had been using it on his duty tour and thus it was considered a Department's vehicle. Hank got everything done and precedes home.

Grace had an unusual day as well. VCU, where she works, requires her presence at a meeting with a contractor's representative. It seems that the contractor's workers had reached a problem in tearing down an old building. It meant more time would be required to finish construction of the new building. Grace had to attend. The contractor's representative told the Dean about the problem and the fact the road would need to be closed an additional two weeks. This meant more time for students to struggle to get a parking place, which was already a problem. The meeting took two hours and Grace had to cancel one of her classes. It was a hectic day for her. Grace could not understand the importance of her being there other than the fact that her classroom was right next to the construction area. She finishes out her day and goes home. She arrives before Hank and Conrad.

Conrad leaves work and goes directly to the hospital to see Sylvia. When he gets there, she was missing. He goes to the Nurse Station and asks "Where is Sylvia Reed? She's not in her room number 213." Nurse Valery Bass tells Conrad, "She is at the beautician's having her hair done. She should be back anytime. She has been gone about an hour. You can wait in her room if you like, Mr. Thomas." "Thank you," says Conrad. He goes back to her room and turns on the TV. It is tuned to one of the music channels that play oldies (50s, 60s and 70s). It has been awhile since he heard music of the nature now playing.

Conrad wonders if Sylvia likes it or did someone else turn it to that channel. He did not have long to wait. Sylvia returns to her room in a wheel chair. She gets up from it and climbs into bed. Sylvia asks "Have you been waiting long?" "No. I just got here a few minutes ago. I asked at the Nurse Station where you were and I was told you went to the beautician's shop. I like the way your hair looks," Conrad says adoringly. Sylvia took note of the way he says it.

Sylvia asks him "Why did you bring me here?" Conrad saying with concern "I really was concerned about your well being. You needed help." "Why here? Why not some other hospital? Surely, Richmond has other hospitals," comes back Sylvia. Conrad says "This was the closest hospital. Besides, it is easy for me to get here from work or from home. I just take Parham Road." "Can you do me a favor tomorrow? Bring me something to eat. I am tired of this hospital food, already" inquires Sylvia. Conrad states

"I'll be happy to. After all, I want you to learn more about me." Sylvia took note of that statement.

Sylvia, being full of questions, asks "So, you are pleased with my hair? What do you think about the rest of my body?" "Well, you have pretty feet and what I could see of the rest of it through your gown; I'm pleased with it too. I would like to see the rest of it in another way" comments Conrad curiously. Knowingly, Sylvia replies, "Maybe someday, you will get the chance." "That would be very enlightening. I can hardly wait for it to come true," responds Conrad happily. Sylvia took note of his response again. They are getting closer together without Conrad really knowing it. But, Sylvia does. And she is completely charmed.

Nurse Valery enters and says "Hello, Mr. Thomas. How are you tonight?" Without waiting for an answer, she goes to Sylvia and states "I am going to take your bandages off to see how well you have healed." After removing the last strip, she moves strands of Sylvia's hair and says "It looks good. Since the doctor could not and cannot see you today, he will see you tomorrow. With your head looking the way it does, he will probably say you can go home. I am sure he will be surprised." Sylvia turns to Conrad and asks "What do you think of my hair now?"

Conrad immediately comes back with "It makes you beautiful. Doesn't it nurse?" "Yes, it does," put forth Valery just before she leaves. Sylvia is filled with joy to the comments made by both of them. She, especially, took note of Conrad's revelation. She realizes she is beginning to like him unlike any other boy or man she knew before him. She wonders 'How did I know that?'

Conrad moves closer to Sylvia and takes her hand and says meaningfully "When you are discharged, you are going to need a place to stay. We have a spare bedroom. Maybe, I can get my parents to agree to it, at least until you get a place of your own. To do that, you will need a job. To get a job, you will need a Social Security Number and maybe a car with a driver's license. It all will take time. I'm sure you will be able to wait" relates Conrad.

"I really have no other choice. As far as the bedroom at your house, I think I would like that most of all. The other things we will do one at a time. It may not be in the order you stated, but we will get it done together because I am already dependant on you,' empathizing is Sylvia.

The time to leave arrives. Conrad is still holding Sylvia's hand when he says reluctantly "It is time for me to leave and I hate to go. There is always tomorrow. I'll be in early to see you" he enjoys as he leans over and gives her a kiss on the cheek. Conrad says his goodbye and leaves. He goes straight to his Viper and straight home. He wants to ask his parents about the spare bedroom.

Conrad arrives home, takes off his coat and sees that both of his parents are at home. Eagerly, he tells them about Sylvia's possible discharge tomorrow and the fact she has nowhere to go. He puts it to them "Can she live here until she gets a job and her own place? We do have a spare bedroom. It won't put us to any trouble." Grace opens with "It will be a task I feel that is not worth taking. We know nothing about this girl. Besides we need the bedroom as a guest room." "Grace, Dear that is exactly what she would be. I'm in favor of it. We have taught Conrad to be helpful to others including strangers. If we let her have the spare bedroom, we would only be doing what we have taught the boy. I suggest and want you to rethink it," demands Hank. Grace does what he advises her to do. She cannot bring herself not to face the fact that they have taught Conrad to be helpful.

Grace says "I have faced the facts and realize that you are right, Honey. If the girl needs help, then we should give it to her if it is in our power. I guess the bedroom is it, but only until she gets a job or some other form of income." Conrad reiterates "The bedroom is needed by Sylvia and we do have it available." Hank confirms "Then, we give it to Sylvia for the time being." With that settled, Conrad asks "Dad, can you go with me tomorrow morning to see Sylvia so I can introduce her to you?"

Hank comes back with "Sure, but it will have to be short. I can't be too late to get to work." "We can make it early. What if we make it 7:30 in the morning? I can introduce you and after a few minutes, you excuse yourself and leave for work," states Conrad. Hank declares "That will be acceptable. If I leave early enough, I won't be late." They agree on it. Conrad is real satisfied with his parents, especially his father.

Conrad tells his parents that he is ready for whatever is for dinner. Grace tells him it is in the kitchen waiting for him. It turns out to be hot dogs, baked beans and a salad. He eats three hot dogs, a helping of the beans and the salad. He, then, says to his mother "Mom, it was good. We haven't had hot dogs for some time. I really liked having them for dinner."

Conrad goes to the family room. There, he gets on the computer to see if there are any jobs available in Richmond. He does not find one suitable for Sylvia. Most of the jobs were for men anyway. He looks up employment agencies and finds three. One, however, is extremely far south from downtown and especially from where he lives. He makes a note of the two other agencies. Conrad, also, makes inquiry as to any girl maybe missing from home. He is directed to the national listing of missing children. That is not what he wants. He decides to quit for the night and go to his bedroom. He lays out a black striped suit for tomorrow. He wants to look good for Sylvia. He, then, goes to bed.

Day six arrives with the morning and Conrad is ready to leave at 7:00 o'clock. He checks to see if his dad is ready to go as well. Hank is ready also. The two say goodbye to Grace and leave for Henrico County Doctors Hospital. They each drive their own vehicles and arrive at the same time. Conrad lets out "Dad, we go to room 213. Sylvia will be awake. We will be a little early for visiting hours, but I'm sure we can get into see her." "Okay son," acknowledges Hank.

The two enter and go up to Sylvia's room. Once inside, Conrad says "Sylvia. I want you to meet my dad. Hank Thomas, this is Sylvia Reed." Sylvia asserts "Glad to meet you Mr. Hank" cutting his name short to provide a sense of familiarity. Hank, also, asserts "Well, it's glad to meet you Ms. Sylvia. Conrad hasn't told you yet, but we are going to let you use our guest room until you are able to get your own housing. Is that acceptable to you?" "Why yes, Hank," getting even more familiar replies Sylvia "thank you very much. Conrad, did you do this for me?" "Yes, I did, but mom was a bit hesitant about the idea. We had to remind her how I was raised. I hope the doctor allows you to leave by giving permission for your discharge" confirms Conrad.

RN Georgia St. John comes in and tells the son and father "Gentlemen, you are here too early, but I will allow it this one time. No more incidents of this nature will be allowed." Georgia checks out Sylvia's monitor and everything looks normal. She disconnects the unit with "You no longer need this, or the IV," as she turns off the monitor and removes the IV from Sylvia's arm. She leaves telling Sylvia to have a nice day. Sylvia thinks 'It already has been a nice day. Conrad is visiting me'.

Hank announces "It is time for me to go to work." "Where do you work, Hank?" requests Sylvia. Hank responds "I'm a Lieutenant on the Henrico County Police Force. I've been there for 30 years. I'm thinking about retiring soon." "Dad, you haven't told mom and me. When are you going to do that?" commands Conrad. Hank says "Sometime this month or next. I haven't made up my mind." Sylvia relates "'The sooner, the better' they say." Hank tells Sylvia and Conrad goodbye and that he must get to work.

Conrad takes Sylvia's hands and requests "Well, what do you think of my dad?" "He appears to be quite a man. I will bet he is good to you. When will I meet your mom?" questions Sylvia. Conrad iterates "Soon, very soon. As a matter of fact, you will see her when we pick you up after you're discharged. It's time for me to leave for work. I'll be back this afternoon" he says as he leans over and kisses her cheek again.

Afternoon arrives and Conrad leaves work headed for the hospital once again. This time, he stops and gets Sylvia a McDonald's Big Mac and fries with a Diet Pepsi. He gets to the hospital and goes in with the drink and bag in tow. Conrad goes to room 213 again and finds Sylvia laughing. "What's up with the laughter? I like it," queries Conrad.

Sylvia states "It is the TV. I had some time to use while waiting for you to get here. So, I turned on the TV and found a channel that has comedy shows. I see you brought me McDonald's. What do I get?" "I've got you a Big Mac, fries and a Diet Pepsi. I couldn't think what to get you. I hope this will do!" says Conrad. Sylvia responds "That sounds better than this hospital stuff they call food. I have had my fill of it. Bring on the Macky D's."

Conrad hands her the drink and the food. Sylvia tears open the bag eager to get at the food. She goes for the fries first. The Big Mac comes after the fries and she drinks the Diet Pepsi along with eating the food. Sylvia is delighted with the treat and is looking forward to possibly going out to eat with Conrad. She lets him know "Conrad, I hope one day we can go out to eat together. I am looking forward to the opportunity. Do you think it can happen?"

"Why yes, of course. I am looking forward to the occasion as well. I want to take you to my favorite place to eat one day. I'm not sure yet when that will be, but it will happen," speaks Conrad to her affectionately for he meant it that way. Sylvia took note of this statement as well as having done so with the other comments. Her feelings for Conrad were getting stronger by the minute.

Sylvia finishes her food and drink and thanks Conrad. She tells him Doctor William Spears had been in to see her and was really pleased with her progress. She says "Spears thinks I am a medical miracle. He also says I can go home tomorrow. He has already signed the discharge notice and the nurses have been made aware of it. I will need a pair of shoes though." "I'll see to the getting of your shoes first thing tomorrow morning. It will be Sunday, but Talbot's will be open around 10:00 o'clock. I can get you anything there. The store even carries bathing suits in the spring. I might even get you a new dress," informs Conrad.

Sylvia relates "You do not have to go to that expense. A pair of shoes is all I need." "You will need more than that. Leave it to me. I know your shoe size by looking at the one you had left. I can guess your dress size just by looking at you. Like I say, let me take care of it. I will be here about 11:00 am," expresses Conrad.

Conrad says it is time for him to leave. He holds Sylvia's hands and kisses her on her lips. She is well pleased with that and tells him so. He makes up his mind to do it again at the first opportunity tomorrow. Conrad leaves her room and goes to his vehicle, but instead of going home, he heads for Talbot's. He figures he has an hour at most to get what he wants for Sylvia.

Once there, he parks his car and goes directly to the women's department. He is greeted by Angela North. Angela asks "What can I do for you, sir?" Conrad expresses the need for women's clothing. His first choice is a dress. Angela leads him to the dresses with "What size sir?" Conrad says "A size five and make it green." North finds one and Conrad states "That dress is exactly what I want. If you weren't married, I would like to be married to you. You listen so well." "I'm not married, but I'd like to be. Are you asking?" comes Angela North.

Conrad responds "No, I don't know you. But that could change." Then Conrad remembers Sylvia and asks "Can we go to the shoes. I want a black flat pair." Again, Angela gets exactly what he wants in the size he told. A size six. Conrad remarks "You did it again. Those are exactly what I want. Can we now go to the coats?" "Yes. Follow me, please" commands North. Conrad follows her to the coats. Angela, then, asks "What style are you interested in? Long, short or in between? Fur, leather or cotton? What size?" Conrad is at a loss for a moment. Out of the corner of his eye he sees a fur collar, medium length coat that is black. He checks the size and sees it will fit Sylvia. He demands "I want that one" pointing at the coat. "And I need a hat." Angela goes to the hats and gets one that is furry to go with the coat's collar. It too is black. Conrad is well pleased and tells Angela just that. He decides to get a pair of black gloves.

"Will that be all, sir?" asks North. "I am ready to check out. It is almost 9:00 pm. We need to get this done so I can go home," commands Conrad. Angela leads him to one of the registers in the store. There were several, but she chose the one closest to them. "Will it be cash, check or charge?" comes Angela North. "It will be Visa," he states. Conrad gets the card out as Angela tallies the items on the cash register. "The total comes to $319.87. May I have your card?" Conrad complies with the request from Angela. Angela swipes the card and gets the approval and has Conrad sign the receipt. She says "Thank you, sir. Come again, please." Conrad replies "I will." He, then, leaves with the goods and places them in his trunk.

Going home, he thinks of kissing Sylvia hoping she was pleased as much as he was. He thinks it was kind of rash of him to do that without knowing her better. He gets home, goes inside, takes off his coat and says "Sylvia gets discharged tomorrow. I have gotten some things she will need. I have them in my trunk. I think she will be well pleased." His mother says "Conrad, what have you done now? What does she need that you had to buy? I know you paid for them with your money because Sylvia does not have any as you say."

"Mom, I bought only what she needs right now. I also told you that she doesn't have any clothes except for a dress. She will definitely need a coat due to this October weather. I got her a coat, gloves, shoes, a dress and a hat," Conrad relates. His dad agrees with "I think you have done the right thing. It's just a matter of helping her. Once she gets a job, Sylvia can pay you back. You do have the receipt, son?" remarks Hank. Reluctantly, once again, Grace agrees with Hank. Conrad tells his dad that he does in fact have the receipt.

Conrad goes into the kitchen for something to eat. He does not really care what it is. He is that hungry. He has two hamburgers, corn and boiled potatoes. Conrad then goes to his room, undresses and goes to bed leaving his parents downstairs discussing what is to be done tomorrow.

CHAPTER 6

The Discharge

The start of day seven has Conrad rising at 6:00 o'clock am. He takes a shower and gets dressed. Conrad goes downstairs and sees that his mother is already awake and cooking eggs for breakfast. She asks "Son, how many do you want this morning?" "Two will do me, mom. Can I have some orange juice?" asks Conrad. "Sure thing" comes back Grace as she heads for the refrigerator. She gets the juice and a glass, pours the OJ into the glass, and hands it to Conrad. He begins to drink the juice as his mother gives him his eggs and two slices of toast. The bacon is not done yet.

"Mom, there is something we didn't talk about last night. It's semi-important. You have yet to meet Sylvia. I would like you to go with me this morning using your car. It has the room for all three of us. If she is going to live here, you should at least meet her first," reports Conrad. Grace is in somewhat of a shock. She realizes she should have seen this coming. She ponders for just a moment and then says "I guess you are right about meeting her. And the Sorento would be the thing to use. When do you want to leave? Your father has to work today. It is something about two men he arrested in a shoot out yesterday. He has three bullet holes in his GMC Sierra as a result."

Conrad asks "Why didn't dad say something last night?" "Because you were busy with your details for today, we did not say much. Dad and I talked about just this occasion. I knew you would get up early and go see her. So, I arose early too. We can go to lunch somewhere and eat. That would be better than the hospital food" replies Grace "but you still have not said when we will go." "Visiting hours start at 8:00 o'clock this morning. We could leave at 7:30." responds Conrad.

Hank is coming through the doorway with "Good morning all. I have to deal with those two culprits that put bullet holes in my 2009 Sierra. It makes me mad. This is the first personal vehicle that I have had shot up. Well Grace, did he ask?" "Yes and we have it worked out already this morning. We will leave before you. How many eggs do you want, Honey?" "Two over easy, yellows not broken and whites all done," reports Hank. "Coming right up with coffee for you to go with your eggs. Anything else?" requests Grace. "No." Grace gives him the eggs, toast and coffee.

Conrad requests "Mother, it is 7:30 o'clock. We need to be going. I want to stop and get her a Sausage McMuffin with cheese and a Diet Pepsi. That shouldn't take us too long. It will depend on the line at the drive thru." "Alright. Get my coat from the closet and you better get yours. It is quite nippy outside. I have been out to get the paper," gives Grace. Conrad says "Bye, dad. See you sometime this afternoon." Conrad gets the coats and helps his mother put hers on. He then puts his coat on and they leave.

Fortunately, the Sorento was not blocked in. However, after the Sorento is moved, Conrad must move his car so that his dad could move his truck when he came out. After moving his Viper and getting the clothes, the two go to Henrico County Doctors Hospital via McDonald's where the Sausage McMuffin with cheese and a Diet Pepsi to drink are picke up and paid for by Conrad.. Getting at the hospital, they go inside to the elevator and Conrad tells his mother to punch two. She does and they arrive shortly going to room 213.

Sylvia is awake and watching TV. She sees the McDonald's bag with "Another treat for me?" "Yes, little one. A Sausage McMuffin with cheese and a Diet Pepsi," relates Conrad. "Aw, you should not have done this. But, I am glad you did. What else do you have in the Talbot's bag? Did you go shopping for me?" inquires Sylvia. "Yes." First, Conrad pulls out the dress. Sylvia loves it. Next, he gets out the shoes. Sylvia loves them. Next, the coat comes. She thinks that is adorable. Last, he shows her the hat and gloves.

"It is all so wonderful. Do you want to help me put them on?" asks Sylvia. Conrad's mother is flabbergasted at the very idea of such a thing. But before she says anything, Sylvia interrupts with "I was not serious Mrs. Thomas. You are Conrad's mother, right?" "Why yes. How did you know?" Grace states. Sylvia merely says "A little bird told me to ask" replies Sylvia "you did not have a part in it." Grace replies "How did you know that?" "A sparrow told me," responds Sylvia, "but I do not know your first name.". "Why, it is Grace." "Thank you" conveys Sylvia.

Sylvia gets out of bed and lays out the clothes. She takes the dress and goes into the restroom with it. When she comes out, Grace comments "You are beautiful like Conrad says." "Thank you. Now, for the shoes. By the way, this dress is a perfect fit. I hope the shoes fit as well" relates Sylvia. She puts them on and those are a perfect fit as well. Grace says "How did you know?"

"A little bird told me," copies Conrad. Finally, she tries on the coat, hat and gloves. "These all fit as well. I am going to have you as my permanent dresser" hopeful is Sylvia. She takes off the coat, hat and gloves for the time being, but keeps the dress and shoes on.

"I should be discharged in about an hour or two. Tell me Grace, why is your son so thoughtful?" "For one thing, he was raised to be as helpful as possible. Secondly, you were in need of clothes so he bought them for you last night. It made him quite late getting home. Third, he convinced his father and I that your needs could be met by us and him. He is that way," gives forth Grace.

"I should have known that from the McDonald's he brought me yesterday. It was a lot better than the hospital's food. I ate it only because there was nothing else that I liked. Did you know the first thing I had to eat was a sandwich? It was not good at all, but I was hungry," comes back Sylvia.

"I do not know about hospital food now. The last time I was in a hospital I was giving birth to Conrad's sister. She is deceased now. The food was not all that bad back then," says Grace. "I liked bringing you the food. It was my pleasure. I wouldn't have done it had I felt otherwise. After all, you're my find" relates Conrad. The three talk about the upcoming stay, the rules of the house and Sylvia's bedroom. Time passes swiftly. RN Georgia St. John is the one to come in and tell Sylvia she is free to go after signing a paper. Sylvia gets and signs the document.

Conrad leads the way because his mother and Sylvia were not familiar with the hospital's way to exit via the ground floor. Once in the lobby, the receptionist that had been watching Conrad every day, comes over to him and gives a big hug saying "I'm going to miss you. I've enjoyed seeing you come in to visit. Was it this young lady?" Conrad says "It surely was. We're taking her home." After Conrad disengages the receptionist, the three go to the 2007 Kia Sorento.

"Before we go home, how about us going to Red Lobster? I have not been there in quite some time," asks Grace for she loved seafood. Sylvia says "That sounds good to me. That McDonald's was good, but that was some time ago. I am hungry again." Conrad retorts "Well then, Red Lobster it is." The three head for the restaurant and get there in 15 minutes. It was not very far away from the hospital. Going in, they are greeted by a hostess "How many, please?" "Three" gives back Conrad. The hostess says "Follow me, please." She takes them to a table along one wall near the back of the restaurant. It is dimly lit. But, Conrad thinks that makes it more romantic. So does Sylvia and remarks "This setting is really enjoyable. It is almost romantic." "I agree," says Conrad.

Grace, on the other hand, declares "The restaurant does this to lower the electric bill. The lower wattage means less expense." "Even so, it is still romantic," Sylvia comments. The waitress finally comes. "My name is Tuesday Wells. I will be your waitress today. Can I get you something to drink?" introducing states Tuesday. "I will have coffee," says Grace. "I want a Pepsi and my lady friend will have a Diet Pepsi," Conrad says. Wells leaves for the time being. The three go back to talking about the upcoming days.

Tuesday returns with the drinks and places them correctly in front of the one that ordered. She says "Are you ready to order your food?" Grace asserts "I will have the Lobster Lover's Dream." Sylvia comments "I want the seafood platter." Conrad orders the Shrimp combo. Wells leaves again. This time the wait is longer. Sylvia iterates "I am a senior in college, but I cannot remember where I go." "There are three here in Richmond: Virginia Commonwealth University, Richmond University and Union University. Maybe we could check them out to see if you attended any of them," comes Conrad. "What good would that do? We do not know my real name to look up for verification," returns Sylvia.

Tuesday returns with the food and places each plate where it is supposed to go asking "Will there be any desserts?" Conrad states "We will let you know later." Grace is the first to start eating, Sylvia is second and Conrad is last. Grace is really getting into her lobsters. She has two pieces. Sylvia likes her seafood platter with the variety of food. Conrad, on the other hand, while eating the shrimp wishes he had ordered the seafood platter. They all finish about the same time and Tuesday Wells notices the event. She arrives and asks about desserts again. Only Sylvia orders cake ala mode. Tuesday leaves and comes back almost immediately. "Why were you so fast" asks Conrad. "I don't know how, but I had it prepared before the young lady ordered it," concedes

Wells. Conrad asks for the bill. Tuesday goes and gets it taking a few minutes to tally and then deliver.

After Sylvia finishes her cake and ice cream, the group goes towards the checkout. Conrad leaves a five dollar tip. Once at the register, the cashier says "The total of your meal is $55.15." Conrad hands her his Visa card. She swipes it to get payment, gets a receipt for Conrad to sign and thanks Conrad. The three leave for the Thomas' house. 20 minutes later, Sylvia notices the street name is Cadbury and the house number is 5695. Grace pulls the car into the driveway next to Conrad's car. They get out of the Sorento and go in. Once inside, Conrad takes the coats and Sylvia's hat with the gloves and places these into the closet. Sylvia immediately notices the home is immaculate. "Who does the cleaning?" asks Sylvia.

"I do it all," tells Grace to Sylvia. "It must be a hard job," comments Sylvia. "Not as hard as you might think. Hank and Conrad are very organized and take care of cleaning behind themselves," gives Grace. Conrad says "By the way, mom. My sports jackets need to be picked up at the cleaners. Can you do that for me?" "When I get the chance I will. Do you have the money to pay the bill?" Grace asks. "Yes, mother. Here, let me give you $40.00 to cover the costs. It should be less than that amount. At least, it was last time," conveys Conrad.

Sylvia asks "Can I see the rest of the house?" Grace answers "Of course. Let us start right here in the living room. That recliner there is Hank's. He gets picky when someone else sits in it. The other one is mine. The couch is for everybody else's use. Now, let us go into the kitchen." In there, Sylvia sees how clean it is as well as the living room. She is amazed again. Grace states "Let us go to the utility room. This is where I do the laundry. There is not much to see here. So, let us go to the family room. Here we have the television set, computer and library. You can make use of any of these items any time that you feel like it."

Grace says they are ready to go upstairs. Once there, "This is Hank's and my bedroom. There is a whirlpool in the room that we find enjoyable. It is the largest room in the house. Off to one side is an office of sorts for Hank to use. Sometimes, he brings work home with him. Not often, but often enough. Let us go now to Conrad's room. It is the next largest room." Sylvia sees that it too is immaculate. It has the masculine look to it. She gets ideas in her head about the room.

Finally, they get to Sylvia's room. It is plain and gender free as was the master bedroom. She notices that it is a little smaller than Conrad's room. The last thing they look at is the bath room. It too is quite large. Sylvia notices the shower is large enough for two people to use at the same time. She gets ideas here as well. She also sees that there are two wash basins—one for Grace and one for Hank or one for Conrad and one for her. Ideas are running through her mind again. Some of the ideas seem familiar, but she does not know why.

They finish with the house tour and find that Hank has come home. It is early afternoon. He asks Sylvia "What do you think of the house?" "I think it is beautiful. I cannot imagine why it is so neat. Nothing looks out of place. I particularly like the family room. I like my room as well. It looks like it was made for me. I can hardly wait to sleep in a bed that does not belong to a hospital" with enjoyment, speaks Sylvia. "Well, tonight is the night you get to try it out. We hope you will enjoy your stay with us," states Hank.

Grace says to Hank "Honey, I do not feel up to cooking tonight. Can we go somewhere that Sylvia will find enticing?" "I know just the place. We'll go to Hank's Barbeque on Parham Road. It's been a while since we were last there. Besides, we all like barbeque, even you Grace. We need to get there by 6:00 o'clock to beat the evening crowd by about an hour," demands Hank. That means we need to leave by 5:30," gives Conrad, who is somewhat enthused. Sylvia says "That sounds really nice. Barbeque is my second favorite food." Nobody thinks to ask what her favorite food was. They were amazed that she could remember what her second favorite food was.

Hank says "its 4:30. I want to watch the 5:00 o'clock news. Then we will leave." Sylvia says she would like to use the computer for a while. There was something she wanted to see if she could find. Conrad invites her "Well, Sylvia let's go and use it." They are off. Grace goes into the kitchen and prepares two cups of coffee. Hank and she would sit in their chairs for a while. He tells her about his off day work and she tells of her day with Sylvia and Conrad. She, particularly, tells of going to Red Lobster and having the Lobster Lover's Dream.

Meanwhile, Sylvia and Conrad are in the family room. Sylvia sits in the computer's chair and Conrad stands behind her. He is interested in what she is up to using the computer. He also did not know if she had ever used a computer, but he found out rather quickly that she was good at it. Sylvia searches a missing person database. She is interested in finding if she is missed somewhere. Hopefully, she will get a description of someone who looks like her. She sees several possibilities, but none really matches her description. She is a 5' 6", 110 pound, red head. And that hair was bright red. She reminded Conrad of Maureen O'Hara, the movie star, that was seen opposite John Wayne in movies such as *McClintock*.

Conrad knew what she was up to as soon as she typed in the search block 'Missing Persons'. He somehow hoped she would not find a person matching her description. The search was futile. Sylvia, then, searched Richmond for anybody that might have a missing daughter. It was a futile search also since she has already searched the missing person web site on the Internet. She gives up and turns to Conrad and hugs him saying "Will I ever find out or remember who I am?" Conrad likes the hug and hugs back as hard as is Sylvia. He looks down at her and she looks up at him. Then, unexpectedly by both of them, they kiss again and again. The romantic relationship has begun to the liking of both of them.

About that time, Hank comes in to watch the news and sees the two hugging. He says "I know what is going on in here and

Grace would not like it." Conrad says "But, mom doesn't know. Don't tell her, dad. I will when the time is right." "It better not be too long. You know how your mother gets when she finds out something she doesn't like," offers Hank to the couple.

The couple sits in a love seat and pretends to watch the news while holding hands and thinking of each other. The main thing Hank wanted to see was a news commentary on Henrico County Police. The news teams had conducted a surveillance of a few officers and were unhappy with their findings. They felt one of the officers should have been arrested for stealing from a Wal-mart department store. He had blamed it on his diabetes low sugar level. Sometimes, a diabetic person will have a memory loss for a short period of time. Hank was not satisfied with the coverage.

The news was over and Hank says it is time to leave. They all get into the Kia Sorento. It is the only vehicle the Thomas' owned that would haul four people. It would actually hold five. The drive to Hank's Barbeque was uneventful. It took them 20 minutes to arrive, so they beat the 6:00 o'clock deadline. They go in and are greeted by Hank Woodson, owner of Hank's Barbeque. He says "Welcome Hank. It's good to see you again. Your usual table is available. Who is the young lady you have with you?" "This is Sylvia Reed. She is a friend of Conrad's. Sylvia will probably be coming with us for a while until there is an end to her staying with us. Their romance has to end for that to happen" says Hank Thomas. Grace immediately jumps on Hank's comment "What do you mean with romance?" "Ask your son" returns Hank. "Dad, you promised not to say anything" retorts Conrad. "Well, I want to know. Tell me or I go to the car" demands Grace.

Conrad is in a spot and knows it. He was not prepared to tell his mother of the deal. But, he thought it is now necessary. So, he says "Sylvia turned to me in tears crying 'I feel lost' and we hugged each other. One thing led to another and we kissed. Dad saw us, but that's all there is to it." Grace tells Conrad "Well, I never thought you would get involved with Sylvia like

that, especially so soon." "It just happened" commends Conrad.
"Don't let it happen again" commands Grace. Conrad returns
"Mother, I can't say it will not happen again. We both felt it
necessary at the time."

Hank Woodson gets their waiter, Clyde Harris. He shows
them to their table. After the group is seated, he asks "What can
I get you to drink?" Hank Thomas is the first to answer with "I'll
have black coffee." "I will have the same," speaks Grace. Conrad
says "Sylvia will have a Diet Pepsi and I will have a Pepsi." Clyde
leaves the table. After five minutes, he returns with their drinks
and places each one where it should go. Hank states "That was
quick. You're new here aren't you?" Clyde answers "Yes, it has
been just a week total. What would you like to order?" questions
Clyde Harris. "We all will have two barbeque sandwiches. Make
us each a salad. I'll have French. My wife will have Ranch.
Conrad will have red wine and vinaigrette. As for Sylvia, you
will have to ask her," instructs Hank. Clyde asks "And what
type dressing will you have miss?" "I will have the red wine and
vinaigrette. It is the only dressing I have ever had," gives back
Sylvia. Clyde leaves to get their salads. Conrad took note of
'only dressing I have ever had.'

In just five minutes, Clyde returns with the salads with the
dressings on the side so that each person could place as little or as
much as they wanted on their salad. Each of the eaters pours all
of the dressings on their individual salads. They begin to eat and
Hank has a feeling that only a police officer can get. He excuses
himself and goes out the front door. He had parked the car in
a dimly lit area. He looks in the direction of the car and sees a
black man at the Sorento. Hank pulls his gun and yells "Stop.
Police." The perpetrator shoots at Hank. Hank gets behind
the wall at the entrance and shoots back wounding the guy and
causing him to drop his gun right in the line of fire.

Hearing the gun shots, Conrad runs out the door. Hank
tells him to go back inside and call for backup. Hank was not
going near the man until backup arrived. Conrad does as he was

told. In a couple of minutes there were two squad cars at the scene. Officers advanced to where Hank was at. Hank identifies himself as a lieutenant. With gun drawn, one of the officers advances to the wounded man. He tells him to stand up with his hands in the air. The perpetrator complies with the order. One of the other officers, seeing that the man was wounded, calls for an ambulance to come to the scene. It takes five minutes for it to arrive. Meanwhile, a crowd starts to develop and Hank Woodson arrives at the door. He sees the crowd and gets Clyde to come and assist in the crowd control.

Conrad comes back out and yells "Dad, are you alright?" Hank tells Conrad "Yes, son. Go to your mother. Tell her what has happened. I'll be in after I look at the car." The sergeant with one of the officers turns out to be George Harris, Hank's friend. He is also Clyde Harris' father. Clyde goes over to his father and says "Dad, what are you doing out here this time of night?" George begins "I am with a new man. I am giving him a ride with training in how to react to calls for assistance. It is his first night out since graduating from the academy."

Hank Woodson comes outside and sees what a job Clyde had done with the crowd. He is well satisfied that an employee of his could be so responsible. He calls Clyde inside to have a talk with him. "Clyde," Hank says "I am well pleased with the job you did out there tonight. I want you to tell Janice Henry to take over the Thomas table and I want you to take the rest of the night off with pay. I am also giving you a $.50 an hour raise effective tomorrow." Clyde says "Thank you, boss." And he leaves to tell Janice Henry and then, leaves for the evening. He goes back outside to tell his father.

Meanwhile, the ambulance has arrived. The paramedics ask George where the injured person is. They are directed towards the Sorento. The officer who had originally approached the man had cuffed him. The guy says "These things is tight man, Can't ya do somtin' with 'em?" The officer responds "The cuffs are on for your protection as well as ours. There is no adjustment available to the cuffs. Quiet down and let these medics look you over and tend to your wound or you might bleed to death." The fellow complies.

Hank goes to the Sorento and sees the driver's side window has been broken out. The man was after his wife's purse. She had left it because she did not need it in the restaurant. Hank thinks that now he has two vehicles needing repair work on them. His insurance was bound to go up as a result. He goes back inside and everyone is talking about the happening outside. The people look in Hank's direction and point. He became the talk of the night. He could hear people talking about how the police had responded so well. They were proud of their officers.

Janice Henry comes, introduces herself and is with the barbeque sandwiches. All four are ready for the food. Hank is especially ready after the happening. They begin to eat in spite of the talking and watching that was going on around them. Sylvia tells Hank "I am sure you had a time out there. Did everything work out okay? I heard three shots. At least one had to be yours. What became of the culprit?" Hank tells Sylvia "The man will be taken to the hospital. I got lucky with one shot. I wounded the guy in his right arm and he dropped his weapon. The other two shots were his and those weren't even close. I don't know why he even had a gun. He sure didn't know how to use it. Everything eventually worked out okay. Clyde did a good job of controlling the crowd so well his father was proud of him. He is George's son. Mr. Woodson also told me he gave Clyde a raise and the rest of the night off."

About then, George Harris arrives and asks "Hank, who is going to take responsibility for tonight's incident? And who is going to do the paper work?" Hank tells George "You're lucky. You take responsibility and do the paper work, George. Your boy did a good job out there tonight. If you aren't already, you should be proud of him. He's a fine young man." "I must agree with you on all accounts," says George "and I will see you tomorrow." George leaves. The Thomas' finish their meals.

Janice comes back with three cakes. Grace asks "Who ordered these? We did not." Janice Henry remarks "One is from Mr. Woodson. One was from table five. And one was from Sylvia." This got Conrad's attention. He asks "How did you know her name? You weren't here earlier when it was mentioned and she hasn't gotten up from the table." "You know, I don't know how I know her name. I must have met her before. As far as ordering, I had it in my head that she did" states Janice. The last statement really hits Conrad.

Hank speaks this time "Well, let's dive in and eat some cake. Which one do we eat tonight? The other two will go home with us and I can take a piece to work with me tomorrow." Grace says "Let us start with the coconut. You like that most of all." "So do I" says Sylvia. Conrad takes notice of that as well as the other times and comments "Sylvia, how is it with your amnesia that you can order things, remember that you like things and can almost act like you have ESP?" Sylvia, being a little sarcastic says "I guess my memory is not as bad as the doctors thought. My ESP is not of my doing. I do not know how I do it. Just like Janice did not know how she knew my name. We never have met before that I can remember. I have been in the hospital for seven days and four of those I was unconscious. Maybe she entered my room by mistake and saw me then somehow."

"You can try and explain your way out of this, but I'm going to watch you like a hawk" argues Conrad. "That sounds fine to me because I do not know when I do it" asserts Sylvia. The cake is cut in to four large slices and each person receives a slice. The talk had calmed down some, but it did not bother the Thomas table people. They enjoyed the cake and when done Hank goes to pay for the meal. Woodson will have none of it. He insists the meal is on the house. Hank takes out $50.00 and told Woodson to divide it between Clyde and Janice. He also tells Woodson they will be back shortly despite the evening's events.

The Thomas family, along with Sylvia, headed for home. Hank drove the Sorento in a somewhat slowed manner due to the wind that came into the car's broken window when he goes faster. He tells Grace that the car really is not that drivable in this kind of weather and the car's glass would need fixing tomorrow. That means he will have to drive her to the university in his truck. It also means he would have to take some time off work to get the vehicles squared away. As they go to the house, Sylvia says again that she was looking forward to sleeping in a bed other than one belonging to a hospital.

The four arrive home at 10:00 o'clock with two cakes in hand. Hank opens the door and lets the two women in first for they each had a cake. They go into the kitchen to put the cakes away for the night. Conrad collects the coats and puts them in the closet. It is decided that they all would retire for the evening. Sylvia is first up the stairs and into her room. She just lies on the bed for a few minutes. Conrad comes in and she arises. They come together and kiss each other goodnight. Conrad leaves and Sylvia gets into bed. Hank and Grace come up shortly and find that Sylvia and Conrad are in their rooms attempting to go to sleep. The married couple goes into their room and get undressed to get into the whirlpool to relax for a bit. Afterwards, they dry off and retire for the night.

CHAPTER 7

The Next Day

Conrad is the first to arise and get a shower. Sylvia follows him. Grace and Hank have their own bath room. Sylvia is the first downstairs and goes into the kitchen to make a pot of coffee. When Conrad comes down, he is amazed to see that Sylvia has beaten him downstairs. He asks "How did you get down here so fast?" "I am a fast dresser. I only have one piece and shoes to put on," states Sylvia. That last statement caught Conrad by surprise. Sylvia asks "What does your mother usually fix for breakfast?" "Eggs over easy and bacon" reports Conrad. "I am not that good of a cook, but I can scramble eggs real well" brings back Sylvia. "That will do," says Conrad taking in the comment about scrambling 'eggs real well.' About then his mother and father arrive.

Sylvia has already started cooking scrambled eggs. She has placed bacon in the microwave. Sylvia gets four glasses down with one larger than the others. She had checked out the cabinets before starting to cook. With the eggs and bacon done Sylvia announces "Breakfast is ready." She pours orange juice into each glass and gives the big one to Conrad. She also gets two cups of coffee for the parents. She places the eggs and bacon on the table and they all eat. Grace asks "What did you do to the eggs? They taste better than mine." "I use some milk and cheese. The cheese gives it the extra boost to the eggs. I learned that from

McDonald's Sausage McMuffin with cheese. It does a good job on the eggs. The bacon I cooked in the microwave. I placed paper towels under and over it. As you can see the bacon came out quite crisp" tells Sylvia.

Conrad announces that he is going to take a two week vacation starting today. He states that his intentions are to help Sylvia find a job and a place of her own. Sylvia tells Conrad that she thinks it is a good idea. So do Conrad's parents, except Grace thinks Conrad should only take one week. She lets her son know her feelings. Conrad comes back "Mom, I've already decided on two weeks. My job will be covered most of the time. I will only need to stop in occasionally to see what is up." She inquires "What do you plan to do with all that time? You have never taken two weeks before."

Things were beginning to get a little touchy. Conrad tells his mother "Mom, enough is enough. I am going to help Sylvia find a job, get an apartment and settle down. Whatever time I have left, I will spend with Sylvia showing her the city." After that encounter, Grace remains quiet. Hank, on the other hand, speaks up with "I think it's a great idea. Maybe you two will get to know each other immensely better. I'm sure you two think the same way. Here's to you two" as he lifts his cup of coffee. Hank turns to Grace "I'll take you to work so I can get your window fixed after I call the insurance company. My truck is going to take longer and I'll deal with that later."

The group finishes breakfast and Sylvia begins to put things in the dishwasher. Grace says "You do not need to do that. I normally do that." Sylvia comes back "Normally, you say. Well today is not one of those 'normally' days. I fixed breakfast, so I cleanup. You need to get out of here to go to work. I can handle all the cleaning which needs to be done." Grace, feeling a little inadequate, says "Dinner will be my responsibility"

Grace and Hank leave. On the way, Hank says "I could use another cup of coffee. I'm going to stop at McDonald's. Do you want anything?" Grace responds "No." Hank gets to

McDonald's and orders his coffee. It takes a long time for there are cars in front of him to get his order. He feels he would have done better if he had gone inside. Finally getting his coffee, he continues to drive Grace to VCU. She arrives a little early. Hank, then, drives to work at Henrico Police Headquarters. He wants to see what has been done with the culprit from last night at Hank Woodson's barbeque.

Arriving at work, he asks the desk sergeant what happened to the guy he had shot last night. The officer says "George Harris brought him in and the man is in lockup." Hank goes to see the guy, but his lawyer, Devlin Masque, is with him. So, Hank cannot see the prisoner just yet. He returns to his desk and sees that he has a woman waiting to talk to him. Hank gets the woman to the chair next to his desk. He asks "What can I do for you, miss?" "My 11 year old son was killed in a drive-by shooting this morning while waiting for a friend to go to school with him. Joseph couldn't have been the target. He has done nothing wrong" relates the woman.

Hank tells her he will need her name, address, and any description on the men and their vehicle. She provides her name and address and speaks afterwards "They're two African American men in a big black sedan. They used a gun that shot a lot of bullets in a short time. I didn't get the license number."

Hank asks "Is there anything else you can tell me?" "Well, there was a German Shepherd in the rear seat" she replies. "Madam, we will do everything we can to catch the perpetrators. You have given me more information than you may realize. Go home and we will be in touch. You may have to come and identify the men," tells Hank. "Well, I hope you catch them soon," says the mother.

Hank had made a special note about the dog and the black car. He goes to the computer and calls up the licenses for German Shepherds. Getting a print out of the addresses and owner names, he next does a listing of black cars and identifies two locations which match on the list of dog licenses. He gets into his car and drives to the first address. It turns out to be the home of an Asian family. He next goes to the other address and notices a black man in the yard playing with a German Shepherd. He calls for backup to arrive in an unmarked car.

Hank does not see the other man. But, Hank is positive this is the house. There is a black Lincoln parked in front of the house. Hank's backup arrives and all three men get out of the vehicles and approach the man. He notices them coming towards him and he runs to the back of the building trying to escape, but the other two officers get him down and bring him cuffed to Hank. "Here he is lieutenant," directs the officer with culprit in hand "There is supposed to be two. Check in the house. I'll take this one to your car," orders Hank. The officers go into the house with guns drawn and yell "Police" and they notice a man sleeping on the couch. As he wakes up, he is seen reaching for a Gluck 9. One of the officers says "Don't do it or we will be forced to shoot you." Fearing death, he raises his hands and demands "What is all this about? I haven't done anything. My brother and I have been here all morning." The last statement was his demise. "Who says anything about this morning?" asks the other officer who is cuffing him. They take him to the car as well.

Hank tells the two officers to take the men to Headquarters and lock them up. He calls the impound lot to come and get the car. He knows he needs the lady whose son was shot to come in and identify the men as well as the car. He also calls animal control to come and get the dog since its master will be in jail for a long time if identified. After those two requests are completed, Hank goes back to the office. He calls the mother of Joseph to come in for identification via a lineup.

The woman arrives. Hank has three plans for her. First, she goes to the lineup. Both brothers are inside the lineup. She identifies one of those in the lineup. Secondly, she is taken to see the car. "That's it. I remember the dent in the rear bumper" states the mother confidently. Third, is a bit more difficult. He takes the woman to the dog pound. He wants to see if she can identify the dog. She does saying "That's the one. See his orange stripe down his neck. That's unusual for a dog." Hank takes her back to the office and tells her she will need to re-identify the man, car and dog in court. He thanks her and says "Goodbye, have a good day," as if she could. Hank sets about questioning the one identified shooter.

"Where were you and your brother this morning about 8:00 o'clock?" questions Hank. "We weren't nowhere. We was at home," says the culprit. "What if I tell you a woman has identified you, your car and the dog as being the ones doing a drive-by shooting causing the death of her son?" inquires the lieutenant. "Your brother as the driver won't get as stiff a penalty as you. If you want to write a confession, I'll talk to the DA" informs Hank. The shooter, knowing he is a goner, is quick to make a deal. He writes out the confession and is returned to his cell. Hank has a good day for the rest of his shift.

Grace did not have a very good day to start either. When she had finished her second class of the day, she had some free time. She was in her office and a student comes in saying "I have been raped." "What did you say?" queries Grace to the black-haired young lady. "I said I was raped" says the girl. When did this happen?" asks Grace. The lass comes back with "About fifteen minutes ago. It was Gary Fielding." Grace gets on the phone and calls campus police.

An officer arrives very shortly wanting to know "What is the problem, Mrs. Thomas?" "Officer Tang, this young lady says she was just raped a few minutes ago by Gary Fielding. I do not know the boy. What is our next step?" informing and asking speaks Grace.

Officer Tang directs Grace to take down as much information as she can and he will be back to pick it up. Meanwhile, he goes to the Administration Office to seek Fielding's schedule. With the paper in his hand, Tang heads for the Mathematics Building in search of Gary. He finds him and tells him he is under arrest. Fielding asks "What for?" without putting up any fight.

"Rape" is all Tang gives Gary. He takes Fielding to the English Department and places him on a bench a short distance away from Grace's office.

The girl had told Grace, "I was in the computer room working on a five page paper that is due this Friday. The classroom was empty for the time being and I was the only one there. Then, Gary comes in and sits behind me pestering me with sexual taunts. I turned around to tell him to please be quiet so I could do my work. He jumps over the table, pushes me to an empty table and pulls my dress up. He had heard that I do not wear any under garments. Then, he asks 'You want it don't you?' and I told him no. He raped me anyway."

Tang informs Grace "Mrs. Thomas, I have Fielding here. Can the girl identify him?" "I am sure she can. Laura, come here, please. Is that the boy right there?" Grace puts the question to her. Laura answers "Yes. That is the boy that raped me." "Am not" responded Gary "it was consensual. I said 'you want it don't you and she nodded her head. As I penetrate her, she says 'oh'" "I said 'NO!'" Laura countered.

Grace says "I can see finger bruises on her legs. That is not a sign of consensual sex. I think he needs to be in jail. You both realize you will have to go before the Council and tell your sides of the incident. Their decision will be binding as far as the university is concerned. Officer Tang, remove the boy from my sight." Tang takes him off. The rest of Grace's day was uneventful, but the incident was enough to ruin her day.

Meanwhile, Sylvia and Conrad are busy getting ready to go out for the day and try to get some things accomplished. The first place they go is to the Social Security Administration's office in Richmond. If Sylvia is going to work she will need at least a Social Security number. They arrive two minutes early and decide to wait at the door. There is already some people at the door. Sylvia asks Conrad "How will I prove my identity? I do not have a birth certificate." "Leave that to me" says Conrad.

The door opens and they get in line to use the sign-in computer screen. It has five choices. Their choice is *A New Card*. They were given a receipt. They took seats to wait their turn. Almost immediately, Sylvia's receipt number is called. Conrad and she go to the window. The clerk asks "Do you have any identification?" Sylvia answers "No. I have lost my purse with my driver's license in it." Conrad takes note of that statement. "I can vouch for her. I'm Conrad C. Thomas, Manager at Wachovia Bank. Her name is Sylvia Reed and her date of birth is October 22, 1988" complies Conrad. "How long have you known this woman?" asks the clerk. "A while" reports Conrad. "Sir, if you will sign this affidavit and the young lady as well. We can begin" orders the clerk.

Conrad takes the form, reads over it, and fills in the blanks. Sylvia and he sign the affidavit. The clerk takes back the form to a computer search and finds no Sylvia Reed. She, then, goes to another computer that prints the card for her. The clerk takes the card to Sylvia and says "here you are."

Being done with the Social Security, they proceed to an employment agency on Midlothian Turnpike. They go inside, take a ticket and she has to wait her turn which was short. Some people got upset that she was called before them. The clerk asks her what her name, address and Social Security number with phone number. She gives it all to them using Conrad's address and phone number. They ask her what skills she has and Sylvia says "I can use a computer completely and I have worked in a library." Conrad has another statement to take note of. He is beginning to wonder if Sylvia is getting her memory back. He decides he will just have to wait and see. The clerk tells her they will call her if they have something come up.

Conrad takes Sylvia to his car and says they are going to his bank. At his bank, Conrad tells Sylvia to open saving and checking accounts. He gives her $200.00 and says "Put a $100.00 in each account as you open it." They go inside and Conrad takes her to a teller. "Kitty Calhoun, this is Sylvia Reed.

She wants to open checking and savings accounts. Will you take care of her, please?" directs Conrad. He, then, goes into his office to check on mail and notes. Having none, he returns to Sylvia. Kitty tells Sylvia "The checking account has starter checks and you will receive a box of 250 checks in about 10 days along with your debit card. I need a PIN number for the debit card." She accepts the checks, gives a PIN number of 4546 and turns to find Conrad right behind her. "Kitty, this is my new girl friend, Sylvia Reed" states Conrad.

Sylvia tells Conrad she is all through. The next place they go is Falling Creek Apartments on Marina Drive. They want to get a low price place for her. The two go into the manager's office and Alexander Pence asks "How can I help you?" "We want an apartment. Can you show us what's available?" asks Conrad.

"At the present time, I only have one apartment available. It is room 213" tells Alexander "if you will come this way." Pence takes them to the room. They notice that it is of the kitchen/living room variety with one bedroom. The apartment is furnished. Before Sylvia can say anything, Conrad informs Pence "We'll take it." Pence comes back with "I haven't told you the rental price. It is $550.00 a month. You pay the utility bills. Do you still want it?"

Conrad advises Alexander "Yes. We can pay the first month's rent today." "Then, let us go sign the contract. It is on a tri-monthly basis. In other words, you must agree to pay rent for a three month term and renew the contract or move out" reports Pence. The three go to the manager's office and Pence gets the contract ready for their signatures. Sylvia and Conrad sign the paper and hand over $550.00 to Alexander Pence. He gives them two keys and says "I hope you enjoy your stay." The pair go up to room 213, go inside and look the place over. They find that there is very little silverware, no cleaning detergents of any kind and few plates and bowls. A skillet, pots and pans were adequate. Sylvia vows "Honey, it is OUR place." She approaches him and kisses him fully on the lips with her hands and arms around his neck.

Sylvia's actions caught him totally off guard. He has a thing about the statement 'OUR place'. Was it a statement of her intent or just a quick comment because he would be paying the rent? He decided to wait and see. Now they would need to go and get things for the apartment. He noticed only two glasses and two cups indicating the apartment is for two people or a single, but no more. They felt they would change that.

Their first concession is to go to Wal-Mart. Since they were on Midlothing Turnpike, they go to the big Wal-Mart next door to Sam's Club. They manage to get a parking spot close to the door. They park the Dodge and go inside. Getting a cart, Conrad and Sylvia head to the house wares aisle opposite the food department. Doing this reminds them they need food. Sylvia decides on the silverware first, then, they will do the plates and bowls. At the house wares aisle, she finds all she needs in the things she originally came for. She decides on an 8 piece setting of plates and likewise for the silverware.

Going down the food aisle, she starts with the raw vegetables. She gets a 5 pound bag of potatoes, two tomatoes, lettuce, celery, grapes, apples, and salad mix. She proceeds to the canned goods. In this aisle, Sylvia gets two cans each of corn, green beans, great northern beans, chili with beans, beef stew, tuna, and a jar of jelly. She fills the need to get cereal and milk. Sylvia gets a box of frosted flakes and in the dairy area a dozen eggs, butter, cheese and milk.

Meanwhile, Conrad has been busy getting the meats. He got five pounds of hamburger, two pork chops, 2 pounds of stew beef, two sirloin steaks, 10 pounds of chicken legs and thighs, one package of Polish sausage and some fish. In the drink aisle, Conrad gets one carton of Pepsi and two cartons of Diet Pepsi. He goes to the frozen foods and gets two pizzas, Brussels sprouts, French fries, and TV dinners. Each of the two, thinking they had enough food in their carts, head for the checkout lanes and they meet there. They find a line that is just emptying out and shove their carts into it. Sylvia begins unloading her cart first. When she is finished with hers, she turns to Conrad's cart. Sylvia places the items from his cart onto the conveyor belt. Once totaled, the checker says your total is $276.11. Cash or charge?" Conrad gets out his Visa and pays for the groceries and house wares with it.

The pair pushes the loaded cart out to the car and places the items in the trunk. Conrad says "Let's get these foods to the apartment and into their storage areas before we go anyplace else." Sylvia and Conrad get into the car and drive to Falling Creek Apartments. As they pull into their parking space, they see a young lady standing there doing nothing. They get out and before they can get to the rear of the car, the girl states 'You must be the new couple that just moved into 213." "How did you know that?" asks Conrad. "Simple, I'm Rosalyn Pence. My dad is the apartment complex manager. He told me a new couple had moved into 213. Would you like some help?" "We could use it. There is quite a bit" requests Sylvia.

The trio begins the lugging up the stairs of the food. After two trips, the goods are all in the apartment. So is Rosalyn. Sylvia and Conrad think it kind of odd that she remains. Sylvia asks "Is there anything we can do for you?"

"I just want to get to know you. I don't get many friends in the complex. I would like to try becoming yours," responds Rosalyn. Sylvia decides "That would be nice indeed. I have no friends other than Conrad. Sit down on the couch and we can talk." Rosalyn asks "How is that possible? As old as you are, you should have some friends. Sylvia responds "I had an accident and I have lost my memory. Conrad was the one that rescued me and took me to the hospital. I do not know how or why I was where he found me. The accident was seven or eight days ago. I just do not know."

"Well, I'll be your friend. I can visit you when you're alone or Conrad is here. I don't have any male friends," says the long black haired Rosalyn "I'm nineteen and out of school. My mother and dad are divorced. My dad and I share apartment 100. I have my own room. It's a good thing because dad brings home these obnoxious women to spend the night. It's not every night, but it's too often for me," gives Rosalyn. Conrad states "We are the friendly type. I'm not married to Sylvia, yet. I don't really know our future." Sylvia notices the second sentence with 'yet' in it.

Rosalyn ends with "I need to go. My dad wonders where I disappear to and he gets mad. He does that a lot with me." "You come anytime and we will talk about your dad, if you want" speaks Conrad. Rosalyn says "Bye" and leaves the apartment. Conrad comments "She's almost as pretty as you are beautiful. If I didn't have you, I might want to get involved with her." "You can have us both. I am not the jealous type. I heard you say 'yet' about being married to me. Is that your ultimate goal?" inquires Sylvia. Conrad returns "Before I can have both of you, both of you will have to agree on it, independently and in unity. You have agreed on it independently just now," says Conrad as he moves to take Sylvia in his arms. He gives her a very passionate kiss. "I guess we're more than a couple as of now," continues Conrad. Sylvia gives Conrad a similar kiss, then, states "Yes. We are." They take the time to put away the groceries, the drinks, the plates and silverware.

"Let's go get some lunch at my favorite eatery," says Conrad. Conrad takes Sylvia to his favorite restaurant Bandito's Burrito Lounge. Sylvia immediately says "This is my favorite kind of food. I particularly like burritos." Conrad takes particular note of both sentences. He parks the Dodge and they go inside. They are greeted by Jose Emanez, owner. He welcomes Conrad with "It is so good to see you again Senor Thomas. And, who is this?" "This is my girlfriend unlike any other girl I have dated, Sylvia Reed," speaks Conrad. Jose tells Sylvia "Welcome senorita. Let me show you to a booth." Alvarez leads Sylvia and Conrad to a booth and they sit opposite each other.

Their waitress, Juanita Gomez, arrives. She has had a crush on Conrad for some time. Juanita asks "Conrad, why have you been away so long? It has been over a week since you were last here. That's not like you." Conrad tells Juanita "This is the reason. Juanita meet Sylvia Reed. I found her unconscientiously lying alongside Mount Holly Church Road and took her to the hospital. I have visited her every day she was in there. We have become good friends." The last statement did not set well with Juanita.

"What will you have to drink?" asks Gomez. Conrad responds "I'll have a Pepsi and Sylvia will have a Diet Pepsi." Juanita leaves. Sylvia reaches for Conrad's hands and takes hold of them in her own hands. She looks him squarely in the face and reminds Conrad "She has had a thing for you for some time." Conrad cannot do anything except reply "I guess so. But, I haven't had a thing for her. She's not my type."

Gomez returns with the drinks and asks "What is it you want tonight, Conrad?" "I'll have a Burrito Supreme, two Soft Shell Tacos and nachos with cheese" demands Conrad. Before Juanita can ask or do anything, Sylvia states "I will have the same." Juanita makes a note on her tablet and leaves.

Sylvia is still holding hands with Conrad even through the ordering ordeal. She asks Conrad "Why are you so interested in me? I am a total stranger. I have never been to Richmond before." He mentally notes the last statement again and gives forth with "You are my dream come true. I've always wanted a red-haired doll. You're her. I have a question for you. How do you know you have never been to Richmond before?" "I just do. I do not recognize anything we have seen. I do not know where Henrico Doctors Hospital is from here, much less our apartment" gives back Sylvia.

Juanita arrives with their orders, places Conrad's down first and then Sylvia's. Sylvia notices that her tacos bear no tomatoes, while Conrad's do. She was wondering what else might be different. After Juanita leaves, Sylvia brings the difference to

Conrad's attention. He wonders "Do you think she did that on purpose?" Sylvia knowingly says "Yes." The two eat their meals.

After they have finished, Conrad leaves a $5.00 tip for Juanita. Sylvia questions Conrad "Why did you leave so much?" "That's what I always leave when I come here regardless of who may or may not be with me and regardless of the bill. They go to the register and Senor Emanez tells Conrad the amount due is $18.28. Conrad gives him the exact amount.

Sylvia wonders to Conrad "Why did you give him the exact change?" "Because, it is a game we play. He tells me the amount and I see if I have the exact change. Only once did he catch me. I keep a pocket of change just for Alverez" returns Conrad. They go to the car and decide that it is time to go to the electric company and have the electricity put into Sylvia's name. Sylvia and Conrad go inside the building to find a line of people waiting at one cashier. There are three other booths, but only the one cashier is maintaining the service available. Just then, another cashier enters and opens her booth. Sylvia is first to get there even before Conrad.

The clerk desires information by asking "What can we do for you today?" "I need the electricity at my apartment to be put into my name. I live at Falling Creek Apartments, Marina Drive, Apartment 213," gives Sylvia. The clerk asks "And what is your name?" Sylvia responds "Sylvia Reed."

The clerk makes a note, leaves to go to a computer and does a name search. She finds no record of a Sylvia Reed and tells Sylvia "Since you have never had service with us before, there will be a $150.00 deposit that will be refunded at the end of the first year of service provided you are never late with a payment." Conrad gets the money out and hands it to Sylvia who, then, gives it to the clerk. The clerk says "You're service is on. Is there anything else?" "No" answers Sylvia as she turns to leave. She grabs at Conrad's right hand wanting to hold it as they walk out to the car together.

The duo gets into the Viper and start to leave when an idea hits Conrad "We need to get you a cell phone. Let's go to AT&T." Conrad takes her into the exact place where he got his phone. He parks the car and they go inside. Conrad puts his name on the list of people waiting to see a representative. When his name is called, he gets Cheryl—the same girl that waited on him when he got his phone. He says "Cheryl, this is a friend of mine and we need to get her a cell phone. Can you help us out?" "Yes. What type of phone do you want? We have several varieties to pick from," says Cheryl. Conrad tells Cheryl "Give her the Blackberry 8530. I have that type and enjoy using it." Cheryl goes into the stock room and returns with the Blackberry. She also has the accompanying Bluetooth ear piece for hands free communication. It is what Conrad has with his cell phone.

Cheryl begins telling Sylvia how to use the phone, particularly, how to use the Bluetooth functioning of the ear piece. After showing her all the functions, Cheryl asks "Are there any questions?" Sylvia says "I think I have it all in my mind. If I have a question, I can ask Conrad." Cheryl, then, says "Now, let us get you a number. I need only look at the computer to see what the next number that is available will be. Here, 804-555-2126." "That is one less than my number. How did that happen?" asks Conrad.

Cheryl states "The number was given up just yesterday. It became available because the computer picks the lowest number to assign to a phone. You were just lucky, I guess." Cheryl, then, tells Conrad the price and that there is a $100.00 mail-in rebate. Conrad gives her his Visa card and she deducts it from his account. Cheryl checks out the phone by dialing Sylvia's number. The phone rings in Sylvia's hand. She answers it to find that the phone does work. In addition to the phone and ear piece, Sylvia gets a charger, holster and instruction manual. Conrad and Sylvia leave pleased with the phone.

This Monday has been a full day for them. Instead of going to the apartment, they go to Conrad's home. His mother and father are there. He fills them in on the day's events, especially the apartment. Grace asks Conrad "And, who paid for all this?" "I did. It's just a loan until Sylvia gets her a job. Like I said, we went to an employment agency. We had to give them our phone number, but now Sylvia can call them and give the agency her number" answers Conrad.

Sylvia mentions how pleased she has been with Conrad. That did not set well with Grace. Conrad tells his mother and father about the developing relationship between Sylvia and him. Grace is not too thoughtful of that statement as well. She seems to not want to 'cut the apron strings' and let her son be a man. Grace has prepared steak, baked potatoes and corn for dinner. They all go into the kitchen to eat. When dinner is over, Sylvia helps Grace with the clean-up.

Hank and Conrad go into the family room and begin watching the TV. After the clean-up, Grace and Sylvia go there as well. Sylvia gets on the computer and finds a blog about celebrities and the cars they own. Of particular interest to her was the President's daughter owned a 2009 red Dodge Viper. She tells Conrad of the incident that the President's daughter and he owned a Dodge Viper. She thought it quite a coincidence and told Conrad that. Conrad was, of course, not really interested in the fact. He had gotten his Dodge before she did. It was if she were copying him. Sylvia continues to search and surf the Internet. Conrad, Grace and Hank watch TV. Time arrives for them all to retire for the evening.

CHAPTER 8

The Day After

Sylvia and Conrad come downstairs at the same time with Sylvia leading the way. Grace is in the kitchen fixing breakfast. "What will you two be up to today?" asks Grace. Conrad responds "We need to do some more shopping, not much though and we need to get Sylvia a driver's license. So we will be going to DMV." "What is for breakfast?" asks Sylvia. Grace tells her "Pancakes. We have not had these for some time. Conrad really likes it when I make them my special way." "What is that special way?" questions Sylvia. Grace gives back "I use butter in the mix with a bit of sugar. That way not as much syrup is needed to make the pancakes taste better."

Hank arrives and sees that Grace is making pancakes and goes "Mmmmm ... Those smell good." Conrad tells his father good morning. Hank says the same to everybody. With a large stack of pancakes done, Grace questions "Who wants how many?" Hank asks for four, Conrad asks for four and Sylvia asks for only two. Grace takes three. They all use the Maple syrup to cover their pancakes. Sylvia takes very little syrup and Conrad asks "Why so little syrup? Why not a bit more like us?" Sylvia answers "I have to save my girlish figure for you."

That was about all Grace could handle. She demands "What is going on with you two? I want to know now. Give me all the details." Conrad retorts "Mother, we are just good friends. There has been no hanky panky of any kind. We are just spending a lot of time together." Sylvia gets it in her mind that the 'no hanky panky' is going to change real soon. Grace is satisfied for the time being. Hank enters the conversation with "Grace, you're at it again. Leave the boy along. He's a man and he knows what he wants. If it be Sylvia, so what? We've gone over this before. I'll have no more of it. Is THAT understood?"

Grace and Hank say their goodbyes and leave in Hank's truck. Grace's car is still at the body shop getting the window replaced. The company did not have the window in stock and had to order one from the KIA dealership. They go to VCU and Hank drops Grace off at the English Department. He, then, heads for the Henrico County Police station to start a relatively normal day. Grace expects hers to be the same. Like minds think alike.

Conrad asks Sylvia "What are our plans besides going to DMV for your learner's permit?" Sylvia reacts with "I intend to get my license today. We also need to get me some more clothes and sheets and a comforter for the bed at the apartment. Besides, we need to spend a little time there. You did tell Rosalyn you would talk to her." So, Sylvia cleans up from breakfast while Conrad gets the coats and hat out for Sylvia and a coat himself. When finished in the kitchen, Sylvia comes with "Let us go and get me some clothes first." "Okay" replies Conrad.

Getting in the car and backing out, Conrad sees a neighbor across the street waving her hands. He stops and goes to her "Mrs. Crawford, what's the matter?" "It is my husband. He is lying in the living room floor. I think he has had a heart attack," states Mrs. Crawford. Sylvia, by this time, is out of the car and hears the conversation.

Without waiting, she dashes into the house to find Mr. Crawford exactly where Mrs. Crawford says he would be. She checks for breathing and he is not. She checks for a pulse and finds none. Sylvia begins CPR—15 pushes on the chest and 2 puffs of air in between compressions—on Mr. Crawford. Mrs. Crawford follows Sylvia by a couple of minutes. They enter and find her doing CPR on Mr. Crawford. In between puffs, while doing compressions, she says "Call 911. Tell them the address and to bring a defibrillator. Sylvia continues until the rescue arrives and relieves her of her heart felt duty.

Using the defibrillator three times, the rescue workers bring Mr. Crawford back to life. One of them turns to Sylvia "I don't know where you learned CPR, but he would have been unrecoverable if you had not intervened." The rescue squad places him on their gurney and lifts him to roll out the door. They place him in the ambulance and drive off. Mrs. Crawford closes the door and locks it to follow them in the family car.

Sylvia and Conrad get back into the car and drive to the apartment first. They see Rosalyn standing on the sidewalk as if she had been waiting for their return. She walks up to Sylvia and asks "Can I hang out with you guys today? My dad is in one of his worst moods and he is taking it out on me." "Come on up. We will talk" responds Sylvia. The trio goes up to the apartment. Going in, Rosalyn sits right down on the couch without asking or saying anything. It is as if she were a mute who belonged there. Sylvia breaks the silence with "Tell us about your dad's problem. I am sure we can help."

Rosalyn begins "Dad gets angry with me the day after a night he has to spend alone. He is over sexed and hates it without a woman to satisfy his need. I guess he picks on me because I'm a woman in the house and I won't have sex with him. Now, I wouldn't mind having sex with Conrad. But, he's yours."

Sylvia says "You need to get out more in the day time and maybe even at night. If we are here, feel free to join us. I am not jealous of Conrad and he is not jealous of me. We have an open relationship. We would enjoy your company and your thoughts about life." "Well, right now, I don't have too many thoughts on life. That is a whole issue unto itself. Maybe if I spend time with you, it will become clear as to what I want and who I want to spend my life with," gives Rosalyn.

Conrad, hearing the note about him and Rosalyn getting together makes him really wonder what Sylvia would think if he was to do it. He tells Rosalyn to come anytime. Rosalyn willfully accepts the invitation. Sylvia puts forth "Conrad, we need to go get me some clothes. Let us take Rosalyn with us. It will be a tight fit, but I think we can work it out. Rosalyn is small enough, I think. How about you go with us to get me some clothes, Rosalyn?" Rosalyn agrees it would be a real diversion. So, the three get into the Dodge and it is a tight fit just as Sylvia says it would be. They head for Talbot's—a place where Conrad likes to shop.

Arriving at the store, the three bail out of the Viper, which normally only sits two. They go in and Conrad sees Angela North again. He goes to her and says "This is the young lady I bought the other clothes and shoes for," as he points to Sylvia. "We need more dresses for her." Angela takes him to the women's department once more. Sylvia immediately sees a sky blue dress that she wants. She takes it on her arm. Looking more, Sylvia finds a yellow dress, a red dress, a white top with dark blue skirt, a light green top with forest green skirt and a black dress. She hands some to Rosalyn and some to Conrad. Sylvia asks Angela where the fitting rooms are located and Angela shows her to them.

Sylvia first takes in the two piece green outfit and puts it on. It fits her perfectly accenting her waist and breasts. She goes out to where Conrad is at. He goes "Wow. That is the best I have seen on you yet." She turns around and Rosalyn, with envy, remarks "It really is a beautiful fit on you." Sylvia goes back into the fitting room this time taking the sky blue dress. Again, it is a perfect fit. She returns to Conrad, who says "You fill that out quite well. Keep that up and we will be in trouble." Angela questions "What kind of trouble?" Conrad does not answer. Sylvia takes the yellow dress into the fitting room for her next try out. Once more, a perfect fit.

Sylvia goes out for the other three to see her. Angela comments "That is a fine dress for spring, but there wouldn't be too many times to wear it in the winter." "I like it a lot. It fits you to the 't'. Get that one too," states Conrad. Rosalyn just looks on. This time, Sylvia takes the white top with the dark blue skirt. Putting it on is easy. This one did not fit exactly right. So, she goes to Conrad and asks "What do you think of this one?" "It doesn't fit you as well as the others, but I like it" remarks Conrad. Rosalyn, on the other hand states "I wouldn't be caught wearing that with the way it fits. It looks too loose." "I agree," says Sylvia.

Sylvia has saved the red and black dresses for last, because she knows what these will do to Conrad. She puts on the black dress first. Sylvia heads out to the viewing area once more. This time, Conrad is shocked speechless. His jaw drops open. It is the most perfect fit showing off her features—all of them. Rosalyn, seeing gaping Conrad, states "That is a must have. Just look at the expression of Conrad. I would love to have that dress." "Maybe, I will let you borrow it" gives forth Sylvia. Finally the red dress is selected. She takes it in and switches clothes. It is a knockout. Sylvia returns to the viewing area. Conrad is speechless again, but this time manages to say "That dress makes me want you, here and now." Rosalyn and Angela agree to the looks of the dress as being phenomenal. Sylvia decides to leave the white top and blue skirt. She takes the rest of the clothes. Before going to the register, Sylvia asks Conrad "Can we get me a pair of sport shoes, Dear?" Conrad notices the 'dear' remark and says "Certainly."

Angela takes the group to the shoe department. She shows Sylvia a variety of shoes in all kinds of designs and fitting styles. Sylvia makes up her mind on a white and green pair of Nike's. She, then, says "I am all through shopping here today. We can checkout now." Angela leads them to the nearest register and rings the total up. It comes to $472.19. Conrad reluctantly gets out his Visa card and hands it to Angela North. North scans the card and gives a receipt to Conrad for his signature. After signing, he returns it to her. Angela says "Thank you. Come again, please. I have enjoyed this experience."

The trio goes to the Viper with clothes in tow. Conrad opens the trunk and places the things in there getting what the other two had carried in addition to what he had. The three, once more cram into the Dodge. Conrad heads for the apartment. They arrive and Mr. Pence is looking for Rosalyn. When he sees her, he tells her to get in the apartment meaning theirs. She looks at Sylvia and Conrad for help. Conrad speaks up "Sir, we took your daughter with us so that she could help Sylvia shop for new clothes. We still need her to help carry some of the items upstairs to our apartment. Rosalyn will be down when we are through with her." "Okay, but make it quick," says Alexander.

Rosalyn, Sylvia and Conrad get the clothes and head up to 213. They enter and take the clothes to Sylvia's bedroom. Conrad takes Sylvia into his arms and passionately kisses her lips as he pulls her tight against his body. He whispers "I want you tonight." "Why wait?" asks Sylvia. Conrad responds "Do you mean now? What about Rosalyn?" "She can watch, join in or do nothing. It really is her choice," offers Sylvia. Sylvia calls for Rosalyn. Rosalyn comes into the bedroom after having nearly left to go home since she has to. "What is it?" Rosalyn asks. Sylvia questions "Do you want to watch, join in or do nothing? We are going to have sex."

Rosalyn is dumbfounded stating "You mean I can join you?" "It's your choice" says Conrad. Rosalyn asks "Can I wait and have a turn at it with Conrad alone?" "If that's your choice, it is fine with me," says Conrad and, then, asks "Okay with you Sylvia?" "Why yes. If that be your choice," Sylvia expresses herself. Rosalyn goes into the living room and waits. Sylvia and Conrad have their turn at intercourse. When finished, Conrad calls Rosalyn and tells her it is her turn. Rosalyn undresses and Conrad sees a body that was somehow hidden by the clothes she had on. He made up his mind that Sylvia and he would buy Rosalyn some clothes.

Rosalyn gets in the bed with Conrad. It is not her first time with a man, but she thinks it will out do any previous time. She finds she was right in thinking that. Once over, they get dressed and go into the living room with Sylvia, who had put on her light green top, forest green skirt and Nike shoes. Conrad was thinking it would be nice to do it again. Rosalyn asserts herself "I think I really am going to be your friends. Maybe, we can do it again sometime. I better leave and see what father wants." Rosalyn leaves in a hurry.

Sylvia takes Conrad and kisses him while holding him in her arms. He says "You were great. Better than Rosalyn. You should see her body when she is nude. It almost matches yours. I'd guess you're a 36-24-34 and Rosalyn is a 34-25-35." "You are right about me. I am a 36D with 24 inch waist and 34 inch hips" reminds Sylvia. She also reminds Conrad that they need to go to DMV for her license. So, they leave.

Conrad drives to DMV and parks. The two go into the office and wait to get attended by the information clerk. When their turn arrives, Sylvia states they are there to get her license. "Do you have a learner's permit? You will need that for the road test," asks the clerk. "No, I need that first. I have had a license before, but I have lost it and have not driven since" declares Sylvia. "In that case, you take the learner's permit test, get issued a learner's permit and drive with a licensed driver beside you. After you feel comfortable, you can take the driving test," declares the clerk.

Sylvia gets a numbered ticket and is told to wait until her number is called. It is just a very short wait and her number appears over clerk five. She goes to that window and the clerk asks "You are here to take the learner's test?" "Yes," says Sylvia. The clerk directs Sylvia to a computer and tells her there will be a test for her to take on the computer. Sylvia is also told she must score a 75 or better to pass the test and that she had 30 minutes to take the examination. Sylvia is told to begin. In 20 minutes, she is finished and calls to the clerk telling her so. The clerk comes to Sylvia's side and checks her score. It is 100. The clerk says that is the highest score the department has had for the day and it was late afternoon. The clerk advises Sylvia "Come to the window and I will get you a learner's permit."

Sylvia complies with the advisement. Once there, the clerk asks for Sylvia's name, address and date of birth. Sylvia provides as requested giving her apartment address. The clerk leaves and goes to another computer behind the counter. She enters the data and prints the permit. The clerk gives the permit to Sylvia and tells her to have a nice day. It is a nice day for Sylvia in more ways than one. Sylvia asks Conrad to let her drive his car. Conrad lets out "You yourself said it has been a while since you last drove. With all this heavy traffic, you want to drive?" "Yes, I do," states Sylvia.

Conrad hands her the keys and gets in the car on the passenger's side. Sylvia gets behind the wheel. She starts the car, adjusts mirrors and feels the steering wheel by turning it to check on the tension. There is none. Sylvia advances the car out of the DMV parking lot on to the street. It is an easy task for her. She asks "Where shall we go?" "We still need sheets and a comforter for your bed. Conrad tells her the directions as they go to Bed Bath and Beyond on Brook Road.

Sylvia parks the Dodge without any effort. The two enter the store. Sylvia is not content with just white sheets. She picks out the comforter first. It is shades of blue and green. Sylvia tells Conrad "I want blue sheets to go with this comforter." They find them and go to checkout. The clerk scans the items and says "The total is $89.23. Will that be cash, check or charge card? "Visa," says Conrad back to the clerk. She takes his card and swipes it through the reader. She, then, hands him a receipt for him to sign and give back to her. He complies. They leave with the goods.

Sylvia calls the employment agency to see if there is a job available. She finds out there is none. She gives them her cell phone number so they can call that instead. Conrad tells Sylvia to drive to his house so they can have dinner with his parents.

Sylvia starts the Viper and drives effortlessly to the house on Cadbury Street. Conrad notices that his parents are not home. He advises Sylvia they will go in and wait. Sylvia goes right to the family room and gets on the computer. She hopes desperately to find out who she really is. She is on it when Grace and Hank arrive home.

Conrad calls "Sylvia, mom and dad are home." She goes into the living room. "Hello mom and dad," says Sylvia without batting an eye. This takes Grace completely over the edge "How dare you call me mom. I am not your mother." "Not yet," says Sylvia. That statement also gets Grace riled, but Hank intervenes with "Grace, it is okay for her to call us mom and dad. She doesn't know who her parents are. As it is, we are the only family she has. Now, apologize to Sylvia." Grace apologizes, but is still upset. She is thinking 'does this girl think she is going to marry Conrad?'

Grace goes into the kitchen. She has a big meal in mind for dinner. Her plan includes a tossed salad, eight pieces of fried chicken, mashed potatoes, corn and peas. For dessert she has coconut pie. Sylvia enters and offers to help. Grace tells her to mix the tossed salad. Sylvia does an excellent job. Grace notices it. Grace, then, asks her to mash the potatoes which had cooked to tenderness. Sylvia did a fine job at that as well. Dinner is complete and Grace calls the men into the kitchen. The salad is served first. Each has their own salad dressing. Grace .had especially bought red wine and vinaigrette for Conrad although she knew Sylvia would use it as well. The men say the salad is exceptionally good. It made Sylvia feel good. It made Grace feel bad. To each, their own.

After the meal, Sylvia helps Grace clean the kitchen. It was something she had done before and thought nothing of it. Grace, however, was thankful for the help and told Sylvia. They cleaned up everything and go into the living room. The men were discussing their day of events. Grace listened and, then, offered her day. Sylvia just listened and felt a part of the family.

She had felt that way when she called Grace and Hank mom and dad. Conrad asks "Mom, was the boy the campus rapist?"

"The police believe so. They have him in custody for questioning. If he is the one, they have 21 charges against him. So many times, he would get the girls in the dark and they would not be able to recognize him. When he did it in the day time, he usually wore a mask. This time, he just thought he could make it appear as consensual sex. It did not work with me and I do not think it will work with the police," Grace gives her day.

The time arrives for retirement for evening. Sylvia has feelings of belonging, not only to the family, but to Conrad in particular. She thinks she is actually falling in love with him and today's event was not a mere sample. Sylvia says goodnight and heads upstairs. Conrad is right behind her. He catches her in the upstairs hallway and kisses her. "Tomorrow is another day we will be together" says Conrad. This made Sylvia wonder if it only meant they will be together or did it also mean they will be together sexually. Sylvia asks Conrad "What did you mean by that remark?" "Wait and see" is all Conrad says. They each go to their room before Conrad's parents come upstairs. The night goes quickly by.

CHAPTER 9

Back in Washington

Four days have passed since Sylvia Redman's disappearance. The FBI has no leads as to where she may have gone. They think she may have gone to Baltimore because there were reports of a red-haired girl driving a red Dodge Viper. It could not be confirmed or denied. Senior Agent Ginger Ales calls Jim Duffy to her office. Glen Underwood and Ho Wong, after getting through with Yodel and Marvin Cookson were reassigned to normal duties, while the other six were still investigating the D.C. area. Duffy was called to take on a new assignment. Jim was going to go to Baltimore and work with the FBI agency there. His task will be to confirm Sylvia's presence there or not. Agent Duffy leaves for Baltimore.

President Sylvester Redman has had reports from Director Charles Edwards. Some have been encouraging, but in the end, there was no Sylvia. He calls Edwards on the phone and says "Edwards, are we still using that satellite monitoring system at police headquarters?" "Yes, Mr. President. We have not seen a single thing other than one red Dodge Viper. It turned out that a blonde lady owned the car. She bought it because your daughter had one. Why do you ask?" "I want the agent with it to take it to Baltimore and set it up there. We have received possible reports of a red-haired young lady driving a red Dodge Viper. I want that satellite to find the Viper," commands Sylvester.

Edwards's response is "I will get with Agent Ales and have it done today. It should take about two or three hours to dismantle, move and reassemble the unit putting it to use. Ales is sending an agent to Baltimore anyway to work with our agency there. I will have her informed of your demands immediately, Mr. President." "Keep me informed about everything, especially Baltimore. Have the agent going there report back daily. It has been four days and I am getting worried to no end. Do you understand about Baltimore?" "Yes, Mr. President," responds Director Edwards.

Charles Edwards calls Senior Agent Ginger Ales into his office. "Have you sent an agent to Baltimore yet?" he asks. Ales answers "Yes, Jim Duffy is on his way as we speak." "Who is with the satellite monitoring system?" "That would have been Duffy. He left ten minutes ago" says Ginger. "Well, call him and tell him the satellite system will be coming to Baltimore Police Headquarters. He is to help them to learn and use the system. Understood?" "Yes sir," responds Ginger Ales.

Senior Agent Ginger calls Duffy, "Jim, you are to help the Baltimore Police with the satellite system. We are sending it up there today. Once installed, show them how to use it, especially the zoom in feature to look at humans. Once you are done with the installation, work out a system to check out the identified Dodge Vipers that the system shows." "I want the satellite to find Sylvia because no one else seems capable," demands Charles Edwards. "We are trying Director. It is a job that is bigger than anyone can imagine. With the media blackout, there is little information to go on," gives Ginger. Director Edwards tells Ales "Get busy by getting back to your job." Ginger Ales seeks to comply with his requirement.

Director Charles Edwards calls Chief Travis "Travis, this is Edwards. I'm sending a man to help with the dismantling of the satellite monitoring system. We are having it moved to Baltimore today. The system has not proved useful enough to warrant its continued use at your facility. Agent Ho Wong should be there within 30 minutes. I want the unit in Baltimore and working by 12:00 o'clock. Wong will accompany the monitor system and see to the fact a technician does get it installed by my deadline. Do you have any questions?"

"No. As a matter of fact, I was going to ask that it be moved. We have used a large amount of manpower to monitor the streets of D.C. with little production," directs Chief Travis. Edwards says "It WILL be taken care of in a short time and you can tell your officers they no longer need to be on the lookout for the President's daughter's Dodge Viper."

Edwards calls Ales and tells her "Get Ho Wong to D.C. Police Headquarters to assist with the dismantling of the satellite monitoring system. Further, he is to accompany it to Baltimore and see to its installation with the technician that goes along with him. They should have it up and running by noon. Do this immediately." "Yes sir," is all Ginger Ales could say.

Agent Ales calls Ho Wong and orders him "Go to the D.C. Police and help the technician. The Smithsonian will send a technician, to dismantle the satellite monitoring system. You and the technician are to go to Baltimore with the unit and see to its proper installation. Jim Duffy will be there already. After the installation, work with Duffy on his assignment. You both can stay overnight to get the job done and more if need be. I will wait for a report from both of you by five today."

Ho goes to D.C. police headquarters and waits for the technician. They dismantle the system and load it onto a Smithsonian truck with the help of three other officers. Wong and the technician drive to Baltimore.

CHAPTER 10

Baltimore

In a city with over a million people, Duffy almost feels lost. He arrived in a 45 minute trip up I-95. Duffy goes to the Police Headquarters and advises the chief, William Morrison, that the facility will be getting a satellite monitoring system to assist in the search for Sylvia Redman's red Dodge Viper. He states "Chief Morrison, the system should be here shortly. I am to help train your people how to use the system. You will need four people assigned exclusively to it. There is to be one on each shift and one as a relief person. I know this is added manpower to your workforce, but it is necessary."

The Chief responds "My budget was cut at the beginning of the fiscal year. I'm not sure I can spare the manpower. What authority am I to use to justify the extra man-hours?" "This is a Presidential problem and it is on his authority I am telling you this. Keep track of the hours and funds may become available. It is important to find Sylvia. There has been no communication from her and no use of her credit cards. She has four and you would think she would use one for gasoline, but her car did have a full tank of gas. On a full tank, one can go 400 miles. There has been no sight of her either. That is the reason for the system coming here. We heard there have been reports of a red-haired woman driving a red Dodge Viper. We need to find that car and the vehicle will lead us to Sylvia Redman. There is to be no media leaks on this to the news media or television stations," directs Agent Duffy.

About that time, Wong arrives with the monitoring system and the technician for installation. He asks "Where shall we install the system? I will also need a space for the satellite's antenna dish." "I have a debriefing room right next door where the monitor can be set up. The dish will have to go on the roof. Duffy and Wong were real familiar with a debriefing room and knew that it would work out greatly. Chief Morrison shows them to the room. The technician, then, asks "Which wall do you want it on?" "Use the outside wall. It has a window whereby the cabling from the antenna can be routed through," states the Chief pointing to the wall with the only window.

The technician and Wong go to the truck to get the system. The Chief had provided two helping officers. They all haul it up to the chief's debriefing room and the technician begins the installation. Wong assists having learned about the system having been present when a problem developed and a technician had to come to D.C. Police Headquarters.

Ho asks "Is there any way I can help?" The technician tells him "Go to the truck, get the cabling and antenna. Find a place on the southern corner of the roof and install it. Connect the cabling and drop it down to this window. It may be a long run of wire, so take the whole roll. We can figure out how much is needed.

Ho Wong goes to the truck as requested. He gets the roll of cable, a pair of wire cutters and the dish with mounting hardware. Wong, then, heads to the roof. He finds a very good spot on the southern end of the roof and begins installation. Meanwhile, Duffy is talking to the chief about how to schedule the people to be used to monitor Baltimore's traffic. He shows the Chief a user's manual and states "If you have any questions look in here. If you cannot find an answer, call the Smithsonian Institution and ask for the satellite monitoring technician. After hearing your problem, he will either advise you on what to do or he will come and work on it. The system is very reliable. There was only one problem that developed in D.C. It turned out to be a user miss used the system causing it to jam up."

Wong, on the roof, finds the wall that the window is on and begins dropping the cabling over the edge. The technician, standing by the window sees it and pulls in the end. When he feels he has enough wire, he gives two tugs to let Ho know that he has enough wire. Wong cuts enough on his end to loop the cable for rain purposes and to connect the dish's receiver and transmitter. After Ho is done, he returns to the debriefing room. Once there, he tells the chief "You will need a dispatcher here as well to direct the closest squad car to the Dodge Viper's location. If the car is moving, it may be difficult to keep up with. A Viper can outrun a squad car as if the officer had purposely slowed down."

Chief William Morrison contacts his radio technician and tells him to bring and set up a dispatching system in the debriefing room. The radio technician brings it in and asks "Where do you want it sir?" "Right by this device so the people doing the work here will have a way of telling some squad car where to go. The radio man gets it set up and tries to use it. He sees that it is working and tells the chief that. He, then, asks "Will there be anything else, sir?" "That will be all," confirms Morrison.

Duffy, seeing that the technician has gotten the system installed and running tells the Chief "We are ready to instruct your users." "I'll have to get one up here. Let me go make a phone call," says William. The Chief calls the Sergeant's desk in the lobby and orders "Send the next officer to come in up to my debriefing room." "Well sir, there are two here right now: Ashley Powers and Nicholas Anderson. Do you need both of them?" "Yes. Send both up right now."

Powers and Anderson arrive at the debriefing room, look in and Ashley asks "What is that and why are we here?" "You are here to learn to use this satellite monitoring system to check on Baltimore traffic looking for a red Dodge Viper. When you find one, you will use the dispatch radio to contact the nearest squad car to go to the location. Powers, you are senior to Anderson aren't you?" instructs Morrison. "Yes sir," comes back Ashley. "You will have the day shift. Anderson, you will be the relief person. I know that is going to change your work schedule, but it is necessary and better that the evening or midnight shifts will have a relief," tells Morrison. Anderson says "Thank you, sir."

Duffy takes Ashley and Wong takes Nicholas. Each agent describes the working system to their counterpart. Neither of the officers have any questions when the training is through at 11:30 am. Wong turns to Duffy and says "Jim, one of us needs to call Ales and tell her the system is up, manned and running. "I'll do that Ho," retorts Duffy. Agent Duffy says "Excuse me," and leaves the room. He goes where he can get some privacy.

Duffy calls Senior Agent Ginger Ales "Hello, I want to speak with Agent Ales, please." He did not recognize the voice on the other end. "This is Agent Ales speaking. How may I help you?" "It's Duffy, ma'am. I'm here with Wong. The satellite monitoring system is up, running and manned for the time being. Chief Morrison still needs to find two other officers to take the evening and midnight shifts."

Ales orders Duffy "After you train the other two officers, I expect Ho and you to work out a schedule whereby one of you will be there at any given time. If a Viper is spotted and dispatch is made to follow up on the finding, then whichever one of you that is working will call the other and give the location. Everybody in the system wants Sylvia found. She is not to be arrested, but it may be necessary to take her into custody if she refuses to call her parents. The President and First Lady are extremely anxious to find out something. Give it your best. Give me a call if you find Sylvia."

Duffy responds to the orders "We will do our best, ma'am. I think we will split the shift from 3:00 o'clock to 3:00 o'clock. That seems best to me. I'm sure Ho will go along with it." "Well, Ho is senior to you. Let him pick whether am or pm. I will expect a report every day before 5:00 o'clock pm," directs Ginger Ales. "Oh, by the way, get the other two officers trained rather quickly. We want a full staff on the monitoring system." 'Yes, ma'am," says Duffy.

Ho has been busy showing the two how to zoom in on a location and be able to identify whether the person is a woman or man and what color hair they have. However, facial features would not show. Duffy comes back and gets Chief Morrison. "Chief, we need the other two officers to train. Will you get one off the evening shift and one off the midnight shift? And could you get them here now?" queries Jim. The Chief calls one of his officers and says "Lieutenant, get me two officers and send them to the debriefing room now. Get one off the evening shift and one off the midnight shift. They are to be trained on this new piece of equipment. You can come and take a look at it. It is a satellite monitoring system. It's really neat."

The lieutenant does as he is told and gets hold of two junior officers. He feels it better to lose their service than one of the more experienced officers. He tells the Chief what he has done and the Chief tells back that it was a good idea. He asks "About how long before they get here?" "Collins says it will take her about 20 minutes and Fuller says 25 minutes. So, both of them should be there within half an hour," states the lieutenant. Chief Morrison turns to Duffy and says "The two other officers will be here within half an hour."

Officers Jane Collins and Arthur Fuller arrive about the same time. The two are told to take the place of the two that have been trained. Collins is given the training first while the other three watch. Then, Fuller is given the training. All four were asked by Ho "Are there any questions about how to use the system or what to do if you see a red Dodge Viper. Collins raises her hand and speaks "I'm not sure what a Viper looks like. I haven't seen one that I know of. Can I be shown a picture?"

"It so happens we do have a picture of exactly the car you are looking for," responds Ho. He pulls out a picture of Sylvia and her red Dodge Viper. Collins mouth drops a bit and says "That's the President's daughter, isn't it?" "Yes, it is. That is who should be driving the car we want found. As you can see, she has red hair. It has happened in D.C. that a blonde lady was stopped for driving a red Viper, but when the officer saw she was a blonde he had to let her go on her way. Any more questions?" solicits Wong. There are none.

To show them more of the uses of the monitor, Duffy focuses in on a yard with a family having a cookout. He iterates "There are four people. The man is cooking on a grill, the woman is placing plates on a table, and a boy and girl are sitting at the table. Notice the man's hair is brown and the woman's hair is black. The two children have their father's, I assume, hair coloring. This is not what this system is to be used for. You may have a tendency to want to use it in this manner, but then you would be in violation of orders."

"Since it is only 2:00 o'clock, Powers, you take the first crack at using the system and the rest of us will watch," remarks Ho Wong. Ashley takes the seat and begins observing downtown traffic. She sees a red car and zooms in for a closer look, but it was not a Viper. She continues to expand her search outward from the downtown area in a spiral manner to keep from overlapping searched areas. Duffy tells her "That is a good method to use. You get to see more and more of the city by using this method. But, don't stop at the city limits. There are plenty of areas to search other than merely Baltimore city."

Powers continues her search and does find a red Viper in the Park Circle area of Baltimore. She gets on the radio and orders "All cars in the vicinity of Reisterstown Road and Park Heights respond." "This is car 29. We are in the 2400 block of Park Heights and can get there in two minutes. What's up?" "Car 29, you are to stop a red Dodge Viper traveling north on Park Heights as I speak. The car should be in you sight in less than a minute," tells Ashley. "This is car 29, we see the Viper coming now. We will stop it. What other orders are we to follow?"

"Check to see if the driver is a woman with red hair. If it is such a person check her identity to see if she is a Redman," states Powers. Car 29 stops the vehicle with no problem. The two officers get out of the car and advance on the Viper. They see it is indeed a red haired woman. The senior officer asks "Ma'am, can you give me your license?" "What have I done officer?" asks the woman. "Nothing. We are just checking your license." He sees that the woman's last name is Johnson, not Redman. He tells her everything is okay and she can leave. Ashley sees the car leave and immediately says "It probably is not the woman we want."

Powers goes back to searching. "That was done exactly as needed. Good job Ashley," states Wong. "It couldn't have been much better." Ashley keeps expanding her area of observation. She sees a car parked in the 3500 block of Virginia Avenue. "All cars in the area of Virginia Avenue please respond" demands Powers. "This is car 35. We are about 5 minutes away. We are up Reisterstown Road." "Go to the 3500 block of Virginia Avenue. You should see a red Dodge Viper parked along the curb. Find out who the owner is and call back." "This is car 35. ROGER."

Before they get there a red-haired woman comes out of a row house and gets in the car, starts it and drives off going south on Reisterstown Road. Powers tells car 35 to continue south until they catch up to the car. Car 35 stops the car and asks for the driver's license. Upon seeing the license they call bask "This is Car 35, we have stopped the car the woman is a Redman, but her first name is Sondra. What shall we do?" "Car 35 let her leave," states Ashley.

Powers has expanded her search to Towson. She looks over the area and finds no Viper. Going west, she comes to Reisterstown. Again, nothing. She continues her search going south and does see another Viper traveling along Highway 50 on its way westward. "Any car in the vicinity of highway 50 at the city limits please respond" asks Ashley one more time. "This is car 10, we are about 7 or 8 minutes away." "Is there any other car closer?" "This is car 76. We are at the city's limits on highway 50." "You should see a red Dodge Viper coming at you. Stop it and ascertain who the driver is," comes back Ashley. "Roger.' Car 76 waits about 4 minutes and the car approaches. The officers stop the vehicle and ascertain that it is a man driving the car. They report this back to Headquarters. "Ask to see the registration of the car. Determine if it is in his name," asserts the operator of the dispatch. One of the officers asks to see the registration. They see that the car is definitely in his name and call the information back to the dispatcher. She says simply "Let him go."

Ashley Powers gets an idea. She shares it with everybody watching her. She explains her plan and gets approval from Duffy. "Calling all cars. Be on the lookout for a red Dodge Viper. Stop it and ascertain who the driver is. Ask for the driver's license and registration. Keep on the lookout for a Sylvia Redman. If you get one as described call dispatch," informs Ashley. For a while, there is no response. Ashley continues her search. While she is searching the south side of the city, car 44 calls to report it has stopped a red Dodge Viper with two occupants. "Car 44, determine the identities of both persons and ask to see the registration," asserts Powers. ."This is car 44. We have a John Wilson and Sylvia Redman in the vehicle. The car is register to Sylvia Redman. "Is she about 21 with red hair?" petitions Ashley. "Car 44 yes she is." Ashley calls back "Hold the car until an FBI agent arrives." "Very well done Powers," relates Agent Duffy.

Ho and Jim get in their car and head to the west and get to the stopped car in 10 minutes. "Office, this is agent Wong and I am agent Duffy of the FBI. We are here to look at the person you said was a Sylvia Redman." The two agents ask the woman to step out of the car. "What is this about? I have done nothing wrong. I was wearing my seatbelt. How long are you going to keep us here? We've been here 20 minutes already," inquires the woman. Duffy takes out his photo of Sylvia Redman. There is a lot of similarities between the woman and the picture. "How old are you? asks Ho. "I'm 28 years old, if it's any concern to you," reports this Sylvia. Ho turns to Jim and states "Well, it was close. But, our Sylvia is only 21. Get their address" commands Duffy to one of the officers "and then, let them go." Turning to Ho, Duffy clarifies "This is probably the report of a red head driving a red Dodge Viper."

Ho says "This is the closest we've been to discovering Sylvia. We need to put this in our report to Agent Ales." Jim agrees with Ho, but states "We need to tell of all the stops so she gets the idea that the satellite is working out well here." Wong agrees. Duffy takes Wong aside and announces his discussion with Ales earlier. He reports "Ales and I had a discussion and for the time being, one of us is to be here so the unit is covered by us 24 hours a day. I suggested we make the schedule 3:00 o'clock to 3:00 o'clock. She also says you were senior, it would be your pick as to which tour of duty you want." Ho says "I'll take the am to pm shift and you can have the pm to am shift." "That works for me. We will start it today. We can share expenses on a room with two beds. You pick out the place we will stay and call me here with that information," concedes Duffy. Time passes and Ho leaves at 3:00 o'clock. At 5:00 o'clock, Duffy calls Agent Ales and tells of the system is working out, gives a report on the Vipers stopped, especially the Sylvia Redman, and the tour assignments. Ginger tells him to keep up the good work and that Ho and he should stay at least a week or less if Sylvia is really found.

CHAPTER II

Back To Sylvia.

It is day ten. Sylvia and Conrad arise at the same time to go downstairs and see his mother and father already up and eating. Conrad goes to the table and gets his food. Sylvia goes to the refrigerator and gets a bottle of Diet Pepsi and, then, goes to the table. After sitting next to Conrad, she begins to eat. The four are having scrambled eggs, bacon and toast. The last person to finish eating is Conrad. The four had been talking of the day's events. Most important was getting Sylvia's driver's license. She wants it quite bad. Among other things is to see about a job. With that, Grace tells Sylvia that "VCU library is looking for additional help. You said once that you had worked in a library. Maybe, that will qualify you for this position."

Sylvia says "I would love to have that job. It is right up my alley. I volunteered quite often at our library. I think it will fit my plans quite well." "I will bring an application home with me. By the way, how am I getting to work today with my car still in the shop?" inquires Grace. "Mom, dad will take you to work and after he gets your Sorento home, Sylvia and I will come and get you in it," informs Conrad. Hank states "I'll try to get it done on my lunch hour. I'll need you, Conrad, to ride with me to drive the Sorento back here to the house. Sylvia can come along. Hank grabs the coats and Grace and he leave for VCU.

Sylvia says "Can we go to DMV first? I want to get my driver's license. If I get any job, I will probably need to drive to work and that means I may need a car. After DMV, can we at least go and look? I want a Viper like you have." ""Well, let's get the driver's license out of the way first. Then, we will have plenty of time to go wherever we want including a Dodge dealership or maybe shopping for you" comments Conrad. "There is always the apartment to go to. Besides, you told Rosalyn you would talk to her and I mean more than sex, although that is on your mind quite a bit lately," speaks Sylvia. "Well Love, you are my inspiration with a body like you have and that gorgeous red hair.

Conrad gets the coats and helps Sylvia into hers. She places the hat on her head and tells Conrad "Let us get under way. I am getting anxious to take my driver's test." Conrad leads her out the door and they get into the Viper. He drives to DMV and they get there just as the doors are unlocked. They go inside and take a ticket. After sitting down, Conrad exalts "I hope this will go fast." Just as he spoke Sylvia's number comes on over desk window four. "I am here to take my driving test," requests Sylvia. The lady behind the counter says "Weren't you here just yesterday to get your learner's permit?" "Yes, and I am ready for my driver's test to get my license," demands Sylvia. Conrad intercepts with "She has driven before. It was quite easy for her to drive again."

The clerk says "Normally, we expect a person to take 30 days before taking the test. However, with your previous experience being the case, I will send you to Xavier Dawson. He is our driving examiner. She says to Sylvia "Follow me, please." The clerk takes her to Xavier. He tells Sylvia "You will need a car. Where is it at?" "In the parking lot out front," replies Sylvia. "Get the driver to bring it here," says Dawson. Sylvia goes and tells Conrad to bring the car around back. He leaves for the car and she leaves to be with Xavier. Conrad shows up with his

Viper. "I've never had one of these as a test car. It is bound to be different. Get in the driver's seat."

Xavier with his clipboard gets in the passenger's seat. He starts giving instructions "Go around front and leave by turning left." Sylvia starts the engine and uses her turn signal and does as instructed. "Go to the light and take a right." Sylvia complies and after a short distance of sorts, she uses her right turn signal. She has to stop for the red light, but turns right on red when the way becomes clear. "Go through the next two lights when green until you come to the third light." After having to stop for two red lights, the last light is green when she comes to it. She proceeds to the next light. Before getting there, Xavier tells Sylvia "Take a right." She uses her turn signal, but sees that it is a bear to the right with yield sign. She yields until the way is clear. She sees a Shoney's Restaurant, a Mi Chachia Mexican Restaurant, a McDonald's and Burger King. "At the next light turn right." She does as instructed. The light was green. "Go through the next light and I will tell you when to turn." She proceeds following his instructions completely perfect.

After going about a mile he tells her "Turn left at the entrance to the hospital and go to the patient entrance." Sylvia does that and stops. "Go to the parking lot." She completes the instruction. "Now, park the car and get out." She does, takes the key and locks the car after Dawson gets out. "Okay, now what" asks Sylvia. "We get back into the car; you start it, leave the hospital parking lot and go to the left." With a little effort, she accomplishes these acts. "Turn right at the light." The light is red, so she waits for turning traffic to clear. After using her right turn signal, Sylvia turns right on red. "Continue to DMV and make a left" She proceeds to complete the driver's test. Sylvia scores a 100% on the test. Xavier gives her the results and she goes into another window. This one had no light, but was taking customers. Sylvia gives the record to the clerk, who goes and enters her data and gets a print out. "Come with me, please," instructs the clerk. Sylvia follows and is led to a picture taking area. She gets her picture taken and is told to wait 15 minutes. Sylvia gets her license with the alcohol breath test built in. She shows Conrad.

Sylvia and Conrad leave DMV and head for the apartment. Once he parks the car, Rosalyn comes to them and says "Is there anything I can do to help." "No, but you can come up if that be your wish," tells Conrad with anticipation. Rosalyn with eagerness beats them to the apartment's door. Rosalyn waits for Sylvia and Conrad. The duo finally arrives with the key. The three go inside and to the couch. Rosalyn relates "It is my dad fighting with me. He had a mistress last night and expects me to clean up behind them. I don't feel like it's my job to clean after the slob and him." Conrad tells her "Just stay up here as long as you like and maybe he won't bother you." Rosalyn chooses to do so thinking it would be best.

After talking to Rosalyn, Sylvia fixes ham and cheese biscuits. She gets out a Pepsi and two Diet Pepsis giving one to Rosalyn. She is thankful for the drink and ham biscuits. Conrad gets him a biscuit and devours it. Sylvia sits down beside Rosalyn so that Rosalyn ends up in the middle between Sylvia and Conrad. Rosalyn asks "What am I going to do?" "We will work on it. Perhaps you could move in with Sylvia" relates Conrad. Rosalyn says "That would be good."

Sylvia says "When is a good time to go get your clothes? You are over 18 and have the right to live where you want to be. When will your father be gone?" "Why he is gone right now. Why do you ask?" questions Rosalyn. "We can go get your clothes now," responds Sylvia. Rosalyn gets up to go with Sylvia and states "Let's go before my dad gets back." "Conrad, you come too" demands Sylvia. The three go down the stairs until they get into the Pence's apartment. Sylvia tells Conrad "Go wait outside. If we are not out in 20 minutes, come and get us." Conrad accomplishes the task whole heartedly waiting. Sylvia and Rosalyn go into her room to do the move.

Sylvia begins gathering Rosalyn's clothes into a 33 gallon trash bag. Alexander Pence comes in. He pushes his daughter out of her room and locks the door. Alexander attempts to rape Sylvia. He tears her dress off of her and sees she has no underwear on. Sylvia fights back. It is a match enough to hold Pence back. Meanwhile, Rosalyn goes and gets Conrad. Conrad enters the apartment, goes to Rosalyn's room and after trying to open the door kicks it open.

Alexander is caught completely off guard. Conrad hits him hard in the stomach and then in the jaw. Pence goes unconscious. Conrad tells Rosalyn "Go get some rope or duct tape so I can bind him up. Where's the phone?" Rosalyn points to the phone and says "There." She leaves to get what Conrad asks for. Shortly, she returns and Conrad tells her he has called 911 for the police and for her to go watch for them. Conrad takes the rope and binds Pence's hands behind his back. The entire time, Sylvia had been standing naked. She takes a pair of jeans and a blouse that belongs to Rosalyn and puts those on before the police arrive. She recovers her torn dress.

The police arrive and ask "What is the problem here? We got a report of a rape." Before entering, Rosalyn speaks "This way officers. Sylvia says "Here is my dress. He torn it off of me and was attempting to rape me when Conrad entered and stopped him. See, the door frame is busted where Pence had it locked shut and Conrad kicked it open. One of the officers turns to Rosalyn and asks "What is your part in this young lady?" expecting her to say nothing. Rosalyn states "I am Rosalyn Pence. That is my father. He threw me out of my room and locked the door behind me. I went and got Conrad." Turning to Conrad, the office says "You must be Conrad and that must be Pence."

"That's correct officer. I'm Conrad Thomas and this is Sylvia Reed. The incident was as told to you. I bound up Alexander Pence and called 911," returns Conrad. "What exactly did you do?" queries the officer. Conrad divulges "After Rosalyn came and got me, I tried the door, but it was locked. I then kicked it open, go in and caught Pence by surprise. He was on top of Sylvia, but she was fighting him. I pulled him off slugging him in the stomach and jaw. He goes out like a light. I then tied him up and called 911," relates Conrad. After listening and taking notes, the officer says "We have enough to place him under arrest. You three will have to appear in court." The officers wake and take Pence. They place him in their squad car and leave for the station.

Sylvia says to Rosalyn "I am sorry that I took some of your clothes, but I was in need. It is a shame that he tore my dress and the police took it as evidence. It was not wearable again anyway. Sylvia, again, starts packing clothes into bags. Once all of the bags are full, the three go up to 213. Going inside is a bit difficult with the two bags of clothes, mostly jeans and tops. It is typical teenager things. Sylvia and Rosalyn take the bags into Sylvia's room. "I guess you officially become our friend," states Sylvia. Rosalyn responds "Well, I'm glad of it. I can see Conrad when I want and you too Sylvia." Sylvia knew what that statement meant.

"Let us go through your clothes and see what we can donate to Goodwill. I am sure there is quite a lot that you do not need now that you are 19," reports Sylvia. They sort the clothes and a small pile remains for Rosalyn to wear, mostly tops. The rest will go to Goodwill. "Conrad, we need to get Rosalyn some new clothes. I guess it is back to Talbot's," comments Sylvia. They get their coats because the temperature has dropped to 35°. It is a cold day indeed.

The three get into the silver Dodge Viper and Conrad drives to Talbot's. They go inside and are again greeted by Angela North, the sales clerk. "And what do you want today? Angela asks. "We need women's clothes again, but for this young lady" says Sylvia. The three know where to go, but Angela goes with them. Sylvia does the picking of clothes for Rosalyn. The first thing Sylvia does is tell Rosalyn they will not be getting any jeans. Sylvia is more interested in getting some dresses, pants, jerseys and a skirt or two for Rosalyn. Sylvia picks out a yellow dress similar to the one she had gotten for herself. Next is a light aqua that looks good to Sylvia. She picks three more dresses: red, beige; magenta. Then, she goes to the skirts, tops and pants. She picks a green skirt first. Then she picks a blue and red. At the tops, Sylvia gets one jersey and one blouse to start. The jersey is dark blue and the blouse is white. For pants, Sylvia picks a medium blue and a black.

Sylvia commands Rosalyn "Get in the fitting room. I will give you the outfits as I want you to wear them. Here, take the yellow dress first." Rosalyn takes the dress into the fitting room and takes off her jeans and sweat shirt. She puts on the yellow dress and goes out to the viewing area. "Wow. You look great in that. It is definitely a take home," speaks Conrad excitedly. Sylvia tells her "The dress is a very good looking piece of clothing on you. We will get that one, especially for church." Rosalyn is a bit perplexed over the 'church' statement. Sylvia hands her the aqua dress. Rosalyn takes it to the fitting room and changes dresses. She, then, goes out to Sylvia, Conrad and Angela. This time Angela speaks "You definitely want that. It goes well as a contrast to your hair." Sylvia and Conrad agree with Angela. Next, Sylvia hands her the red dress.

Again, Rosalyn goes into the fitting room. She is beginning to feel like a woman instead of a teenager. Swapping dresses becomes an adventure and not a mere task. Rosalyn enjoys going out this instance. Conrad says "The red is a big complement to your hair. It looks quite well on you and accents you figure." "We will keep that one as well. I particularly like it on you" defines Sylvia "and now take the beige." Once more, it is into the fitting room, swapping dresses and going back to the viewing area for comments. Sylvia says "That one just does not look right on you. We will pick something else." Conrad and Angela agree with Sylvia. Last of the dresses, Rosalyn takes the magenta. She hopes the three will like it because she wants it. She takes off the beige and hangs it up on a hook. Then, she puts on the magenta dress and goes out. "Wow!" goes Conrad. Rosalyn is well pleased with the impressive response from Conrad. "Turn around in it so we can see the full fit," quips Sylvia. Rosalyn smiles to herself at the comment. She spins once slowly. The three take it in and Sylvia declares "This one is a definite as well. Rosalyn is well pleased and says "I'm glad you like it. It is my favorite."

"Here, take the three skirts, the blouse, the jersey and the two pants. I want to see all ten combinations of the colors" directs Sylvia. First are the medium blue pants and the dark blue jersey. Wearing those out of the fitting room, Sylvia says "You can wear it like that, but I would not." "It looks well and fits well," says Conrad. Rosalyn goes back and puts on the white blouse. Back in the viewing area, Sylvia comments "That is a winner. You could wear that combination for everyday wear." Conrad just looks. "Go in and change pants." Rosalyn complies. She returns in the black. Again, Sylvia says "We have another winner. You could wear that to church with us when we go." Conrad and Rosalyn, both, again, wonder what is up with the going to 'church'.

Conrad asks to see her with the blue jersey on. Rosalyn goes and changes. Finally, Sylvia says the same about the outfit with the other pants and the skirt combinations, especially likening the red skirt with the white blouse saying "They all are everyday combinations" Sylvia demands "stay here, all of you. I am going to get another dress to replace the beige. I saw one I started to get instead." She goes back to the dresses and picks out a lilac. Getting back to the fitting room area, she hands it to Rosalyn; she states "I like this one even before I put it on." She goes in, changes and comes back out. Conrad says "I like that one best of all. It contrasts the darkness of your hair, but also compliments your complexion." "I agree. This dress is the best for you. It compliments your figure quite well," gives Angela. "Okay, then, we are done for the day," instructs Sylvia.

Angela says "Well then, let's go to the register. The trio is carrying the clothes that they decided upon. Angela has the beige dress and will hang it back up later. Conrad puts his load down first. Conrad prepares to get his credit card out. He reminds himself the balance is getting up there and he will need to use his Master Card in the future. Sylvia puts her load down after Angela rings up Conrad's load and bags those. Angela proceeds on these. Finally, Rosalyn puts hers down on the counter. North rings these up as well. "Mr. Thomas, your total comes to $531.22." Conrad hands her his Master Card. The charge goes through. Conrad was a bit worried. He had been using it too quite a lot lately.

With bags of clothes in hand, Rosalyn, Sylvia and Conrad head for the Dodge Viper. Conrad opens the trunk and all the clothes are placed in it. The three make their way into the car and head for Burger King. Once there, the three go to the door to go in and Conrad notices a man with a gun aimed at one of the cashiers. He tells the girls to wait, but Sylvia does not. As Conrad goes in and gets a little closer, Sylvia yells "Conrad." The gunman turns without turning the gun. Conrad slugs him forcefully. The man goes down and hits his head on the counter. Conrad yells "Call 911, now."

One of the cooks heads for the telephone and dials 911. The operator, Judy Crenshaw, asks "What is the problem?" "This is Burger King on Midlothian. We have had an attempted robbery and a customer took the man down. The man had a gun, but no one was hurt. Send the police now, please." Before the man regains consciousness, the Henrico County Police arrive asking "Is that the perp?" "It is indeed the perpetrator. One of the cahiers has his gun. It was a Gluck 9" tells Conrad. One of the officers retrieves the gun. "It is indeed a Gluck 9. How did you know that?" questions the officer. "My name is Conrad Thomas and my dad is Lieutenant Thomas on the Force. He owns one." "I know your father," says the officer. The other officer putts cuffs on the man as he regains consciousness. "Where did you get a kick like that from?" the perp asks Conrad. "I've had a lot of practice lately." The police leave with the culprit.

Conrad starts to order, but the manager interrupts and turns to the cashier "Give him whatever he wants and it's on the house." Conrad orders three Thick Burgers with fries and drinks. The manager asks "Is that all you want? I'm amazed you don't want more." "That will do for us," states Conrad. They are given large cups to fill while they wait for the food. Sylvia and Rosalyn get their Diet Pepsis and Conrad gets plain Pepsi. The girls go sit at a booth side by side leaving a space for Conrad opposite them. The other customers are heard talking about Conrad and Sylvia entering the way they did. Conrad gets the burgers and fries and carries the tray to the booth. He sits down and Sylvia says "Let us say grace and give thanks that no one was seriously hurt." This too, caught Rosalyn and Conrad by surprise. Sylvia says the grace giving thanks and, then, says "We can eat now." The trio does just that. They enjoy the food amid the chatter.

Conrad finishes first and gets another drink filling his cup. Sylvia is next to finish and she too goes and gets another fill up. Last to finish is Rosalyn and she says "This is the first time ever I've been to a Burger King. The food was good." She does not refill her drink having some left in the cup. They go to the car and squeeze in. Conrad is finding it easier to drive having gotten use to the arrangement. He drives to their apartment, gets the clothes and goes up the stairs. Sylvia and Rosalyn follow. Conrad opens the door with his key.

Once inside, they all head to the bedroom. Conrad, for the first time notices Rosalyn is about the same size as Sylvia when it comes to dresses. He knew their bodies were about the same, but never thought about the clothes because Rosalyn always wore jeans. Sylvia pushes her old clothes to the left leaving the right side for Rosalyn's new clothes. They begin putting them up, but instead of all the clothes, Rosalyn keeps out the white blouse and medium blue slacks. In front of Sylvia and Conrad, she strips and they notice she is not wearing underwear. She slips on the blouse, buttons it and then puts on the pants. Conrad sees she is a well figured young lady. He says "Wear that until tonight and you'll get a surprise." "It won't be a surprise to me," suggests Rosalyn. After the clothes are hung, Conrad suggests Sylvia call the employment agency.

Sylvia dials the number. "Hello. This is Exclusive Staffing Agency. How may I help you?" asks the clerk. "I am Sylvia Reed. I left my name and number to be called if there were any jobs I might qualify for. Is there at least one?" queries Sylvia. "I am sorry Ms. Reed. There is nothing today, but we are expecting something from Virginia Commonwealth University tomorrow morning. It should be something you are qualified for," announces the clerk. Sylvia says "Thank you" and hangs up. "The agency is expecting a job from VCU tomorrow. It must be the job your mother told us about at the library," tells Sylvia. Conrad speaks about more shopping, but the girls do not know what he is talking about.

CHAPTER 12

The Car

Conrad queries Sylvia "What are the things you need to get now?" "I could use a used car," states Sylvia. Conrad states "That's where we're going. Not to get you a used car, but a brand new one." "Conrad, you should not do that for me. I can get by with a used vehicle. I kind of like a Dodge. Can we go there?" inquires Sylvia. "We'll go to Chesterfield Dodge on Midlothian. I've dealt with them before," declares Conrad. This time, Conrad lets Sylvia drive. She gets them there. A salesman, Jack Newman, comes out. He is surprised to see three people get out of a Viper. He knows it is meant only for two.

Newman asks "How may I help you today? Are you interested in new or used? What model would you prefer?" "We are interested in only one model. We would like to see a Dodge Viper," Conrad says. "Oh, that does present a problem. We only have one Viper and it is red. We haven't been able to sell it because of the color. Few people want a red vehicle. Just look at the lot. There are plenty of silver, black, white, gold, and blue, but not one red. We normally don't stock red. This one is on special though. The regular price is $93,000.00. This one, however, we will let go for $80,000.00 with only $1,000.00 down payment. There is also a rebate of $5,000.00 that will also go to your down payment. Are you interested?" inquires Jack. "Yes, we are," demands Sylvia before Conrad can even ask.

Jack Newman takes them to the back of the lot and there sits the only red car—the Dodge Viper. It is a 2009 model. There is a layer of dust on it. Sylvia wants to look it over and heads for it. Jack says "I'll go get the key." He is anxious to make a sale, especially this one. His commission would be high and the lot would be rid of the one red car they had. Meanwhile, Sylvia is looking the car over from the outside. She looks first at the front, then, the driver's side, the rear and last the passenger's side. She wants inside the car. Conrad says "Just wait. Newman has gone after the key. When he gets here, you can get inside. Dear, I think this has got to be the one." Sylvia says "Honey, I think you are right. I just love this car and it is so similar to yours."

Newman arrives with the key and Sylvia gets in the driver's seat. She puts the key in the ignition and starts the car. She, then, checks all the controls that need the ignition on. After a couple of minutes, she turns the ignition off. Sylvia checks out the eight positions of the driver's seat. She turns to Newman and says "I want it." Conrad says to Newman "Let's go make a deal." The four of them go into the showroom to Jack's desk. Sylvia and Conrad sit down. Rosalyn goes to the drink machine. Newman asks "Now, whose name will this machine be in? 'My name. Sylvia Reed.'" "Your address is?" inquires Newman. "213 Falling Creek Apartments, Marina Drive, Richmond," answers Sylvia. "Haven't I met you before? You look familiar," inquires Jack. "No, I really do not think so," answers Sylvia. "I have calculated your total at $77,738.00 which includes tax, title and license. I need the $1,000.00 down and your signature. Sylvia says "You can make the pric lower by lowering your commission. I have had that done before." Newman declares "If I cut my commission in half, I would only get $3,887.00." "So be it" demands Sylvia. "I still need the $1,000.00 down payment. Conrad gets out his Master Card and says "Charge the $1,000.00 to this." "Very well, sir. Does this mean you will be making the payments?" queries the salesman. "We will be making the payments. You can add my name to the loan if you so desire. It's

Conrad Thomas." "Thank you, sir. I now need to send you to our Finance Department. Go all the way to the far wall, turn left and it will be straight ahead" states Newman."

Rosalyn joins Sylvia and Conrad as they head to the Finance Department. They enter and are greeted by Zyva Kaplan. "Good afternoon. This will be a relatively simple process. I look at your cost and verify your rebate as a down payment. We also look at your down payment and calculate what the monthly payments are. I see that Newman has calculated the total that is due. He was not supposed to do that. The calculations are my job. Give me a minute and I will recalculate the total owed by you," informs Zyva. "You owe the $72,861.00 that Jack calculated for you. He could have given you a better deal, if you were to bicker with him more. He could have given a portion of our commission. As it is, we offer a 72 month financing rate. Your payments will be $1,060.00. I hope that you can handle that."

"I am Manager of a Wachovia Bank Branch. I could finance this at a better rate where payments will be less than $800.00. Let me use your telephone," states Conrad. He calls his office and tells them to set up a loan for $72,861.00.over a 120 months. Conrad learns the payments would be $650.00 per month. He tells Zyva "We will have the payment for the balance in a few minutes. Girls, I want you to stay here and keep an eye on the car and the contract while I go get a check for the whole amount." Conrad leaves in his silver Viper, goes to the bank and gets the check after signing a few pages. He, then, heads back to Chesterfield Dodge Motors and into see Zyva. He hands her the check for the full amount. Kaplan states she will have the car prepped and temporary tags installed on the vehicle.

After waiting half an hour, the car is brought to the front. It had temp tags, been washed on the outside and vacuumed on the inside. A full tank of gas is also provided. Sylvia was ready to leave "Rosalyn, who are you going to ride with?" "I'll ride with Conrad. We have something to talk about. It is things concerning me." "Okay. I will meet you at the apartment."

Sylvia leaves driving her red 2009 Dodge Viper—the sportiest car on the market. Conrad and Rosalyn get into his car and he begins driving to the apartment. Rosalyn asks "Conrad, tell me, please, that our time together in Sylvia's bed was not a onetime act. I want to have your baby." Conrad is caught off guard, but manages to come back with "As we said once before, it is your choice. You bear the responsibility for your own actions. If you want to have a relationship with me, you might have to have one with Sylvia as well." "I can do anything to have a relationship with you that will allow me to bear your child. I don't think I'm quite ready to do that so I must get on contraceptives. I'll do that tomorrow," responds Rosalyn.

Sylvia beats the other two by ten minutes. She parks her car and locks it tight. Sylvia goes up to the apartment and gets in the bedroom and undresses waiting for Conrad. It was going to be her way of thanking him for the car. Sylvia thought about the fact she always liked a red Viper. Her wish for one had come true. Conrad and Rosalyn enter the apartment and Conrad does not see Sylvia. He has seen her car outside with the temporary tags on it. So, he yells "Sylvia, where are you?" She returns "I am in the bedroom. Come see what I have to thank you for getting me the car I truly wanted."

Rosalyn waits in the living room as Conrad goes to the bedroom. Upon entering, he sees Sylvia nude. He knows what she has in mind. Conrad undresses and lies her down gracefully. They have a heartfelt time together. Rosalyn, meantime, wonders what is going on. She goes to the bedroom and looks in. She sees Sylvia and Conrad going at it. When they are finished, Rosalyn, too, is nude and simply states "My turn now." Conrad obliges her.

Conrad informs the girls that his mother's car is ready for pick up at the glass replacing shop. He tells them also that "I'm to pick her up because dad is working late. We need to get dressed and go after her at VCU." The three get dressed and they head to the red Viper—Sylvia is going to drive. Conrad tells her where to go. They get there in 15 minutes. Conrad goes in and asks for the Sorento which had the broken driver's side window. The shop informs him the insurance covered it all and if he will sign a release, the car will be his. Conrad signs and picks up the car. They decide to temporarily leave Sylvia's car at the house. So, Sylvia drives back to the house and Conrad follows. He is somewhat surprised that she remembers how to get there.

The three get into the Sorento and Conrad drives with Sylvia beside him and Rosalyn in the rear. He gets to VCU just five minutes before his mother walks out the door. He sees she is carrying a large brown envelope. When Grace gets in, Conrad asks "What's in the envelope, mom?" She responds "Something for Sylvia. It is an application for a job in the library. She says she had some library experience, so I thought this would be a good opportunity for her."

Grace hands the envelope to Sylvia, who opens it and gets the application out. Grace informs Sylvia "You need to be there with the application as soon as you can. The University will have the job posted for one week only starting tomorrow. If you are first to get it in, then, you may be first to be interviewed after the week is up."

"You hear that, Conrad. We need to be here early to get the application processed. I will be able to give my own address at Falling Creek Apartments and my cell phone number. I should not have any trouble getting the job tomorrow. Grace interrupts "How are you going to get the job tomorrow? The University will not close the posting for a week and only then will they do the interviews." Sylvia continues "I have the experience that is wanted by VCU. The University anxiously wants the job filled. I will fill it tomorrow." "How do you know that?" says Conrad. It is also echoed by Rosalyn. This gets Grace's attention "Who is this? Why is she here?"

Conrad reports "This is Rosalyn Pence. She is the daughter of the apartment complex manager, Alexander Pence, who by the way is in jail for attempting to rape Sylvia. We have taken her in for the time being because she doesn't know where her mother lives." Rosalyn says "Hello, Mrs. Thomas. I've heard quite a bit about you from Conrad." She is fabricating, but it is to put Grace at ease. Conrad appreciated that. Grace comes back "Your father attempted to rape my son's girlfriend?" Conrad and Sylvia notice the reference to Sylvia as Conrad's 'girlfriend'. That is a word that Grace had never used before in relation to Sylvia.

Rosalyn tells Grace that yes it was her father who attempted to rape Sylvia. And it was her that went and got Conrad to intercept her father before her father could penetrate Sylvia. It is an abbreviated story, but mother Grace gets the idea. Grace requests "How long are you going to let her share Sylvia's room?" "Mother, Sylvia now has an apartment. Didn't you hear her say 'Falling Creek Apartments? Rosalyn will be with Sylvia as long as she needs to until she can get her own apartment. Her father's apartment will go to the next complex manager."

"Well, you two have been busy today. Let us get to the house so we can have dinner," requests Grace. Conrad continues on. There is some other discussion about the day's events, but the red Dodge was overlooked. When Conrad pulls into the driveway, Grace immediately notices the red Viper and questions Conrad "What is that doing here? Did you have a wreck and get a new car? Or did you rent this for Sylvia, and if so, who is paying the lease payments? When does it go back? Why did you get red? Surely, you could have gotten a different color." "Mom, I had no wreck. The car is Sylvia's. It is not a rental car nor on lease. She got a loan from the bank to buy the car expecting to get a job soon. If she is correct, she'll have one tomorrow morning."

"And what part did you have in it?" asks Grace. Conrad retorts "Mother, all I did was act on her behalf to get the loan. The loan is in her name only. I'm not even a signatory to the loan. I will make the loan payments." "Those will only be a little over $600.00 and my job will more than cover the payments as well as pay Conrad back," expresses Sylvia to Grace. They all get out of the Sorento and go inside. As everyone takes off their coats, Rosalyn makes the comment "What a lovely house you have Mrs. Thomas. I bet you spend enough time to clean. It looks immaculate."

"Thank you" says Grace. The phone rings and Grace answers it. It turns out to be a slanderous call. Grace says "That was one of the neighbors. The person accuses you of having Sylvia as a whore and/or your dad has her. Well, I never. It probably was Mrs. Crawford." "No mom. It wasn't Mrs. Crawford. Mr. Crawford had a heart attack and Sylvia saved his life. The rescue squad says if she had not done what she did, Mr. Crawford would have died. Mrs. Crawford is indebted to Sylvia." "If it was not Mrs. Crawford, then, who would it be?" petitions Grace. "It's probably Ms. Stevens. You know the old spinster that lives next door to Mrs. Crawford. She is into everybody's business. If she thinks that, then, it will be all over the neighborhood" tells Conrad.

CHAPTER 13

Day Eleven Evening

Things go pretty smooth for a while and the time to fix dinner arrives. "Mrs. Thomas, I want to help. I'm very good in the kitchen. You just tell me what you want and where the pots and pans are and I'll do the rest," invites Rosalyn. Grace accepts the help "Let us go into the kitchen and get started. I plan on having beef stew on rice and a green vegetable to go with it." "How about a salad instead of a green vegetable? I can fix one up really swell. I had to do all the cooking at our apartment" explains Rosalyn.

Rosalyn begins with the rice and the beef stew on the stove. While these are cooking, she makes a salad with several different vegetables including mushrooms, radishes, black olives, tomatoes, carrots, cucumbers and celery not to mention the lettuce. She even manages to get in some raisins. Having prepared the salad, Rosalyn moves to the range to get the beef stew and rice into bowls. Grace, in the meantime, is getting the plates, coffee, a Pepsi and a Diet Pepsi. She asked Rosalyn what she wanted to drink—a Diet Pepsi. She also gets down the plates and silverware. It is Grace that tells the men and Sylvia to come to the table for dinner.

Conrad is first to speak "I really like this salad. I don't think mom ever put raisins in our salads and all the various vegetables. It tastes delicious. We may have to keep you around a while to cook for us or at least fix the salad." This touched a nerve with Grace. Hank says pretty much the same thing. Sylvia says "I envy you, Rosalyn. I made a salad last night and it was good, but not as good as this is. You have had a lot more cooking experience than I have." That statement hit Conrad's nerve "There you go again. How do you know that you haven't had a lot of cooking experience?" "I just do!" retorts Sylvia.

They all enjoy the salad, even Grace. The beef stew over rice goes well as they all enjoy the food. It has been some time since Grace had prepared it. Unbeknown to the group assembled for dinner, Grace has bought a cake and has it stored under a plastic cover. When all are through eating, she asks "Does anyone want a piece of coconut cake?" Everybody says yes. The cake goes over the best. Rosalyn expresses her desire "I want to do the kitchen clean-up. I have had some experience at that as well. I've learned where everything goes. It shouldn't be a problem. You all go and enjoy the evening. I'll join you later."

Grace goes in the family room gets a book and goes back to the living room to read. Hank goes to the family room to watch TV and Conrad joins him. Sylvia goes to the computer. Once on the Internet, she comes across a blog where two teens are talking about famous people and the cars that they drive. Paul Newman drives a sports car. O. J. Simpson drives a white Jeep Cherokee. The President's daughter drives a red Dodge Viper. Sylvia stops and turns to Conrad saying "We bought the same car that the President's daughter drives. It is here on this blog." "That's nice," is all Conrad has to say.

Rosalyn is busy cleaning the kitchen putting dirty dishes in the dishwasher and wiping down the table cloth. She puts the left over cake back under the plastic it had been stored in. She finally finishes and goes into the living room and asks "Where are Sylvia and Conrad?" "They are in the family room. It is the first door on the left." Rosalyn goes to the family room, sees Sylvia on the computer and grabs a chair to sit next to her. Rosalyn is interested in what Sylvia is doing.

Sylvia is now searching for a site that will say something about missing adults. She had failed at it once before. This night, however, she goes to americasmissingadults.com. There she finds 40 pages of missing adults. She starts with page 1 and continues through to page 40. She found three women who were described as similar to her. Two were much older and one was her age. This one had blonde hair and was thus not a Sylvia look alike. Sorrowfully, she has an iota of luck tonight. The whole time, Rosalyn is watching and looking for just what Sylvia is looking for. Rosalyn remarks "It's a shame you can't find out about who you really are. If you could find your description it will at least tell where you were last seen. That would be a starting point."

Conrad overhears the conversation and states "It may be that you have no family to report you missing. If you were an only child whose parents were deceased there would be no one missing you." This assertion hits a nerve of Sylvia and she comes back with "I do have a family. For some reason, they haven't reported me missing yet. I could be in a dorm room at a university and they wouldn't miss me for a while." Conrad notes the declaration of having a family.

Rosalyn points out "You mentioned you have a family. How do you know? Could it be you are getting some of your memory back?" "I do not know how I know. I just do. It could be possible I am getting some of my memory back like I mentioned a university. Why would I do that if I did not have some connection to a university?" Conrad adds "You have several times made remarks about knowing something and there is no reason except you are getting your memory back. Have you remembered a city that you may be from?" Sylvia nods her head yes and says "several." "Well, let's hear some," wants Conrad Sylvia begins and lists off several names—too many to be of any help.

Hank, having heard all of the conversations, butts in "If you were to ask me, I would say wait and see what else she will remember. Sylvia just might surprise us all and remember where she is from and who she is." This puts a stop to the comments and questions. Rosalyn saves the tension from being excessive with "You're right, Mr. Thomas. We should just wait and see. It might even be tomorrow." Conrad secretly hopes not. He is wanting to get to know her extremely more and intimately as well.

It comes time for them all to retire, but there is Rosalyn as an extra. Sylvia comments "I guess Rosalyn and I will drive to my apartment. She can sleep on my couch." "Have you forgotten my car is at your apartment? The three of us will have to fit into your car," asserts Conrad. "Nonsense. She can sleep on the couch here. I have extra blankets. We did this when Bill and Dave needed to spend the night last year," intrudes Grace. The decision is made for Rosalyn to spend the night on the couch.

Grace goes to her closet and gets an extra blanket for Rosalyn. Grace and Hank leave the three youngsters to themselves. They go upstairs and retire for the night. Conrad takes Sylvia in his arms and kisses her in front of Rosalyn, who envies Sylvia. She makes a remark about it and Conrad takes her and kisses her passionately—more so than he thought he would. Sylvia says "I am glad to see you two getting together on a more personal level. It means the three of us will be together for some time to come, maybe forever. The last word hit a chord with Conrad. He was hoping for that all along. His desire for Rosalyn was almost as intense as his desire for Sylvia. He even starts thinking Sylvia and he will get married.

Conrad says goodnight and heads for his room leaving the two girls alone. Sylvia reaches for Rosalyn who does not fight it. Sylvia, then, plants a kiss on Rosalyn's lips. "This is something of a start between you and I. We will share each other and share Conrad. It is the way it has to be. We have made a commitment tonight. Conrad and I will get married. It will probably be soon. I am going to say goodnight because we all have to be up early. Sylvia leaves and Rosalyn goes for the couch. She has difficulty going to sleep thinking of the things that have happened tonight. She eventually dozes off content with this evening's events growing cloudy in her mind

CHAPTER 14

The Job

Day twelve starts with Rosalyn being the first one up. She goes into the kitchen and begins to cook fried eggs. She cooks a total of ten. While the eggs were cooking, she also baked ten biscuits. Rosalyn gets out the butter, jelly and milk. She makes a pot of coffee. The smell of the coffee goes upstairs and begins waking everyone else up. Conrad is first in the shower. Sylvia is next. Hank and Grace take turns in the master bedroom's shower. Sylvia is the first to get downstairs and see Rosalyn cooking breakfast. She asks can she help and Rosalyn tells her no that she has it all underhand.

Conrad is next to come downstairs and enters the kitchen seeing the same as Sylvia. He comments to Sylvia "You've done it again. This is the second time you have showered after me and beat me downstairs." This makes Rosalyn ask "You two have spent the night here before, haven't you?" "Yes," says Conrad and continues "Sylvia has her room since we were not using the guest room and she had nowhere to live." "But I thought you two moved into the apartment together," comes back Rosalyn. "We did. It will be permanent in a few days. As soon as Conrad and I are married, and maybe before then," affirms Sylvia. Conrad has to speak "When did you make up your mind all this was going to happen? You never told me of your intentions." "I made up my mind the first time we were nude together, which will be more often from today onward."

Hank comes in a good bit ahead of Grace and says "'from today onward' what?" "Oh dad, we didn't know you were there. Sylvia and I were talking about our time together. She meant that we would be a couple from today on until we break up. Maybe only until she finds out who she really is," clarifies Conrad. Grace comes in and asks "What have I been missing? Oh. Rosalyn did you make breakfast and coffee? We all need to be seated and eat before it gets cold." Grace has forgotten her first question and no one, including Hank, says anything about what she has missed.

Hank says "I see you remembered to pick up your mother from VCU. I had all but forgotten it. Her car was available to me, but I couldn't get away from work. I intended on calling you, but I didn't have time for that either." Grace states "It was just as well. I had gotten an application for Sylvia to apply for a librarian position at VCU. It gets posted today. She needs to be as early as possible because they number the applications as each is received. Maybe it will make her first to be interviewed."

Conrad relates to his dad that he had called about the car and was told it was ready for pick up. Hank said that was good in many ways. It had worked out better than Hank had imaged. Rosalyn mentioned that she had gone with Conrad and Sylvia just wanting to a part of the ride. Conrad mentions "Dad, mom got an application for Sylvia to apply for a job as a librarian at VCU. What do you think of that?" Hants exhorts "I hope she gets the job. What about Rosalyn?"

Rosalyn says "I don't have any experience except for keeping house. I would like to get a job in a library, but I just wouldn't qualify for the position. Maybe if I go to college like Conrad, I can get me a good job. We'll just have to wait and see." Conrad remarks "When you do go to college or a university, study hard as if your life depended on it. You never know. It just might. It's true you can get a better job with higher education. I've been thinking of going back to VCU and getting my MBA. I know it would do me good."

Hank says "Yes, it does lead to a better job. Grace, Conrad and I have gone to VCU. I took Law Enforcement, while Grace took English and Conrad took Business Administration. It has made a difference in our lives." Breakfast was over and Grace and Hank have to leave for their respective jobs. Hank tells of his plan to take his truck to the body shop to get the truck's panel repaired or replaced. Conrad tells of his effort to get Sylvia to VCU to put in the application she had filled out last night. Sylvia confirms the assertion.

Rosalyn says "I don't know what I am going to do." Sylvia comes back with "You are going to go through your old clothes and get rid of a lot of things, especially the jeans. You might want to keep some of the tops. Those may go with the skirts which you have."

Hank and Grace leave in their own vehicles leaving the three together. Conrad takes hold of Rosalyn and kisses her and says "You are a part of us now. You will live with us as a member of the family and we will call you our housekeeper since you have a lot of experience at that. Besides, it will keep nosy people from being too nosy." "I will keep house for you. I said I would do anything to be with you and eventually have your baby," puts forth Rosalyn. "A baby? Why have I not heard about this before? I want to have his baby as well," extorts Sylvia. "We had a discussion when we were alone. She doesn't want to have it right away. She intends to get contraceptives today. Are you thinking along those lines?" inquires Conrad. "Hell NO!" declares Sylvia. "When I said I intended to have your baby, I meant as soon as possible, and by the way, we are going to get married soon."

Rosalyn asks Sylvia for a helping hand to get the kitchen clean so they can leave a little earlier. Sylvia jumps in and starts loading the dishwasher. Rosalyn puts the butter, jelly and milk away in the refrigerator. The trio gets their coats and leave. They pile into the Viper and drive to the apartment. Rosalyn goes in to work on her clothes. Sylvia and Conrad go to VCU.

Conrad takes Sylvia right to the Admissions Office. It is where he knew applications were taken. It has not been that long since he graduated from Virginia Commonwealth University. Sylvia enters with application in hand. She has listed her experience in the library stating she knew the Dewey Decimal System and was capable of learning any other method of filing books on shelves. The clerk in charge, Mildred Foster, takes the application and mentions she is first to file. Out of desire, Sylvia asks "Is there a possibility I could be interviewed today?" Mildred looks over the application carefully and takes note. "Let me make a phone call. This is out of the ordinary, but we are desperate for another librarian. When could you start?" queries Foster.

Sylvia comes back with "I could start later today. In, say, three hours." Mildred makes the call "Maryann, this is Mildred. We have an applicant for the vacant librarian position. She was wondering could she be interviewed today. She also says she could start work in about three hours. She has librarian experience. Do you want to interview her?" "Business is slow right now, Mildred. Send her over. I will interview her" says Maryann. "You are to go to the library and see Maryann Witten." Sylvia and Conrad leave for the library.

Part way there, Conrad stops the car and leans over and kisses Sylvia. "What was that for?" asks Sylvia. "Just because I wanted to give you some good luck, Dear" says Conrad. A campus police officer pulls up behind him and Conrad cannot imagine what he has done wrong. The officer states "You can't park here and do that. This is a no parking zone. You'll have to move along. What are you doing on the campus anyway?" "My friend here is applying for a librarian position and we are on our way to the library," responds Conrad. The officer advises "Continue on, but watch the no parking zones." "Yes sir, officer" as Conrad pulls away.

The duo arrives at the library and goes into the desk. "Hi Maryann" speaks Conrad. "This is Sylvia Reed, who is applying for the librarian position." "Well, Ms. Reed let me take you to the office and do the interview there. Conrad, you wait here. Maryann leads the way. Once there, a short walk, Maryann says "Have a seat. I have known Conrad for some time. We have even dated for a short time. If he brought you, he must believe you are qualified. Tell me about your experience." "I have worked in a university library volunteering. I would put in about 30 hours a week. I know the Dewey Decimal System and I can use a computer."

"What college or university did you attend?" inquires Maryann. "It was Georgetown University. I was majoring in something that began with a 'P'. "Psychology maybe? "Yes, that was it" "Well, I can see that you have the skills and in a good way. I think our hunt is over already. Mildred told me you could start this afternoon. That will not be necessary. However, I do need you to start tomorrow at 11:00 o'clock and work to 7:30 pm. Your off days will be Sunday and Monday. I have two other workers here. We will go meet them now," explains Maryann Witten. The two get up and Witten leads her to the employees' lounge. There are two vending machines that Sylvia notices right away. One has a variety of snacks while the other has soft drinks. There is also a coffee pot.

Maryann introduces Alexis Taylor, who is drinking a cup of coffee. "We are a no smoking facility," commands Witten. Alexis, this is Sylvia Reed. She will be the replacement we need to fill Franklin's position," reports Maryann Witten. Taylor says "Hello." Maryann points out the restrooms and 20 fire extinguishers. She notes "Each fire extinguisher is 25 feet from another. That is an OSHA requirement that we had to meet to open the doors. These are checked on a quarterly basis.

"We have 27 computers scattered throughout the building. 25 are for the use of students and two are for the staff to use. One is to check books in and out. The other we use to do research to help students find a book or books. You can see we have another worker; she is our youngest volunteer at 19, Hannah Strong. That is about all I can tell you except report tomorrow at 11:00 o'clock. Are there any questions?" "Do you offer maternity leave? I am not pregnant yet, but I expect to be in the near future," "Our maternity leave is 6 weeks and is only available to employees who have worked at least a year," responds Witten.

Maryann takes Sylvia back to the desk where Conrad is talking to Hannah. "Sylvia Reed meet Hannah Strong. She's the same age as Rosalyn," remarks Conrad. Maryann asks Sylvia to look up a book for her to test Sylvia's computer skills. Sylvia gets on the machine and in a matter of a few seconds; she has the book and tells Whitten where to look. Witten is impressed. Maryann tells Sylvia she has the job. Sylvia is elated. She says "I will be here at 11:00 o'clock in the morning." "Conrad let us go celebrate. They head for the apartment. Upon entering, they find Rosalyn has sorted all her clothes out on the bed. She describes "This large pile is what can go to Goodwill. This other is what I think I should keep." "You 'THINK' leaves a little bit of an exclamation," inquires Sylvia "Do you expect me to go through them for you?" "As a matter of fact, yes I do," comes back Rosalyn.

Conrad quips "There goes our celebration." "Celebration? You got the job, didn't you?" queries Rosalyn. "Yes, I did. It was so easy. All I had to do was show the head librarian my computer skills and that I knew the Dewey Decimal System. It was great. By the way, the head librarian is one of Conrad friends from when he went there. I have Sunday and Monday as off days and I work from 11:00 am to 7:30 pm. That is not the best days to be off, but it is a job. I cannot wait to tell Grace and Hank," informs Sylvia. Then, we do need to celebrate. How are we going to do that? Conrad begins to undress himself. Rosalyn, seeing Sylvia, does the same. The clothes are pushed into the floor in two piles. All three get into the bed together. Conrad cannot believe what is happening. Two girls want him at the same time.

Sylvia is the first one to make a move. She climbs on top of Conrad. She has her way. Then, Rosalyn does the same. The time lasts 15 minutes. Conrad remembers, Rosalyn was going to get contraceptives today. He comments "Rosalyn, you were going to get contraceptives today. Have you done that job, yet?" "No, I haven't had time. Besides, I don't have any money. I was going to ask you. I could go to the CVS after I go to the doctor's office. I won't need to pay him right away. He will wait," announces Rosalyn. "Will you take me Sylvia?"

Sylvia merely says sure thing. Conrad digs in his wallet and pulls out two 20 dollar bills giving these to Rosalyn for her pills. He demands "I expect you to take the pills before next time. Having a baby or not is a two-sided discussion. I will help you have your baby, but WE will decide when."

CHAPTER 15

Shopping Again and More

Sylvia tells the other two she would like to go shopping again, but this time to a mall and take Rosalyn's old clothes to Goodwill. Rosalyn announces "We should go to Willow Lawn. The mall has loads of stores and is not that far from VCU and a Goodwill collection box. Conrad opens his mouth "We can go shopping, but it will have to be short on spending. My Visa doesn't have much left and my Master Card is all that we can really use. Remember to keep it low."

They go in two separate cars. Rosalyn rides with Conrad. She wanted him to take her to the doctor's office after their time at the mall. Upon arriving at the mall, they search for parking spaces. It just so happens, they get spots opposite each other. The two parked as if the cars were kissing. Sylvia decides she wants to shop for some jewelry. She sees a store layout map with a directory. Sylvia finds the Cocoanut Jewelry store. She is mainly interested in a necklace with a butterfly. Butterflies are her favorite design. If she could find a dress with butterflies on it, she would buy it.

Conrad has decided he wants to shop for jewelry too, but neither one knows what the other wants to do. The three some start walking the mall. Conrad says to Sylvia "I am going on by myself. We can catch up together later via our cell phones. There is something important I need to do." Knowing right where

Cocoanut Jewelry was at; he heads there. Meanwhile, Sylvia and Rosalyn go into various stores just looking.

Conrad gets to the jewelry store and asks to see wedding bands. The shop clerk asks "Don't you want to look at engagement rings?" Conrad returns "I had forgotten about that. Show me any combinations you have." The clerk shows Conrad several types at several different prices.

Finally, she comes to one and tells Conrad. This is the only ring of this style we have ever had. For some reason, people just don't want to buy it. We have it reduced to $4,000.00 right now. Notice the stone arrangement; there are ten stones on the top and ten stones on the bottom with a large diamond in the center. To go with it is a three stone ring as the engagement ring. Conrad immediately says "I'll take both of them. It's a bit more than I want to spend, but it is exactly what I like." He is thinking three stones for Rosalyn, Sylvia and himself on the engagement ring and 21 stones for Sylvia's age.

The clerk gets some paperwork to go with the jewelry and tells Conrad the rings are covered by a warranty for one year. She also has a paper which is in triplicate that is the bill of sale. It has a description of both rings and a place for Conrad's signature. He hands her his Master Card and signs the bill. She processes his credit card, puts the rings in separate boxes and places them in a bag. She returns to Conrad and says "Thank you Mr. Thomas. Please come again." Just then, Sylvia and Rosalyn arrive. Sylvia asks "Conrad Clayton Thomas, what have you been up to?" Conrad knows he is in trouble now. No one but his mother has ever said his middle name.

He gets down on one knee right in front of Sylvia, Rosalyn, and the people around the store. He says:

I love you truly
Truly I do.
Love me always

As I do you.

Be my one and only
Only be mine.
Love me always
Ever so fine.

Be there my Dear
Dearest of all
Love me always
My name to call.

Baby of mine
A baby you'll carry
Loving me always
As I ask you to marry
Me.

Several people heard the proposal and started clapping. It made Sylvia blush one of the few times ever. She was speechless at the moment. She knew they would get married, but has not expected this. Some of the comments from the crowd were 'Answer him', 'Tell him yes' and 'show him you love him always'. Rosalyn tells her "Go on Sylvia tell him yes." Finally, "Yes," is said by Sylvia. "Now we can plan the wedding. You need something more than a necklace," says Conrad. Sylvia responds "And what might that be I need?" "A watch"

Conrad takes Sylvia to a display case that contains nothing but watches. At first, she does not know which to pick. Conrad points to one that has three diamonds: one at 3, one at 6 and one at 9. He explains to her the three stones stand for the three of them. She liked the idea and says she would take that one. Conrad calls the clerk "Ma'am, we want this watch here; the one with three diamonds at three, six and nine, if you please. My fiancé is smitten with it." The clerk takes it out of the display case and hands it to Sylvia. Sylvia places it on her arm and it looks like it belongs there.

"We'll take it. There is no need to wrap it or bag it. She'll wear it," says Conrad. "It is a very good choice sir. Will there be anything else?" asks the clerk. "As a matter of fact, Rosalyn, which one do you want?" queries Conrad. Rosalyn answers "Just get me the cheapest they have." The clerk tells Rosalyn to pick from a different show case. Rosalyn picks out one that is cheap and straps it to her wrist. It, too, looks like it belongs there. Conrad questions the clerk "How much do I owe?" "Give me a moment, sir, to tally up your purchases."

The clerk goes to a register and inserts the prices for the rings and the two watches. "Sir, your total comes to $4,413.89, which includes a one year warranty on each of the watches." As Conrad gets his Master Card out, Sylvia demands "Conrad Clayton Thomas, there is no way two watches cost that kind of money. What else did you spend our money on?"

"I forgot to give you these," explains Conrad "but you only get one today. The other will wait until our wedding day. You have said 'soon' and we will decide how soon later tonight." "Oh Conrad, you should have and did. I want to wear it now," commands Sylvia. Conrad slips it on her left ring finger and gives her a kiss. Several people have been watching. One even says "I haven't seen anything like this." Rosalyn kisses Conrad for her watch. The watchers are dumbfounded by the kissing of the second girl. "Thank you, housekeeper," articulates Conrad.

That oration seemed to satisfy the crowd. The clerk comes back with his receipt and papers on the rings—papers that describe the unique rings. "If the rings are ever stolen, these papers will be of value to the police. "Thank you, ma'am," states Conrad. Sylvia tells Conrad "Dear, I am a bit hungry. I saw on the directory a Dairy Queen. I have not been to one of those in quite some time." "Do you remember going to a Dairy Queen?" inquests Conrad. "Yes, my father would take me," answers Sylvia. Conrad comes back immediately "There, you have done it again.

Your memory is coming back. You remember going to a Dairy Queen and you remember your father. How about his name?" "I cannot remember everything at once until I know who I am," gives back Sylvia.

They arrive at Dairy Queen. Conrad only wants a strawberry milk shake. Sylvia wants an Oreo Blizzard and Rosalyn says "Can I have anything I want?" "Of course you can," reports Conrad. Rosalyn orders a Banana Split with nuts. They all enjoy the treats as they continue to walk the somewhat decaying mall. It seems they are getting tired of walking and Sylvia says "I am tired of walking here. Can we go some other place? I prefer one that is enclosed." Conrad answers "We can go to Regency Square. It's not that far and we can get there in about 15 minutes." "That sounds better. At least, it will be enclosed," quips Sylvia. Conrad retorts "How did you know that? Are you psychic?" "A little bird told me," was her response to a question she had not expected to know the answer for the question. Conrad is at a lost to determine how she knew that. They had never even passed Regency Mall. But, they go there anyway. It being enclosed would make it more enjoyable for them.

They arrive in the two Vipers and get to park next to each other; however, it is some distance to the mall's entrance. Conrad takes the hand of Sylvia on his right and Rosalyn's hand on his left. They walk to the mall's entrance and enter to see the directory of 169 different stores. Rosalyn says "This is the first time I've ever been here. And it has two floors to walk. I wonder how far it would be to walk the entire length of both floors, not to mention entering each store?" "I don't know. I've never done that before either. I'm sure it would be quite a distance," implies Conrad. Sylvia just instructs "Let us start walking."

They first enter Sears, and then Macy's, looking at various other shops as they walk. "Conrad, I do not have a pair of walking shoes. Can we get me a pair?" They walk the distance to the other end of the mall to go into Foot Locker. Once there, Sylvia tries on a few pairs and decides on a green accented Reebok.

Conrad notices the price is only $59.99. He goes into his wallet and hands Sylvia $65.00 to cover the 5% tax as well. Sylvia gets the shoes and immediately changes from the flats to the Reebok's. She feels a lot more comfortable. Rosalyn would have a new pair as well, but did not say anything. Neither did Sylvia or Conrad. They are at J C Penny's and decide to go in the store.

At once, Sylvia sees a white gown she thinks will look good on their wedding day which reminded her they have not gotten the license or a minister. She goes to the dress. It is her size "Dear, I want this dress for our wedding and to wear to church," states Sylvia. "Well, how much is it?" inquires Conrad. "It is a mere $149.99," tells Sylvia. Reluctantly, Conrad says "I guess you do need it. It will go well with my black suit." Conrad goes to the nearest register with the dress in tow by Rosalyn. "Dear, we forgot a dress for Rosalyn." Rosalyn feels elated that she is being included as the bride's maid of honor. She sees a pink one that she likes. She brings it to Conrad who sees the price of $59.99. "At least, I'll get by without spending several hundreds of dollars." He gets his Master Card out one more time. He hands it to the clerk and says "Ring the dresses up." She does and takes Conrad's card, scans it and gives him the receipt to sign. He gets done and turns to the girls and tells them both "Shopping is over."

Sylvia elates to Conrad "Dear, we need to get our marriage license today." "You are making it soon, aren't you?" quips Conrad. "We have known for some time we would marry. Do you not remember at your parents' house?" "Yes, but I also said some day. "Dear, today is some day and we are not getting married today, but soon," remarks Sylvia. Sylvia looks at her hand with the ring and holds it up to look at it better. She cannot get over Conrad getting it for her or the way he proposed. Conrad says "Follow me to the bureau and don't try to pass. If you get lost, I may not find you again."

Sylvia and Conrad go to the license bureau to get one. They go in together with Rosalyn close behind. They go to the counter and make their wish known. The clerk tells them that they can have a civil service or a religious service. Whoever performs the service will need to sign the bottom and return it to the county clerk's office for processing. Conrad thanks the clerk after paying the fee. Rosalyn asks "We can't do that, can we?" Conrad says "No. It would be bigamy. I could go to jail for that. Besides, you're our housekeeper. Let's get out of here and go to the apartment."

Rosalyn rides with Sylvia this time. She has been riding with Conrad. "Do you really not mind me having intercourse with you fiancé?" questions Rosalyn. "Not at all. If it is his choice, then, he has the right as far as I am concerned. The same goes for Conrad. If it be my choice, he would not get upset. We have that kind of understanding between us" relates Sylvia. They talk some more about the future and whether she will get her memory back or not. And if she does get it back, will she stay married to Conrad? They arrive at the apartment.

Conrad, in the meantime, sees a decrepit woman beside the road. He stops, being the good Samaritan, and asks if she needs some help. She says "I am hungry. Could you get me something to eat?" "Yes, I can do that," answers Conrad. He drives to a Burger King and gets the woman a Whopper, fries and a drink. He only spends $6.59 on the lady. He notices that although the clothes appear worn and dirty, the woman herself is quite clean. He asks her if she would like to rest a bit and she says that would be great. Conrad heads for the apartment once again. Arriving there, he sees Sylvia's car parked near the stairs. He asks the lady if she needs help up the stairs. She says no. They go up with Conrad in the lead.

Upon entering, he hears the two girls in the bedroom talking about their freshly bought merchandise. He calls to them "Sylvia, could y'all come in here?" Sylvia enters first. Rosalyn comes in with "Mom?" The woman goes "Rosalyn?" Sylvia and Conrad are caught by complete surprise. "If you are Rosalyn's mother, what is your name?" interrogates Conrad. The woman, before

Rosalyn has a chance to speak, tells him "Yvonne Mercer. I went back to my maiden name after I divorced Alexander. Where is he, anyway?" "In jail facing up to 25 years for attempted rape of my fiancé," Conrad informs her. Yvonne relates the fact she divorced Pence because he could not stay away from women, any kind of a woman.

Rosalyn, being in wonderment, questions her mother "Why are you dressed the way you are? Where do you live? What have you been up to? How do you make a living? When will I see you again?" "Whoa girl. You have asked me a lot of questions that will not only take time to answer, but also time to explain. I dress like this to keep people from seeing me as a woman who has money. After I left your father, I got a job that pays me $20.00 an hour. I've saved over the years and have invested some. So, I do have quite a bit of money. I live at 4356 McClellan Drive. It's not big or fancy, but it serves me. I've been trying to save some more money so I can buy a house. As for seeing me again, you now know where I live. It's just a matter of you getting there," answers Yvonne.

Sylvia and Conrad had been listening to the whole conversation. They were quite interested because this was Rosalyn's mother and she had money. Although, the money was not that big of an issue, it did mean that Rosalyn could get some more new clothes. Sylvia asks "Can you spare some money for some clothes for Rosalyn? She is down to just a few items, maybe seven days worth. You will be a big help to Conrad and I because Rosalyn is our housekeeper and we do not pay her. She chose to do it on her own after her father's indiscretion."

"Where does she sleep?" asks Yvonne. "She sleeps wherever she wants to. We are not prudes about Rosalyn. She is going to be my bride's maid at our wedding. She also expects to live with us once we buy a house. Conrad and I have good paying jobs. It will not take us very long to get a down payment together," gives Sylvia. Yvonne, being full of questions, comes back with "What, no hanky-panky going on?" Conrad, this time, speaks "If you must know, some. It was her choice and as Sylvia says we aren't prudes." "I don't have a man. I want in on it. I will give Rosalyn money if you will include me via my house," desires Yvonne. "If that be your choice, so be it," Sylvia says. Yvonne comes back "You don't mind your fiancé having other women? That's why I divorced Alexander."

Sylvia gets inquisitive "Why do you not have a man? You look young enough and pretty to have almost any man you could want. How old are you? 37, 38, 40? You are bound to have an opportunity for a relationship. Why not?" "It just isn't feasible. Any man that isn't married would want me at 36 for my money and sex only. With Conrad, I don't have to worry about that. Besides, I can end it anytime I want and he can end it when he wants. It IS my choice. Does Conrad accept the terms?" probes Yvonne Mercer.

"It is my choice as well. We will need a schedule that is agreeable to both of us and our work schedules. How is a Saturday afternoon? I can bring Rosalyn to see you and that way there will be nothing for anyone to draw conclusions about," offers Conrad. "Saturday it is" says Yvonne.

Sylvia agrees because very likely she will be working every Saturday. It was decided the meetings will start next Saturday. Rosalyn is pleased with the arrangement. It meant that she could, should and would have Conrad again and again. Yvonne gives Rosalyn one of her credit cards and advises "Use it sparingly. It has a high limit, but I don't want the monthly payments to be all that high." "I know. Conrad has been using his credit cards and his monthly payments are going to be high for a while," returns Rosalyn.

Conrad expresses his desire to take Yvonne home "I can take you home now. If you're not ready, you stay with Rosalyn for a while or you can go back to the streets. It's your choice." "You use that phrase quite a lot. Is there some special meaning to it that I'm not aware of?" asks Yvonne. Conrad returns "Only that it means you are free spirited and desire to be able to exercise the right to be." "Take me for example. I really do not know who I am. I was rescued by Conrad and we fell for each other by being together so much. I do not know if I have had other men. I just know I have not since I met Conrad. But, I know I am of the free spirit type. I do not even wear underwear so I can be free to engage in sexual encounters which express my freedom of choice," explains Sylvia.

Yvonne chooses to speak on the subject "I guess I am of the free spirit type as well. Here tonight, I have expressed my choice of having Conrad. In the past, I have signified my desire to not have a man because I wanted to be free. With Conrad, I am free to do as I desire whenever and wherever I want. There are no encumbrances. If I choose not to meet with Conrad on a Saturday, I have that choice. To me, being free is the utmost craving of everyone or should be. I think I have said about all I can on the subject." "It was well defined by you in your wants, desires and needs. I couldn't have said it better mother," discloses Rosalyn.

Sylvia asks Yvonne "What is your choice of going or staying to spend some time with Rosalyn." Rosalyn tells her mother "Mom, it has been so long since I saw you last. Please stay and talk with me. Conrad can take you home when Sylvia and he get back. We could go through my clothes and you can tell me if I have made the right choices for the desires of Sylvia and Conrad. They want me to dress as a woman and not as a teenager. I'll soon be twenty if you remember." Yvonne lets out "I'll stay for a while, but only until Conrad or Sylvia can take me home."

CHAPTER 16

The Minister

Unbeknown to Conrad, Sylvia has already looked for a minister. She found three and that at least one of the three she thought would work out for their needs. One was a Presbyterian, one was a United Methodist and the last was a Nondenominational. Sylvia tells Conrad "Let us go before it gets too late. Rosalyn and Yvonne will be okay here. All they need to do is lock the door after we leave." "How are we going to find a minister this late in the afternoon?" inquires Conrad. ""I have called three and each will be in their respective offices for the next three hours. That should be plenty of time to, at least, get one to say yes to our desire to get married."

Conrad asks "Have you got their addresses and telephone numbers? We might need to call one or more if the traffic gets really bad. Rush hour hasn't come yet, but it will before we are through. Where do we go first?" "The Presbyterian is the closest. He can be first. His name is Reverend Joshua Morgan. He says he would talk to us and we needed to come to his office at our earliest convenience. I asked about this afternoon and he said fine. His office is on Broad Street," exhorts Sylvia.

Conrad drives where Sylvia tells him to go taking each turn as she gives it to him-she had looked at a map of Richmond. The trip only takes 20 minutes. He parks in the lot and they go inside. A greeting is given by a secretary who wants to know "How may

I help you?" "We are here to see Reverend Morgan about getting married," answers Sylvia. "Are you members of this church or another Presbyterian?" "No, but he says that would not really matter," gives back Sylvia. "Wait one moment, please," and the secretary goes to find the Reverend.

"Reverend Morgan, there is a young couple here to see you about getting married. Will you see them now?" asks the secretary. "Yes, Elizabeth, show them in," says Joshua Morgan. The secretary does as instructed and brings Sylvia and Conrad to the minister. "Reverend Morgan, I called you earlier today. I am Sylvia Reed. This is Conrad Thomas. We want to get married. Will you be able to do that for us?" clarifies Sylvia.

The minister answers "Well, it really depends on when you want to be married. When might that be?" "This week sometime. The sooner, the better," desires Sylvia. Conrad remains silent because Sylvia has made the arrangements. Morgan states "I'm afraid that's not possible. You see, I'm required, by our denomination, to give counseling before I marry a couple. The counseling sessions take two weeks. You don't have that time available. I'm truly sorry."

Sylvia expresses her thanks and the couple leave disappointed somewhat. Sylvia advises Conrad "The next minister is the Nondenominational at the Cloverdale Church on Three Chopt Road. The minister there is Reverend Gordon McGuire. You should know where this church is at." "I do. It will take us less than ten minutes to get there," states Conrad. They arrive and the church looks deserted, but there is one car in the lot besides Conrad's Viper. The two go to the door that is marked Pastor and knock.

Reverend McGuire answers the door. "You must be Sylvia Reed. I have been waiting for you. So, you want to get married? My first question is when and my second is why. Answer these two questions and we will go from there." "When is easy. We want to get married sometime this week. The 'why' is a bit harder. We are in love and have been since we first met. Conrad has even bought me an engagement ring and wedding band. We want to share as much of our time together as possible. It cannot be all the time since we both have jobs and Sunday is the only time both of us are off. We want to have children as well," explains Sylvia.

You have answered those questions. I must tell you there is counseling that must be done first. It is not much time. You need only come 2 hours every night for a week. Can you put off the wedding until next week?" "Could we possibly get four hours one night and three the next two nights. That way we will meet the requirements," asks Sylvia. "Yes, that will do. Now there is only one question remaining and I must have a yes answer. Anything else, I cannot do the wedding. Do you plan to join this church as members?" Of course the answer is no. Conrad just is not the church type just yet.

After the encounter with Reverend McGuire, Sylvia and Conrad will need to go to the United Methodist minister, Reverend Garland Dotson. Sylvia tells Conrad "We must now go to the UMC on Gayton Rd. It is not that far from the apartment and we should have gone there first." The rush hour traffic has started. The drive is about 20 minutes. The Viper arrives and is parked. Sylvia and Conrad get out and go to the doors of the church. These are unlocked. They go in and see a rather nice church. To one side of the altar was a room with the door open. The two could hear talking. Almost at once, it quit. The couple goes to the door and sees Reverend Dotson.

"Reverend, I am Sylvia Reed. I talked to you earlier about our marriage," states Sylvia. The Reverend assumes "This must be the groom. Welcome to both of you." "This is Conrad Thomas, my fiancé. We want to be married this week. We have been in love since the moment we met and we want to have children. Can you help us," says Sylvia. "I believe so. My denomination requires me to give you marriage counseling. The length can be 6 to 20 hours. It really depends on you. There are no other requirements other than having a valid license. Have you had intercourse yet?" asks Garland. "Yes, we have, but only a couple of times," states Sylvia. "What about Friday at 10:00 o'clock? Do you have a church?" inquires Reverend Dotson. "No, we do not," gives Sylvia. "Might I suggest our church? The United Methodist motto is: 'Open doors. Open minds, and Open hearts,'" invites Dotson.

Sylvia says "We will give it serious thought. I used to attend a Methodist Church. I enjoyed the worship routine." Comments Conrad "She's never told me that before now. We will be here 10:00 am Friday. Thank you, Reverend Dotson." "You are welcome," says Garland.

CHAPTER 17

Baltimore Again

The President is highly disturbed about Sylvia's missing. He remembers the police saying 'if not found in 48 hours, there is little hope of finding her alive. President Sylvester calls Jim Duffy in Baltimore. "Agent Duffy, tell me what the status is of your search in Baltimore." "Mr. President, we have searched just about all we can search here in Baltimore with the satellite monitor. There may be a way to search that we have not tried yet. We can use the Social Security Administration (SSA) to provide names of any Sylvia or S. Redman. It will be time consuming, but Ho and I can handle it'" informs Agent Duffy.

"Why have you not thought of this before now?" asks the President. "It had not occurred to us to use the SSA until one of the officers mentioned how she found where her ex-husband lives so she could get alimony and child support. We can get on that today. Ho is already at the SSA getting a listing of names," states Duffy. "Well, I am glad to hear that. It is possible she goes to work in Baltimore. Maybe, you will find her this new way," advises Sylvester. "Ho just returned with the list. It is not too bad, but is bad enough. There are 29 Sylvia Redman's and 42 S. Redman's listed. This search method will take us about two or three days depending on traffic and if we can go by way of some order that requires less driving" informs Jim Duffy "and we have already had several sightings of Dodge Vipers, but only a couple of red."

Agents Duffy and Wong get to governmental cars and start on the search. Duffy is going north and Wong is going south. Duffy starts on the east side of town and works his way north from there. The first house he goes to has a red haired lady by the name S. Redman. Duffy asks her what her first name is. She replies "Synthia. Why?" "We are doing a house search for a Sylvia Redman who has been missing ten days now. Thank you, ma'am. Have a good day" relates Jim. Duffy's next house seems to be more of an opportunity to find Sylvia. The woman's name iss Sylvia Redman. However, her hair is blonde and it is not bleached. Agent Duffy tries another address. This, too, has a Sylvia Redman. He arrives and knocks on the door. There is no answer. He starts to leave when a red haired woman comes from next door with "Can I help you?" "I am Agent Jim Duffy of the FBI. I am conducting a search for a Sylvia Redman. You match her description. Can I see you driver's license,' inquires Duffy. He looks at the license and notices her birthday is right. He thinks he has found her and asks "How long have you lived here?" "About two years," comes the reply. "You are not the Sylvia Redman we are looking for. Sorry to have bothered you," confesses Jim Duffy.

Agent Ho Wong, in the meantime, is having very similar problems with the names on his half of the list. He thought he had Sylvia Redman when all of a sudden her husband shows up from work and asks what Ho thought he was doing. Wong told him and that ruled out this particular Redman. Ho continues much in the same way as Duffy. Each man is going down the list. Each has possible hits. Wong goes to one house and the woman was a red head, 5'4", about 110 pounds and had the same birth date as Sylvia Redman. When he asked her where she was born, she replied Greater Baltimore Medical Center. That information ruled her out. Sylvia was born in Walla Walla, Washington.

.Continuing out to Towson, Maryland, Agent Duffy finds another woman at home. Her name is Sylvia Redman. She is the same weight and height as the missing Sylvia. But her hair was black. He thinks it is really the missing Sylvia and asks to see her driver's license. She says she does not have one. Duffy, then, asks "Do you drive at all?" "Yes, when my license is not suspended," comes the girl. "Where is your car and what make is it?" This Sylvia is getting a bit mad about all the questioning "IT'S A CHEVY AND IT'S IN THE GARAGE." "Sorry to have bothered you ma'am."

Duffy crosses her off his list. It is getting to be a long day. Duffy wants to call it quits for the day. He calls Wong "Did you have any luck?" "I had one Sylvia Redman that matched everything except Redman is her married name. I would have called you if I had found her" declares Ho.

They both decide it is a good time to quit. It is getting late in the evening and not a good time to be knocking on doors. Before they retire for the night, they both go to police headquarters to check on the satellite monitoring system. The agents arrive at 8:15 pm. Jane Collins is working the monitoring system. Ho asks "Have you had any luck whatever on finding the Viper? I know you were the one that didn't know what one looked like." Jane asserts "I have seen a few red Vipers. They stand out in traffic. Rush hour is a good time to look because the cars are moving slow. Zooming in helps me identify what the car is, but I still have trouble seeing who the driver is." "Don't be too concerned about that. It happens to all users," announces Ho Wong.

Duffy asks "Have you scanned the Reisterstown area?" "Two days ago Agent Duffy," responds Jane "but we could scan again." "Do it" "We are moving in that direction. Is there any particular area you'd like to see?" asks Collins. "I want just the suburbs. I do not feel the need to scan downtown," relates Duffy. "We're there. I'll start at the north and work around downtown in a clockwise direction. That should cover everything you want to see," advises Jane. Duffy comes back "It should at that. If you see red cars, zoom in on any that you see. It may be a Viper. I want to see for myself. I got a tip from one of the women on my list. She has a cousin named Sylvia Redman as well as herself, but she didn't tell me where around Reisterstown her cousin lives."

Collins starts to see red. There are not that many red cars, but she is seeing some. On each one, she zooms in to look closer at the car. She does spot a red Dodge Viper. She locks on to it because it is moving in a southern direction. "I'll need to call the county police to stop the car and check it out," converses Jane. She has to get up to use the telephone to call the Baltimore County Police station. Ho takes over the monitoring. Jane tells the county police that an FBI agent is interested in stopping a red Dodge Viper heading south on Reisterstown Road about two miles south of the town of Reisterstown.

Jane must wait for the county dispatcher to get back with her. She had been told to hold. This she is doing. Finally, the dispatcher comes back on the line and informs Jane a vehicle has been dispatched. The county dispatcher asks "What do you want with the car or its' occupants?" Agent Duffy instructs "Tell her to stay on the line until the vehicle is stopped." Jane does as instructed. The county police catch up to the car, but it does not want to stop. Duffy sees this and tells Jane pass it on that the officers will follow until back-ups are with them. Jane gives the information to the dispatcher, who tells the officers.

The Viper begins to pull away from the following officers. Duffy says to Ho "Get the Baltimore Police to set up a curb-to-curb road block on Reisterstown Road at the city's limit. The officers will only have about seven minutes to get there and setup. Three cars should be enough, but the more the better." Ho complies. Duffy takes over the monitoring system and zooms in as tight as the satellite will allow. He sees the woman has red hair and she looks young. That was all he could tell from the display of the satellites monitoring.

The city police set up the road block in five minutes using three cars as instructed and two more backups south of the three. The city police officers, on the scene, do not wait one minute before the Viper is in sight. The woman driver of the Dodge sees the road block and attempts to turn around, but the county unit that had been following her has caught up with her. It blocks her off in the county. The city police are at the city's limit. However, three of the city officers go to help the lone county officer. The woman gets pulled out of the car and is cuffed. She says "What have I done? All I was doing was just driving myself to my mother's house. Can't a girl get any respect?" The officers want to know what is next besides arresting her for eluding the police. Duffy takes the phone away from Jane and says to the dispatcher to tell the county officer to check her identity.

The county officer asks "May I have your driver's license?" The woman says "What for?" "I need to check your identity"" "Why? I know who I am." "Ma'am, your license, please." She tells the officer it is her purse and he reads SYLVIA REDMAN. He calls dispatch and tells them her name. Duffy says to the dispatcher "Tell him to check her birth date, ask where she was born, check her height and weight." The dispatcher does so. The officer complies and Duffy is informed. It all matches the President's daughter, Sylvia Redman. Jim tells the dispatcher to have the county officer make out a report and mail a copy to the Baltimore Police Headquarters. He is also to turn this Sylvia over to a city officer, who will bring her to headquarters.

Jane Collins calls the officer that received the girl and he brings her in. She is wondering what this is all about. Duffy gets to her and asks "Are you Sylvia Redman?" "Yes, I am. Will you tell me what this is all about?" asks this Sylvia. Duffy asks "Is your weight 110 and height 5'4"? "Yes. Tell me what is going on?" "You are going to Washington D.C. to see the President and First Lady," informs Agent Jim Duffy. She is pleased to hear that. Duffy calls the White House and gets President Redman "Mr. President, we have your daughter in Baltimore."

"Well Duffy, bring her home." The girl immediately confronts Duffy "I'm not the President's daughter. The only time I have been to Washington was when I was a baby. My father's name is George Redman and my mother is Carol Redman. They live here in Baltimore and that is where I was headed when the police stopped me," explains this Sylvia.

Duffy calls Wong "Ho, you know the President's daughter. Is this her?" "Almost her twin, but Sylvia Redman is a brighter red head and maybe a bit longer hair. They sure could be from the same family," says Wong. Jim Duffy says "Then, I've made a terrible mistake. I'll have to call the President back and tell him a mistake was made in her identity." Duffy calls the White House again and tells the President of the mistaken identity. Redman is highly disturbed that the mistake was made and that his daughter is still missing.

The search in Baltimore resumes with Duffy and Wong using their lists of Redman's
They have no luck by either of them.

CHAPTER 18

Back To the Apartment

Sylvia and Conrad are satisfied by Reverend Garland and decide to go back to the apartment. They get into the Viper and Sylvia drives. She needs to learn the streets of Richmond. She has no trouble finding her way back to the apartment, but Conrad has been quiet, so she asks "Dear, why are you so quiet? We usually talk a good deal. Have I said or did something that has upset you?" "None of that, Sylvia. I am thinking about Yvonne and the mess I have gotten myself into. I like Rosalyn, but I'm not so sure about Yvonne." "Give it a chance. If it does not suit you, then, by all means stop the relationship. The money is not that important to us. We can handle Rosalyn's needs," quips Sylvia. Conrad goes "I guess you are right. I really haven't given it a chance yet. It may turn out to be something I will want to keep doing even if she stops giving Rosalyn money or credit cards."

The duo arrives at the apartment. Going inside, they see Rosalyn and Yvonne sitting on the couch talking. It was a real mother-daughter conversation. Rosalyn sees Conrad and jumps up, puts her arms around him and kisses him right before her mother. Yvonne is somewhat at a loss for words, but eventually states "I thought you said my daughter is your housekeeper. I've never seen a housekeeper kiss her boss in the way Rosalyn did. What is going on here?" "Remember earlier tonight when we were talking about choice and freedom. Rosalyn has made her choice to be with us forever and have a baby by me. In the meantime, we will share each other as the need arises," tells Conrad.

"Rosalyn, you did not tell me about the relationship with Conrad. It makes me wonder if I should not have a relationship with Conrad," Yvonne spills her thoughts. "Mother, give it a chance. If it works out, you may want to keep it going. I'm sure Conrad has had similar thoughts. Haven't you, Conrad?" directs Rosalyn. Conrad remarks "I did have some thoughts about it. Sylvia told me to give it a chance. I'm willing to give it a chance if Yvonne is willing." Yvonne reminds Conrad "We said earlier that we would do it on Saturday afternoons. I want you tonight when you take me home. I want it in my bed, my way. We can leave right now." "Is it okay with you, Honey?" "Yes, Conrad. It is always okay with me if it is what you want. But remember, I get to do what I want even after we are married," confirms Sylvia.

"I love you truly, truly I do, Sylvia. Wait up for me and I'll see you when I get back here. Let's go Yvonne. You'll have to give me directions. I'm not that familiar with that area of Richmond," states Conrad. They leave the apartment in the silver Viper and Yvonne Mercer gives all the directions to her house. He parks in her drive and they go inside together. She turns, grabs and kisses Conrad. He is caught off guard as has happened in the past. Conrad takes her in his arms and carries her to her bedroom on the first floor. The house is two-story with four bedrooms. The master bedroom is downstairs as is one other bedroom. Conrad trips a bit in the hallway, but does not lose his balance and does not drop Yvonne.

In the bedroom, he lowers her down and begins to undress her. She, likewise, does the same to him. When they are both nude, Yvonne tells Conrad she wants it her way—her on top. They have intercourse and satisfy one another. Yvonne says to Conrad "We can do it your way if you want." "My want can wait until Saturday. Remember that for me. We may even do it both ways. Or, there are many other ways that we could try as well," responds Conrad. He, then, gets up and dresses. Yvonne does not get dressed, but does put on a housecoat. She walks to Conrad and tells him "You are the first man I've had since I left Alexander. I want this to be a regular thing and if you want me more often, just call. Here's my personal cell phone number. I keep it on and near me all the time. There are not very many people who have this number, so be careful with it and don't give it to Sylvia or Rosalyn." "If that be your choice, so be it." is all Conrad says. He kisses her goodnight and leaves.

Driving back to the apartment, he feels like he has somehow betrayed Sylvia and especially Rosalyn. However, he remembers that Sylvia told him to do it if it was his choice and that she could have her choice as well. He wonders what that means. He feels the encounter was an enjoyable diversion. He has never had an older woman and she is only 11 years his senior—not enough to be his mother. Besides, Rosalyn shared her beauty. You could tell they were a mother-daughter thing. He makes up his mind that he cannot wait until Saturday for another time with Yvonne.

Conrad parks his car and heads up the stairs to the apartment. Going in, he does not see Rosalyn or Sylvia. He calls "Sylvia, where are you?" "In the bedroom, dear." Conrad enters and sees Rosalyn and Sylvia nude and in the bed together. It does not shock him. He remembers that she could have her choice as well. He asks "Should I get undressed and get in bed too?" "Yes, Dear." They had each other and all retired for the night.

CHAPTER 19

Marriage and Work

It is the morning of day 13. It is Friday. Conrad is the first to get up and he takes his shower. As he comes out after drying, he is met by Rosalyn, who kisses him and says good morning. Rosalyn takes her shower and dries off. Meanwhile, Conrad is getting Sylvia up and getting dressed. Sylvia goes in to take a shower, dry off and, then, get dressed. Rosalyn has already gotten dressed and is in the kitchen looking for something to eat. The trio meets in the kitchen and Sylvia kisses Conrad good morning. Conrad says "It is 6:00 am. I need to get to mom's and dad's for my wedding clothes, after we eat. Rosalyn, you and Sylvia have your dresses here. My suit is at the house. I know the first thing my mother is going to say." "What do you know she will say, Dear?" "'Where were you last night?' is exactly what she will say before anything else. I might as well get prepared for that. It can't be bypassed" tells Conrad.

Sylvia makes scrambled eggs and cooks some bacon. Rosalyn gets the drinks ready and Conrad is thinking what he will tell his mother. The food gets through cooking. Sylvia serves it to Rosalyn and Conrad, while making a plate for herself. Rosalyn, Sylvia, and Conrad eat their fill. The kitchen is then cleaned by Rosalyn. Conrad tells the girls "I am going to face mom while dad is still there. I need to get there before 7:00 am, so I'll leave now. Sylvia, bring Rosalyn with you to the church. I will meet you there at 9:30 am. Remember, you need to be at work at 11:00 o'clock. It will need to be a fast wedding and, then, here to change into working clothes. Conrad kisses both women and leaves.

Conrad goes straight to his parent's house. He sees both their vehicles are parked in the driveway. He does not want to block them in, so he parks on the street. He gets out and goes inside, but stops at the door. He makes sure all his clothes look tidy since he had on the same clothes as yesterday. Conrad enters and true to his thinking, she asks "Where have you been all night?" "Mom, dad, there is something I have got to tell you. Sylvia and I are getting married today at 10:00 o'clock. If you can spare an hour and a half, I would like both of you to attend," panics Conrad. Panic, likewise, his mother asks "What do you mean you are getting married TODAY? Before you answer that, tell me where you were last night and where was Sylvia? Did you two spend the night in bed together? "

"Sylvia and I spent the night together in bed in her apartment. I meant what I said about getting married. We have been planning it for a few days. She is everything I always wanted in a wife. I want to marry her before she remembers who she is and possibly falls out of love with me. I can manage our life together. We both have jobs. Sylvia did get the librarian job at VCU. I have bought an engagement ring and a wedding ring for Sylvia. We were really busy yesterday. By accident, I found Rosalyn's mother. That took quite a while. We went to the minister last night. I was tired so I spent the night there," explains Conrad confidently "we even want to have a baby." "CONRAD CLAYTON THOMAS, what do you think you are doing? Are you out of your mind like Sylvia?" inquires his mother.

Hank puts in his two cents worth "Grace, Dear, our son is old enough to make these kinds of decisions. Look at us. We met and two months later we were married. Our marriage has lasted 28 years. We have managed it quite well. Give the boy a chance.

Conrad, I'm proud of you, but it is a little fast. Couldn't you wait a bit longer? Like, maybe two weeks from now?" "Dad, Sylvia made the calls to three ministers that we talked with last night. I didn't even know she had done that. The minister we found asked us 'How about Friday at 10:00 o'clock?' and before I could say anything, Sylvia says yes. She knew she has to work today. I guess she is in a hurry too. Maybe, I'm the kind of guy she has been looking for and she doesn't want to lose me. The marriage thing started soon after I took her to Mi Hacienda. She noticed that Juanita Gomez has a thing for me, but I don't have a thing for her. It probably prompted her memory or something."

Hank Thomas tells his son "Your mother and I will be there. She can take a half day off. You've told us when but not where." "Go to the United Methodist Church on Gayton Road. Its pastor is Reverend Garland Dotson. I need to change clothes and go by the office. They don't know either. Besides, I need to catch up on my work. I'll meet you there at 9:45 am," gives Conrad. Conrad heads upstairs to change into his black business suit. He figures that will be okay for work and the wedding. After dressing, he heads for work,

He parks his Viper and goes into the bank. Conrad goes to his office and checks the notices on his desk. One is from Yvonne. The note says 'call me. Can't wait for Saturday.' He had other notes about financial services and checking accounts. One of these notes mentions a woman who had posted $1,200.00 to her account, but it did not register in her account. He sees he will have to come into work later after Sylvia goes to work. Having read all the notes and made notes of his own, he goes and tells the working tellers the news of him getting married and that anyone who could take their lunch early is invited. One of you can call the girls that are off today and ask them if they would want to attend. It is at the UMC on Gayton Road. It being 9:30, Conrad heads for the church and gets there at 9:40 am. He meets up with Sylvia and they go to find Reverend Garland, who is in his office.

The reverend welcomes them. Garland states "Are you ready? Time is getting shorter by the minute. We need to get your parties lined up." They go to the foyer and Rosalyn is waiting. The reverend tells Rosalyn she will be first before Sylvia and Conrad. Dotson asks is there a best man?" Conrad answers "No." But Conrad sees one of his buddies and asks him to be best man. He agrees. He will be first to enter before the groom. Conrad looks in and sees several people he knows and one he does not know. He asks Sylvia if she recognized the woman and she says it is Alexis Taylor from the library. Conrad thinks he might want to get to know her.

Conrad also sees his parents have made it. He quickly calls to his dad to come to him. "Dad, can you give Sylvia away? She has no one else." "I would be honored." The five get lined up and Reverend Dotson goes to the altar. He motions for them to start in. One by one the five go in with Hank holding Sylvia's arm. She looks gorgeous in the white dress. Conrad keeps that in his mind through the service. The minister goes through the preliminaries and finally gets to the vows part of the service. He says to the couple repeat after me:

> I, Conrad Clayton Thomas, take thee Sylvia Reed to be my wife, to have and to hold,
> from this day forward, for better – for worse, for richer – for poorer,
> in sickness and in health, to love and to cherish, till death do us part,
> and thereto I pledge thee my faith.

Conrad repeats each line after the minister. He is well pleased that everything is going so well. He can hardly wait for it to be over.

> I, Sylvia Reed , take thee Conrad Clayton Thomas to be my husband, to have and to hold,

> from this day forward, for better – for worse, for
> richer – for poorer,
> in sickness and in health, to love and to cherish, till
> death do us part,
> and thereto I pledge thee my faith.

Sylvia does as Conrad had with each line. She too can hardly wait. They exchange rings. The minister prompts the couple to turn around and says "I now present to you Mr. and Mrs. Conrad Clayton Thomas. Sylvia and Conrad go to the people gathered for the wedding. It is a relatively small crowd. But, they are happy with it. Reverend Garland Dotson invites everyone to the fellowship hall for refreshments. Everyone proceeds to the refreshments except for Sylvia. She has to leave for work after going to the apartment to change clothes. She heads out not even getting to talk with Conrad's parents. He tells them she has to go to work and being there by 11:00 o'clock.

Kitty Calhoun is there. She approaches Conrad."I guess this closes my chance of ever getting you to take me to bed. I am sorry for that, but happy for you." Conrad says "I have had a thing for you as well. We needn't allow this to get in our way. We' will talk when I get back to work." Calhoun leaves Conrad. She is feeling a little better that he will talk to her about a relationship that she will enjoy even though Conrad is now married.

Sylvia arrives at work precisely at 11:00 am and enters. Maryann Witten greets her "Your station will be right here at the counter. Mainly, you will be responsible for checking books in and out. You will have some lookups to do. Use this computer over here. It has our inventory and the ability to access other libraries to see if they have the book requested. If you need any help, Hannah will be in at noon." Sylvia settles in.

The very first student to bring a book to check out says "I know you. You're a student here aren't you? I know I have seen you before." Sylvia says "I am sorry to report to you I have never been a student here. You must have me confused with someone else." The student checks out the book and continues to think he has seen her before but cannot remember where. Except for that one incident she has an uneventful day. She uses her Viper to go to the Shoney's she had seen during her driving test. It was a dual restaurant. You could order from a menu or you could go buffet. Sylvia chooses to go for the buffet. She gets a salad, chicken, rice, potatoes and corn.   She settles in a booth to eat. Having previously ordering a Diet Pepsi, she finds it there with silverware ready for her to devour.

Hannah comes in at noon and they get to talking when they are not busy with a student. It seems Hannah had a thing for Conrad. She got it when he talked to her while Maryann was showing Sylvia around. Sylvia shows her the wedding rings that Conrad bought for her and says "We were married today at 10:00 o'clock. I had to rush after the service to get here on time. I made it exactly on time." Hannah ogles at the sight of the rings and asks "How much did those cost?" Sylvia merely answers "Over $4,000.00."

Maryann saw Sylvia showing off her rings and comes desiring "I want to see the rings. So, you got married today. Congratulations." Sylvia shows her the rings and she is electrified. The rings were gorgeous on Sylvia's hand. "It is a little slow for a Friday afternoon. Business will pick up after classes are over for the day. I expect you two to be hard at it. Call me, if it gets too hectic," expresses Maryann.

The day does get hectic and Hannah, knowing what to do, gets Maryann Witten to come and help. Maryann takes the books and stacks them for Sylvia to check in and a different pile for her to check out. Hannah, in the meantime, looks up books for students and when not busy helps Sylvia. It is almost more than Sylvia can handle, but she does make it through the day. The end of her shift comes rather quickly. She heads for her apartment knowing Conrad and Rosalyn will be there alone.

Meanwhile, Conrad goes to his parents' house. He needs to get some things to take to the apartment. He goes into his room and takes three suits, three sport coats, three pairs of pants, socks and underwear. He heads back to the apartment. He finds Rosalyn is cleaning the place. He goes into the bedroom and puts his clothes in the closet. He asks Rosalyn "What would you like to do today?" Rosalyn answers "I would like to go see my mother."

Conrad says "I had a note at work to answer from your mother. I guess we can go over there and see her. The two go out to the silver Dodge Viper and get in. Conrad starts the car and backs out to go to Yvonne's house. He gets there in a short time. They knock and go in as if they lived there. Yvonne is upstairs and hears the noise. She gets her shot gun and proceeds down the stairs not knowing who it might be. Half way down she yell's "Stop, whoever you are? I have a gun and will shoot." A few steps down she sees it is Rosalyn and Conrad.

"Conrad, why didn't you call? I wanted to talk to you about today. Can we go at it? "Why yes, of course," replies Conrad. "When do you want to do it?" "Now. Rosalyn, you wait down here. Is that understood?" "Yes mother," is Rosalyn's response to the order. Yvonne and Conrad head upstairs. He remembers her way of doing it. Conrad is satisfied with that method and tells Yvonne "We can do it your way, if you want." "I want it a different way. What do you suggest?" comes back Yvonne. Conrad states "We could have you on top facing my feet. That would be different." Yvonne agrees. They get at and satisfy each other.

Rosalyn yells "I want my turn. Yvonne calls back "Come and get it." Rosalyn and Conrad go at it to orgasm for both. Conrad has nothing to worry about for Rosalyn has been on the pill. He asks "Now what?" Yvonne says "We go downstairs and have some lunch. The trio goes downstairs to the kitchen with Yvonne leading the way. Once in the kitchen, she goes about fixing ham, turkey and cheese sandwiches. They eat and Conrad thanks Yvonne who says "No. Thank you, Conrad. We're still on for tomorrow, right?" "Yes," is the only answer to Yvonne. After eating, Rosalyn and Conrad head back to the apartment.

Conrad parks and the two head up to the apartment. Conrad wants a Pepsi and they are out so he goes to the convenience store for a six-pack. He sees Alexis Taylor in the store and approaches her. "You're Conrad Thomas, aren't you," questions Alexis. Conrad states back "Why yes. How do you know?" "From the wedding today. I thought you looked quite handsome," reports Alexis. "Well, you're quite the looker yourself. If I wasn't married and you weren't married, we could get together for some fun." "I am not married. I have never been married. You can have me, if you want," states Alexis. Conrad thinks about his situation. He already has three women and really does not need a fourth. He tells her "Thanks. But no thanks. I have all I can handle." Alexis wondered why he turned her down and why he has all he can handle. She thinks "Does Sylvia provide him with that much?' The two part and go their separate ways.

Conrad picks up the six-pack of Pepsi and a six-pack Diet Pepsi. He checks out and returns to the apartment. He is back with the drinks and offers one to Rosalyn. She accepts the Diet Pepsi. Conrad sees he is going to need two cartons of Diet Pepsi, since both Sylvia and Rosalyn drink it. After a drink, Conrad tells Rosalyn he must go to the office to find out what happened to $1,200.00 that should have gone into the account of a lady. He leaves for the bank. Once there, he calls the lady and asks if she remembered what teller she goes to.

She replies "I don't know her name, but she is the one that is pregnant. Conrad knew who that had to be. He tells Sarah Harper to close her window. He takes her into his office and tells of the mistake made. Sarah asks whose account it was. Conrad tells her. She says she remembers the transaction, but doesn't remember anything wrong. Sarah goes back to her window and checks the receipts for yesterday and finds she had mistakenly wrote one digit wrong. When she shows Conrad the error, he tells her to correct it and to make a note on the wrong account's record. She does that. It is time for Conrad to leave.

When Sylvia pulls up to park, she sees a man trying to push Rosalyn into a van. Rosalyn is fighting mighty hard and the man is having trouble. There is no one else around except Sylvia. She wonders where Conrad is at. Sylvia calls 911 and tells of the incident and the address. Sylvia, then, gets out of her car and attacks the man hitting him with a book she had brought from the library. About that time, Conrad pulls up and sees the fighting. He has a pocket knife and pulls it out to threaten the guy, but it does not work. The man pulls out a knife and puts it to Sylvia's neck. It is a standoff for a few minutes until two officers arrive and both pull their guns.

The first officer, Patricia Garvin, tells the man to put down the knife. He refuses. Pat tells him again and that she will be forced to shoot him if he did not drop the knife. The guy still refuses and presses the knife even tighter against Sylvia's neck. Rosalyn and Conrad look on. Pat Garvin tells him one more time to drop the knife or she will be forced to shoot. "Go ahead. Shoot. You'll hit her instead of me" says the man. Patricia takes dead center ain at the man's head. She takes one shot and hits the fellow dead center of his forehead. He falls dead. Patricia tells her partner "You saw it. He was about to cut her throat. This will mean a lot of paperwork and I'll be investigated by Internal Affairs." She turns to Sylvia "Were you the woman he was attempting to abduct?" "No. That would be Rosalyn. I helped her get away from the man and he grabbed me just seconds before you arrived. My name is Sylvia Thomas." She felt fascinated to be giving the last name Thomas. The other officer has called for an ambulance to get the body to take to the city morgue.

Pat turns to Rosalyn "You were the one he was attempting to abduct. Where was he trying to force you to go?" "Into this van. I fought him the best I could and it was almost not enough until Sylvia came to my aid. And when Conrad came, he put the knife to Sylvia's throat. That was just before you arrived, officer Garvin" tells Rosalyn. "You must be Conrad. You had a knife as well. Did you have it out before he did?" asks Garvin. Conrad states "No. I thought he would drop Sylvia and fight me, but he didn't do that. I think he thought he could make me drop my knife." "Well, we will have this van towed for evidential reasons. Do you all live here? I may need to come back tomorrow and do some more investigating" says Garvin. Sylvia says "Yes, officer. We all live in room 213."

The ambulance arrives to take the corpse to the city morgue. They load the body and leave. The other officer mentions the man had no identification on him and that it could be in the van. Patricia tells the other officer to check it out. He finds nothing and tells Pat. She tells him to run the tags and VIN through the car's computer. He does that and gets a name and address. Patricia Garvin tells the three that her partner and she will check out the address. They leave.

Rosalyn, Sylvia and Conrad go up to the apartment. Conrad inquires "Rosalyn, what were you up to being down there by the parking spaces? Why didn't you stay up here?" Rosalyn comes back with "I thought I could go check on the new couple that moved in to apartment 113. They are older than all three of us, but I thought it would be nice to introduce myself to them. If they were receptacle to the idea, maybe we could have dinner with them sometime." "It is not a good idea to go out alone. What if the man had hit you on the head three times and given you three concussions? You could have been like me—no memory," states Sylvia. Rosalyn speaks "Well, it didn't happen. I fought him the best I could." "And you almost lost, if Sylvia hadn't of jumped in. It was also a good thing she called 911 to get the police here. Let's hope you never face that kind of situation again," says Conrad. They go up to the apartment, talk for a while and, then, retire for the evening.

CHAPTER 20

The House

It is day 14, Saturday. Sylvia and Conrad decide it is time to buy a house. They go to a Remax Realtor. The woman says her name is Judy Diamond. Sylvia and Conrad tell her they are interested in buying a house. Judy's first question is "In what price range are you thinking?" Conrad says "We want to keep it under $175,000.00, if at all possible." "It just so happens that I have five to choose from. The lowest is only $110,000.00 for a two bedroom house," states Diamond. Sylvia responds with "We need at least three bedrooms and maybe four." "Well, I have one four bedroom at $175,000.00 with 3 baths. Will that do?" "We will have to see the house before we can decide. What else do you have?" asks Conrad.

Judy Diamond tells them she has three houses: two with three bedrooms and one with four bedrooms. One of the houses has 2 baths, while the other two only have a single bath. She goes on to explain that the 2 bath, four bedroom is selling for $150,000.00 and the other two are both selling for $130.000.00 each. Sylvia and Conrad ask to be shown the one with two baths. Judy has them follow her to the house. They travel to Genito Road. The property is somewhat in a wooded area, but has a large fenced pasture at the rear. The realtor has a key to the house and they all go inside. The house is fully furnished and Sylvia can tell someone lives there. She asks "Why are the people living here selling this house? It looks too good to be selling for $150.000.00. How much land comes with it?"

Realtor Judy responds "This house comes with 28 acres and a barn, which you should have seen coming in the drive. The owner wants to move to Florida and is anxious to sell. Normally, a house on 28 acres would sell for $169,000.00. But this house is on sale for a particularly needy reason. Let me show you the house. We are in the living room. Straight ahead is the dining room with the kitchen off to the left. Notice the sliding glass door at the back of the dining room. In the kitchen, there is an island that you can prepare meals on. There is also a dishwasher under the island as well as storage space. Notice all the cabinets. There is also a small pantry. Now let us go to the master bedroom.

They walk to the right and the Master bedroom is on this end with the utility room. It is large with a master bath and two sinks. They continue to the utility room. There, they see the washer and dryer. Judy says "Let us go to the family room." Once there, they see it is the biggest room in the house. Sylvia and Conrad are fascinated by the size of the family room. Finally, they are shown the other bath room and three bedrooms. Conrad demands "We will take it. Is there a chance of getting the price even lower?" "Why yes. What made you think of that?" asks Judy.

"You, yourself, made the comment it was a speedy deal and that it was wanted to be sold. If we can get the price down just a bit, our down payment would be less. I can have Wachovia Bank do the financing," reports Conrad. "Let us return to the office and see what we can work out," states Diamond. The three exit the house and head for the Remax office. They park their cars and go inside the office. Realtor Diamond asks them to have a seat. They sit. Judy gets out some papers and begins to sort them a particular way. This has Sylvia wondering, but Conrad knows what is up. Diamond is preparing the necessary paperwork to sell them the house.

She says "I have had five couples look at the house. Not one of them was interested in it. I even offered to lower the price; still it would not sell. You are the only ones to say you would buy it. I am prepared to sell the house for $125,000.00. You will need a down payment of $12,500.00. Are you prepared to pay that amount?" "I will be ready to pay it this afternoon. I just need to get to the bank before noon. It shouldn't take us that much more here. Let me give you $1,000.00 to hold the house for us." "Okay, but we need to sign some papers. The first is the agreement with the seller that the price will be $125,000.00. The second is a statement you accept the house as is. That means furniture and all. The third is an agreement on the monthly lease amount; with a statement you will not sell the house except back to the owner. Sylvia and Conrad sign all the papers and he heads for Wachovia Bank. Conrad makes a loan for $123,500, withdraws $11.500.00 for the down payment and takes it to Realtor Judy Diamond. He closes the deal. Sylvia and he have a new house to live in.

Sylvia and he return to the apartment and tell Rosalyn the news of the house buy. She is elated that she will have her own bedroom. The dishwasher was also an enlightenment. Conrad says to Sylvia "Let's go pay the rest of the down payment before you have to go to work and we can take both cars. Rosalyn can ride with you out and will ride back with me. You can go on to work from there. So they get in their cars and drive to the realtor's office. Judy Diamond is still there hoping they would return. As the trio enters, Conrad says "I've got the rest of the down payment. Wachovia will have a check ready Monday for the balance. We are ready to take possession now."

"I will need one key to get my clothes, jewelry and a few other things. Here is a key to the house. You can enter at any time, but give me about an hour. If you have any problems after you move in, call me and tell me about it. You are buying my house. I am the one who wants to move to Florida," states Realtor Diamond.

Sylvia leaves to go to work. Rosalyn and Conrad go back to the apartment.

Meanwhile, Grace is having one of her nicer days where nothing is going wrong and the students are exceptionally well in their actions. She decides it is time for a treat when lunch time rolls around. Grace has a free period after lunch and thus can be gone for a while. She decides to go to Red Lobster for her lunch. She calls Conrad to join her. He does taking Rosalyn with him. Grace is a little surprised to see Rosalyn in the company of her son. She had expected him to come alone. Grace gives them a hello son and says nothing about Rosalyn. This did not upset Rosalyn, but did hit a chord with Conrad. He tells his mother "Rosalyn came with me because she had nothing to do today. Sylvia has gone to work and Rosalyn and I are alone for the rest of the day until Sylvia gets home. We may go meet her for her lunch which would serve as our dinner. We haven't decided that part yet."

The waitress comes to their table and says "My name is Gloria Swan and I'll be your waitress. Can I get you your drinks or should I come back?" "We will order our drinks now. I want black coffee" tells Grace. Conrad speaks "Rosalyn will have and I will have Pepsis." "You forgot Conrad. I drink Diet Pepsi," Rosalyn retorts. Gloria says "Thank you. I'll be right back with your drinks." Conrad tells Rosalyn "I'm sorry about the foul up. I have forgotten because you haven't been with us that long. "With you? I thought she was your housekeeper and only came by during the daytime to do her work?" asks Grace.

Gloria, the waitress, returns with their drinks right then. She asks who ordered what because she forgot to mark it down. After getting it straight, she inquires "Are you ready to order your meals? Grace, before the other two, states "Yes. I will have the Lobster Lover's Dream with a salad and French dressing." "Mom, I thought you didn't like French dressing?" prompts Conrad. Grace replies "I do eat different dressings from time to time. I just wanted French today." Conrad orders "I'll have the seafood platter. Rosalyn, what will you have?" "I'll have the same as you, Conrad" gives back Rosalyn. Swan says "Very well then. I'll get your orders placed. It shouldn't be very long. We don't have that many people at lunchtime."

Conrad announces "Mom, Sylvia and I have bought a house. It is four bedrooms and 2 baths. There is a living room, dining room, kitchen, and a family room. And we only had to give $125,000.00." "Why could you not wait for your father to retire? You could have our house to live in. Is it not good enough?" desires Grace. "Mom, you know the talk of the neighborhood. We would not have any privacy. Our house is far out in the county, almost to Chesterfield County. It is on Genito Road. It is 28 acres with a barn. Mom, it is a beautiful setting, slightly wooded. I want to buy a horse. We have a fenced pasture where the horse could graze and get exercise." "Conrad, what will you do with a horse?" asks Grace. "Ride it, of course." Rosalyn has kept quiet not wanting to look like she was interfering, but Conrad was holding his own against his mother. So, Rosalyn did not say a thing.

Gloria returns with the food and that puts a stop to the conversation. The waitress gets the orders right this time. She only had to remember who got the lobster. The three begin eating. Grace starts with her salad. She looks at her watch and sees she has an hour left before her next class and tells Conrad she must hurry. So, she stops eating her salad and begins on the lobster. She wanted it more than the salad. Conrad says "Mom, you've got time to eat your salad. Why don't you finish it first?" "I want to get back a little early to set up a display for my next class. That class is ahead of the other classes. If my timing is correct. I do not have time to eat the salad," remarks Grace.

Rosalyn and Conrad eat their seafood platters at a slower rate than Grace eats the lobster. Grace gets done before the other two and sarcastically tells Conrad "I will let you pick up the tab, since you have so much money." Grace has finished her Lobster Lovers Dream and rises to leave. "Mom, when will I see you again?" "Tomorrow, if you come to the house," replies Grace. She, then, leaves. Rosalyn and Conrad are still eating. Gloria comes by and asks "Will there be any dessert?" Conrad turns to Rosalyn "How about it? Do you want any dessert?" Rosalyn answers "Yes. I want ice cream a la mode with whatever pie or cake you have. Surprise me." Gloria Swan asks Conrad and he says no. Gloria leaves to get the dessert.

Rosalyn turns to Conrad "Can we do it today? I'm really in the mood." "I think we can," Conrad returns. They finish their platters and Gloria comes with the dessert—chocolate cake with vanilla ice cream. Rosalyn is thinking more about Conrad than about her cake a la mode. She hurries and finishes the dessert. Conrad leaves a tip as they go to the register for their bill. He pays for it with his credit card. They leave Red Lobster and head for the apartment. Rosalyn and Conrad get out and go into the apartment and into the bedroom. They undress and have each other. Conrad, afterwards, dresses and asks Rosalyn "Would you like to see the house now?" "Yes, I would. Can we go there now? Didn't the realtor say to give her time." "It's been over an hour. She will be done by now," says Conrad.

The duo head for Conrad's Viper and get in. Conrad takes his time to drive to the house. He is in no hurry. It is four hours before Sylvia gets off work. He is wondering what to do with his time. Rosalyn has an idea about that. They arrive at the house. A neighbor, seeing the car, comes over to see who would be at her friend's home. The neighbor has just returned home from work. Arriving, she asks "Who are you and what are you doing here?" "I'm Conrad Thomas. I bought this house today from Judy Diamond at Remax Realtors. My wife and I will probably spend the night and move the rest of our things in tomorrow. The neighbor says "Oh. I didn't know she has sold it. She has been having a hard time getting a buyer. I'm Bonnie Jean Peterson, your next door neighbor. At least, on the east side towards Richmond. Your neighbor on the west side is a half mile down the road from here. Welcome Mr. and Mrs. Thomas."

"This is not my wife. She is our housekeeper. You will see her here in the day time. You're welcome to come over anytime. My wife, Sylvia, goes to work at the VCU Library from 11:00 am to 7:30 pm, Tuesday through Saturday. I work at Wachovia 9:00 am to 5:00 pm, Monday through Friday. Rosalyn doesn't work anywhere except for us." "Excuse me. I thought she was your wife. If you work from 9:00 am to 5:00 pm, how is it you're here now?" "I'm on vacation. I will be off for another week," returns Conrad.

"I'm glad you're moving in, especially with a housekeeper who will be here all day. I'll now have somebody to talk to. My husband, Frank, died in an automobile accident two years ago. I've been alone ever since," tells Bonnie Jean. Rosalyn states "I'll be more than happy to talk with you as long as Mr. Thomas isn't here. We talk over his day's work until his wife comes from work. We may have dinner late to include Mrs. Thomas or leave some extra for her to eat. It all depends on how she feels at work. She'll call to let me know. If you'll excuse me I have some work to do."

Conrad excuses himself too. He tells Bonnie Jean "I need to get in there as well. We want things arranged before my wife gets off work." "Very well. It has been nice talking to you, Conrad," emphatically tones Bonnie Jean. She leaves and walks back to her house. Conrad goes in and does not see Rosalyn. He yells "Rosalyn, where are you?" "I'm in here Conrad," returns Rosalyn. He enters the second bedroom to find Rosalyn lying nude on the bed that will be hers. He knows what she wants and decides to give it to her. They have their enjoyment.

Sylvia calls Conrad on her cell phone. She asks "Where are we going to sleep tonight? Will it be at the apartment or at the new house?" "Rosalyn and I are at the new house. Come on here and we can determine what we'll do for the night," answers Conrad. Sylvia finishes her day at work and heads for the newly bought house where she expects to live a long time. It will be their house; Rosalyn, Sylvia, and Conrad. Conrad shows Rosalyn the house and she is well satisfied that it will be easy to maintain. Conrad notices he has two and a half hours before Sylvia gets there. He remembers to go to Yvonne for his appointment with her. He merely tells Rosalyn that he has something to do and will be back in an hour or two. Rosalyn knows what it is, but does not say anything except "Okay."

He leaves the house and heads for Yvonne's. Once there, he does not knock; he simply goes inside. She has been expecting him to arrive anytime. She is in a robe with no shoes on. She walks up and kisses him passionately. He responds quickly and takes her to her bedroom. She starts undressing Conrad. Conrad merely slips the robe off and Yvonne is nude. Undressed, Conrad tugs her into bed. This time, she is told to get on top and grab his ankles. They do their thing and Yvonne is excited to do it a different way. She asks Conrad "Is there another way you can show me?" Conrad informs her to lie on her back in the middle of the bed and raise just her left leg. He crosses her and they do it again. Conrad announces that he must return home for Sylvia will be there shortly. "You shouldn't have waited so long to come today. We could have had more fun and games," reports Yvonne

Conrad dresses wondering what she meant by games, but does not take the time to find out. He heads directly to the new house. He gets there half an hour before Sylvia does. He is at a loss as to which place they will stay at. Conrad just waits for Sylvia to arrive. "There are some things we need for this house. It has no cable or satellite, no computers, no TV, no stereo, no lamps or end tables for the bedrooms and we need new mattresses as well. Let's go shopping a bit," says Sylvia. Sylvia and Conrad leave Rosalyn behind and head for Wal-mart. They park and go inside. Conrad says "Let's buy the stereo first. We can have music as we move in the other things we buy. He also buys two HP computers with a router. Conrad knows he must call Hughes Corporation for the satellite installation for the computers and

Dish Network for the TV satellite. He feels they have enough for the night and they check out and go home.

The trio decide to spend the night together in the master bedroom's king size mattress. There is no sex this night for both, Rosalyn and Sylvia, are too tired. They retire for the night.

Morning arrives day 15, Sunday. There is no need for either of them to go to work today. Conrad tells Sylvia about the visit of their next door neighbor, Bonnie Jean Peterson, "The woman was quite cordial and she is a widow. Her husband was killed in an accident two years ago. She is a friend with Judy Diamond, the realtor. She says she wants to come over and talk to Rosalyn since Rosalyn will be here all day. Bonnie Jean gets off work about 2:30 pm and is home by 3:00 pm." "Well, there is nothing wrong with that? Did she tell you her age?" inquires Sylvia. "No. But I would guess about 30-35 years old," comes back Conrad. He tells Sylvia "We need to get new mattresses, night stands, lamps, and a TV. However, we need to watch pricing for my Visa and Master Card are getting full. I dread to think what the monthly payments will be."

The duo leaves for a furniture shop. They are met by Crystal Hopkins, daughter of the owner, Daniel Hopkins, at Hopkins Furniture. Sylvia and Conrad express "We want six night stands and six lamps to fit on each of the night stands. If you sell them, we need three mattresses. We will leave the fourth bedroom for a later time. We want a king, a queen and a full." "Come this way. We will go to the night stands first, then the lamps and, finally, the mattresses." reports Crystal "Here we are at the night stands." There were many types to choose from. Sylvia tries to remember the furniture of each bedroom. She remembers oak in the full mattress room, maple in Rosalyn's room and walnut in the master bedroom. She sees its variety is readily available and asks for two of each.

Crystal takes them to the lamps leaving the mattresses for last. Sylvia sees the lamps are different sizes and different styles. She thinks she will go with all the same height, but different styles. The first is for the guest bedroom; it is a glass vase style, about 18" high with a 10" natural linen shade. Second is Rosalyn bedroom; oil rubbed bronze, 18" high with the same shade as before. Last for the master bedroom; antique brass touch lamp, 18" high with the same shade. After ordering two of each, Sylvia and Conrad go to the mattresses led by Hopkins.

Crystal tells them "The best we have is the Posture-pedic. It conforms to your body's figure for an excellent night's sleep. We also carry Sealy, Serta and Simmons. Each manufacturer has their own quality and benefits for their mattresses. What would you like?" "We will take one of each of the sizes we mentioned in a Serta and when can all this furniture be delivered?" queries Sylvia.

"I will have to look at our delivery truck schedule to make that statement positive or negative for next week. Mr. Thomas, will you come with me please? Mrs. Thomas, will you wait there please?" questions Crystal. Hopkins takes him up to the office after going through a gate that is locked. Once through, she locks it back and leads him upstairs. Conrad was concerned as to what that meant. He did not have long to remain in that condition. Inside the office, Crystal begins to undress, but Conrad puts a stop to it. He tells her "I'm a married man and I never have sex without my wife knowing about it. You have her waiting downstairs and locked out of this office." "Conrad, I wanted you. I'm willing to give myself to you and you stopped me. Why? Other men have used the opportunity. It's totally free. I'll tell you what I'll do. If you have sex with me, I will take a $1,000.00 off your bill," offers Crystal

Conrad remains adamant. He will not give himself to Crystal this way. He thought 'if I wasn't married to Sylvia, I would'. He tells Crystal that he wants to go down and pay his bill. She relents and redresses that which she had taken off. They go back downstairs and Hopkins prepares the bill. Conrad gets out his Master Card to charge the items. Crystal says "The furniture will be delivered Monday morning about 10:30."

Sylvia and Conrad go to the apartment to gather things and take them to the new house. Sylvia gets all her clothes and Conrad gets what little he has there. They also get all the food. They just barely fit it all into the silver Viper. She had no room for towels and linens. These would have to wait another time. They drive to the new house where Rosalyn is waiting for them. She helps unload the car. She makes sure the food gets into the kitchen. Sylvia and Conrad get the clothes into their bedroom and into Rosalyn's bedroom. They had left what she will donate to Goodwill.

Rosalyn asks "What is for dinner? Are we eating in or going out? If we go out, should I change my clothes which are a bit dirty from working here?" Conrad answers "We can eat here. Fix whatever you want from what we have. A steak, cooked medium, would do nicely." Rosalyn gets the steak and prepares it. She also makes mashed potatoes, gravy and peas. When finished, she gets the table set and puts the food on it. Rosalyn tells them dinner is ready. Sylvia and Conrad join her in the dining room.

After eating, Conrad goes to the stereo and plays CDs of oldies music. He plays the Beach Boys, the Beatles, John Denver, Anne Murray, The Tokens and Peter, Paul & Mary. His favorite songs were 'Puff, the Magic Dragon' by Peter, Paul & Mary and 'The Lion Sleeps Tonight' by The Tokens. He invites Rosalyn and Sylvia to join him. There is not much else to do. The Hughes installation man and the Dish Network installation man have not come yet. They would be here Monday since Conrad had called each company. Rosalyn and Conrad plan to be there Monday working on the house and putting some things in the barn. After some time, they retire for the evening, all tired.

CHAPTER 21

The Thomas House

Grace and Hank were missing Conrad. Conrad had been there a short while in the morning, but as it turned out, he was gone all day. Grace has to work to replace a teacher that has to take off due to a family death. Grace is more than glad to do that. She remembers the time she needed to take off when her daughter, Lois Jean, died. It had been before Conrad was born. She took three days off and she thanked her replacements for filling in for her. There had been one for each day. She feels it is her duty to replace as need be.

Grace works the entire day without a free period, such was the replacement need. She could have been off, but she would not be spending much time with Hank. He goes to Joe Harper's house to help Joe rebuild an engine for a 1949 Ford sedan. Joe had bought the car from Willington's Salvage Yard in north Richmond. The engine is corroded, but not beyond salvage. Rebuilding the engine is the first thing Joe decides to do to this antique auto.

Hank and Joe start by disconnecting the dead battery, removing hoses, belts, wiring and the carburetor. They, then, dismount the transmission. Finally, they dismount the engine from the frame and using a chain hoist to lift the engine from its mounting brackets. Joe places the engine on a work bench where the rebuilding will occur. Hank gets out the tool box and opens one drawer to gets wrenches and sockets with ratchet to take bolts out of the engine's head.

Hank removes the valve cover and gives it to Joe, who promptly cleans it and mounts a new gasket. Hank, then, removes the timing chain, distributer, valves, thermostat and head. He gives all these to Joe. Joe begins salvaging what he can and starts a list of what is needed. Joe and Hank begin the dismounting of the block to get to the pistons and finally the crank shaft. The engine is apart and five hours have past. Joe figures the most important thing not on the list is a piston hole router to clean these. His list includes valves, timing chain, distributor, spark plugs and wires, piston rings and a host of belts with hoses included. The transmission will be checked after the engine is reinstalled, but it will need new oil—it is a standard transmission.

Joe makes a quick run to Advanced Auto Parts. He is able to get some of the items. The others will need to be special ordered. Joe takes what he has and begins some of the reassembly. Hank and Joe Harper end for the day. Joe thanks Hank for his help. Hank, then, goes to his house and takes a much needed shower. He dries himself and dresses in clean clothes. Hank decides to watch TV and wait for Grace to come home.

While watching TV, Hank realizes it is time for Grace to be home. Shortly, Grace arrives. Hank says "Hello Dear. We are going out tonight to celebrate our anniversary. Where would you like to go, as if I didn't already know?" "Red Lobster," is Grace's answer. It is 4:30 pm—a little early for dinner. Hank gets his coat. Grace had not a chance to take hers off. They leave in the Sorento. Arrival is a mere 20 minutes.

Once inside, they are greeted by a hostess, who says "Follow me, please" and takes them to a booth. The lighting is romantic. Hank reaches into his pocket and gets out a bag. He hands it to Grace to open. She does so getting a small jewelry box, which she opens. Inside is a diamond ring. Grace says "Hank Thomas, you should not have done this. However, it is beautiful. And it fits. How did you know what size to get me?" "I got one of your rings and took it to the jewelers to size it," states Hank. Grace comes back "I thought I had lost that ring. It still has not shown up. What did you do with it?"

"I have it at work. I'll bring it home Monday. It will be safe. It's locked in my gun case, which has my gun in it and I need to bring it home and have the gun cleaned by Conrad. He does such a good job. I can get a spare from the department's inventory," discloses Hank. Just then, a waitress comes and states "I am Tuesday Wells. I will be your waitress tonight. What can I get you to drink?" "Two black coffees." Tuesday leaves. Hank looks at the menu and decides on Shrimp. Tuesday comes back with the coffee and asks "Are you ready to order?" Hank tells her he will have the Shrimp and a salad with ranch dressing. Grace, of course, tells Tuesday she wants a salad with French dressing on the side and the Lobster Lovers Dream.

It only takes 15 minutes for the orders to arrive. Hank had been talking about retirement. Wells notices the ring on Grace's hand and says "That ring is beautiful. I did not see it when you first came in. I will bet he gave it to you tonight." Grace merely replies "Yes, he did." They begin to eat their meals. Grace inquires "When do you think you will retire?" "I have been thinking next Friday and I have also been thinking of moving to Florida near Key West," replies Hank. Grace comes back "That will mean I will have to retire as well. Since they let you retire with 25 years of service, I can since I have 28 years" .They finish their meals and Hank leaves a hefty tip. He liked Tuesday Wells. They go to the register and pay for the bill.

They leave Red Lobster's parking lot, which was starting to get crowded. They go to the house, .go to the master bedroom and get undressed. Grace and Hank get in the hot whirlpool and Hank relates how good it feels to relax. They spend about an hour in the tub. They get out and each dries the other. Both put on under garments and robes. They go downstairs to the library to watch TV and wait to see if Conrad comes home. After two hours of watching TV, they retire for the evening.

CHAPTER 22

Baltimore To Fredericksburg

President Sylvester Redman is getting disturbed that his daughter has not been found. He calls FBI Director Charles Edwards directly. He wants information. Edwards answers. "Edwards, it has been almost two weeks and you do not have anything yet. I want a report of what is going on and where it is happening. Have I made myself clear?" "Yes, Mr. President." Edwards calls Senior Agent Ginger Ales to his office. "Ales, I want the satellite monitoring system moved to Fredericksburg, Virginia today no later than 6:00 o'clock pm. Have Duffy and Wong go with it as before. They have become something like experts on its workings" orders Edwards. Is that clear.

Ginger Ales says "Yes, sir. I am not sure they can make the 6:00 pm deadline, but we will try. My one big concern is that Duffy has not seen his family in over a week. I would like to give him a week off after Fredericksburg is up and running," offers Ales. Edwards directs "Get it done. Then, he can take off. You are excused." Ales leaves Charles' office in a somewhat desperate manner. She knew the Fredericksburg deal needed to be done by 6:00 pm. Baltimore has turned up nothing about the President's daughter for the time the monitoring system has been there and in use 24 hours a day.

Agent Ginger calls Ho Wong "Hello, Wong, this is Ales. We need the satellite monitoring system moved to Fredericksburg,

Virginia today by 6:00 pm. There are to be no excuses. Duffy and you are being reassigned to the Fredericksburg office for the time being. You are to report into that office as soon as you get there. One of their agents can get you squared away with the local police. We will need the same setup as is in Baltimore now.

Wong responds "We will get on it right away, but I don't know that we will make the 6:00 pm deadline. It's 12:00 noon now. Duffy went to lunch with the Chief of police. He should be back in 45 minutes. I can begin the dismantling, but we'll need a truck to put it on." "Rent one and charge it to us. I will write the voucher as soon as I am off the phone with you" orders Ginger Ales. The call ends and Ales writes the voucher putting it into her processing basket.

Wong calls Duffy on the cell phone and tells him Ales has called and given the order of moving the system to Fredericksburg by 6:00 pm. Jim says "I'll be right there. Get started on dismantling it. I'll tell the Chief it is being moved today." Duffy tells the Chief about the moving. The Chief says it will be a blessing to get his officers back and on duty.

Duffy arrives in 12 minutes to help Ho dismantles the system. Ho is getting a good start and now needs the help that Duffy can provide. The duo goes hard at it until the satellite monitoring system is completely disassembled. They now need a truck to haul it on. Wong asks the Chief what company will be best suited for their need. The Chief tells them to use Penske Rentals. He has used it before and told that it was really dependable.

Agent Wong puts in a call to the local Penske Rentals and asks how much is the cost of renting a five ton truck. He also asks will they take a government credit card. The latter response was 'yes' and the former was '$89.00 for one day'. Ho says he will be right there to get the truck. Wong asks Duffy to take him to Penske's to get the truck. Duffy complies with the request. They get the truck and return to Police Headquarters debriefing room.

The time is now for loading the monitoring system and satellite antenna. Duffy and Wong get officer Author Fuller to help them load the system onto the truck. Fuller was working because he is replacing Jane Collins, who is off. With the system loaded, Wong drives the truck, while Duffy drives their car. It takes two hours and a half to get to Fredericksburg from Baltimore.

Once in Fredericksburg, Virginia, Duffy drives to the FBI office and tells the story of the satellite monitoring system and its use. He also asks for an agent to accompany him to Police Headquarters where the system will be assembled and put to use. Agent Roy Williams volunteers. He has a thing for the Chief's secretary. Roy shows Wong and Duffy the way to Police Headquarters.

Upon arriving, Wong parks the truck at the back of the facility. Duffy parks the car he is driving in the front along with Williams. They wait for Wong to join them. The three go in together with Roy leading the way to the Chief's office. At the office, Roy says in a sexy way "Hello Charlotte. Is the Chief busy?" "No Roy, go right on in," answers Charlotte. Williams enters with "Good afternoon, Dave. I want you to meet two of my counterparts that have some work for you. Chief David Connors meet Jim Duffy and Ho Wong."

The Chief promptly asks "What kind of work do you have for me? Ho speaks "We have a satellite monitoring system that we want to install in your debriefing room or similar room. We will need four officers to learn to use the equipment. The purpose will be to look for a red Dodge Viper that belongs to Sylvia Redman, the President's daughter. There is to be no media leak of this search. She has been missing from the White House and the President and First Lady want to talk to her."

Chief Connors calls his secretary in "Charlotte, come in here. I have a job for you. Find me four officers, put their names on a list for me and have them report to me. I don't care which precinct you get them from, but try and make it one from each precinct until you have four. Be sure one of the officers is a corporal. I'll wait in the debriefing room. Do this now."

Charlotte goes to her filing cabinets and pulls a roster for four precincts. She makes a list of eight in case she did not get the first one of each precinct. She takes her list and calls the first precinct. A desk sergeant answers the telephone "Precinct one." "This is Charlotte, the Chief's secretary. I'm calling to see if Michael Pilson is working today. If he is, I will need to talk to a dispatcher."

"Let me have you talk to dispatch because he is working on patrol," says the sergeant. "This is dispatch." Charlotte identifies herself again and tells dispatch to call Michael Pilson. Dispatch does so. "Pilson here" Tell Pilson he is to report to the Chief's debriefing room at once" Charlotte tells dispatch. The dispatcher does so. Pilson answers "10-4." Charlotte does the exact same thing to precincts two, three, and four. She gets Miriam Lewis from two, Corporal Leroy Sharp from three and Clyde Bates from four. All report in to the debriefing room.

The Chief tells Ho "Here are your four officers. Corporal Sharp, you will be responsible for the schedule to be worked by the four of you. All of you will report to these two FBI agents until I say otherwise. Agent Duffy, they are yours to put to work." Duffy tells the four that they need to help bring in some equipment to the room. He also tells them he does not know how long they will work using the equipment.

The two agents and the four officers go to the back of the building and start to unload the equipment boxes. This is done until all the boxes are placed into the debriefing room. Ho says "Agent Duffy and I will assemble this satellite monitoring system. It is used to see the traffic on the street. You can also see people, but not enough to identify them. We will instruct you after we get the equipment working." Jim and Ho get at assembling the unit.

Once the monitor is turned on and begins working, Ho sits down at the console. He focuses the system to get a look at downtown Fredericksburg. He does this without instruction. Ho focuses on a red car. Then, says "This is what you will be looking for. You will find a red car in traffic and then zoom in like this. You will be looking specifically for a red Dodge Viper. As you can see, this car is not a Dodge at all. It is a Ford. The systems focal point can be moved left to right, up and down and anywhere in between. The scroll ball makes that possible. All you need do is use a map of the city and county to observe every street looking for a red Viper. The monitoring system needs to be done every hour because the traffic changes. Cars come from Richmond and D.C. and other areas. Once you see a red Viper, you, acting as dispatch 2, will tell the nearest squad car to investigate and check the license. If it isn't D.C., then it's of no concern. We are only interested in D.C. licensed Vipers. Upon stopping a vehicle of this manner, the officer will check the driver's license. We are only interested in Sylvia Redman."

Ho gets interrupted "That's the President's daughter's name," says Corporal Sharp. "That's who we are looking for. She has been missing from the White House since her birthday. She is 21, so she can do as she pleases except for breaking the law. She is not to be arrested unless breaking the law. She is to be instructed to call her father or mother. The officer will insure that she does. Sylvia is a red head, 5'4", 110 pound woman. There have been reports she was in D.C. and Baltimore, but they all panned out. That is why we are here," instructs Ho Wong.

Duffy asks "Are there any questions about what we are doing?" Pilson raises his hand and asks "If we are on a red car and it's our time to change operators, do we do that or do we finish the contact?" "Finish the stop. Then, change shifts," tells Duffy and continues "Pilson, you be first at the controls. Let's see how good you are. Sit and use the scrolling ball to move the focal point. When you find a red car, zoom in to see what make it is." Pilson sits and gets use to the controls. It takes a while to find a red car. Red cars are not that well liked. When he does see one, he zooms the control as he is supposed to do. He sees it is a Chevrolet. He zooms back out and continues to look until Duffy says "That's enough for you. Miriam, you give it a try. Pick up where Pilson left off."

Miriam sits and takes a bit of time to get use to the controls, but she manages before Duffy or Wong says anything. She looks for about 7 minutes and spots another red car. Zooming in, she sees that it is a Dodge, but not a Viper. She asks "What if I find a Dodge Viper? How am I going to get a squad car to check it out? Are we dispatch 2 or not?" "Good questions," says Wong, "Chief, we need radio dispatch equipment to set up a dispatch 2 unit and tell the present dispatch to start using the identifier Dispatch 1. Can we get that equipment right away?" "Charlotte, get Bronson up here now." Charlotte contacts Bronson and informs him that the Chief wants a dispatch facility placed into the debriefing room. He tells her it will be half an hour before he can get to it, but she tells him that "The Chief wants it done NOW".

Bronson gathers the necessary equipment and gets a helper to carry some of the equipment. The two carry the things to the debriefing room and begin installing the radio equipment. Finally, they are done. Bronson and the helper leave. Miriam continues her search. It is a while before she finds another red car. It turns out to be a Dodge Viper. She has Clyde Bates to be dispatch and get a squad car on it. Bates does it and a squad car pulls over the Dodge Viper. The patrol officer asks "What next?" Bates asks "Does it have a D.C. license plate?" "No." "Then, let the car go after you check the expiration date on the driver's license."

"Good use of manpower there Bates. I haven't thought to do that as a part of the procedure," says Wong. "Being a patrol officer, I know what we should do when we stop a vehicle," informs Bates. Wong instructs "Bates, you used dispatch quite well. Take your turn at the controls. Remember, you're also the dispatcher." Bates expands the area moving away from downtown Fredericksburg and he takes in I-95. His opportunity for a red car increases. To be on the safe side, Bates dispatches a squad car to an intersection with I-95 just in case there is a need. The traffic on I-95 often will go 80 mph. Ho states "Another good idea Bates. You are setting yourself up for a rush hour shift." Bates continues his search, but does not see another red car.

After a while, Wong has Corporal Sharp take the controls. He is given a chance to expand his search area keeping I-95 in view. Duffy sees it is already 6:05 pm and he hasn't called Ales. He leaves the room and goes to call her. "Hello. This is Senior Agent Ginger Ales." "Ales, this is Duffy. We have the system up and running. We are in the process of looking for red Dodge Vipers. One red Viper has already been stopped. The last officer is at the controls now. There is one really sharp officer who came up with two ideas I would never have thought of. We will stay with them on the split shift we had in Baltimore.

After Sharp gets up from the system, he says "I was put in charge of scheduling. Bates, you take the 3:00 pm to 11:00 pm. Lewis, you will take the 11:00 pm to 7:00 am. I will take the 7:00 to 3:00 pm. Pilson you will be the relief person. I'll work on off days later. Bates gets back on the system. He expands his search area even further, but still keeping a portion of I-95 in the scope area. Ho tells Duffy he is leaving for the motel. Duffy remains with the crew.

CHAPTER 23

The New House

It is Sunday, day 15. Conrad is the first up and takes his shower, dresses, and goes into the kitchen. Rosalyn gets at it again fixing breakfast after she has her shower and gets dressed. Sylvia is last to shower and dress. The three sit down and eat. Sylvia suggests they go to church. Rosalyn asks "Where would we go and what denomination would it be?" "We could go to the Methodist Church where we got married," invites Sylvia. Conrad says "Let's make it another Sunday. I just don't feel up to it." "Okay."

Conrad says "We have plenty of things to do here at the house. We don't even need to go anyplace. Besides, there are some things we need to take to the barn. If we work together, it shouldn't take us very long. I want some of the pictures off the walls and I want to move the two mattresses from the two smaller bedrooms to the barn. We can get the master bedroom's mattress and Rosalyn's on Monday. Then, there is dusting everything and mowing the grass. Sylvia interrupts "We do not have a lawn mower. Conrad continues "Yes, we do. There is one in the barn. I saw it when I went out there on a hunch that there might be something to do with the barn. And I got an idea. There's more on that later this week."

Rosalyn states "You tell us what pictures and we will take them down." "Well, let us begin in the living room. There are eight pictures on these walls. I want it down to two on the west wall and two on the south wall. The other four go to the barn. In the master bedroom, the one picture in there has to go. In Rosalyn's bedroom, she can decide on it. In the next to last bedroom, the one picture in there needs to go. And the last bedroom needs the one there to be taken down as well." instructs Sylvia. Rosalyn decides to keep her picture. It has butterflies on it and she likes butterflies. The girls get busy taking down the pictures and taking the lot to the barn.

Conrad tells Rosalyn "We need dusting in every room. Sylvia and you can handle that and handle the two mattresses. I'll get the lawn mower and see if it has gas to mow the full lawn. If not, I'll have to go get some gas. I saw there is a tank in the barn, but it is empty." Conrad goes to the barn. The gas tank on the mower is empty as well as the gas can. He decides to go get some gas at the local convenience store. It is a short drive of only three miles. Taking the gas tank, he goes and gets five gallons thinking that should be enough.

Back to the barn, Conrad pours the gas into the mower's gas tank. He tries to start the mower, but it will not crank at all. Conrad is no mechanic, but he figures there is something wrong with the battery. He checks that and one of the cables is unhooked. He reconnects the line and the lawn mower starts okay. He drives it out of the barn and engages the cutting blades. It was a 42' cut, Troy-Built. He continues mowing until done. While mowing, he sees Rosalyn and Sylvia carrying the mattresses to the barn. He drives the mower back into the barn and parks it in its own special place.

Sylvia approaches him and states "We have got everything done that you listed a while ago. It is lunch time and I want Mexican food. So does Rosalyn. Let us go to Mi Hacienda. We have not been there in over a week." Conrad agrees to the going to Mi Hacienda for the food. So they change from their work clothes into Sunday type clothes except Conrad. He goes casual. They take the two cars and Rosalyn goes with Conrad. She tells him "Since we are sleeping together tonight, Sylvia and I will take you on at the same time." Conrad asks "What about my desires? Don't I have a say?" "Yes, you do, but only after the two of us have our desire."

Shortly, the three arrive at Mi Hacienda for the Mexican food. Ready to eat, they go inside one after the other with Conrad last to enter. Owner Jose' Emanez greets the group and sends them to a table for four. Juanita comes for their drink order "What will you have to drink?" Conrad answers "A Pepsi for me and Diet Pepsis for Rosalyn and my wife." That last word caught a hard hearted chord in Juanita. She demands to know "When did you marry HER? And why did you marry her?"

Conrad responds with "We were married Friday and I married her because she wants to have my baby. That is something you never wanted. You wanted our relationship to be you and me only. I couldn't take that. So I married Sylvia, who I can expect that and more." Juanita leaves mad as a wet hen. She gets the drinks and sets all three right in the center of the table so everyone would have the same reach. This included Conrad. Juanita, then, asks "What will you have to eat?" Conrad orders for all three of them. Juanita writes it down and leaves.

Conrad tells Rosalyn "Juanita has had a thing for me for some time. I have not been interested in her, but it hasn't mattered. I'm wondering how she will mess with our orders." "She messed with mine the last time we were here," says Sylvia. Juanita does return with their food as ordered. There has been no hanky-panky with the food. Conrad is amazed. Juanita states "You will find your food exactly as ordered." The three eat and Conrad leaves a $5.00 tip when they get up to leave. Rosalyn says "Why did you leave that big of a tip? She wasn't all that friendly." Conrad just tells her that is his normal tip. Conrad pays the bill as they leave giving the exact amount. Rosalyn finds that odd too and tells Conrad she is perplexed at why he did that. He tells her the same as he had told Sylvia when last they were there.

The trio returns to the house and Sylvia says "I just thought of something. We do not have enough linen for all four rooms. We will need to do that today or tomorrow." "You and I will go get linens while Rosalyn does whatever she wants," responds Conrad "She could go through the pantry and make a shopping list of what we need. She could also check her clothes for need such as underwear, socks, or maybe shoes. She has only one pair." "I'll look at my clothes and shoes," says Rosalyn."Well, we better get going Conrad," commands Sylvia.

The two take the red Dodge Viper and go to House of Bedding. Conrad parks and they go in. Before them are vast colors of linens. Sylvia has made up her mind to get some different colors. She did not want white even though there was a wide selection of whites. She gets three greens, three blues, three beige and three reds. They check out and the total comes to $86.75. They, then, head back to the house. On the way, Conrad decides he wants a Big Mac from McDonald's. Sylvia decides on a Big and Tasty. He goes through the Drive Thru and pays $11.59. They finish the drive to the house.

Rosalyn is busy entertaining the next door neighbor, Bonnie Jean Peterson. They have been talking about her husband's life. Rosalyn has been telling her of her father's jail time and her rich mother.

Conrad enters the house and sees what is transpiring. He asks "How has your day gone so far?" Rosalyn replies "We have been talking and Bonnie Jean mentioned that she thought you were quite handsome and how lonely she is. She would like to come and have dinner with us tonight."

Sylvia inputs "She is entirely welcome to come and have dinner with us. Have you decided on what is for dinner?" 'I think spaghetti will be fine for the four of us." Conrad states "I'm interested in Bonnie Jean and how she is making enough income to pay all her bills and living expenses. She will need to share that with Sylvia and I."

Rosalyn explains "I have gone through my clothes and decided all I need are some socks and a pair of shoes. I don't need these today. I see you got the bed linens. Which are mine? I like the red best of all." Sylvia tells her she gets one of each color. Rosalyn is elated at getting new linens. She never had that in her apartment with her dad. Rosalyn counts her blessings. When she wanted to be friends with Sylvia and Conrad, she had no idea it would lead to this.

Bonnie Jean decides it is time for her to leave. She gets up and says "I am looking forward to having dinner with you. Just give me a call and I will come straight over." Bonnie Jean leaves. Rosalyn explains "We had a good time talking. She came over shortly after you left. She gave me her phone number in case I should need something. Bonnie Jean is only 26 years old. Her husband was 30 when he was killed in the accident."

Sylvia asks "Have you fully decided on what you need Rosalyn? We best take you to get the items before it gets too late. We can go to Wal-mart. It is not that far to it." Conrad says "You two go without me. I'm going to do some checking of the barn." Conrad has it in his mind to get some chicks and build a yard for them with a roost inside the barn. He needs to do some measuring to determine how much lumber and wire he will need.

The girls go to Wal-mart for the items Rosalyn needs. They first go to get socks. Rosalyn gets a pack of six. The girls, then, go to the shoe department. Rosalyn tries on four pair before she decides on a pair of Nike. Rosalyn and Sylvia look some more in Wal-mart since they had the time to do so.

Sylvia chooses to get a camera. She cannot ever remember whether or not that she had one. Sylvia gets a clerk to explain the differences after arriving at the display. She looks at all the digitals. The clerk shows her a Cannon that has caught her eye. It has the LCD screen on the back that shows you what you aim the camera at before taking the picture. It also has a limited zoom lens. Sylvia becomes so infatuated she tells the clerk she wants it. The clerk gets her the Cannon. Sylvia pays $649.00 plus taxes for it with her VISA credit card that Conrad had set up for her.

The pair next goes to purses. Since Sylvia had lost hers, she does not have one. She sees there are many styles. She has seen many women with different styles and it made her choice even harder to make. Finally, she decides on a black with white trim. It is not too large or too small. Rosalyn points out the fact they need spaghetti noodles for dinner. They go to the grocery aisles and see a placard that says noodles. The pair goes down that aisle and gets the noodles. Sylvia determines the time in Wal-mart has been enough for now. They check out and head to the house.

Meanwhile, Conrad is in the barn. He measures off an area for the roost and determines he needs 64 feet of wire inside plus 16 2x4 lumbers for the frame. He goes out of the barn and on to the west side of the barn to measure off the scratch area for the chicks. He decides on a 24' by 24' square. He determines he needs 72 feet of chicken wire, four 2' x 4' boards and 12 posts. He will also need to get a posthole digger, gate hinges, a gate latch and 'u' shaped nails to attach the wire to the posts.

Rosalyn and Sylvia see Conrad in the pasture next to the barn doing his measuring. Sylvia asks "What do you think you are doing in this portion of the pasture? "I'm measuring for a scratch yard for some chicks. I'm thinking 15 chicks will be plenty. I can get them Monday or Tuesday. It will probably be Tuesday, since I need to build a roost and scratch yard. I'll start on that Monday afternoon. I've got to watch my time. It is getting short. I only have a week before I start work again."

Sylvia responds ""If you get 15 chicks, I want a dog and a horse." "Okay Dear. You pick the dog and we will pick the horse together," relates Conrad.

Rosalyn fixes dinner. She prepares spaghetti and a salad. Rosalyn calls Bonnie Jean to come for dinner. The four sit down to eat. After the meal, Bonnie Jean leaves and Rosalyn, Sylvia and Conrad go to bed. It has been a long day.

CHAPTER 24

Monday, Day 16

Grace and Hank get up. They shower, dress and go downstairs for breakfast. Grace fixes eggs over medium, sausage and coffee. She also gets out two glasses for orange juice. When the food is done, Grace and Hank eat discussing retirement. Hank has enough time for a full retirement benefits program. However, Grace has only 28 years—two years shy of a full retirement. Both decide to retire and move to Key Largo, Florida. They will sell their house.

Hank goes into work and tells his captain that he wants to retire. The captain has him go to the Administration Department. Once there, Hank must fill out some papers. He does this and is told his retirement will be effective tomorrow. He leaves and goes to find George Harris, his friend. Finding George, Hank fills him in on his own retirement. George asks "What prompted you to come in and seek retirement? I know you've got enough years, but why today?"

Hank tells him "Grace and I were discussing it at breakfast and we both decided we would retire. We plan to sell the house and move to Key Largo. We spent a little time on the Internet and found a web site dealing with Key Largo. Did you know Key Largo has 50 restaurants and one of the best places to stay is the Holiday Inn Motel? I plan to go down and talk to a realtor after I put our house on the market."

Meanwhile, Grace knows where to go to file for retirement. She knows she will lose a part of her retirement due to leaving before 30 years, but it will only be 4% less. She goes to Administration and tells them of her desire to retire. Grace is given some papers to fill out. She is told her retirement will be effective next Monday. She goes to teach her classes for the day.

Rosalyn, Sylvia and Conrad get up and shower, then, dress. Sylvia is off this day and is looking forward to spending it with Conrad. Rosalyn has her own plan for the day with Conrad. The three have breakfast of cereal and muffins. Afterwards, Rosalyn cleans up the kitchen. Conrad tells Sylvia and Rosalyn that he plans to work on the chicks' yard and roost. This is not how Sylvia wants to spend her day, however, it is what Rosalyn wants.

Conrad asks Sylvia "Do you want to ride with me to get my dad's truck? I'm going to the police station to get it. I just called dad and he told me it was okay. Can you guess what else he told me?" "He is taking today off?" "No. He is retiring today. It will be effective tomorrow."

Sylvia inquires "Will we be able to see him?" "I think so." "Well, let us go and see your dad." The day is looking brighter already for Sylvia. She will spend some time alone with Conrad. Rosalyn would stay to work around the house. She would also be there when and if the two installation men show up and the furniture delivery takes place. Rosalyn asks "What if the installation men show up? Where do you want the wires and connectors?" Conrad says "In the family room for both. Have them connect up to the TV I bought and to the computers."

Sylvia and Conrad leave for the police station. After a 15 minute drive, they arrive. Both go inside to the sergeant's desk and ask for Lieutenant Thomas. The sergeant calls Hank and tells him his son is waiting to see him. Hank arrives shortly.

"Dad, how's it going today? I'll bet they are keeping you busy," states Conrad. Hank says "Not really. I have been reviewing some open case files and making notes on how to progress with the case as I read each one. How's your day been going?" "Well, I haven't really done anything yet. I'm in the planning process of building a chicken coop and making a scratch yard. That's why I need your truck. I've got to go get the lumber and fencing" gives Conrad.

"Here, take the key and you can bring it to the house later tonight. Where is your car parked?" states Hank. Conrad tells his dad it is parked out front. Conrad says "Have a good last day, Dad." "I'll try."

Conrad leads Sylvia to his dad's truck. They get in and Conrad starts the vehicle. It is another 15 minute drive to the new house. Conrad drops off Sylvia to look for a dog and a horse while he goes to the farm supply place he read about in the newspaper. It is in Goochland about 45 miles away. It takes him 50 minutes to get to Goochland and find the store. Once there, he tells the clerk he wants 21 2 x 4 x 8', 72 feet of chicken wire, gate latch with hinges, 12 posts and a pothole digger. In addition, he wants 15 chicks. The salesman says "You are in luck. Our chicks are on sale this week. You will save $7.50 on the chicks."

The clerk begins by getting the lumber, then, the chicken wire, posts, staples, gate hardware and finally, he gets the 15 chicks. He totals the bill and it comes to $237.62. Conrad pays with his Master Card. The clerk helps load the equipment and chicks. Conrad drives back to the farm. He first unloads the chicks and sets them aside, then, he gets the lumber off, posts, posthole digger, and gate hardware with the staples. He feels the scratch yard should be first. Conrad gets Rosalyn to help. He first digs the post holes while Rosalyn measures the length between the posts. After anchoring the posts with Quickcrete, he gets the chicken wire and staples. He spreads the wire and Rosalyn begins to staple.

The duo stretches the wire and staples it to the last post. Conrad gets the lumber for the gate and makes a gate by cutting the boards as necessary. After nailing the gate hardware, Rosalyn and he put on the chicken wire. Finally the gate hardware is placed on the gate and the gate is hung. Conrad gets the chicks and sets them free. The chicks begin to wander the yard.

Rosalyn and Conrad go into the barn and measure off the first wall. Conrad gets the lumber and Rosalyn holds for Conrad as he nails the first wall together. Then, he nails the second wall to the second and third corners. Finally, he nails the last wall to the third and final corner. Next is the chicken wire over the walls and a gate he had made for access to the eggs once the chicks grow into chickens and begin laying eggs.

The last thing to have a door is to cut a doorway into the barn from the scratch yard. He shows each of the chicks how to use the passage way.

Meanwhile, Sylvia has been searching for a Newfoundland shepherd. She finds a breeder at Brookstore Newfoundlanders in Chesterfield, Virginia. She goes there and sees just the dog she wants. The breeder says the name is Bella; a solid black newfoundland. Bella is full grown and trained. Sylvia asks "Can the dog be trained further? I want it to be somewhat of a guard dog." "Yes. By all means, Bella can be trained in about 15 minutes. He is very easy to train of all dogs," comments the breeder.

"I want to buy him. Here is my credit card. Can I change his name?" mentions Sylvia. "Yes, but his name for the AKC will have to be Bella. What nickname will you give him?" asks the breeder. "Bear because he looks like one." "That seems like a good nickname for him. It will take about a day for him to recognize the new name," tells the breeder. Having paid for 'Bear', Sylvia loads the dog and heads to the house. She is anxious to show off the dog.

She calls Conrad "You need to build a dog pin. I have the dog with me. I named him 'Bear'." Conrad begins as instructed by Sylvia. He has some left over fence and lumber. It takes him about half an hour—the amount of time Sylvia needs to get to the farm. Rosalyn helps Conrad and asks "When can we do it again? I'm getting horny. I need you." "We'll see," is all Conrad can answer.

Sylvia arrives with Bear and he is placed in the dog kennel as Conrad calls it. Bear at once takes an interest in Conrad. Conrad notices it and thinks about taking Bear for a walk later. He will need a strong leash. Sylvia mentions the need for a leash. Rosalyn mentions "What are we going to feed him? Will it be bought dog food or table scraps? I could cook an extra helping of meat for the dog," "Table scraps for now seems to be our only choice until I can get out and find what feed to get him," says Conrad.

At that time, the Hughes installation man arrives. Conrad goes to show him where he wants the dish established on a pole. The installer gets the pole out of his truck. He digs a hole for the post and anchors it with Quickcrete. He, then, attaches the dish, gets out his meter and aligns the dish. Next, he runs the cable into the library where Conrad wants it connected to his computer via a modem. The installer gets it done and tells Conrad it will be $650.00 for the dish and modem. Sylvia is pleased for she now has her own computer to search the web. Conrad pays the man.

Rosalyn tells Sylvia of her need for Conrad. Sylvia says for her "Take it up with Conrad. If it be your choice, so be it if Conrad agrees." Rosalyn, once more, approaches Conrad with her desire. Conrad says "We can do it now.

The two go into Rosalyn's bedroom and undress. It is easier for Rosalyn because she was not wearing underwear—a trick Sylvia taught her for freedom to do as she chooses. The two get into the bed and go at it for about 15 minutes. Afterwards, they dress just as the furniture arrives. Sylvia shows the men where everything goes as they unload. The new mattresses are installed and the old Master bed mattress is put on the truck to be hauled away. Sylvia thanks the men.

Next, the Dish Network installer arrives. Conrad goes to show him where to put the satellite dish next to the Hughes

Dish. The man does as the Hughes installer had done. He digs a hole and anchors the post with Quickcrete. He attaches the dish and aligns it with his meter. It is different than the Hughes dish. Next, he connects the wires to the dish and begins to run it to the house. Conrad shows where to enter the house and the installer bores a hole the same as the Hughes man. He connects it to the receiver box and that to the TV.

The Dish Network man says the installation is included with the first month's bill. Rosalyn, Sylvia and Conrad are satisfied with the installation. Now, they can watch TV at night when not doing something else. Rosalyn turns the set on to see the HD for a program. She likes it and decides to watch the soap operas during the day.

Sylvia thanks the man and he leaves three satisfied customers. The group decides to watch a western on the Encore network's programs. It runs until dinner time. Rosalyn gets into the kitchen and prepares four pork chops, mashed potatoes and green beans. She also gets out one Pepsi and two Diet Pepsis. After dinner, Rosalyn and Conrad go to watch TV. Sylvia gets on the computer and the Internet.

Rosalyn and Conrad watch a movie on the Lifetime Movie Network. It is a premier showing of the movie. Sylvia surf's the Internet again looking for lost adults, but finds nothing other than what she has already seen. So, she chooses to view blogs. It proves interesting, but that is about all. Finally, she looks up Key Largo because that is where Hank says Grace and him would move to. She finds that real interesting and spends time reading about living there and tourism. It takes her up to bedtime. Rosalyn and Conrad have finished watching the movie. So, all retire for the night.

CHAPTER 25

First Retirement Day for Hank

It is Tuesday, day 17. Grace and Hank arise. Hank talks with Grace about selling the house and moving to Key Largo in Florida. He tells her he will work on packaging up miscellaneous items such as pictures, what knots and memorabilia. She tells him that would be fine and that he should start upstairs as to leave the downstairs presentable to any guests. Grace is expecting some work now that Hank is in retirement.

Grace gets ready, grabs her coat and leaves for work after kissing Hank. Hank rounds up boxes and goes upstairs. He, then, remembers he still has Conrad's Viper. He makes up his mind to get the GMC back from Conrad. He calls Conrad "Son, I need to get my truck back. And you need your car. You are finished with my truck, aren't you?"

Conrad tells his dad that he is indeed finished with the truck. He asks who should do the driving? Hank says to Conrad he will come to their house so he could see the layout of the house. Hank drives the Dodge Viper to Conrad's house. He finds it easily. Once there, he goes in to find Conrad at the TV. Rosalyn and Sylvia are fixing breakfast. Sylvia asks Hank if he would like to join them. He says he would like a cup of coffee which Sylvia makes for him.

Rosalyn and Sylvia finish the eggs, bacon and toast. Rosalyn calls the men in for the breakfast. Rosalyn chooses to sit between

Conrad and his dad. Sylvia sits opposite. Hank says "It really feels different to be retired. Today seems like it is Saturday. I wonder what I'm going to do with my time." Conrad tells his dad "Take up fishing or remodeling an old car, like a '56 Chevy. There are lots you can do if you put your mind to it. How about learning to play a musical instrument?"

Hank, drinking his coffee, says "I could take up salt water fishing from the shore. We want a shore front piece of property with a house already on it." Conrad points out "That sounds like a good idea. When you want to stop after looking just go in the house. I'm sure there is somebody who can teach you to fish like that. Maybe you'll catch a Blue Marlin."

Rosalyn states to Conrad "You can't catch a Blue Marlin from the shore. The water would be too shallow. Besides, your dad doesn't have a boat." "That doesn't mean he can't rent or buy one."

Sylvia jumps in with "Are you guys finished with breakfast? We need to clean up the kitchen. You can take your drinks into the living room." The guys get up and go. The gals get busy on the kitchen. Rosalyn and Sylvia clean fast and are done in 15 minutes. They join the boys. Hank and Conrad were talking sports. Sylvia joins in while Rosalyn just listens.

Sylvia brought up the fact that Billie Jean King had played softball in her youth as well as tennis. The men were surprised that Sylvia knew that. Was her mind coming back? The men turned their attention to the Atlanta Braves. Sylvia butts in with "I know Jason Heyward and Martin Prado. Again, the guys are amazed. She seems to be full of baseball info.

Sylvia says it is time for her to go to work at the library. Hank says it is time for him to get to his house and do some more packing. Conrad asks "When do you think mom and you will move?" "Only after we find a home in Key Largo, then, we will move" responds Hank. Sylvia leaves for work after getting her coat, hat and gloves. Hank says goodbye and leaves for his house in his GMC. Conrad and Rosalyn go to her bedroom and get at it. It lasts 30 minutes this time.

After getting dressed, Conrad asks Rosalyn if she would like to go with him to buy a horse. She says yes she would. That, however, leaves Sylvia out of the picking of the horse as she had wanted to do. Conrad drives to Brandywine Farm in Chesterfield, Virginia taking about 45 minutes to get there. Conrad tells the breeder he wants a riding horse and asks what they have for sale. The breeder tells him they will need to go to the stables. After looking over several horses, Conrad sees a golden Palomino that has caught his eyes. He tells the breeder he wants that one. The breeder says "The horse sells for $8,000.00 not including tack. We rent horse trailers for you to take the horse to your farm. You do have a farm with pasture?" "We have 28 acres some of which is pastures and some wooded," answers Conrad. "That's fine." "When can I pick up the horse?" "As soon as it is paid for."

"I'll need to get my dad's truck here to hook the trailer up. Let me call him. Okay?" Conrad calls his Dad "Dad, I need your truck again. Can you drive to Brandywine Farm in Chesterfield? Take route 288 and it will get you here. Call me when you get close and I'll give you directions." "Okay, son."

Hank stops the packing and gets in his truck to go to the farm in Chesterfield. He takes route 288 to Chesterfield and gives Conrad a call. Conrad tells him the directions to the farm and Hank continues on. Arriving, Hank finds he must pull a horse trailer with his truck. He realizes that it should be no problem for his GMC. Conrad signs the contract and has 30 days to pay for the horse. He pays for the trailer which rents for $25.00 an hour or $100.00 for a day. He uses his credit card for a one day rental. Rosalyn has been quiet because she has not known what to say in this venture of buying a horse.

Conrad and Hank get the trailer hooked to the truck. The breeder brings the horse and loads it onto the trailer. Rosalyn, Conrad, and Hank are ready to roll. Conrad asks Rosalyn "What should I name the horse?" "Goldie." Conrad agrees with Rosalyn as to the name for the horse. The GMC truck and Viper arrive at the farm belonging to Conrad and Sylvia. Hank and Conrad get the horse to the pasture. Conrad tells him the horse's name that Rosalyn came up with. Hank agrees it is a good name for a golden Palomino.

Hank asks his son is there any other need for the truck and Conrad says just to take the trailer back. The rental time had already been three hours and it is a 45 minute drive. Hank draws the trailer and leaves. Bear raises a fuss over the horse and Conrad goes to calm the dog down. Bear accepts Conrad's petting as most dogs normally do.

Rosalyn walks to Conrad and gives him a passionate kiss. Conrad knows where Rosalyn would like to go, but tells her not right now. He asks Rosalyn "Do you want to go with me to have lunch with Sylvia? You can tell her about the name." "Yes, I do want to go." They get in the Dodge and drive to the library getting there just as Sylvia is going to lunch.

Sylvia asks Conrad where they should go and Conrad tells her they can go to the Sino American Chinese restaurant. It was not that far away. Sylvia knows she must take her car because Conrad would go home as soon as her lunch time is over. The three get to the restaurant and go in. They are given a table by a hostess who asks what drinks they will have. The girls both get a Diet Pepsi and Conrad gets a regular Pepsi.

They go to the enormous buffet and see all kinds of food—American and Chinese. Each of them loads up a plate and returns to the table where they find their drinks has been delivered. Rosalyn says "This is the first time for me ever being in a place like this except for when I went with you." Sylvia states "You have nothing over me. This is my first time to a Chinese restaurant." Conrad notes Sylvia's statement and tells them he has been here before.

Rosalyn, Sylvia and Conrad finish eating their selections and each goes back for more. Again, they fill their plates because things were so good the first time. After finishing their plates again, Sylvia and Conrad cannot eat any more. Rosalyn, however, decides to get some dessert and ice cream. She goes and returns with another plate full.

The time comes for Sylvia to return to work. She leaves Rosalyn and Conrad because Rosalyn is still eating. When Rosalyn gets done, the duo is ready to leave and pay the bill. The waitress brings the bill and they get up to leave. Conrad sees a friend of his and goes to say hello. The friend recognizes the presence of Conrad and introduces his wife. The friend says "I heard you got married. Is this your Mrs.?" "No. This is our housekeeper. I just had lunch with her and my wife who had to return to work.

They talk just a bit more and Conrad says his goodbye. Rosalyn comments "Why did you say I was your housekeeper?" Conrad comes back "Because, in a way, you're our housekeeper. I can't introduce you as my sex partner, my mistress or my wife. People know I'm married to Sylvia." "How long do you plan to keep calling me your housekeeper?" queries Rosalyn. Conrad responds "I don't know. Probably, for some time to come, I will keep it up."

Conrad pays the bill being the only one in line. They get out of the restaurant rather quickly. Rosalyn asks Conrad "When can I get off the contraceptives and have your baby?" "We can do that after Sylvia is pregnant which I hope will be soon." They leave for the farm.

Having eaten, Conrad feels it is time to feed Bear. He gets some scraps and goes to the dog. Bear is happy to see Conrad and jumps all over him. Conrad thinks it is time to teach Bear not to do that to the family members. It takes 15 minutes and Bear has it down. After Bear finishes eating, Conrad takes Bear for a walk around the yard and down the street to the east.

Next door neighbor Bonnie Jean comes out and talks to Conrad about how life is going in their new house. Conrad relates to her that everything is going fine. She asks Conrad to come into her house to see what it looks like on the inside. Conrad says he will as soon as he gets though walking Bear. Conrad walks the dog for 20 minutes and returns Bear to his pin.

Conrad goes over to Bonnie Jean's house. She invites him in. She shows him the living room, dining room, kitchen and one bedroom which is not the master bedroom. Getting there, Bonnie Jean says "This is where I sleep alone. I long for someone to share it with me if only for 15 minutes Do you understand what I am talking about?" "Yes, I do. But I'm not your man. I have Sylvia and she gives me plenty every day," replies Conrad. Bonnie Jean says enticingly "I will give it to you anyway you want. I am desperate. Look, I will take off my clothes and show you my body. It is yours and you do not have to ask."

Conrad stood and watched. Her body, to him, was something to see. Yet, he had made up his mind he would not give in to the urge Bonnie Jean was placing on him. Conrad turns to walk away and she grabs his arm to say "Look. Look at me. I am here for you. You are the first man to see my body since my husband died. Do you want me or not?" "No, Bonnie Jean. You are very enticing, but I can't let myself be so enticed. As I have said, I have Sylvia every night." "What about her period? You can't have her then. Do you get it from your housekeeper? Why not get it from me? I want you in a very bad way" brings forth Bonnie Jean.

Conrad takes her hand off his arm and leaves. He goes to the house and tells Rosalyn. This entices her to ask for Conrad to take her to bed, but Conrad tells her not now once more. It is getting close to the time for Sylvia to come home, so Rosalyn begins to fix dinner. Tonight will be pork sirloin with mashed potatoes and corn on the cob. There will also be some chocolate ice cream for dessert.

Rosalyn finishes the fixing of the meal just as Sylvia arrives. She talks about how she had gone to lunch with Rosalyn and Conrad telling them she had told Witten, the head librarian. Witten had thought it was a nice event and asked could she go the next time. Sylvia had told her yes. The three sit at the table and begin to eat their meal. Sylvia tells Rosalyn "The pork sirloin is extremely tasty. It tastes as if you did something to it." Rosalyn replies "I did put some sage on it as it was cooking. It does taste well."

Conrad finishes his meal and relates "Rosalyn, you have done an excellent job with dinner. I'm ready for dessert. What have you got?" "We have Butter Pecan and chocolate ice cream." "Well, I'll have some right now. I want two scoops of the Butter Pecan and get the chocolate syrup," begs Conrad. Sylvia finishes and asks the same thing. Rosalyn gets the three of them two scoops each. She also brings the chocolate syrup that Conrad has asked for.

Rosalyn, Sylvia and Conrad talk about the dinner and the dessert. Sylvia and Conrad mention how well the dinner turned out and that the corn with mashed potatoes were an added treat. The three finish their ice cream.

Sylvia states "As a treat, I will cleanup. Just leave everything where it is and I will take care of it. There was one sirloin left to go to Bear. The corn and mashed potatoes were finished off. There was nothing to put away. The dishes go in the dishwasher and Sylvia joins Rosalyn and Conrad in the family room. The two were watching an Encore western.

Conrad says "Now that you have finished in the kitchen, let's go out to the barn. I want to show you something before it gets totally dark." Sylvia and Conrad go outside and Conrad shows her the horse. "Rosalyn picked the name of Goldie. What do you think of the horse?" "I think it is a good pick of both the horse and the name. However, I was suppose to go with you to get the horse and maybe name it as well. When can we ride it?" "After tomorrow. I have to buy the tack for the horse. That is going to run about $350.00. I must get a bridle, a blanket and a saddle."

The two go back to the family room. Conrad sits back down to watch the western getting updated by Rosalyn. Sylvia goes to the computer to surf the web. She finds one thing interesting. There was a comment that the President's daughter had not been at school for two weeks and no one knew why. She tries to join the discussion, but it is for naught. So, she reads what is being discussed. They say her car had not been seen either. Sylvia gets a shiver over her body. But, she does not know why.

Conrad asks "Are you finding anything interesting?" wanting to know about her experience tonight. Sylvia responds "The President's daughter has not been to school in two weeks. Is that not interesting? Here I have been for over two weeks. If it had been the same time, I would think I was the President's daughter."

Conrad retaliates with "You know you're not the President's daughter. You're my wife. Let it go at that." Sylvia complies knowing something is not right. She quits the computer and goes to watching TV with the other two. They have an enjoyable time due to Rosalyn going and popping some popcorn.

After watching the western that came on at 8:00 pm, the trio goes to bed. Rosalyn, instead of going to her bedroom, goes into the master bedroom behind Sylvia and Conrad. She reminds Conrad of what he said earlier about 'not now'. Conrad satisfies both women and they all sleep together.

CHAPTER 26

The House in Key Largo

It is now Wednesday, day 18. Grace and Hank arise early. They come down for Grace to fix breakfast. It is merely scrambled eggs and bacon. Hank tells Grace he has finished the packing of the upstairs and some of the downstairs. Grace is well pleased with his efforts. She even gives him a kiss. They finish their breakfast and Grace does the cleaning of the kitchen as usual.

After breakfast, Hank tells her he is flying to Key Largo to check on some housing. He also tells her he should be back by dinner time. Grace gets her coat and leaves for work. Hank gets his and leaves for Richmond's airport in his GMC. It takes him about an hour. He had checked the flight time on the Internet and knew he had half an hour before he needed to get his ticket. He stands in line waiting. When his turn comes he asks for a round trip First Class ticket to Key Largo, Florida. He pays for the ticket with his Visa card.

The flight number and destination are called for boarding. Hank has been waiting in the lounge area and gets up to get on board the plane. He has a First Class seat and is among the first to board. He takes his seat and has more waiting—this time for the take-off. It comes and Hank is on his way by 9:30 am. The flight arrives in Key Largo at 12:00 noon. Hank rents a car.

Hank looks in the yellow pages of a phone book for a realtor. He discovers a Remax Real Estate office and notes the address.

Hank, then, needs to get a map. So, he asks the clerk, who rented him the car, if she has one. She gives him one. Hank looks for the street name and finds it on the map. He heads there and it only takes half an hour. He goes inside.

Hank is greeted by Carol Ann Trump. She is one of the realtors working there. She asks "How may I help you today?" Hank responds "I am looking to buy a house here in Key Largo. I now live in Richmond, Virginia. Do you have anything available on the gulf side on the shore line?" Carol Ann replies "Why yes. We have only one house available at the present and it happens to be on the beach." "Can we go look at it?" "Yes."

Carol Ann takes Hank to 105 N Bounty Lane. It is a two bedroom, one bath, single level house. It is selling for $135,000.00. After Hank looks the house over, he tells Trump "I'll take it. How much is the down payment?" Carol Ann states "The down payment is 10% or $13,500.00 to be paid today, if you want the house." Hank writes out a check knowing it will be deposited against his $20,000.00 bank balance.

He calls Conrad and tells him the news and "I need a loan for $121,000.00 for the balance until our home is sold. I'll be home this evening about dinner time. Come see me then. Get the loan started today." Conrad relates "I will, Dad. You will have to sign the note tomorrow at the bank." After getting the tack for the horse, Conrad goes to Wachovia and gets the loan started. He will have it ready for tomorrow when his dad comes to the bank.

Carol Ann says "That is the fastest sale I have ever had. Are you married?" "Yes." "And you did not bring your wife?" asks Trump. Hank tells "My wife had to work today. She will come and see it Saturday. I'll have the rest of the money tomorrow. I can mail it to you or you can wait until Saturday." "Saturday will be soon enough."

Hank has Carol Ann take him back to the Realty office. He gets in the rental car and drives back to the airport. Hank turns in the rental car, but keeps the map to show Grace. He then goes and checks the next flight to Richmond. He sees one leaving at 3:30 pm with a transfer in Atlanta. That is the flight he was looking for. He has an hour to wait.

Hank gets on the plane and flies to Richmond via a transfer in Atlanta. He gets in his GMC truck and drives to see Grace. It is 6:00 pm. Grace has dinner waiting. Hank and she talk over his trip and the house in Key Largo. He tells her it is a beach front house right on the gulf coast and they will be able to walk the beach in the evening's twilight.

Conrad comes in and asks "Dad, did you tell mom everything?" "We just finished talking about it. She is excited. We are going to Key Largo Saturday to check it out. I will need the balance check then," comments Hank. "Well, the check will be ready tomorrow. You will have to come in and sign some papers for the loan. I put your house as collateral for the loan. You will need to get your house on the market as soon as possible. Do it tomorrow, if you can," advises Conrad.

Conrad tells his dad about his day and getting tack for the horse. Grace asks "When did you get a horse? Why did you not tell me?" "Mom, it was a busy day yesterday. We got the horse and named it Goldie yesterday. It is a golden Palomino. She is 3 years old. I went to a tack shop and bought a blanket, a bridle and a saddle just today. Sylvia wants to ride the horse already, but she will have to wait until Sunday unless she rides before she goes to work in the morning. She might do that without having to wait," relates Conrad.

Conrad says good night and leaves. Grace and Hank talk over the selling of the house. He states he will get on that tomorrow. Afterwards, they retire for the evening.

Conrad arrives at the house and sees the two girls watching TV. He asks has either of them fed Bear and taken him for a walk. Rosalyn tell Conrad that she had done both. Conrad kisses Rosalyn for her work done on his behalf. The three settle to watch the ending of the move and then, the 10 o'clock news. Afterwards the three retire for the evening.

CHAPTER 27

Thursday, Day 19

Rosalyn is first to rise and she goes to the other bathroom to shower. Afterwards, she dresses and goes to the kitchen to fix breakfast. Conrad and Sylvia get up at the same time and decide to take a shower together—something they had not done yet. Conrad washes Sylvia and Sylvia washes Conrad. When they are through, they dry each other and think it a great way to start the day. They dress and Sylvia comments "I need to go buy me some jeans so I can ride Goldie. You do not expect me to mount a horse with a dress on, do you?"

They go into the kitchen and see Rosalyn has fixed breakfast already—pancakes. She used Grace's method just for Conrad. The three enjoy their pancakes and Conrad tells Rosalyn the pancakes are as good as his mom's. They finish and Rosalyn cleans up.

In the meantime, Grace and Hank get up, shower and dress. They, then, go downstairs and have breakfast and coffee. Grace tells Hank that she can hardly wait to go to Key Largo. He says "You only have to wait until Saturday. We can even stay overnight. The house comes furnished. We won't have to move everything. But, I do want the library, computer and Dish network."

Grace gets her coat and leaves. Hank goes to Remax Realty. There, he asks for Judy Diamond—the same realtor that Conrad had when he bought his house. Hank says "I'm Hank Thomas.

My son bought a house from you. I want to put my house up for sale. It is 3 bedrooms, 2 baths, with living room, dining room, kitchen and family room. I want $135,000.00 for it. Can you help me sell it?" "I'm sure I can. We can have it listed here and on the Internet under Houses for Sale. We need you to sign some papers for us to begin" comes back Judy Diamond.

Hank is pleased that she is going to take the house and put it on the market. He queries "About how long does it take to sell a house?" "Well, Mr. Thomas, it can be as early as a week. Houses are selling fast right now. We will need a key to show your house to prospective buyers. It helps sell the house," comments Judy.

Hank gives her his key knowing there is a spare outside the house under a rock in the garden. She thanks him and tells Hank "We will do our best to get you a buyer. Your asking price is quite acceptable. How soon can we show it?" "Today, if you want"

Conrad spends time talking to Rosalyn and Sylvia about his parents moving to Key Largo. He says "We may have to help him load the truck and Sorento depending upon what he wants to drive to Florida. But, that won't be for another week or so. It may even be a Sunday and/or a Monday." Rosalyn asks "How much does he plan to take?" "I'm not sure yet. It could be all or he could sell the house furnished. I know he is asking for $135,000.00. Dad is going to use the same realtor that I used to buy this house" states Conrad.

Sylvia inquires "Does he expect us to help or is this your idea to help your parents?" "It is my idea." "Then why do we have to help them pack up? It may be your dad has a plan already. Movers will come and do all that for you if it's paid for," informs Rosalyn. "Dad says he was going to take some of the things with him on the flight to Florida. He has memorabilia packed already. It is mainly from the upstairs. We can do the downstairs while they are in Florida," explains Conrad.

Sylvia says "It is time for me to go to work." She gets her coat, hat and gloves. She, then, kisses Conrad goodbye. It is something she has made up her mind to start doing every day she goes to work. She gets in her car and drives to VCU. Conrad tells Rosalyn they could go help his dad today. So they grab their coats and leave.

Hank is back to packing. Breakable items he is wrapping in newspaper to help keep them from breaking. Rosalyn and Conrad arrive and go inside. "Dad, we are here to help. What would you like us to do for mom and you?" remarks Conrad. Hank states "The library books need packing. That is a two person job. Start in there. I'll give you something else when you're finished in there."

Rosalyn and Conrad go into the library and find boxes already there to pack the books in. They begin working on packing the books. After about 45 minutes, they are through. They go to Conrad's dad to get another assignment. Hank tells them the computer and modem need dismantling and packing. They proceed to do that. But, before they begin, Rosalyn reaches for Conrad and gives him a kiss saying "That's for being a good son." They get done with the computer in half an hour. It took so long because they had trouble packing the keyboard with the computer.

The two go back to Hank and ask what is next. Hank states "Lunch." Hank decides they will go get some barbeque sandwiches. They get into Hank's truck and drive to Hank's Barbeque Restaurant. It happens to be Conrad's dad's favorite place to eat. They enter and are met right off by Hank Woodson, owner.

Woodson shows them to a table. Clyde Harris has not started working yet. So, they get Janice Henry. Janice queries "What will you have to drink?" Hank responds "A black coffee, a Pepsi and a Diet Pepsi. Janice now remembers the Thomas'. She tells them she will be right back with their drinks. Conrad asks his father "Dad, what more do you have to get done that we can help you with?" "There isn't much left to do. I'm about ready to quit myself," replies Hank.

Henry returns with the drinks and asks what they will have. Hank says "We'll have a barbeque sandwich each." Janice leaves to turn in the order. Rosalyn states "I'm ready to quit too. It hasn't been much, but I agree there isn't much left to do given what you have told us Mr. Thomas."

Janice arrives with the sandwiches. They begin eating. Hank mentions about the last time they were here and the attempted robbery of Grace's purse. Conrad questions "Dad, did you get into trouble for wounding the man?" "No. I didn't even have Internal Affairs ask me any questions." They finish the sandwiches and prepare to leave. Conrad, this time, reaches for his wallet to leave a tip of $10.00 for Janice. Hank goes to the register and pays for the meal. They leave and return to the house.

Hank informs Rosalyn and Conrad they can go. He tells them he will do the rest of the packing. They leave in the Dodge Viper and return to the new house. Hank, in the meantime, gets two suitcases and packs some of Grace's and his clothes to take to Florida on the flight. He knows the boxes will cost extra to be sent as luggage.

Hank hears a car outside and goes to the door. It is Judy Diamond with a couple of perspective buyers. Hank is more than glad to show them in and show them the house. Judy states "It looks as if you have been packing. When do you think you will get everything out?" Hank informs "We won't be taking everything. The house will come furnished with mostly all the furniture. The house I've bought in Key Largo is furnished as well."

Hank begins showing the couple around the house. He gets into the library and tells them "The TV is a 52' Sanyo LCD HD. It will stay also. "It cost me $1,100.00. But, I have no real way of moving it." "Are you not having movers move you? They are not that expensive," declares Diamond.. Hank replies "No. We decided against movers. There is no real need for them. As I said our house in Florida is furnished. We will be going down

214

Saturday and Sunday to check it out and pay the balance on the price."

Judy tells Hank "Thank you" and leaves with the perspective buyers. Hank is finished with what packing he is going to do for the day. He decides to go over to Joe's and see how the 1949 Ford is coming along. Since Joe works the second shift, he is at home working on the Ford. He says hello to Hank. Hank asks "How's it coming? Did you get the engine done?" Joe informs "I have finished the engine. I'm not putting it in yet because the wiring all needs replacing."

"Do you want to help me with the wiring? It would be faster if two of us were to do it. One of us can pull from the passenger side and the other can guide the wires through from the engine compartment" declares Hank agreeing to help. It was his intention all along. They begin the replacement of the wiring harness.

Rosalyn and Conrad arrive at the house and go inside. They have nothing to do so they go to the family room and watch a movie on the Lifetime Movie Network. This takes up their time for about two hours. The movie is romantic and has sexual overtones. This gets to Rosalyn. She asks Conrad can they do it in her bed. He says "Let's go. It should be interesting with you on top."

Rosalyn and Conrad finish their thing and go back to the family room. This time, they watch the Investigation Discovery channel with a segment of Deadly Women. It takes them to dinner time and Sylvia's arrival time. Conrad tells Rosalyn "I'm going to take Bear for a walk. I shouldn't be gone long." Conrad gets Bear. He walks east again and Bonnie Jean comes out. She says "I still want you Conrad. Please come in and take me."

Conrad determines he will walk Bear to the west from now on. He tells Bonnie Jean "No. I've told you twice already I've got my wife. I'm content with that. If I were single, it would be an entirely different way. But, I'm not." Bonnie Jean claims "I will always want you. I'm only 26. I work in a factory that has mostly women. The men are a lot older than me. So, you see, I can't get a man. I want you." "You can keep wanting, but unless something happens to Sylvia, I won't be available," maintains Conrad.

Conrad finishes walking Bear and puts him back in his pin. He goes and checks on the chicks and sees they are beginning to clear the scratch yard. Conrad knows he will have to get some chicken feed for the chicks. Sylvia makes her arrival. Conrad goes and gives her a kiss feeling he has missed her for the day. They enter the house and Rosalyn has dinner ready—steak, baked potatoes and green beans. Dessert will be a pecan pie.

Conrad tells Rosalyn and Sylvia about Bonnie Jean offering herself to him. Sylvia wants to know why he has not taken her. Conrad says "I have Rosalyn, Yvonne and you. What more could I want?" Sylvia states "It is a matter of want; it is a matter of choice. You could choose to have her and I would not get upset nor would Rosalyn." Conrad reiterates his previous statement. He is trying to convince Rosalyn and Sylvia it is not his choice.

They eat their dinner and, then, have the pecan pie. Conrad comments "Rosalyn, I've got to keep you satisfied so you'll remain our cook. The steak was awesome as was the pie. Keep up the good work, my dear." Rosalyn realizes that is the first time Conrad has called her something besides her name and housekeeper. She is gratified that Conrad has chosen such a word to land on her.

Conrad tells the girls he will do the cleanup and take Bear the remaining steak. Rosalyn had cooked more steak than needed just so Bear would have some too. Rosalyn and Sylvia go into the family room and watch the show Deal or No Deal on the game channel. Conrad, when finished, joins them.

After the show, Conrad announces he wants to watch NCIS. The channel gets changed. Sylvia is not all that interested, so she goes to the computer to surf the Internet. She is not looking for anything particularly. Sylvia wants to use up time until they go to bed. She comes across the blog she had read before and she reads the President's daughter's car had been spotted in Baltimore. This convinces her she is not the President's daughter.

The time comes for them all to retire for the evening. The TV gets turned off, but Sylvia leaves the computer connected to the blog she read. Rosalyn goes to her room while Sylvia and Conrad go to the master bedroom. They go to sleep as should be.

CHAPTER 28

Richmond

It is Friday, day 19. In Washington, the President has had enough of the Fredericksburg operation. He calls Agent Ginger Ales to his office. The President declares "I want the satellite monitoring system moved from Fredericksburg, Virginia to some other more likely location. Try Richmond. That ought to be a good place to have it."

"Yes, Mr. President. It will be accomplished today. All I need do is tell agents Duffy and Wong. They will take care of it," announces Ginger. Ales goes back to her office and calls Duffy "Duffy, I want Wong and you to move the monitoring system to Richmond, Virginia. Do it today. It is a presidential order. Call me when it is done."

Duffy tells Wong the news. Ho leaves to tell Chief Connors the news about leaving. Connors tells Ho "You mean I get my people back? This is wonderful. What can I do to help?" "We need some people to help move the system once we get it dismantled. That should be in two hours, Chief," responds Ho.

Jim Duffy begins the dismantling of the system. He is helped by Miriam Lewis, the present operator. Ho Wong arrives to help. Instead of taking two hours, it only takes one and a half hours. Ho goes to Penske Rentals for the truck they need. He drives it to Police Headquarters. Jim gets the help they need for loading the system. Miriam helps with that also.

Loaded, Ho drives to Richmond. It takes an hour. Duffy and Wong report to the local FBI office. Again, they need someone to take them to Police Headquarters. Wong asks "Can we get one of you to take us there and introduce us to the Chief of Police. They get William Anderson to take them to the Chief. Anderson has them follow him to Headquarters.

Once inside, Anderson introduces them to Chief Patrick Ray. Ray asks "What can I do for you gentlemen?" Ho tells him "We need four of your people to use a satellite monitoring system to check on vehicles in Richmond and the surrounding areas. You can get your people while Jim and I assemble the system. What room can we use? Ray declares "I can give you my office staff meeting room. It is down the hall on the right."

"We will also need dispatch equipment for the operators of the system. It will be dispatch 2. That will meet our needs once we have the system operating. This will be a joint FBI and Richmond Police operation," states Wong. Jim asks for help to unload the truck. He gets it.

Duffy and Wong work on assembling the system while the local office works on setting up dispatch 2. The dispatch is ready long before the system. Duffy and Wong continue until the system is in operation. They wait for the four officers to arrive. Wong is on the system when the first officer arrives. He merely says "Watch closely what I do." The officer does so.

. Duffy checks with the Chief to see when the other officers will arrive. Chief Ray tells him when the next shift comes on he will get two more officers and the last will be from the midnight shift. This is not to Duffy's liking but, it is what Wong and he are stuck with. Jim returns and tells Ho what has happened. Wong is not thrilled either.

Wong shows the officer how to use the system. He tells him to first find a red car, then, zoom in to see if it is a Dodge Viper. Ho continues to tell him that if it is a Dodge Viper, the driver's license is to be checked for Sylvia Redman. Ho says the car should have D.C. plates on it and if the car does not match all the criteria, it is to be let go.

Wong gives the system over to the officer. The officer begins the search. He sees a few red cars but no Dodge Viper. He is starting from the downtown area and moving outward in a spiral technique. When he does spot a red Dodge Viper, he gets on the dispatch and calls "This is dispatch 2. Any car near 12th and Broad, respond." "This is car Alpha 13." "Proceed to 12th street and heading west on Broad you will see a red Dodge Viper. If it has D.C. plates, stop it and check the driver's license for a Sylvia Redman." "Car Alpha 13, it has Virginia plates." "Do not stop it. It is not what we are looking for."

The officer continues his search, but he does not find another Dodge Viper of any color. He is replaced by the evening shift officers—one female and one male. Wong must train them to use the system, use dispatch and tell them what they are looking for. Duffy tells them that the junior officer will be a relief person. The female is senior officer.

After watching Wong, the female takes control of the satellite monitoring system. She finds a few red cars, but zooming in provides no Dodge Viper. The male is given a chance to use the system. He has the same results. Duffy and Wong are beginning to wonder if Richmond is a good idea. They could have gone to Manassas, Lynchburg or Roanoke. Duffy thinks these will be future endeavors.

The shift for the two officers ends when the midnight shift officer arrives. Duffy tells Wong he is going to find a motel for them and get to bed. He also tells Ho to come to the motel after he gets this officer squared away on the system. Ho agrees. Duffy checks into a Quality Inn on the north side of Richmond. He calls Wong to tell him where to come and that a room is reserved for him in his name.

Wong goes back to watching the midnight shift officer use the system. She checks out to be quite good at it. She finds more red cars than either shift before her. It seems odd to Wong since this is the midnight shift. There should have been more during the rush hour traffic or so he thought. But, all the red cars are not a Viper.

Wong feels it is now safe for him to leave the female officer on the system. He goes to the motel and checks in. It is 2:00 am. Duffy gets up at 6:00 o'clock am and decides to let Wong sleep. Duffy goes to a Shoney's and has breakfast, then, to Headquarters. When he appears in the staff room, he sees the female officer is still at it. He asks if she saw any Dodge Vipers and she says no. Wong arrives at 8:00 am and the female is gone. They have the same male officer they had yesterday. He is at it because the morning rush hour is in effect.

The officer does see some red cars, but no Dodge Viper of any color. The search area reaches the city limits and the officer determines he needs to start at downtown again. Duffy and Wong say nothing. If he is going to find a Viper, they think he will need to repeat the search area. This goes on for the rest of the day and continues into the future always stopping at the city limits.

CHAPTER 29

Rosalyn Sick

It is Saturday, day 20. Sylvia Redman has been missing almost three weeks. Sylvia Thomas rises at 7:00 am and prepares breakfast. Rosalyn is still in bed. She hasn't told anyone that she is running a fever. She feels too weak to get up. Conrad gets up showers, and dresses. He then goes into the kitchen to find Sylvia fixing breakfast. He asks "Where's Rosalyn? Shouldn't she be up by now? Will you go check on her?"

Sylvia finds Rosalyn still in bed and shaking. She feels her forehead and it is quite warm. Sylvia goes and tells Conrad. Conrad tells Sylvia that Rosalyn needs to see a doctor. Sylvia looks in the phone book under yellow pages for a physician near them. She calls and is told the office is not taking new patients. Sylvia tries again and explains what the problem is. The secretary says "Bring her in and we will try to work her in. Her visit is subject to payment today, at least the insurance co-pay.

Conrad gets Rosalyn up and Sylvia helps her dress. Sylvia tells Conrad "You take her because the waiting could last until after my reporting time. I cannot be late yet. I need to put in more time before I can afford to be late." Conrad agrees with Sylvia. After Rosalyn is dressed, Conrad gets her to the car with Sylvia's help. They put her in and Conrad gets in as well. He starts the car and drives to the doctor's office. He sees a sign that states the office will close at noon today.

Meanwhile Grace and Hank load the Sorento and go to the airport to fly to Key Largo. They have just barely made it on time. They have their tickets and head for the gate after checking the packages. Since they have First Class tickets, they get on the plane ahead of many other passengers. The flight is uneventful and takes two and a half hours. Hank rents a car and loads the luggage and boxes. They go right to the Remax office and present the check for the remainder of the balance for the house. Grace and Hank, then, go to the house. Grace is fascinated by it.

Back in Richmond, Conrad gets Rosalyn registered and they begin the wait. It takes three hours to get to Rosalyn. It is 11:30 am. Rosalyn's name is called. Conrad helps her up and the nurse seeing the trouble Conrad is having helps to take her to exam room 6. The nurse, first thing, takes Rosalyn's temperature. It is 101°. The nurse, then, takes her blood pressure and pulse.

The nurse puts all the information on Rosalyn's chart. She tells Rosalyn and Conrad "The doctor will be right with you." It does not take but a couple of minutes and the doctor is in the room. She reads the chart and says "You are having a problem. Your temperature is 101°. You will need a prescription. Wait while I go and get you one. The doctor leaves for but a moment and is back with the prescription. She tells Rosalyn "Take one tablet every six hours. Do not miss taking a dosage. You will not be cured if you do miss. Take this to the reception desk."

Conrad, again, struggles with Rosalyn. This time he does it alone. He gives the sheet to the receptionist who says "That will be $50.00." Conrad gets the money out of his wallet and gives it to the clerk. He takes Rosalyn outside and has her sit on the concrete wall while he goes and gets the car. With the Viper, Conrad gets Rosalyn into the car. They go to a CVS pharmacy and get the prescription filled.

Conrad gets home at 12:30 pm with a struggle. Rosalyn is getting worse. He sees the need to get her inside and back to bed. Bonnie Jean sees what is happening and comes to help. The two get Rosalyn into the house and into her bed. Bonnie Jean helps

Rosalyn out of her clothes while Conrad gets some water for her to take the medicine. Rosalyn, with effort, takes the tablet with water. She lies down completely and drifts off to sleep.

Bonnie Jean says "I've helped you. Now you help me." "What kind of help do you want?" asks Conrad. Bonnie Jean tells Conrad "I want you in bed with me, now. You're wife is at work and your housekeeper is asleep. There is no better time." Conrad feels obligated and says "Okay, but this one time only. Conrad and Bonnie Jean go into the spare bedroom and get at it. They stay at it for over an hour. So was the need of Bonnie Jean.

Bonnie Jean dresses as does Conrad. She, then, says "Until next time" and leaves. Conrad thinks there will be no next time. He settles down to watch TV. He is not concerned at what he watches. He begins thinking about Bonnie Jean and her need to go so long. Maybe she has not had a man like she says thinks Conrad.

Conrad, so bewildered by Bonnie Jean, goes without eating any lunch. He begins to think maybe there will be another chance with Bonnie Jean. He loses interest in the TV and decides to go outside and check on Bear, Goldie and the chicks. This undertaking uses an hour for Conrad. He sees Bonnie Jean watching him. He stares back. They stand in this position for 15 minutes until Bonnie Jean goes inside her house.

Conrad goes back inside as well. He thinks more about Bonnie Jean. It is if he cannot get her off his mind. He checks on Rosalyn and she is still asleep. He goes back to watching television. He thinks this will get his mind off Bonnie Jean. He cannot believe that she is taking up so much of his time thinking. When he makes up his mind there will be a next time, she leaves his mind.

Conrad, then, remembers his appointment with Yvonne. It is now 5:30 pm. He has enough time to go see her. He gets in the Viper after checking on Rosalyn. He drives to Yvonne's who is waiting for him. All she has on is a robe. She removes it and Conrad sees what he likes about Yvonne. They go into her bedroom and go at it for 30 minutes. After all, it has been a week since she last had it.

Conrad tells her about his experience with Bonnie Jean. Yvonne tells him that Bonnie Jean must be a lot like her—in desperate need of a man. Conrad acknowledges the fact and says "I've made up my mind there will be a next time and probably on a Saturday morning." Conrad also tells Yvonne about Rosalyn being sick and him taking her to the doctor's office this morning.

Yvonne and Conrad spend another 30 minutes talking about Rosalyn, Sylvia and him. He tells Yvonne "I can't say I love you, but I can say I enjoy you. You will talk to me and listen. I feel I am also a help to you. I hope you never find another man." Yvonne declares "I am not now looking nor will I ever look for another man. You light up my Saturdays and other days we make it."

Conrad sees it is 6:30 and he must leave. He kisses Yvonne and she kisses him back to the point he wants her again, but realizes he must go. Conrad leaves in his Viper. He gets to the house and checks on Rosalyn. She is still asleep. But Conrad knows it is time for another pill. He wakes Rosalyn up, hands her a glass of water and the pill. She swallows it down and lies back down to drift off to sleep once more.

Sylvia comes to the house and asks 'How is Bonnie Jean doing?" Conrad thinks it is asked because she knows, but, then again, how did she find out? Conrad just comments "Fine. Aren't you interested in Rosalyn?" "She is doing okay. I know you will see to that. I was interested in **B**onnie Jean because she waved at me when I drove up. She has never done that before."

Conrad tries to change the subject with "How did work go? Did you have a good lunch?" That did not work for Sylvia kept hinting at Bonnie Jean. So, Conrad changes the subject by talking about his mom and dad going to Key Largo. He tells "They left at about 9:00 am and arrived in Key Largo at about

12:00 noon. They took a lot of stuff with them in luggage and boxes. Dad had the Sorento filled. He had to rent an SUV to haul the stuff. They made it to the house and are planning on spending the night and coming back tomorrow about 5:30 or 6:00 pm. Mom is fascinated by the house. They want us to come down the first chance we get."

Sylvia wants to know who is going to fix dinner. She was not going to do it. Conrad says "Since Rosalyn is asleep and will stay that way for some time, why don't we go to a restaurant and eat?" Sylvia agrees with that and Bonnie Jean is forgotten for the moment. Conrad gets his coat and Sylvia still has hers on. They leave. He takes them to Strawberry Street Café'.

Sylvia and Conrad enter the establishment and see it is a really nice restaurant. They are shown to a booth where Sylvia sits opposite Conrad. They are given menus. Sylvia decides she wants Broiled Maryland Crabcakes. Conrad decides upon a Top Sirloin Steak. The waitress comes and asks for their drink order. They each order their drinks as well as their entrees.

The duo waits for their drinks and meal. It does not take long for either to arrive. Conrad is amazed at how fast the service is and tells Sylvia. Both of them relish the meal. They have no dessert. They leave and go to the new house. There, they retire for the evening after giving Rosalyn another pill.

CHAPTER 30

Sunday, day 21

Wong is at the monitor and sees not only a silver Viper, but a red one as well. He sends a squad car to check out the plates. The officers report that both have Virginia plates. So, Wong has the squad car move on. He was sure that was going to be the car he was looking for. He continues to monitor since the office due in had not shown up yet.

Conrad gets up before Sylvia. Rosalyn remains in bed. Conrad gets another glass of water and pill for Rosalyn. She accepts those with a bit more enthusiasm. Conrad sees this and goes to tell Sylvia. She was not in their room or in the master bathroom. He hears water running in the other bathroom and goes to check it out. It turns out to be Sylvia taking a bath instead of a shower.

Conrad tells her about Rosalyn's seemingly recovery. He is hopeful she will get well soon. Conrad asks Sylvia "What's for breakfast? I'm kind of hungry. I could eat a horse. But, not Goldie, of course." "You will have to wait until I am finished here. I have not had a bath since coming to Richmond, only showers" states Sylvia. Conrad takes notice of the fact she says she was 'coming to Richmond.' He tells Sylvia of it. She just brushes it off as a spoken mistake.

Sylvia puts in bubble bath and finishes filling the tub. Conrad asks "Why did you take your bath here instead of our whirlpool?"

"Because I wanted to leave it for Rosalyn and you," gives Sylvia. Conrad declares "Rosalyn is not physically able to get up and take a shower or bath." "I did not say shower or bath. She will make her choice and make it known to you," relates Sylvia "go check on her. She is up now."

Conrad does just that. He finds Rosalyn in the shower. She says to him "Join me in here Conrad. I need the physical support to finish my shower." He undresses and joins her. She tells him to wash her because she does not have the strength. Conrad washes her whole body. In the process, he washes himself. When both are finished, they get out together and Conrad dries Rosalyn and himself.

Rosalyn and Conrad go into the kitchen after dressing. They see Sylvia has made it there ahead of them. Conrad knew that would happen. When she dons a dress, it is the only thing she puts on and besides her shoes. Conrad had noticed that Rosalyn is doing the same.

Rosalyn asks "What is for breakfast? I want something easy to chew. I don't have much strength and will go back to bed after I eat. I haven't had anything to eat since yesterday morning." Sylvia says "We will have scrambled eggs with buttered toast. How does that sound?" Before Rosalyn says anything, Conrad states "great." Rosalyn agrees. Sylvia gets the eggs and some cheese to mix so the eggs have a flavor worth eating. She toasts eight slices of bread and butters them. The food becomes ready and Sylvia fixes a plate for Rosalyn.

Conrad is told to fix his as does Sylvia. They eat all the eggs and all the toast. Rosalyn says "Excuse me; I'm going back to bed. I may go to sleep. If I do, wake me for my next pill. I don't want to miss one." Conrad tells her he will when the time comes. Conrad remembers he has not fed Bear last night. He gets out some hamburger to take to Bear. When with the dog, Bear jumps on Conrad in favoritism. Conrad gives Bear the meat and goes back inside. He also remembers he needs to get the chicks some feed, but that will have to wait until tomorrow.

Conrad tells Sylvia of his remembrances. She says she will want to go with him. She tells him she needs to spend more time with him alone. It is implied that Rosalyn is getting more of his time than her. Conrad mentions to her he must go back to work tomorrow. Sylvia becomes upset a little. She is hoping for more time with Conrad. She must wait until next Sunday.

Grace and Hank are up by 7:00 o'clock am and both are hungry. There is nothing in the house to eat. Hank suggests they go find a restaurant to get some breakfast. Grace says "We need to do that in case at some future time we will need or want to do it again." Grace and Hank get in the rental car and go looking for a restaurant. The two go to Key Largo Conch House Restaurant for their breakfast. It becomes a dining feast.

Grace and Hank have the Cajun Omelet with potatoes. It is a new experience having breakfast in Key Largo, so they have a new experience at eating. They talk about the place and it being one of the few restaurants they found open on a Sunday morning. It becomes an instant favorite for the both of them. After breakfast, Hank pays for the meal with his Visa card. They leave and return to their beach front house.

Grace spends the morning telling Hank what kind of changes she wants to make. She tells him the sea border can stay, but the ocean green must give way to a sky blue in the living room. In their bedroom, she wants an off white instead of the white there now. In the other bedroom, she wants the same thing. She mentions that the kitchen should be a soft yellow like the early morning sun.

In the afternoon, Grace and Hank take a barefoot walk in the beach's water with it being much warmer in Key Largo than in Richmond. It is the one thing Hank has always wanted to do with Grace. They walk about a mile and turn around to walk back. Once at the house, they go to the bath room and rinse their feet off and dry them to put shoes back on. They realize that it is time to get ready for the flight back to Richmond. They could have stayed another day because Grace's retirement starts tomorrow.

Grace gets the empty luggage, while Hank gets the car. They drive to the airport, return the rental car and check in. They find they have an hour and a half to wait. Hank tells Grace "We will have us a sandwich for lunch from one of the vendors here at the airport. What type of sandwich do you want to have?" "I will have a club sandwich, if it can be found" states Grace. Hank goes looking and finds the club sandwich at one of the vendors. He goes and gets Grace to have her sandwich. He has the same. It costs Hank $12.90 for the two sandwiches and no drinks.

The time passes quickly; too quick for Grace. She has gotten to the point she really wants to be in Key Largo. Hank feels the same. After all, it was he that picked Key Largo as their retirement place to live. The flight number is called for boarding. Having First Class seats again, Grace and Hank are among the first to get seated again. The stewardess, Peggy May, asks "Can I get you something to drink?" Hank immediately says yes. He wants coffee black while Grace wants a Coca Cola. Peggy gives them their drinks from her cart. She moves on to the next passenger's seat.

The flight takes off and lasts only an hour until they get to Atlanta and have to change planes. This is done with no hassle. They are on the flight to Richmond. This flight takes an hour and a half. Grace and Hank arrive in Richmond at 5:30 pm. They get their luggage bags and go to the Sorento. Hank tries to start the car, but the battery is dead. He calls Conrad "Son, we're at the airport and our car won't start. We need a new battery. Go to Wal-mart and get me one."

Conrad instantly gets in his Viper and goes to Wal-mart. He finds a clerk in automotive with a badge name of Margie. He asks "Margie, I need a battery for a 2007 Kia Sorento. Can you help me find one?" She shows him the book with battery listings by car make and model. He checks for the one to match his need. After getting the number, he does not see one on the shelf.

He calls "Margie, there isn't a battery of the type I need. Would you have one in stock?" She says she will go look. Margie comes back and tells Conrad they have none. She suggests Advance Auto Parts.

Conrad goes to Advance Auto and finds out they do not have one either. The parts clerk suggests going to Napa Parts; the only other place that may have it. Conrad goes there and much to his delight they have it. He pays for it and heads to the airport. He finds his dad and mom in the lot. He drives right up to the Sorento with the battery. His dad has already taken the dead battery loose from its cables. Conrad gives his dad the new battery and Hank gets it put in quickly. He starts the car to Grace's desire.

They get in and Conrad moves his Viper out of their way. He follows them all the way to their house. Once there, he asks about their stay in Florida. His father tells him it was great and that they had a long walk in the beach's water. Grace tells him about their breakfast of Cajun Omelets and how different and enjoyable it was.

Conrad tells his parents that he must leave. Sylvia has been wanting more of his time he tells them. He leaves to return to Sylvia. At the house, he asks Sylvia how Rosalyn is doing. Sylvia informs Conrad "She is better and I gave her a pill about an hour ago. She is in the family room watching TV." Conrad goes to the room and sees her sitting there. He asks her "How are you feeling?" Rosalyn tells him "I'm much better. I'm able to sit up now. I think the doctor had it right when she wrote the prescription. You know that doctors make their best guess based on their training and experiences. No one else could do that."

Sylvia becomes a little jealous of Rosalyn because she thinks Conrad is giving her too much attention. Sylvia pulls him aside and asks "What do you think you are doing spending so much time with her?" "I'm only finding out how she is doing." "I already told you that I want time alone with you."

Rosalyn cannot but help hearing the conversation. She knows she has been spending too much time with Conrad. She speaks up "I heard what you are talking about. I have spent more time with Conrad. You have been working and he has been here on vacation. That all changes tomorrow and I will spend about the same amount of time with both of you. Sylvia, I'll spend the morning with you after Conrad leaves for work. Conrad, I'll spend time with you after you get here and before Sylvia gets here. Let's end this now."

Sylvia and Conrad agree with her on all accounts. They sit down and watch TV with Rosalyn on one side and Sylvia on the other. They were sharing Conrad.

CHAPTER 31

Back to Work

It is Monday and the day Conrad's vacation is over. He rises at 6:30 am to prepare for going back to work. He takes his shower, dresses and goes to the kitchen. He makes his own breakfast out of cereal that they had gotten from the apartment before returning it to the new manager. Conrad enjoys the difference. He is eating Kellogg Sugar Frosted Flakes.

Sylvia is next to rise at 7:00 o'clock am. She takes her shower and dresses. Going into the kitchen, she sees Conrad has already eaten by the used bowl, cereal and milk still on the table. She asks "Why did you eat already? Could you not wait for me?" "I'm going in early. I've a lot of work to catch up on. Besides, I can take a long lunch and get the chicken feed and maybe go to a tack shop," answers Conrad.

Sylvia gets the cereal and has a bowl as well. She, too, likes the difference. She had almost forgotten what cereal was like. Rosalyn gets up and before taking a shower goes into the kitchen to get a pill. She is feeling much better. After taking the pill, she returns to the bath room to shower. When done, she puts on a dress and goes back to the kitchen. She decides to have a bowl of cereal as well.

Rosalyn is thankful there is not much to cleanup with only three bowls and three spoons to clean and the milk and cereal to put away. It will be a fast morning and she can go back to bed.

Conrad gets him a Pepsi and determines it is time to leave for work. He kisses Sylvia and Rosalyn goodbye and leaves.

Rosalyn goes back to bed after cleaning the kitchen. Sylvia goes into the family room and gets back on the computer where she was last night. She was still connected to the blog. She sees some information has been added. Mainly, the report of the President's daughter's car being in Baltimore had proven false. It was just someone's car that looked like hers.

There is not much else to read, so she leaves the computer connected to the blog site. Sylvia turns the TV on and watches the Good Morning America show. She finds it interesting and stays there for about an hour. There is a knock at the door Sylvia goes to see who it could be. It turns out to be a Girl Scout selling cookies. She asks Sylvia if she is interested in buying a box.. Sylvia decides it would be a real treat for Rosalyn and Conrad. So, she buys two boxes of the caramel chocolate variety.

The time comes for her to go to work, so she takes a glass of water and a pill to Rosalyn. She has to wake Rosalyn who takes the pill and lies back down. Rosalyn seems a bit better. Sylvia gets her coat and leaves for work. She sees that Bonnie Jean has left already and figures she must go in early.

In the interim, Conrad has gotten to work and sees a pile of notes on his desk. These are notes he will have to deal with after 9:00 o'clock am. He spends time dealing with those that he could. When the tellers arrive, he has a talk with all of them telling about his new house. He does not mention Rosalyn as the housekeeper. He does mention Goldie, Bear and the chicks.

Conrad gets to work on the notes. The first he tackles is about a financial investment. The person wants to know what would be best for investment. Conrad has several more just as well. He gets all of them done and tackles the loan applications. Included amongst these is his father's application for the $121,500.00 he needed for the house in Key Largo. He gets on the phone and calls his dad to come in and sign some papers. Mainly, Hank will be putting his present house up as collateral.

Hank makes it in to the bank in 15 minutes. Conrad has him come into his office. There, Conrad explains the loan's workings and asks his dad is there any questions. Hank says no. Conrad, then, asks his father to sign in three places. He gives his dad back a copy of the loan contract. Conrad says goodbye to his dad who is going to do some more packing.

Kitty Calhoun comes to Conrad's office and tells him she came up $400.00 short on Friday and there was no discovery as to why that occurred. Conrad asks to see her receipts for Thursday and Friday. After receiving these, he goes over them with a fine tooth comb insuring that all the receipts are accounted for. To Kitty's delight and amazement, Conrad found the error. Kitty had put down $4.00 as a payout when in fact it was only $404.00. That made her $400.00 short.

Conrad sends her back to her window to wait on account holders. He sees one note that he is supposed to attend a meeting at another Wachovia branch at 1:30 pm. Conrad marks that down on his desk calendar. He has another teller, Greta Parks, come into his office. She tells him "Mr. Thomas, as you know I'm pregnant. What you don't know is my water just broke and I'm having contractions. I think I need to go to the hospital."

Conrad calls 911 and informs the operator of the situation. She responds with "I will send a Rescue Squad immediately." Greta starts having more contractions closer together and says "If they don't hurry, I'll have the baby right here." It does not take very long for the Rescue Squad to get to Wachovia. The two EMT's come in with the stretcher to get Greta on it and take her to the ambulance. They load her and upon leaving use the lights and siren. That told Conrad that Greta was real close to having the baby and may not make it to the hospital before having the baby.

The rest of the day goes uneventful except for a lunch with Kitty Calhoun. It was her treat for Conrad finding the error that no one else could. She has had a thing for Conrad and wanted to tell him about it. She tells him it will never be now that he is a married man. Conrad agrees with her. It also meant Conrad did not get the time to go to a tack shop or get chicken feed. Conrad does both after work on his way home. Another saddle was the most expensive thing he bought.

Sylvia has an uneventful day except for a lunch with her boss, Maryann Witten. The two go to Shoney's—a place that was becoming a favorite of Sylvia. Sylvia has the Shoney's Big Boy sandwich while Maryann has the Soup & Salad Bar. They both enjoy their meal as they talk about Conrad. Maryann tells of a date she had with Conrad. Sylvia tells of their wedding day after the ceremony and her work on that day.

Sylvia works to the end of her shift and heads for home. She gets stopped by a police officer for no apparent reason. He asks to see her license and it has the name Sylvia Reed. He tells her she looks awful familiar. She states it was probably because she has since married Lieutenant Thomas' son. Conrad, and has been to the police station several times. He assumes that must be it. He lets her go. Sylvia had no idea why he stopped her even after talking to the police officer.

Sylvia gets home to find Conrad out in the barn. He has Goldie in the barn in a stable that has not been used for some time. He is brushing the horse down and Sylvia asks why. Conrad says "I bought the tack we need for Goldie and I took her for a ride. She is a very responsive horse and handles quite well, even extraordinary. Wait until you ride her. She will be ready for you when you get home tomorrow." "Conrad, I do not have any jeans. I cannot ride a horse in a dress. We need to go buy me a set of jeans. Why not go to Wal-mart after the jeans after dinner?" blatantly states Sylvia.

Conrad says "Let's go eat then." Sylvia sees that Rosalyn is much better and has fixed dinner. It is hamburgers, Brussels sprouts and corn with Hawaiian Dinner Rolls. Sylvia is amazed at the Brussels sprouts; there was cheese on them. Conrad says that is the way most people in Richmond eat their sprouts. Rosalyn tells "That is the way my mom always fixed Brussels sprouts. She learned it from my grandmother."

They eat enjoying the meal. It seems to taste better when Rosalyn fixes the meal. Sylvia asks what Rosalyn did today while Conrad and she were at work. Rosalyn replies "I just watched some TV and did some dusting. There wasn't much else to do.

Dinner is over. Sylvia wants to go to Wal-mart. Rosalyn does too to get out of the house for a change. Conrad tells them to go without him. He needs to feed Bear and the chicks. Sylvia and Rosalyn leave in her Viper. They get there and go in the store for the jeans. While looking at the jeans, one of the clerks tells Sylvia "You look familiar. Where have I seen you before?" "It was probably right here. I shop Wal-mart a lot. I do not know where else it could have been" states Sylvia.

After selecting a size five of jeans, Sylvia heads for the checkout. She goes to one of the registers that say 20 items or less. Sylvia is waited on in just a few minutes. Her price for the jeans is $15.70. She pays with her Visa card. They head for the car.

Once in the car, Sylvia tells Rosalyn "That clerk in there is the second person today to say I looked familiar. The first was a police officer that stopped me for no reason." "Did he ask for your license?" asks Rosalyn. Sylvia says "Yes, he did. Does that mean something?" "It only means that he was checking to make sure you had a valid license. You do look kind of out of place in a sports car that costs so much money," states Rosalyn.

The two girls arrive at the house and see Conrad giving Bear a walk to the west of the house. He hurries back with Bear to meet the girls as they go in. He asks Sylvia to try on the jeans. The jeans show off her body even more than any dress did. They fit her body perfectly in form as well as size. Conrad gets excited over the look and tells her she needs to buy more jeans. Sylvia tells him no and that one pair is enough.

The three go into the family room and watch TV. They watch Rosalyn's favorite show 'Dancing with the Stars'. When the show is over, they retire for the evening.

Hank and Grace have been busy packing what they would take with them the next trip and last trip to Key Largo, Florida. They finish in time to go to dinner. Hank wants his barbeque and Grace wants Red Lobster. It becomes a coin toss and Grace wins. They go to Red Lobster. Grace has the Lobster Lover's Dream and Hank has the seafood platter. After their meal, Grace and Hank return and retire for the evening.

CHAPTER 32

Preparations

Hank and Grace arise for breakfast. They have fried eggs and sausage with coffee. They do not have plans for the day. All the packing was mostly completed yesterday. So, they go into the family room and watch Good Morning America. There is a talk with Britney Spears and with the weather. It now being November, the forecast on the weather portion of the show says the temperature high for the day will only be 40 °. This will be the coldest day yet. It has been in the upper 40s.

Sylvia and Conrad get up, shower together, and dress. They go to the kitchen where Rosalyn is busy fixing breakfast. They were going to have oatmeal and orange juice. She asks "Is there anything in particular you would like done today? I will have some free time." Conrad says it would be nice if she did the laundry.

After breakfast, Conrad leaves for work. He arrives at 8:30 am. He learns that Greta Parks had a baby boy weighing 8 lbs and 15 ounces with a length of 22 inches. She had named the baby Braelyn Parks. He is also back to financial counseling. His day is a normal run of the mill. There is nothing to disrupt his day.

At lunch time, he gets some roses and takes them to the hospital for Greta. He sees her and she is feeding the baby. The father, Charlton Parks was there with his wife. Greta says to Conrad "You didn't have to do this. But, thank you." Conrad tells her "Congratulations on having a healthy baby boy. I think you will take the six weeks maternity leave, yes?" Greta says she would.

Before he leaves, Conrad leans over and gives her a kiss on the cheek. He, then, leaves to return to work. Along the way, he gets himself a hamburger and French fries with a Pepsi. He eats while driving. He returns to the bank to find a couple waiting for him.

They identify themselves as Ralph and Wilma Barker. They have come for a mortgage. Conrad learns that the house they want to mortgage is his parents' house. He asks have they seen the house completely through and Ralph answers "Yes. It was a dream house. Everything comes with the house which to us is a thoughtful event. We presently live in a furnished apartment at Falling Creek apartments."

Conrad draws up the papers for a loan of $120,000.00 which is all they need. He has them sign three papers. After that, he presents them with a check for the amount they want with the house going as collateral and a copy of the papers. Conrad knows the house is worth more, but his parents were asking for a price that would sell the house quickly. Evidently, it works.

In the meantime, Judy Diamond arrives with the Barkers and tells Hank the house has been sold. Grace and Hank could not believe it had gone that fast. Judy Diamond and the Barkers are shown in and go to the kitchen table where Hank takes them. He knew there would be papers to sign because he had to do that in Florida. They sign the papers and Hank and the Barkers each get a copy. Hank is asked when he can be out. Hank replies "We can be gone by the end of the week. This is more than acceptable to the Barkers. They thought they would have to wait the normal 30 days. It turns out they only need wait about eight days.

The Barkers ask "Is there a church nearby?" Hank says "You know what; you have got me on that one. My wife and I haven't attended church since our wedding." Ralph Barker says

"That's okay. We will find one nearby." The Barkers and realtor Diamond leave.

Grace wants to celebrate. Hank says "We can go out for breakfast at Shoney's. They always have that breakfast buffet in the morning. You can get what you want and I can get what I want." So, the couple leaves in the Sorento. They take 15 minutes to get there and find it is not crowded as they expect. They go in and are met by a waitress who takes them to a booth. Another waitress comes and asks "What would you like to drink?" Hank says "Two coffees. We'll go buffet this morning." Grace and Hank get up and go get the plate they need and they each fill their plate. When they get back to their booth, the coffee is waiting. Breakfast costs $13.15.

Hank calls Conrad and tells him the news about the house selling for the $135,000.00 he was asking. Conrad says "Congratulations, dad. When will mom and you move to Key Largo?" "We're expecting to move one day this week. You and I need to go to DMV and get the title for my GMC truck transferred into your name," relates Hank. Conrad asks "Why do you want to give up your truck? It's almost brand new. Are you sure you want to do that?" "Yes, I'm sure. I have no use for the truck in Florida. Grace and I are both retired. We only need one vehicle now."

"Dad, you go to DMV and call me when you get there. I'll leave work and can only be gone briefly. I'll be there about 10 minutes at most." "Okay son." Hank hangs up and tells Grace what he will be doing for about 30 minutes. He leaves for DMV and gets there before Conrad. He sees there is quite a line, so he waits for his number to be issued to him. He is given D-105. He waits for it to be called and for Conrad to show up. Conrad shows before his father's number is called. They wait patiently. It does not take very long for Hank's number to be called.

Hank and Conrad go to the window and the clerk asks "What can I do for you today?" "I want to transfer the title on my truck to my son," states Hank. The clerk declares "I will need the present title. Is your son with you?" "Yes. This is him." "I need his name and address. .I would also like to see his driver's license" requests the clerk. Conrad provides all that is requested.

The clerk enters the name and address into the computer and gets a title printout when done. She, then, says "A transfer within a family is free." She hands the title to Conrad. He thanks his dad and heads back to work. He is gone 30 minutes. No one says anything about the absence.

Sylvia gets to work finding that Maryann has left for the day and has left a note giving Sylvia complete control of the library for the week. She is to change her schedule today for work for the rest of the week. Maryann has a death in the family and needs the time off. Sylvia is sorry for Maryann, but is happy for the schedule change. She tells her coworkers and shows the note.

Alexis Taylor is not at all pleased with the assignment. She voices her concern "I think I should have been the one to get the job. I have more experience than you. It just isn't fair." "Well Alexis, you will have to take that up with Maryann when she gets back. Right now, you need to get to work. I cannot have dissention among employees," demands Sylvia. Alexis returns to work.

Sylvia has no more disruptions from the other worker. While Sylvia is handling the workings of the library, Conrad has another couple who seek financial advice. He works with them settling the matter of $900,000.00 to be invested and some placed on CDs. He tells them that is the largest sum of money he has ever dealt with.

Conrad leaves work for the day and heads for the house. Once there, Rosalyn embraces him and gives him a kiss. "What was that for?" asks Conrad. Rosalyn replies "Just because I love you. I've been lonely since Sylvia goes to work at 11:00 am each day. I don't know whether I can stand the schedule of you two as it exists now." Conrad asks her if she would like to go to college and she responds saying "Do you think I can handle it?" Conrad assures her that she can. He says Sylvia can take her to VCU to enroll in basic classes and that her major can be decided in a year or even two years. Rosalyn is so impressed, she kisses Conrad again.

These two go into the family room and get on the Internet and access VCU's web site. Conrad sees that registration has already closed for VCU, but sees there are some 1 credit courses that start in a week. He tells Rosalyn what these are and that she should go register with Sylvia tomorrow. Rosalyn is elated at the opportunity to go to a university. She has no idea what major she wants to try for.

Rosalyn begins dinner cooking. Conrad takes Bear for a walk to the west of the house. There is no one close to interrupt his pursuit. Bear and he have a good time together. He notices a police car pass slow by his house, but does not think anything about it. He continues with Bear on the walk. Sylvia arrives from work and goes looking for Conrad to share the news about her reassignment. Sylvia asks where Conrad is at. Rosalyn tells her that Conrad is walking Bear.

Sylvia waits for his return knowing he would feel hurt if she told Rosalyn before telling him. Conrad returns shortly and puts Bear in his pin. Going in the house, Conrad is met by Sylvia. She hugs him dearly and tells him the news. He kisses her and congratulates her. Conrad tells Sylvia about what Rosalyn and he were up to a few minutes ago. Sylvia thinks it is great and agrees to take her with her when she leaves for work tomorrow. Rosalyn had been listening and says to herself 'yes'.

Rosalyn tells the two lovers that dinner is served. They are having beef stroganoff. This was something really different for Sylvia and Conrad. Sylvia asks "Where did you get the idea for this?" "I got it from a book in the family room. It has several suggestions for meals. I plan to use some for our meals. There is lasagna I intend to do for tomorrow night." Conrad says "Bear should find that interesting as much as we will."

After dinner, the three go to the computer again and Conrad shows the courses to Sylvia. There were three. Conrad relates that these will be a start for Rosalyn and that she does not need to have a major for these classes. One of the classes Conrad says he wishes he had taken it, but was too busy with Business Management. He informs Rosalyn that it was those courses that got him the job he has now.

Sylvia says "Even I have gone to a university. I studied Psychology." This caught Conrad's ears. He says "Why haven't you told us this before?" "I forgot." "Well, don't let it happen again." She says she will try not to. Rosalyn queries "What was that all about? Is something going on between you two that I don't know about? Will you please tell me?" Conrad comments "Sylvia has a way of coming up with things that have no explanation. It is as if she has ESP or something. Sometimes I think she is getting her memory back. Other times, I am at a complete loss of words for an explanation. Maybe we will find out soon. I really don't know what is going to happen or what is going on with Sylvia."

The three settle down and ease tensions between themselves. Rosalyn is the first to speak after a short quiet period "Let's watch some TV to get our minds on something else. I like the western channel. It has some old movies, including ones with Tom Mix." Conrad and Sylvia agree it was a good idea and join Rosalyn in watching TV. After a movie, the three go to bed.

Hank and Grace have been busy packing and throwing things away that they will no longer need. Grace sets out all the canned goods and nonperishable food for Conrad to pick up tomorrow. She reminds Hank they need to call Conrad about the food and to tell him to bring a cooler for the frozen foods. They have a good time together and decide they are ready to move to Florida. They retire for the evening.

CHAPTER 33

The Move and Trouble

The Thomas' and Rosalyn all rise at their own respective houses. Grace and Hank have for them today, the moving to Key Largo. Conrad has his job to go to. Sylvia and Rosalyn will get Rosalyn registered for classes. Hank and Grace have fried eggs and bacon for breakfast. Rosalyn, Sylvia and Conrad have pancakes and waffles with fruit jams. They all enjoy their breakfast.

Hank calls Conrad and comments casually "We are moving today. It is just a matter of packing up the Sorento and leaving. We should be on our way by 10:00 o'clock am. Come over later and get whatever you want. We have sold the house furnished, but you can take some things if you want them. Conrad tells his dad okay and to have a safe trip. Further, he tells his dad he will pick up the truck with Sylvia.

Conrad and Sylvia are ready to leave for work. It is another cold day. Conrad leaves in his car while Rosalyn and Sylvia leave in her car. Sylvia talks to Rosalyn about getting her driver's license. Rosalyn states "I really have no reason to have a driver's license. I've got through until today without one, besides I don't have a car to drive." "That is all going to change. You get your license and Conrad and I will see to it that you have a car. It will have to be used, but it will be a dependable one. Conrad knows a dealer from Wachovia who can get you one. Besides, with you attending classes you will need your own transportation."

Rosalyn is flabbergasted. She cannot believe her ears. Sylvia and Conrad were actually going to buy her a car. She sees a certain amount of freedom. She asks can she pick out the car she wants. And Sylvia says yes. It turns out to be a glorious morning for Rosalyn.

They get to Virginia Commonwealth University Office of Records and Registration. Sylvia takes Rosalyn in and leads her to the clerk that will register her. The clerk is surprised that someone has come to register. Sylvia tells the clerk that she works at the Library and Rosalyn wants to register for three 1 hour credit classes coming up in a week. The admissions clerk tells her that she must fill out an application.

Rosalyn eagerly accepts the application, fills in all the blanks and returns the form to the clerk. The clerk tells them to wait a few minutes while she makes a phone call. The clerk calls the high school that Rosalyn graduated from wanting confirmation that Rosalyn had graduated from that school. Satisfied, the clerk returns to Rosalyn and says fill in this form with the classes she wishes to take. Finished, the clerk takes the form and registers Rosalyn for the classes. She says there is one course she will need a computer to take—a laptop. Then, the clerk says what Sylvia was afraid of "The cost of the courses is only $24.00 each, since Miss Pence is going to be a part-time student and live off campus.

Sylvia pays the fee. Rosalyn is accepted into the university. Her classes will start in one week. Sylvia and Rosalyn leave the office and go to the library. Sylvia tells Rosalyn "Unfortunately, you will be here the rest of the day. We can go to lunch together." Rosalyn is introduced to the staff as Sylvia's housekeeper. A joke is made about housekeepers sleeping with their employers. It was not funny to Rosalyn or Sylvia. Of course, they had reason to be upset with the comment.

Rosalyn picks a table and reads a book for a while and uses one of the computers for a while as well. Her time to her goes swiftly by. It becomes lunch time. Rosalyn goes to Sylvia and they leave for a quick lunch. Sylvia is having a problem with Alexis.

They go to a McDonald's for burgers and fries. They eat hurriedly so as to get back to the library in as little time as possible. Rosalyn asks Sylvia "Do you have problems out of Alexis all the time? She just doesn't look the type to cause trouble. What are you planning to do?" Sylvia answers "I plan to tell her to shape up or ship out. It is as simple as that." They finish their lunch and head back to the library.

Sylvia gets Alexis aside and tells her "If I continue to have problems from you, I will put you on unpaid leave until Witten returns. Is that understood? I cannot have trouble here in the library. Many students come in and go out. Any trouble would be noticed. Do I make myself clear?" Alexis returns "Yes. I'll attempt to be what you want." Sylvia is satisfied with Alexis' response.

The rest of the day remains uneventful. The talk with Alexis has done its part. Rosalyn and Sylvia head for the house. Conrad has had a filled day of counseling customers. It becomes time for him to leave and he is ready for it. He drives to his parent's house and gets his father's—now his—truck. He remembered that he needed to get some wood to build a water trough for Goldie. He drives the truck to Lowe's and gets the lumber and nails. He plans on finishing it tonight.

He gets home after Rosalyn and Sylvia. He is interested how the registration went. Conrad asks "How did it all go? Did you get registered? How much did it cost?" Rosalyn responds "It went extremely well. I am registered as a part-time student for three classes and it only cost $24.00 each." "Good for you."

This Tuesday has been the hardest day I've had in quite some time. I did counseling most of the day. One couple had $900,000.00 they wanted invested and CDs bought. That was a nightmare unto itself. I'll be out in the barn. I've got to build a water trough for Goldie. I think it'll be better than carrying her buckets of water twice a day." "Before you go, we need to get a cell phone for Rosalyn and buy her a used car so she will have her own transportation. On top of that, one of her classes requires a lap-top computer. When can we go get all that?" points out Sylvia.

Conrad says "Let me unload the lumber and we will go in the truck first to get the lap-top and then go to Carl's for a used car. Rosalyn agrees to help unload the lumber. The two get it done rather quickly. Conrad calls Sylvia and the three leave for Wal-mart. They check out the lap-tops and determine the $899.00 would be best suited to Rosalyn's need. Upon paying for it, they leave for Carl's Auto Sales. Conrad knows the man from his banking at Wachovia.

Arriving, Conrad goes and finds Carl. He tells Carl "We want a car for our housekeeper. Make it a 2003 or newer. The make and model will be up to Rosalyn. Rosalyn, come here and tell Carl what you want exactly." "I don't know exactly. I'll need to see what he has available and what the price range is." Carl leads them to several cars and it is not until they come upon a 2004 black Mustang that Rosalyn makes up her mind saying "This is the one I want if the price isn't too high. Carl offers the car at a reduced rate saying he will not take a commission on the car. It becomes likable to Sylvia and Conrad.

Sylvia drives the Mustang with Rosalyn accompanying her. Conrad drives the truck. The two vehicles arrive at the house at the same time. It is late enough that Conrad suggests they get to bed. He is the first to head towards the master bedroom. Sylvia follows and Rosalyn, happy with the car, goes to her bedroom. The cell phone will have to wait until tomorrow, day 24.

CHAPTER 34

More Trouble and the Phone

Rosalyn, Sylvia and Conrad get up about the same time. Sylvia and Conrad shower together. Rosalyn uses the other bath room to shower. The three dress and go into the kitchen. Breakfast again becomes cereal, but this time it is Shredded Wheat—one of Rosalyn's favorites. They each have a bowl and Rosalyn gets a second helping.

Sylvia answers Conrad's phone. She tells Conrad "It is Mrs. Crawford." Thinking it might be Mr. Crawford having trouble, Conrad asks "Is there anything wrong?" "Yes, Conrad. Someone stole your car last night. Conrad asks "Did you see them? Do you know what time it might have been?" Mrs. Crawford states "No, I didn't see them and it was sometime after 8:30 pm and before 7:00 o'clock this morning.

Conrad tells her he will be right there and thanks her for calling him. Conrad and the two girls get in the truck and go to his parents' house. Conrad calls 911 to report the theft of his Dodge Viper. The police arrive to take a report. Conrad tells them what Mrs. Crawford told him. Rosalyn pulls one officer aside and tells him "I used to live at Falling Creek Apartments. There was a man in the complex that use to steal cars. You might want to check that area out." The officer thanks her and makes a note.

The trio returns to the house and with Sylvia and Conrad getting ready for work. The time had creeped up on them quite fast. It was now 8:30 am. Sylvia and Conrad needed to be at work by 9:00 o'clock. Rosalyn was going to stay at the house all day. She had dishes to do and laundry to take care of. That would be her day's work. Sylvia and Conrad leave for work. They both have relatively normal days. Sylvia takes a short lunch to get home before Conrad.

Conrad leaves at his normal time and makes it home before Sylvia. He asks "What kept you from getting home before I did?" "I had a flat tire. I got one of the male students to change it for me. He did it for nothing accept wanting to look under my dress. I could not let him do that. I told him I was grateful and would help him out anytime he needed some help in the library." "Did that satisfy him?" asks Conrad. "I really do not know," replies Sylvia.

Conrad gets a call from police Headquarters. They have recovered his Viper. There would be a $60.00 towing fee. Conrad gets the girls and leaves for the station. Once there, he goes in to see the desk sergeant. Before he could identify himself, the sergeant says "You're Hank Thomas' son. I've seen you here several times. What can I do for you?" Conrad reports "Someone called and told me my car had been found. It was stolen yesterday." "You need to go to the impound yard. Go through that door over there and see the officer in the yard. He will be able to help you.

Conrad does as instructed. Seeing the impound lot officer, he asks about his car. The officer tells him "The silver Dodge Viper you speak of is not in the lot at the moment. It is being tested as a possible squad car. It should be back shortly. Sergeant Harris has been gone about 15 minutes." As they speak George Harris drives in with the car. He tells Conrad one like it may be a squad car after he makes his report. Conrad pays the $60.00 towing fee and Sylvia gets in to drive it back to the house.

Rosalyn chooses to ride with Conrad. He goes to the AT&T cell phone store. Inside, he gets Cheryl once more. He tells "We need a phone for this young lady. How about getting us the Blackberry 8330?" "Alright. Do you want the earpiece as well?" responds Cheryl. Conrad merely says "No." She gets the phone, sets up the account and gets the cell number of 804-555-1568. Last she instructs Rosalyn on how to use the phone and states "If you have any questions, ask Conrad. He has had his 8330 for two years now."

Cheryl turns to Conrad "Conrad that will be a total of $179.00 with a chance at $100.00 rebate if instructions are followed. Conrad uses his Master Card to pay for the phone. They get the phone and charger with it and head for the truck. Then, Conrad drives to the house.

It turns out that Sylvia has started dinner. Rosalyn and Conrad sit in the living room and talk about Yvonne. Rosalyn says "Now I will be able to go see momma whenever I want thanks to you buying me a car. I am going to enjoy driving it. But first, I need to get my driver's license. When can I do that?"

Conrad tells her Saturday. She is appeased with that. Sylvia calls them for dinner. Tonight is Texas Burgers. Rosalyn had never seen a concoction like this before. Rosalyn asks "What did you do to get these?" "It is really quite simple. You cook the burgers, place them on a slice of bread, cover with chili and beans and finally put shredded cheese on top, You can add onions" tells Sylvia. Rosalyn asks "Where did you learn to do this?" "At the library. You do not think that all I do is sit there do you?" comments Sylvia.

They eat the meal and Conrad is real pleased with Texas Burger. It reminds him of Mexican food. Rosalyn tells Sylvia "This is good. I want to try this one night. It's a kind of food that you could eat two nights in a row."

For dessert, they have a chocolate cake that Rosalyn had made earlier in the day. Sylvia and Conrad have learned that Rosalyn is a good cook by the meals and desserts she has come up with.

After eating the cake, Conrad says "Rosalyn, once more you have done it. You have given us a sample of your cooking abilities. They say the best way to a man's heart is through his stomach. You certainly have my heart."

They finish eating and Rosalyn starts the cleanup. Conrad takes some hamburger to Bear. The dog wags his tail when Conrad gets near him. While outside, he checks on the chicks. They have taken to eating the feed he had bought. He sees Goldie is hanging close to the fence. He goes over and rubs her head. Conrad looks to the east and he sees Bonnie Jean watching him. She raises her dress as an invite to her body. He goes back inside.

The three join together to watch TV. Tonight, they watch a movie about the disappearance of Natalie Hathaway—a teenager in Mexico with her graduating class. Sylvia says "My parents must be going through the same thing that her parents are going through." Rosalyn states "That may well be true if you have parents still alive. You don't know. Don't worry about it. You will eventually get your memory back and you will know who you really are and where you belong." After the movie, the three retire for the night.

CHAPTER 35

Saturday

The rest of the week is uneventful except for Bonnie Jean trying her best to get Conrad to come to her house. Conrad effectively ignores her. He knows that he could have her any night he wanted to. He even tells Sylvia about Bonnie Jean making the advances. She tells him it is his choice to do it or not.

Saturday morning comes and the three get up at the same time. They each shower and dress going into the kitchen. Rosalyn reports "There isn't anything for breakfast. We ran out of eggs yesterday. We need to do some shopping." Sylvia takes the day off as would Maryann Witten would want her to do. Conrad says "Let's go to breakfast at a restaurant. Shoney's sounds good. Then we can go to DMV and get Rosalyn a learner's permit. After that, we can go shopping. We will take the truck so we all can go."

Conrad drives the truck to the restaurant. The three go inside and are shown to a table. Rosalyn chooses to sit opposite Conrad leaving the left or right for Sylvia. Sylvia takes the right. The waitress comes and takes their drink order. Sylvia asks Conrad "Are we going to eat the buffet or choose from the menu. Conrad says "You two can eat from wherever you choose. I'm going to eat from the buffet." Rosalyn chooses the buffet, but Sylvia takes a look at it first and then looks at the menu. She finally chooses the buffet.

Rosalyn, Sylvia, and Conrad basically get the same things: scrambled eggs, potatoes, biscuit and gravy and sausage. When they return to their table, their drinks are waiting as is the silverware. They eat heartily. They each return for more selections such as fruit, pancakes, French toast and bacon. After eating, Conrad leaves a tip and then pays the bill. They make the choice to go to DMV next as they had planned.

They get to the DMV office and go in to get a number and sit waiting on the number to come up. When it does, the three go to the counter and Rosalyn states she would like a learner's permit. The clerk says we will need proof of age. She does not have any except for a certificate from a Driver's Education class. She tells them she has never had a birth certificate. Conrad says he can vouch for her age. The clerk is adamant about the birth certificate. Conrad points out that he knew they did not always need a birth certificate. But, the clerk insists by telling them "You need to go to the Division of Vital Records at Willow Lawn Mall on Broad Street. They can give you a certificate. It costs $20.00. You will have to wait until Monday."

Sylvia tells Rosalyn and Conrad "I go in late Monday. I can take her." So, the three give up on the learner's permit for the day. Rosalyn is disappointed in the wait until Monday. Conrad tells the girls they will go shopping, but asks where. Sylvia states "I want to try Ukrops. I hear they are lower than Wal-mart on some things. We do not need to get everything there though."

They go to Ukrops. There, they do find some things cheaper, but the meats are more expensive. Sylvia is picky over what she buys from Ukrops and saves her buying power for Wal-mart. After they get eggs, some canned goods and cereal; they go to Wal-mart.

Arriving at Wal-mart, they find the lot quite full. Conrad has to park a good bit away from the store. Upon entering, they find there are no carts. Conrad goes back outside and brings one in. He finds the girls waiting for him just inside. The group head for the food section of the store. The first thing they get is a loaf of bread. Rosalyn acts as the picker since she is in the kitchen the most. They continue to the canned goods and get what they did not get at Ukrops. In the cereal section, Rosalyn selects shredded wheat, Conrad selects sugar frosted flakes, and Sylvia selects cocoa puffs. Each has picked their favorite.

The main reason for coming to Wal-mart is for the meats. In that section, they get bacon, chicken legs, hamburger, steaks, pork loins, and sausage. Next is the dairy section. Here the three decide on milk, eggs, cheese, sour cream, butter and cottage cheese. As a final selection, they go to the fresh vegetables and fruits. Here selection is made for lettuce, tomatoes, potatoes, celery, radishes, cucumbers, cauliflower, broccoli, apples and bananas. Rosalyn points out they did not get orange juice. Conrad walks back and gets that.

As the group heads for the checkout lines, they see that all of them are full Sylvia decides she would like some socks since the weather has gotten quite cold. Rosalyn agrees. So they head for the clothing area and find an aisle that is loaded with socks. Sylvia selects crew socks and Rosalyn selects ankle socks.

Conrad says "Since we are in this section, I could use a package of underwear and one of T-shirts. He gets his desire. He also finds the need for some dress shirts. He does not want white. He has many of those already. He picks out three: a light blue, a light green and a pale yellow. He decides to get a belt as well. Rosalyn, Sylvia and Conrad having been satisfied in all ways of shopping in Wal-mart, head for the checkout lanes. They have a full cart. None of the lanes are empty. So, they pick one and wait. It takes about 20 minutes for the line to get to their cart.

Rosalyn starts placing the clothes on the conveyor belt. Then, Sylvia starts helping Rosalyn put the food on the belt. It takes 10 minutes to checkout. The total comes to $198.89. Conrad pays and instead of pushing the cart all the way to the truck, he goes to get the truck and bring it to the girls. They load all the bags into the rear of the truck. The back seat already had Ukrops purchases.

Sylvia says "Let us go to the Division of Vital Statistics. I think they are open today." "How do you know that" asks Conrad. "I just do." They arrive at Willow Lawn. Conrad states he will stay with the truck while the girls go to the Vital Records. Rosalyn and Sylvia go to find that it is open. They enter and have to wait in line. They are given an application to fill out for requesting a birth certificate. They turn it in; after a 5 minute wait, they receive a birth certificate for Rosalyn. It cost $20.00 as the license clerk said it would. The two go back to the truck.

It is now back to DMV to get Rosalyn a learner's permit. Rosalyn gets a number and she must wait again with Sylvia. When her number comes up the duo go to the counter.

. After telling the clerk she wants a permit, the clerk asks for a birth certificate. Rosalyn produces the one they had just got. The clerk types in her name and asks for the address, weight, height, hair color, and eye color. All of this gets typed in. The clerk takes Rosalyn to take a test on a computer. Rosalyn passes quite well. The clerk, then, sends the information to a printer and comes back with the permit. The clerk states it will be 30 days before she can take her test. She must also be accompanied by a licensed driver until the test is passed.

Rosalyn is enraptured. Her merriment is easily seen. Conrad drives back to the house. They proceed to unload the purchases. Sylvia hands Rosalyn her socks and takes the other clothes to the master bedroom. Rosalyn and Sylvia begin putting groceries away. It takes 20 minutes to clear things up. Rosalyn asks Conrad if he will go with her so she can drive to her mother's house. Sylvia does not get asked to go along. Conrad says he will a little later.

Sylvia chooses to go put her jeans on and go for a ride on Goldie. Out at the pasture, Sylvia gets Goldie, saddles her and then goes for a ride. There were also trails through the woods that she took as a diversion. She spends over an hour riding. In the meantime, Rosalyn and Conrad go to Yvonne's house.

Rosalyn drives quite carefully at first. She gets her feel for the car and drives more diligently while increasing her speed. They make it in an hour. Conrad normally takes half an hour or less.

Upon entering her mother's house, Rosalyn sees her mother is in a robe. She asks why. Yvonne simply says "It's beside you" meaning Conrad of course. Rosalyn tells her mother to look out the window at the Ford Mustang. Yvonne does so. Rosalyn tells her "That's my car. Sylvia and Conrad bought it for me." "That's nice dear. What have you done to deserve that?" asks Yvonne. Rosalyn comes back with "And what's that suppose to mean?" "Well, I just thought you would have to do something to earn it."

"Mother, I'm their housekeeper. I fix meals, I do laundry and I clean the house. What more do you expect?" "Oh, sex maybe." "Mother, I have sex with Conrad because I want to. I don't do it to earn anything. Why do you have sex with Conrad?" "That is an entirely different story. One you do not need to know right now," answers Yvonne, "I'm your mother and that's all there is to it."

Conrad interrupts and says "We came to visit you. Not to have a family discussion over sex. Although, that was an intention of mine. I know what. I'll do both of you." With that Yvonne opens her robe and lets it drop. Rosalyn takes off her dress and shoes and turns to Conrad asking "What are you waiting for?" He undresses as well. The three go into the bedroom and get at it.

When they are finished, Rosalyn and Conrad dress to leave. Yvonne tells Conrad "Come back anytime. It doesn't have to always be on Saturday." Conrad drives the Mustang back to the house. Sylvia has returned from her riding, unsaddled Goldie, rubbed her down and sits waiting in the family room on the computer. She is playing a logic game called 'Sherlock'.

"Sylvia, we're home, Dear," yells Conrad. She answers back "I'm in here. Are you finished with Yvonne?" "Yes, Dear." Conrad sits down to watch TV. Rosalyn goes into the kitchen and pops some popcorn and takes it to the family room. She sits beside Conrad. They share the popcorn. She had also brought three drinks and gave these around. They watch TV for a while until Conrad gets an idea.

"Sylvia, I told you once before, a long time ago, that we would go search for your purse. Let's drive up to where I found you and look around," commands Conrad "Rosalyn can help us look. It will be easier for us that way." "Okay. That sounds like a marvelous idea." So, Conrad drives the 2004 Mustang up to Mount Holly Church Road. It takes half an hour.

Conrad states "This is where I found you; right by this dirt road. Let's look around here first." They search to no end. Conrad, then, declares "We probably need to go down this road."

So, all three go down searching as they go. Sylvia finds her shoe. Conrad says "Search both sides and look under the brush. Rosalyn finds the purse and calls Sylvia. Conrad hears the call and comes running back to the girls. Sylvia opens the purse, finds her $1,000.00 and her driver's license. She sees she is Sylvia Redman. Conrad is the first to speak "You are the President's daughter."

Rosalyn asks "What do we do now? How are we going to explain her being in Richmond?" Conrad says "Let me call my dad and see what he has to say." Sylvia is dumbfounded by the development. Conrad calls "Dad, I've something to tell you. My wife, Sylvia, is actually Sylvia Redman, the President's daughter. What should we do? How am I going to explain she has been here for over three weeks?"

Hank tells him "You need to notify authorities. They are bound to have been looking for her. I'm amazed they haven't found her yet. Notify the FBI in Richmond first. Then, notify Henrico Police. Talk to the Chief. He knows you. Before nightfall, you will be surrounded by law enforcement. Get use to it. They won't go away." Grace interrupts "What is all this about the FBI and Henrico police? Hank tells her "Conrad has married the President's daughter, Sylvia Redman. Conrad, I can't give you any more information on what to do. It's your choice. Let her live with you as Sylvia Thomas or turn her in so she can be Sylvia Redman." "Thanks dad."

Conrad drives the three to the house. He discusses with Sylvia what she wants to do. It becomes a long drawn out affair that neither can make up their mind until Rosalyn butts in "Sylvia, you need to at least talk to your mother and father. They are bound to be worried about you and may even think you are dead. You need to let them know you are here." Sylvia makes up her mind that she will at least talk to them.

Conrad calls the FBI office in Richmond and tells them he lives with Sylvia Redman. They at first do not believe him. He tells them her hair color, her height, her weight, and eye color. They, then, believe and send four agents out to Conrad's house. Conrad calls the Henrico Police Chief and tells him the same thing. He comes to Conrad's house with six other officers. The road gets blocked off. Bonnie Jean sees all that is going on and calls WRIC channel 8 news and tells them of the commotion going on next door. The channel dispatches a news truck with portable broadcast capabilities.

An FBI Agent is the first on the scene with three underling agents. This agent identifies himself "I am FBI Agent Mark Nugent. I am here to talk to Sylvia Redman. Where is she?" Sylvia has been in the master bedroom, but comes out when she hears her name being called as to where she is. She tells the agent "I am Sylvia Thomas or Redman whichever you want to call me by. This is my husband Conrad and this is our housekeeper Rosalyn Pence. What do you need of me?"

Agent Nugent states "Ma'am, we need to let you parents know you are okay and where you are. Do you understand that?" "If it is necessary, then, let it be done. I am anxious to talk with them as well. I have had amnesia for the past three weeks and do not wholly remember who I am or where I come from," relates

Sylvia "and I have a job and a car that Conrad and I bought just two weeks ago."

"Pardon me while I call our office in Washington," declares Nugent. After dialing the FBI number in D.C., Nugent informs the office that he has located Sylvia Redman. The office notifies Ginger Ales, who in turn notifies the President. President Redman orders Ales "Take Air Force One, go to Richmond and get her. I want to see her tonight." Ales did not know that Sylvia was married or that there is a housekeeper. She takes a government car to Andrews Air Force Base. Ales contacts the pilots in route to the base telling them they will be needed to fly to Richmond immediately.

Senior Agent Ginger Ales arrives and gets aboard Air Force One. It takes off and in 45 minutes, it requests landing instructions from Richmond Airport Tower. The tower immediately has all landings and takeoffs put on hold. Air Force One is given instructions on landing. After touchdown, the plane is directed to an area that is used very little and is reserved for special flights. Air Force One is one of those flights.

Agent Ales calls Agent Nugent and asks will anybody else be going back to D.C. Mark Nugent tells her about the housekeeper and the husband and that one or both may go back. Ales rents a van with a government credit card. She has gotten instructions on how to get to Sylvia's and Conrad's house. Ginger makes it in 40 minutes using I-295 to get to the other side of Richmond in Henrico County.

Arriving, Ales is blocked from going to the house until she shows her FBI badge and ID. Once inside, she discovers Sylvia. Without delay, Ginger introduces herself and declares "Young lady, do you have any idea of the effort that has been spent in trying to find you?"

Before Ales can make another statement, Rosalyn interrupts with "Agent Ales, do you have any idea what Sylvia has been through the last three weeks? First off, she has an accident and is found unconscious on the side of Mount Holly Church Road.

Secondly, she remained unconscious for four more days. Thirdly, she suffers from amnesia. And last, she is married to Conrad Thomas, who found her at the side of the road. They own this house." "Who are you?" asks Agent Ginger Ales.

"I'm Rosalyn Pence, their housekeeper. I have been since they bought this house. Where they go, I go," states Rosalyn. Agent Ginger tells Sylvia "Your parents want to see you tonight. I have Air Force One at Richmond Airport to take you there. You are expected to stay. So, you might want to pack a suitcase or two. We leave here in 20 minutes. There will be four FBI agents here to watch your house every day and every hour. If you go somewhere, I or one of the other agents will go with you. You are not to travel alone. Do you understand what I just told you?" "Yes," says Sylvia "does that apply to Conrad and Rosalyn as well. "NO. Just you."

Rosalyn and Sylvia pack clothes for themselves and Sylvia packs Conrad's as well. The three announce "We are ready to go." Ginger shows them to the van. Rosalyn gets in the front passenger seat with Ginger; while Sylvia and Conrad get in the back seat, another FBI agent gets in the third seat. The news channel crew from WRIC tape and broadcast this happening. Nobody in the news crew knows what exactly is going on. But, with all the police and FBI agents, they figure it must be something important and that is why they are here to get the news for broadcast later that day.

Agent Ales drives the van to Richmond airport to the special gate near Air Force One. Sylvia says "I remember this plane. It is like a lounge on the inside with very comfortable seats. Ales and the three get on the plane. The other agent holds onto the van and returns to the Thomas house. The plane taxis and then takes off after the tower holds all air traffic from landing and taking off. The flight only takes an hour and they land at Edwards Air Force Base near D.C.

Ginger gets her car back and loads the three and she drives to the White House. She is let in through a gate guarded by a Marine corporal. Ginger Ales takes Rosalyn, Sylvia and Conrad into the White House into the Oval Office where President Sylvester Redman is waiting with First Lady Mary Redman. "Sylvia, we have been worried about you. Where have you been these past three weeks? And why did you leave in the first place?" asks Sylvester. Sylvia responds "I do not know why I left. I have had amnesia for the last three weeks. I have been in Richmond and I do not know how I got there except for what Conrad told me." "Is this Conrad?" "Yes, he is my husband." Mary asks "Why did you get married and when? I really need to know why."

Sylvia answers "The why is simple. I love him. He stayed with me through all the time I was in the hospital, even when I was unconscious. His family provided me a place to stay not knowing who I was or where I came from. We fell in love rather quickly." "And who is this young lady?" asks Mary. Sylvia reports "This is Rosalyn Pence, our housekeeper. Her only pay is a place to stay and eat. She has been with us for two weeks. Rosalyn is very important to Conrad and I. Conrad has a job as a manager at Wachovia Bank and I have a job as a librarian at Virginia Commonwealth University Library."

Sylvester imparts "Tell us the whole story from the time you left." "Dad, I do not remember leaving. The hospital told me I was unconscious for four days. I stayed two more. Conrad was there all six days. I told you about living with his family. Conrad bought me clothes, a car, and a cell phone. He helped me open a checking account and a savings account. Conrad helped me get a credit card. He helped me get a new driver's license because I had lost my purse." Sylvester interrupts "That explains the fact you did not use your credit cards. Go on." "Conrad helped me get an apartment and his mother helped with the job. Dad, mom, I have a home where I feel loved and comfortable. I cannot live in Washington anymore," completes Sylvia.

"Well, at least you will stay a week with us. Your husband and Rosalyn can see the sights. We can get you squared away at Georgetown University. There will plenty for you to do as well," demands President Redman. "We cannot do that. Conrad has to be at work 9:00 am Monday morning. We have animals that need attending. Goldie is our golden Palomino and Bear is our Newfoundland dog. We also have 15 chicks to feed. I need to be at work Monday at 11:00 am. I am afraid we can only stay overnight. We will need to leave Sunday afternoon," declares Sylvia.

Conrad speaks up "I would like to have a tour of D.C. I have never been here before. I am sure Rosalyn will agree." Rosalyn says "Yes, I want to see the Washington Monument and Smithsonian Institution."

"Ales, get Geoffrey Riggins over here tomorrow morning to act as a tour guide for these two. Have him here at my office by 9:00 am," demands Sylvester. "Dad, I want to go with them. I can be the guide for Conrad and Geoffrey can be the guide for Rosalyn." "Ales, take note of that."

Rosalyn asks "Why can't Ginger be my guide? I've taken a liking to her. I think I would enjoy that better." Sylvester states "Ginger, you heard the lady. Forget about Geoffrey coming and you be here at 9:00 am." "Yes, sir" replies Ginger Ales "I will be here as you ask." Conrad says to Sylvia "I'm getting tired. When and where do we go to bed?" "We can all sleep in my room. It is the Lincoln Bedroom. We will need a cot for Rosalyn. Dad, can you fix that?" announces Sylvia. Sylvester gets on the phone and has one of the servants get a cot for Sylvia's room.

Sylvia states "Dad, we are going to go to bed now. We will see you in the morning." "Okay, Sylvia. Have a good night's sleep," says her Dad. They go to the Lincoln Bedroom and the cot is already there. They undress and retire for the night.

President Redman tells Ales "I am glad that you were able to find her. What did it? Was it the satellite monitoring system?" "No, Mr. President. Conrad Thomas called our office in Richmond and reported he had Sylvia. We have an FBI force surrounding her house in Henrico County outside the western part of Richmond," reports Agent Ales. "I think we have her pretty well covered." Sylvester commands "Ales, you will stay down there two days coming back Tuesday night. Take a regular flight back to D.C. Try to get to know this Conrad and Rosalyn. I will want a report from you when you get back." "Yes sir, Mr. President."

CHAPTER 36

Washington D.C. The Next Day

Rosalyn, Sylvia, and Conrad get up and dress from the luggage bag they had brought with them. They go to the dining room and are met by the President and First Lady. Mary asks "Did you sleep well?" Rosalyn is the first to speak. "Yes, the cot was extremely comfortable. I look forward to it the next time we come." Mary adds "Oh, you talked about coming back? That is wonderful. We look forward to your coming again. Perhaps next time it can be for a week." "That is what we talked about last night. I need to get some more time in on my job before I can take leave, Conrad has two weeks' vacation time left for the year" explains Sylvia.

Conrad asks "What is for breakfast?" Mary Redman states "I really do not know. We get a surprise every day of the week. Our chef employs a wide variety of foods that he uses to satisfy our needs." About that time, the breakfast arrives for all of them carried by two servants on trays. The breakfast turns out to be eggs Benedict, bacon, sausage, hash brown potatoes and orange juice. The President and First Lady each have coffee.

Rosalyn comments "This is quite a breakfast. I'd never have thought about eggs Benedict. We would have fried or scrambled eggs. I'm a relatively good cook or at least Sylvia and Conrad think so." Sylvia adds "She genuinely is. Conrad and I have gained a little weight due to her cooking." Sylvester says "Well, maybe when you come back we can have a meal cooked by your housekeeper. I am sure it will be interesting. What do you think mother?" "I am looking forward to it," adds Mary.

They all finish breakfast. Senior Agent Ginger Ales arrives at 8:30 am. She is dressed for an outing. She asks "Where shall we go first? I am driving a government vehicle and it can park anywhere. I heard the Washington Monument mentioned last night. We could start there. We can also visit the Jefferson Memorial and the Lincoln Memorial. The Smithsonian has several museums. The latest of which is about Native Americans—Indians. We will have a full day. For lunch, we can eat from one of the vendors that are on various corners."

Rosalyn is first again to speak "I do want to visit the Washington Monument. I want to go to the top and see all around D.C." Sylvia comes back "You can see into Maryland and Virginia from up there." "That'll be interesting, I'm sure," returns Rosalyn. Conrad says he is interested in the Smithsonian museums, especially the one on Native Americans and the one on Air and Space. Agent Ales states "It sounds like we have an agenda to complete. Let us get started. We can take the car I have reserved for the day."

The group goes to the Washington Monument first as planned. Rosalyn and Conrad are amazed. Sylvia and Ginger are not. They have both seen it before. Sylvia realizes that she is getting her memory back and tells Rosalyn and Conrad. Both sound agreement and are delighted. At the top of the Monument, Rosalyn makes the comment "It is so beautiful up here. It makes the trip to D.C. worthwhile. I could do this again sometime."

After coming down, the group goes to the Lincoln Memorial. Again, Rosalyn is enchanted having never been there before. She comments "This is what is on the back of a penny. What a delight it is to actually be here. Conrad agrees with Rosalyn. Sylvia and Ginger remain quiet. Conrad asks why. Ginger answers "We both have seen all this before. The only place I have not been is the Native American Museum. I am looking forward to that visit." Sylvia also answers "I have not seen it either. I will like it, I am sure."

Conrad mentions "I've noticed that Ginger and you don't use contractions. Why not?" "We both have attended Georgetown University and they teach you to speak proper English. Contractions are not part of proper English if you are dealing with important people. The President and First Lady also speak proper English. "I have noticed my mother speaks this proper English. She, however, is an English professor for VCU in Richmond. I will make an attempt to speak this proper English," insures Conrad.

Sylvia suggests they move on to the Jefferson Memorial. Rosalyn says "This is what is on the back of the nickel. That is the only place I have seen the Memorial. I would like to go to Monticello to Jefferson's home. I haven't been there yet either. I hear it has an actual dumbwaiter from the kitchen to the dining room. I would like to see that." Conrad comes back "That is a place we can go to after we get home and we can plan it for sometime in the future."

Sylvia comments "I have never been there before either. I am sure it would be interesting. They say you can see downtown Charlottesville from Jefferson's house," After leaving the Jefferson Memorial, the four go to the Smithsonian museums on the plaza. The first they go to is the Native American display. It has all kinds of panoramas of Indians in hunting, village and family settings. It covers just about all the Indian tribes including Algonquin, Iroquois, Cherokee, and Eskimos just to mention a few.

It gets to be lunch time. The group arrives at a street vendor area on the plaza. Rosalyn and Conrad select to order hot dogs with mustard and sauerkraut. Sylvia orders a plain hot dog. Ginger orders a hot dog with mustard, onions and chili. She likes hers done completely with the condiments available. They all get soft drinks and have a good time at eating a lunch snack. Rosalyn states she will need more later in the day. Ginger says that is no problem for them.

Sylvia says "Let us go to the Air and Space Museum. There is a copy of the Wright brothers' airplane. There is also a mock up of the space shuttle and you can walk through it." Ginger says "There is also a display of the solar system. You can see all the planets in their proper perspective to one and another." The four go there and take advantage of all the displays.

After their enjoyment at this museum they go to the African Art Museum, American Art Museum, American History Museum, Anacostia Community Museum and the Natural Science Museum. Rosalyn and Conrad are flabbergasted. They have enjoyed the day and return to the White House. Rosalyn and Conrad relate the excitement of their adventure for the day.

The Redman family, the Thomas group and Ginger Ales have dinner together. Sylvester says "We had planned a surprise birthday for you on Sunday after your birthday. It has been postponed. The invitees were all notified. When you came up missing, we started a search here in D.C. and it goes to Baltimore, Fredericksburg and Richmond. We searched for your car with a satellite monitoring system. Richmond police say they had stopped a car like yours, but it was not the one we were looking for." Sylvia remembers the policeman stopping her, but does not say anything other than he checked her license.

Conrad says "When do we get to go home? I miss Bear and Goldie. What do we need to do?" Sylvester says "We will get you on the road home in a few minutes. You will be on Air Force One in a short amount of time. Do not fret. It is no kind of audacity." Sylvia states "We do need to get going. We have to prepare for work tomorrow. Why do you not come with us to see our home?" "We could do that. We will take Air Force One and get us a rental car once there and spend a short amount of time with you."

The group goes to Edwards Air Force Base and into the plane. The President goes first and Ginger Ales goes last. The plane begins to taxi and once more it is on a flight to Richmond. The flight takes slightly over an hour. The Richmond tower puts landings and take offs on hold for Air Force One once again. It lands and taxis to the special discharge area. Ginger rents two cars—one for her and one for the President. She lets Conrad drive her car while she drives the President and First Lady. They arrive at Sylvia's and Conrad's home. Some of the police are still there as are the four FBI agents.

Arriving with the President and First Lady, the news casters have a field day covering the coming of the two. Conrad, wanting to show off everything takes the President and First Lady to the back of the house to see Goldie, Bear and the chicks. The President asks "Who put up the fence around the scratch yard? It looks sturdy." Conrad responds "I did with some assistance from our housekeeper, Rosalyn. It took us about three hours. The chicks were boxed up the entire time." "It looks as though you are quite the farmer. A horse, a shepherd dog and chicks all to keep you busy in your spare time," states the President. Conrad shows them indoors.

Sylvia takes the lead "This is our living room. Notice there is no TV in this room. This is our dining room with the kitchen off to the side. Rosalyn likes the idea of an island in the middle of the kitchen. Coming down the hallway, the first room is our family room. Here, we have a small library, the TV and two computers. Next is the master bedroom where Conrad and I sleep. Across from the family room is Rosalyn's room and next to her room are two guest rooms. We have not finished off the one room because we are not sure that it will be or not, a nursery. The only other thing is the basement, but we have not done anything to it yet either. We plan another guest room and an activity room to take up half of the basement"

Rosalyn, in the meantime, has been making coffee. She asks "Mr. President, First Lady, would you like a cup of coffee?" They both say yes and Rosalyn proceeds to pour them each a cup of coffee. "Would you like sugar and/or cream," asks Rosalyn. The President says "Make mine black." Mary, the First Lady, says "I will have two sugars, please." Rosalyn fixes up the cup going to Sylvia's mother. She gives each their cup of coffee. After drinking some of his coffee, he states "Sylvia, I can see why you have Rosalyn for a housekeeper. This coffee is better than what I get at the White House. I would say she cooks as well also." "That she does Dad. She fixes all our dinners. If I am first up, I sometimes fix breakfast" reports Sylvia.

First Lady Mary inquires "Where did you learn to cook? You have not been that good of a cook ever. Is it possible you learned from Rosalyn?" "Well, some I did learn from her. But, mostly, I learned it at the library at VCU," tells Sylvia. Conrad comments "Your daughter is learning to be quite the cook. One night she fixed us Texas burgers. It was almost like eating Mexican food. It had a slice of bread with a large hamburger on the bread covered with chili beans, cheese and onion."

"Ales, you are to stay two days, at least, to see no harm comes to my daughter. Before you come back to Washington, get an agent to accompany her to work. Is that understood?" orders the President. "Yes, sir" "We will now leave to go back to Washington. I have meetings early tomorrow morning. Sylvia, give us your phone number so we can call you," demands the President. She does as told. The President and First Lady leave and go to the Richmond Airport. There, they get on Air Force One and head back to D.C.

Bonnie Jean has been watching all that she could, including the President being next door. She is anxious to find out what it is all about. Bonnie Jean becomes determined to talk with Conrad at his work Monday afternoon after she gets off work. She figures she will have an hour and a half to talk to him if he is not busy. Yvonne calls to find out what has happened that Conrad had not visited her on Saturday. He explains everything to her including that Sylvia is regaining her memory and is the President's daughter.

Conrad makes the comment to Ginger "You did not bring any clothes with you. How are you going to stay two or more days? Sylvia will have to take you shopping tomorrow. Will that be okay?" "Why yes. I had not thought about it until you said something. I could use another suit and possibly a dress," speaks Ginger in return. Sylvia explains "We can go to Talbot's or Wal-mart, whichever one you want. Both have quality merchandise, but Wal-mart has the lower prices. Ginger remarks "I think Wal-mart will do."

Rosalyn shows Ginger where her bedroom will be—the one prepared guest room. Ginger says goodnight and retires. The other three talk a bit about today's events. Conrad says "If we had not found your wallet, you would still be my unknown bride—Sylvia Thomas. I think that would have been better. We would live happily ever after much like we will be able to do once your father gets out of office." Sylvia informs Conrad "That will not be the case. I will have a body guard as long as my father lives. I could be taken as a hostage by some terrorists and used to get the U.S. to give into something as long as my dad is alive."

The three finally retire for the evening.

CHAPTER 37

The Stay of Ginger

Conrad is the first to arise this Monday morning. He showers and dresses in one of his new suits. Rosalyn is next and she does dress in a similar manner. Next are Sylvia and finally Ginger. They all meet in the kitchen for breakfast. Rosalyn prepares scrambled eggs with cheese, bacon and fruit. Ginger is amazed at the taste of everything once she starts eating. She tells Rosalyn "I am going to stay long enough to learn a few tricks with food. I am not married and I am already 30 years old. If I do not get married soon, I may wind up a spinster."

Sylvia returns "You do not have anything to worry about. As good looking as you are, you should get a man quite easily. There are plenty of men available in Richmond. They hit on me all the time. I just tell them I am happily married." "Yes, but I do not live in Richmond. I must deal with the few that are in D.C. Most, I have already dated. All they really want is my body." "It is worth having. I am sure Conrad would want you if he did not have me," states Sylvia.

Conrad leaves the girls and heads for work. He gets there on time. He has no business to address this morning. Sylvia tells Ginger and Rosalyn they should all go shopping. They could take Ginger's car. Going out, Ginger tells the FBI agents around the house that they will be back in about an hour. They can relax for that time. The three women get into the car with Rosalyn next to Ginger and Sylvia in the back seat.

Ginger looks a little out of place because she is dressed in a woman's business suit. No other woman in Wal-mart is dressed that way. It does not matter to Ginger, she is there to shop. And shop the girls do. Sylvia gets two new skirts and a blouse. Rosalyn gets a blouse and pair of slacks. Ginger finds a dress that can be worn for casual or business and she finds a business suit that she likes. The women continue to look around to find if there is anything else they want or need. Coming up with nothing, the three head for the checkout.

At the register, Sylvia pays for Rosalyn and her purchases. Ginger pays for her purchases with a government credit card. The clerk had never seen one before and Agent Ales had to explain to her about the card and show her FBI ID card. The clerk accepted the card and the sale is approved. The clerk gives her a receipt to sign. It is something they had all been through at one time or another. They, then, go to the car and Ginger drives them home.

It becomes time for Sylvia to go to work at the library. Ginger, Rosalyn and she go in her red Dodge Viper. Sylvia and Ginger get to the library and Sylvia says "I am going to introduce you as a visiting friend. In essence, that is what you are. You can use any of the computers to surf the Internet or access any web site. You will be able to keep an eye on me very easily if you take a computer that when you sit you face the counter." They go in. Ginger gets introduced. Then, she comments about Sylvia's Viper being just like the one she had in Washington. Rosalyn starts her classes.

The morning appears uneventful. Ginger, Rosalyn and Sylvia go to lunch at Sino American Restaurant. Ginger says it is the first time she had been to an oriental food establishment. As they enter, Ginger notices Goldfish in the indoor pond. She finds it hard to believe these have grown so large. After they enter the food area, they are shown to a table. They sit opposite each other and talk about Sylvia's life from now on. Sylvia learns for a fact that she will have a body guard for some time to come. The body guard will almost have to live with her.

The waitress takes their drink order and leaves. Ginger and Sylvia get up, get a plate and start filling it with various foods. Getting back to the table, their drinks are waiting for them. They eat enthusiastically. The time together does draw them into a friendship status. One that Ginger knew she should not do, but could not help herself. Such was the impact of Rosalyn and Sylvia on Ginger.

The meal being over, they return to the library. Agent Ales says "I want to watch you and make sure no one gets at you. If I see something that does not look right, I will be forced to draw my gun and intervene. Let us hope you have an uneventful day." Ginger takes a computer close to the counter. Being 30, she did not look her age. She looks more like 21 than anything else. Ginger was even hit upon by some male students that if she were a few more years younger. The boys could almost have been her child. She passes them all up saying she is married.

The day ends and Maryann telling Sylvia "Thank you for taking my place. I hope we do not have to do it again, although I know you can handle it." Maryann has stayed over to catch up on some work that Sylvia was not authorized to do. Ginger and Sylvia go to her car and get in. They go to get Rosalyn. As Sylvia backs out, her car is struck by a young man. There is no damage to either vehicle.

The young man states "Since we have had this accident, I will need your name and license number." He really wants to get into an intimate relationship with either of the two ladies. Ginger jumps in with "I am a federal agent. There is no damage here and if there were, it would be your fault for not stopping. I suggest you leave. The young man does just that not wanting any trouble with the law.

Meanwhile, Rosalyn has taken her three classes and needs a ride home with Sylvia and Ginger. Ginger, Rosalyn and Sylvia return home. Meanwhile, Conrad has a visit from Bonnie Jean. She tells him "I saw all the police and those federal men at your house Saturday and there are still some there today. What exactly is going on? Since I am your next door neighbor, I have a right to know." Conrad returns "Did you watch the 11:00 o'clock news? There was bound to have been a story. It really is none of your business, but I will tell you anyway. As you may know, Sylvia has had amnesia and did not know where she came from. It turns out she is the President's daughter, Sylvia Redman." "You mean I've had sex with the President's son-in-law?" "Yes, unfortunately for me," states Conrad. Bonnie Jean comes back with "I won't tell anybody, if you will give me more. That's a simple offer."

Conrad tells her "Tell anybody you like. They will not believe you. All they have to do is ask me and I will deny any knowledge of it. I will just say that you are an envious widow who cannot find a man since your husband passed away." "You would say something like that? Why I never thought you would be like that. Why can't we have a relationship?" asks Bonnie Jean. "We do have a relationship. You are our neighbor who can come and visit us as soon as we introduce you to the FBI agents guarding our home."

Bonnie Jean is a little upset and it shows. Conrad comments "Your disappointment is showing. I will tell you what. When Sylvia will not give it to me, I will come and get it from you. How does that sound?" Bonnie Jean perks up. She has a smile on her face and hope on her mind. She actually believes that Conrad will be coming to her. She decides to leave and compliments Conrad "You are a fine gentleman to look out for the needs of a neighbor."

Time has rolled around for Conrad to go home. He leaves work a bit concerned over Bonnie Jean's comments. He begins to think she will be trouble. He also is wondering what Yvonne is going to have to say about Sylvia being the President's daughter and his not showing up on Saturday. He makes up his mind he is determined to go by her house today. As he enters her house, she says "Hello, lover boy. It's going to make our time together all the more fun. I know you are married to the President's daughter." "Who told you that?" asks Conrad.

"Word gets around. Besides, I have a friend that works for channel 8 and he talked to one of the police officers he knew. For a little bit of romance, he told me everything. It really doesn't matter to me. I'll like it all the more. You did come for some fun, didn't you?" Conrad answers "No. It is not Saturday. I told you we would have each other on Saturdays." Yvonne interrupts "And I told you to come anytime you wanted to have some. So, what else am I to think, my love?"

Conrad says "You are right you did tell me that. I guess we will have to go at it for another time today. They go to her bedroom, undress and get in the bed. She gets on top and goes at it.

When finished, Conrad dresses and leaves going straight home. Rosalyn asks "Where have you been? You're an hour late. It won't be long before Sylvia and/or Ginger ask the same question. What do you want for dinner? What should I fix something special for Ginger?" "Fix something special that I am sure she would like and like you for cooking it."

Rosalyn goes into the library and gets a cookbook. She looks up several entrees, but cannot make her mind up as to which she should prepare. She resolves to cook T-bone steak with sautéed mushrooms, mashed potatoes with cheese, and asparagus. Conrad has to take her to Wal-mart to get the food. When back home, she prepares the food and it becomes ready just as Ginger and Sylvia arrive home from going to the Richmond FBI office to establish a replacement for Ginger.

Ginger says "You did this for me? T-bone is my favorite food and with sautéed mushrooms to boot. Girl, you are something else." Rosalyn took the latter as a genuine compliment. She feels she is getting to be friends with Ginger. They eat with everyone enjoying the meal. After dinner, Rosalyn questions the rest "Who wants dessert? We can have ice cream, cake or a la mode."

Ginger answers with enthusiasm, "I want the a la mode." Both Sylvia and Conrad just ask for ice cream. Rosalyn has the same as Ginger. Rosalyn gets it out and serves it with pleasure as asked for. After dinner, Rosalyn begins to cleanup alone, but Ginger cuts in with "Here, let me help. You did such a good job cooking. You can use the help, I know." Rosalyn accepts only because it is Ginger.

They all go in to watch the TV. They watch Law and Order: Special Victims Unit. It is a new episode that they have not seen. Ginger has some insight as to how the series episode is developing. She shares with the others. They are surprised that she could do that. Ginger explains "Each episode is based on laws and the discovery of evidence. Without evidence, a crime cannot be solved. I have had some training in evidence recovery."

They continue watching television to see the 11:00 o'clock pm news. There turns out to be a clip on Sylvia, but not who she is as a Thomas. She felt the TV channel had done that on purpose to keep her identity a secret. But, mouths will be mouths and Bonnie Jean could not help but tell her co-workers that she lived next door to Sylvia Redman, the President's daughter. Word travelled quickly and another channel had the news she was married to Conrad Thomas.

The police were put to the test with sightseers wanting to catch a glimpse of Sylvia. The Henrico Chief felt he would need to add four officers just to block off the street. Bonnie Jean would bring to her house co-workers so they might get a glimpse of Sylvia. For quite some time it remains thus. Conrad, Sylvia, Rosalyn, Ginger, and Bonnie Jean with a co-worker were the only ones to get in that particular part of their road. An official detour was established so cars would go another route.

After watching the news, the four decide it is time for bed. Sylvia and Conrad go to their room. Rosalyn asks Ginger to talk to her. Rosalyn tells Ginger that she is really Conrad's mistress in addition to being the housekeeper and that Sylvia knew all about it. Ginger states "I thought that all along. You spend so much time alone with Conrad. Why do you not make it known?" "Mainly, I want to not have them hurt because of Conrad's and Sylvia's positions. It would be hard on them. Now, I also have the reason Sylvia is the President's daughter. Besides, all that matters is the three of us know. I really am their housekeeper. I do the laundry, all the cleaning and most of the cooking. My pay is Conrad and Sylvia buy me what I need and want. They even bought me the extra car outside. I haven't got my license yet, but I do have my learner's permit."

Ginger inquires "Why did you want to talk to me? At most, I am only going to be here a week. Then, it will be someone else, we talked about it probably being a woman near Sylvia's age. We have agents fresh out of college." "I need someone other than Sylvia and Conrad to talk about my problems. You just answered one of my questions. You do take people straight out of college. I've wanted to do something like this for some time. If I go to college, do you think you can help me get a job with the Richmond FBI?"

Ginger responds "I may be able to help some. But, the main point will be your college time. We expect our agents to have a GPA of 3.0 or higher. Do that and your chances will be greatly improved." "Can I call you from time to time? I do need a different friend" gives Rosalyn. "And I need to learn to cook like you do. You help me and I will help you."

After a bit more talking, they retire for the evening with Ginger going to the guest room to sleep.

CHAPTER 38

Tuesday

All four wake at the same time. For Sylvia and Conrad, it is no problem. They take a shower together. Rosalyn allows Ginger to take a shower first. She gets her shower afterwards. They all dress for the day's events. Ginger puts on her new business suit which she likes quite well. Her other clothes she gave to Rosalyn to wash. They have pancakes for breakfast. All enjoy the pancakes that Rosalyn made. She tells the recipe to Ginger because she cooked them like Grace has taught her to do for Conrad.

Conrad, before going to work, calls his dad in Key Largo "Dad, hi. How is it going down there? Listen, it is a big task living with four guards and four police officers around us around the clock. In addition, we have an FBI agent, Ginger Ales, that goes to work with Sylvia. She also eats with us. How long do you think this will last? The President says it would last as long as he is alive."

Hank replies "Well, the President is right. I should have told you about the bodyguards since Sylvia is the President's daughter. I knew that was going to happen. It happened with Bill Clinton and Chelsea. She couldn't go to school without a bodyguard. Try not to worry. They won't interfere with your lifestyle. They are mainly there to insure your privacy. The police will handle traffic and the FBI will handle anyone who gets past the police."

Conrad returns "I am glad that I had a talk with you. It has been three days now. I went to D.C. and met the President and First Lady. I also got a tour of the D.C. monuments and the Smithsonian Museums. It was a nice time there. How are mom and you doing down there in Florida?"

"We are doing quite well. We walk on the beach every evening and go out to eat when we want. There are quite a few restaurants that serve lunch and dinner. But, there are only a few serving breakfast. So, we usually have breakfast at home. The house looks well since your mother had some modifications and renovations done to it. You really need to come here and see the house," tells Hank.

"Well Dad, it is time for me to leave for work. I cannot get out of it anymore. I took my two weeks and the work piled up for me. You and mom take care. We love you. Bye" relates Conrad. He leaves for work telling Sylvia "I love you." He gives her a kiss and leaves.

Sylvia asks Ginger what she would like to do. Ginger tells her she wants to learn more about cooking like Rosalyn does. This kind of hits a kink with Sylvia, but she thought it good since she is a house guest of sorts. Rosalyn likes the idea immensely. She gets the cookbook from their library. Rosalyn shows Ginger page after page of recipes and tells Ginger what to do to change the flavor for the better. Things like adding butter and sugar to the pancake mix, adding sugar to cornbread, adding Worcestershire sauce to steaks when cooking, and adding a can of beer to hamburger when making a meatloaf. Ginger gets excited about it all, but really wants to try the beer and hamburger plus ingredients to make a meatloaf that they could have for dinner.

. Rosalyn says "We have all the ingredients for the meatloaf except the can of beer. Get that on the way home. When you get here, you, while I watch, can make the meatloaf." "That sounds great. Here I am being a bodyguard and learning to cook at the same time. It is a marvelous thing. I have never had an assignment like this before," returns Ginger Ales.

It becomes time for Sylvia to go to work. Ginger and Rosalyn accompany Sylvia in Ginger's car. Just out of curiosity, Ginger asks "Are you sure the Viper is not the car you had in Washington?" Sylvia tells her no. Conrad and she picked it out about two and a half weeks ago. Ginger was not surprised at all. The FBI had been looking for a red Dodge Viper with D.C. plates on it. Sylvia's car had Virginia plates. Ginger asks what happened to it and Sylvia tells her she does not know.

After getting to VCU Library, Ginger calls the local FBI office and identifies herself. She tells an agent to start calling salvage yards, particularly on the north side of Richmond, and ask if the yard has any Dodge Vipers. Then ask if they have a red one. If you find a red Dodge Viper, go check the VIN against the title of Sylvia's car in Washington. She tells the agent she wants to know what happened to Sylvia's Washington car. Sylvia heard none of this, but asks why Ginger was on the phone with Richmond FBI. Ginger fills her in on looking for her Washington car that appears to be missing.

Rosalyn is taking her classes again today and will ride home with Ginger and Sylvia. She uses the lap top in all three classes to take notes. She knows it will improve her grades.

Sylvia hears about a Gary Fielding, who had been charged with rape and was expelled by the Council Board. He had raped a girl name Laura Billings. She remembers Grace telling the event at home. She also heard the boy was going to trial on the rape charge. Otherwise, Sylvia's day was uneventful except for a female student who says "You're Sylvia Redman, the President's daughter." Sylvia did not respond. She will leave the girl wondering if she were. Sylvia and Ginger go to eat at Friendly Restaurant and each have a sandwich with chips and a drink.

Going home, Ginger reminds Sylvia they need to get a can of beer. Sylvia asks why and is told it is for the meatloaf she is going to make. They stop at a connivance store and go in. Ginger goes and gets a can of Coor's. Sylvia, on the other hand, buys a $5.00 lottery ticket. She scratches it off and finds she has won $7,777.00. She will need to go to a lottery office to get it redeemed and the office will hold out taxes. The rest will go in the bank.

The trio gets home. Ginger takes the can of beer into the kitchen. Rosalyn gets everything else ready to go. Ginger washes her hands and, then, takes the ingredients and mixes with the hamburger. She saves the beer for last. After mixing all of the items, Ginger places it in the oven at 350°. It bakes for half an hour. Then, Ginger gingerly takes the meatloaf out of the oven. It is ready for dinner which is 45 minutes later than usual.

The meal is ready. With the loaf, they have baked potatoes, corn and green beans. Conrad bites into the meatloaf and smiles saying "Ginger, you have done it. I can taste the hops, but not the alcohol. It is great. Did Rosalyn show you this or did you just know to do it?" "Rosalyn showed me the recipe in a cookbook, but told me about adding the beer. I am glad you like it." Sylvia empathizes with Conrad on the meatloaf. It turns into a glorious evening for them all. They talk about the meal all through the process of eating it.

Ginger and Rosalyn do the cleanup. All four go into the family room. Rosalyn, Sylvia and Conrad sit to watch TV, but Ginger goes to the computer and logs onto the FBI's personnel site. She is interested in Jim Duffy and Ho Wong. She sees they are back in D.C and the satellite monitoring system has been returned to the Smithsonian Institution. That satisfies her to no end. Ginger, then, logs out and joins in watching 'Ponderosa.' After a couple more shows, they all go to retire for the night in their respective bedrooms.

CHAPTER 39

Ginger Leaves

This is not a normal Wednesday. It is normal for the four to get up, shower and dress. They each go into the kitchen and Rosalyn makes oatmeal. It is a real cold day outside and she feels this is needed to ward off the cold. What is not normal is Ginger is to return to Washington. When she tells them, the three get upset and it shows. They want her to stay the entire week. She says she cannot and that her replacement will be there at 9:00 am. Ginger also tells them she will not leave until about 8:30 pm. They eat the oatmeal in remorse.

Rosalyn says to leave the dishes. She will get to them later. They all go into the living room and begin talking about the last four days. Ginger relates "I, being a Senior Agent, was placed in charge of a ten person crew to look for Sylvia. I had them looking everywhere, including Georgetown University. Two men were assigned to a satellite monitoring system and had it working in four localities including Richmond. You cannot imagine the relief I had when I was informed that Sylvia Redman was alive. I have enjoyed my stay with you and look forward to the time I can be with you again."

Conrad talks about finding out who Sylvia really is "I remembered where I had picked Sylvia up at and we went there. We did not see her purse at first, so we went down the gravel road searching both sides. We came upon her missing shoe and then her purse. In the purse were her driver's license, credit cards, and $1,000.00. It was I who called the FBI and the police." Conrad tells the three girls that he has to go to work.

Rosalyn talks on helping with the search. She did not have much else to say except she really enjoyed her trip on Air Force One and the tour of D.C. Rosalyn gets ready to leave with Sylvia for her university classes.

There is a knock at the door. It is 9:00 o'clock am. Sylvia thinks it must be the replacement. It is. Ginger invites her in and introduces her to Sylvia "Agent Gloria Townsend, this is Sylvia Redman Thomas. You will be guarding her for quite some time to come. You may need to move in with them. They have a spare bedroom. I have used it the last two nights. In two hours, Sylvia must be at work. I think I will delay my return and will go with you to show you the ropes. She works until 7:30 pm. Are there any questions?" "No. Not right now" says Gloria Townsend.

Sylvia becomes determine to fill Gloria in on everything since the accident. She tells her she did not know of the accident because she had amnesia. Sylvia points out she was watched over by Conrad for the six days in the Henrico County Doctors Hospital. She tells of the courtship, short though it was and their marriage. Sylvia relates how they got her temporary ID, SSN, and driver's license. She tells about the apartment and the resulting house. Finally, Sylvia comments on the job of a librarian at VCU.

Townsend says that is quite interesting. However, it really had little value in her present assignment. It did give her an idea why they were where they are at in the social structure of life. Sylvia and Rosalyn were willing to relate more, but Agent Gloria says it would not be necessary. Gloria's main concern is moving in with the Thomas' and where she might put clothes that she did not bring with her. Sylvia shows her the guest room and the other bedrooms pointing out the master bedroom is where Conrad and her sleep. Gloria was satisfied with the closet, but was not too happy with the size of the room after looking at the others. However, she relates she is happy to be with them and it is a totally different assignment unlike any she has had so far with the Richmond FBI.

Time was fast running out. Sylvia says they should go to a restaurant and eat. Sylvia decides on Red Lobster. It will be a quick, yet, enjoyable time. Gloria, Ginger, Rosalyn and Sylvia get into the car that Townsend drove. It held five passengers total. Sylvia sits next to Gloria and asks "Where did you go to school and what was your major?" "I went to Richmond University and I majored in Criminal Justice. I received a Bachelor of Science Degree with a 3.62 average."

Sylvia gives directions to Red Lobster which Gloria Townsend did not need. Gloria was familiar with Richmond already, being a four year on campus student and then getting a job with Richmond FBI. Gloria turns into Red Lobster and parks the car. All four get out ready to go eat. Time is short for it is 9:45 am. Inside, they are led by a hostess to a table. Each sit, with Gloria and Ginger opposite each other. This arrangement puts Sylvia and Rosalyn on the side between the two FBI agents. It did not matter to either of them.

The waitress comes with the menu and asks for drinks. They each order their favorite. In a relatively short time, the drinks arrive. The waitress says "Would you like to order now?" Ginger quips "I will have the shrimp special and a baked potato. Sour cream with that, please." Townsend says "I will have a salad and a fish sandwich." Sylvia tells the waitress "I will have the seafood platter." Rosalyn says "I will have the same." Their orders in, the four talk about Sylvia, her husband, and the housekeeper. Gloria just wants to know so she can get use to the family group.

The waitress returns with the food giving each order to the right person. Thus, she was a good waitress. Sylvia took note. Ginger did not notice, but Gloria did commenting "Did you see that? She remembered exactly who ordered what." Sylvia states "That is the sign of a good waitress—keeping the drinks and meals to the right person." Ginger says "We need to leave her a tip. How much?" Sylvia comes back with "Conrad usually leaves about 25%, if the waitress proves worthy for the entire meal doing things like checking on you and refilling your drink."

They begin eating and continue talking about upcoming things. It is a fabulous time together even though it is the next to last meal with Ginger for the time being. She makes known her plan to come occasionally to check on things, especially Gloria Townsend and Rosalyn's cooking. Gloria comments "I look forward to more lunches like this one, without Ginger of course. And I am sorry about that." "Well Gloria, you and I have something to look forward to. Lunch for me is usually a little later, ordinarily at or around 3:00 o'clock pm. I get a half hour." Rosalyn says "It is unusual for her too. Rosalyn has three classes that total four and a half hours."

Ginger advises "Ladies, it is time for us to leave to get Sylvia to work on time." Sylvia gets the bill and charges it with the tip. The four leave for VCU and the library. Gloria has not been on the VCU campus and must be told where to go. She gets them there with time to spare. Ginger tells Gloria "Go ahead of us and act like a student. Get on a computer that faces the checking counter. You will have a better view of Sylvia and the door. Be ready to pull your weapon if anything highly unusual comes up. Any questions?" "Won't that break my cover?" asks Gloria. Ginger explains "Yes, but do not worry about that. Your most important role is to guard Sylvia. If it means putting someone under arrest, do it." Rosalyn says goodbye so she can get to her next class.

Sylvia remarks "I do not expect anything unusual to happen. The library is normally quite quiet. I enjoy working here." Gloria asks "Do you ever get frightened?" "No, of course not. The students are all young, under 22 years old. If you see someone older, then, you should take notice in particularity. That person may be a problem, but then watch me because it could be a professor," reiterates Sylvia.

Gloria does as instructed. Then, Sylvia and Ginger enter. It has been an uneventful morning just like most mornings. Just 10 minutes later, the girl that had told Sylvia she was the President's daughter comes in with three other girls and they go right to Sylvia. "See. I told you she was the President's daughter," says the young lady. Sylvia confronts her "I am Sylvia Thomas. The President's last name is Redman. Do you see any men standing guard? No. Sylvia Redman would have guards. I just look a lot like her. And why would Sylvia Redman work in a university library when she could get almost any job with the federal government." That confrontation shuts the girl up. She looked mad at being rebuked in such a way. The girls leave the library.

Ginger comes up to Sylvia and says "You handled that quite well. You did it without lying. I liked that. It was close to a lie when you said that you looked a lot like her. You look exactly like her because you are her. The comment about men was a good detour from women." Ginger goes back to a computer next to Gloria.

The actual lunch time arrives and Sylvia just goes in the staff lounge. She gets a Diet Pepsi. Ginger and Gloria remain on computers for they can see the lounge quite well from where they are seated. The lunch time is over and Sylvia returns to the counter. Other than doing her normal duties, there is nothing wrong for the rest of the day.

Time comes for the three to leave and get Rosalyn who has been at a computer laboratory taking typing lessons. They get into Gloria's car and she drives Sylvia home after picking Rosalyn up.. Rosalyn gets dinner ready. It is lasagna made a special way with three cheeses. This excites Ginger, who says "I would never have thought of using three cheeses. You continue to amaze me with your cooking techniques."

The five eat and it comes time for Ginger to leave. She gives her phone number and address to Rosalyn. Rosalyn has been hoping Ginger would do that. The Thomas three say their goodbyes to Ginger as does Gloria and especially Rosalyn. Ginger leaves for D.C. and takes a commercial flight.

Rosalyn begins the cleanup and Gloria says "Let me help. Ginger told me she helped you sometimes with the cleanup after meals." There is plenty of lasagna left over. Rosalyn gets the idea to share it with the men on guard. She gets four plates and has Gloria her deliver the food to the men. They are extremely grateful for the dinner having not eaten yet. Rosalyn takes the remainder to Bear. He gobbles it up like there is no tomorrow.

Conrad asks Gloria to join the family in the family room to watch TV. They watch NCIS rerun they have not seen before. After that, the group watches Steven Seagal in Under Siege 2. When the movie is over everyone retires for the night.

CHAPTER 40

Epilogue

Years pass. Gloria Townsend remains the personal body guard of Sylvia until President Redman leaves office. Sylvia, then, gets another bodyguard. Rosalyn gets pregnant and has a baby girl. She names it Ginger Thomas. Rosalyn also goes to VCU and earns a degree in Criminal Justice with a 3.12 average. Ginger Ales helps her get a job with the Richmond FBI office. Rosalyn only has the one child.

Conrad gets promoted to President of Wachovia. He remains with them until he retires from the work.

Sylvia continues to work at VCU in the library. She becomes the Head Librarian when Maryann Witten moves on. This upsets one of the workers who felt she should have gotten the job. Sylvia also finishes her degree in Psychology having credits transferred from Georgetown University in D.C. to Virginia Commonwealth University. She also has four children, two boys and two girls.

The farm continues to grow and the chicks become chickens having their own chicks. Goldie and Bear remain. Sylvia lets Gloria ride Goldie after a bit of instruction for she has never ridden a horse.

Life for the Thomas clan has gone well. Sylvia has said to Conrad several times "Home is where the heart is."